MARK OF THE FALLEN

A Fallen Novel

Tanisha D. Jones

Cover designed by Cover Fresh Designs

This book is a work of fiction. Names, characters, places, and incidents either are products of the author's imagination or are used fictitiously. Any resemblance to actual persons, living or dead, events, or locales is entirely coincidental.

Tanisha D. Jones

Visit my website at www.TanishaDJones.com

Printed in the United States of America

First Printing: Aug 2016

ISBN-**978-1-7338085-0-7**

PROLOGUE

Once Upon A Time
High above Mount Olympus

T
he cooing and gasps of awe were annoying. She rolled her eyes, her hand on the crib as she gently rocked it back and forth, lulling the fussy infant. She glanced down at the plump little creature and frowned. There was nothing maternal in her, and the birth of her daughter had not remedied that fact. She absently rocked the crib, an absurd concoction of ruffles and lace that nearly swallowed the tiny babe, rolling her eyes as her family moved in to gift the child. She never bothered meeting their eyes; they were all excited about the new arrival, all smiling. The great hall of Zeus' Temple was full of milling deities, drinking wine and enjoying the celebratory mood. The usually stark white room held a warm glow; the floors were covered in thick rugs of deep blue and gold, and the drapes were long silken swaths of the same soft gold and white. Tables were lined with wine, nectars and fruit, fabulous sweets, and roasted meats. Servants stood near every station, ready to serve the deities. She looked at the small plate of cheese and fruit that her handmaiden had insisted she eat and turned up her nose in disgust. She had no taste for food or wine. She wanted to be left alone. She wanted to go to her bedroom and hide her face, yet she was put here on display, the child a constant breathing reminder of her humiliation.

She turned once more to look at the child and fought the angry tears that threatened. She had gone to the father, a man she had truly cared for, excited, and giddy with her news. But the look, the look had been one she would never forget.

* * *

"Anhur," she'd called as she entered the small alcove just outside of his temple. In the heat of the desert, the oasis was lush and green with tall palm trees that shaded the small freshwater pond, keeping the crisp blue water cool. She sat on a stone bench and waited for him. This was their place; this was where they had spent some of the best times she had known. This was where it had all begun. Wistfully, she twirled a deep auburn curl around a finger, waiting for her lover.

She had taken extra care with her appearance today, having her hair brushed until it shone. Her gown was of the most profound cobalt to match her fierce, wide-set eyes.

Nemesis was never considered a great beauty, but she did have a lovely face. Soft-featured with rounded cheeks and a straight nose, her lips were like a perfect Cupid's bow, the bottom slightly larger than the top, giving her a perpetual pout. Her eyes were strikingly vibrant, unlike her mother's softly swirling silver. Hers were so bright they glowed. She stood when she felt him coming near, her heart thudding in her chest.

He'd materialized almost the moment his name left her lips, and as always, a rush of lust washed over her at the sight of him. He was beautiful as ever. His muscled chest was bare, the white linen of his loincloth draped over muscular thighs gilded with gold leaves that caught the sunlight haloing him. His skin was golden, his eyes bright amber with thick dark lashes, and his head was shaved clean, but when he let his hair grow, it was a mane of the softest ebony curls she had ever laid her fingers upon. He had a somewhat feline look, almost like a lion, with his strong jaw and his mouth set. Being a God of War had left him with a long scar along his jawline, which he could have quickly healed, but it remained. She found him more beautiful for it. She went to him, her arms open for the inevitable embrace, but he did not open his arms to her. Instead, he stood firm, a look of distrust and confusion on his face.

"Why do you not embrace me, my love?" She asked in a lightly teasing tone. "Do you not miss your lover?"

"No," he said, and her smile faltered, but only for a moment. He was teasing. He had to be. They had done this before, he would feign anger, and then after a quick yet heated argument, he would take her hard. She preferred the roughness of his lovemaking than any gentle, sweet talk. Today she had no time for the foreplay; today, she had news, exciting news.

"Do not be angry, Anhur. I have come with the news." She smiled.

"What do you want, Nemesis?" His tone was sharp, curt, and she felt a slight sting in it. This was not his usual flirtatious arguing. He was truly angry with her, and she could not understand why.

"What is wrong, my love? Why do you speak to me in such a way?"

"You have been away from me for months, Nemesis. Months without a word, and now you show up, and I'm supposed to be excited. I waited for you."

"I'm back now. And now we can be together forever. I told Nyx. I told them all, Anhur. And I have a baby. We have a baby." She watched him narrow his eyes, and then his massive shoulders dropped. He had reached his limits with his lover, his heartbroken by her constant deceptions; even now, he was not sure what was true when she spoke.

"You left me no choice," he sighed, his shoulder slumped in resigned defeat.

"Did you hear what I said? We have a baby. That's why I stayed away. I was with a child. Your child. I have your child." She touched his arm, gently placing her fingers on his bicep, then on his cheek, turning his face so that he could look into her eyes.

"We have a child, my love," she said, tears in her eyes, joy filling her heart. He pushed her hand away from his cheek. It wasn't a harsh movement, nor was it done in anger. But the gesture made her feel alone, dismissed. He was not looking at her, not really. He was staring past her, beyond her beauty, and she gently touches. His body no longer craved her, and she could feel the complete loss of his affections. He no longer wanted her.

"You were gone for so long. Months. I summoned you, and you ignored me, and now you come after all of this time as if I were frozen in place waiting for you. I am not a toy to be pulled out for your amusement, Nemesis. I have other responsibilities. And I have a heart and a body that needs the feel and taste of his woman."

"And I am here," she purred, trying to wrap her arms around his neck. He backed away, holding her arms away from him.

"But you are not my woman. Not anymore, and you never will be again. I have taken a wife. There is no place for you in my life or my heart. Leave this place and never return."

She was stunned and felt for the first time that she had gone too far. She had finally managed to push him away.

"What about the child?" she pleaded. His ire flared, and for the first time since their affair had begun, she saw the man who was the God of War. His eyes blazed, his nostrils flared, and he looked even more lion-like than ever. He loomed over her, every muscle in his body taut with rage.

"Is there even a child? How do I believe anything that you say? You have never been truthful with me, you are a spiteful woman, and I curse the day you ever crossed my path. Just another of your playthings until you become bored and move on to the next. Leave this place before I lose my patience and snap your neck," he growled, his hands clenched into fists as he fought the urge to strike her.

"That new wife has poisoned you against me," she choked.

"You have poisoned me against you. Only you and your

venomous black heart." He left then, disappearing in a swirl of golden air and heat, leaving her with heart in her throat.

"You will regret this, Anhur! You will taste my vengeance!" She screamed at the air. "You will regret this day. I promise you this!" She bellowed before she faded from the oasis.

* * *

Now she sat a raw nerve to be poked and jabbed for the amusement of those around her, her family. Gods were petty and childish if nothing else, and seeing her in pain only fueled their admiration over the babe that had become her greatest regret. She even looked like Anhur with that sun-kissed skin and soft dark curls.

A small woman with long curling dark hair and shimmering silver eyes approached, staring at Nemesis for a moment, her swirling eyes narrowing with disapproval. Nyx, the embodiment of night, looked down at the babe then up at the sullen mother and frowned. The goddess sighed, her ageless beauty unmarred by her ancient age.

"Smile, daughter," she prodded, "at least pretend you like the child." She scolded her daughter, who stared off into nothing. Nyx reached past the ruffles and held up a squirming bundle of pink. She smiled down at the child who looked at her as if she hung the stars, which she had a hand in. She turned to the gathered crowd and held the little girl up for all to see. Nemesis absently brushed her hair over her shoulder. Her skin was smooth as porcelain, her eyes crisp wintery blue and her face serene and beautiful, yet she was mean and as vicious as they came. She removed her hand from the now-empty crib, smoothing the silk of her gown over her knees. Her stony expression never lifted, matching her dark mood.

* * *

The three entered, moving across the floor as one, as they did most things, to get a closer look at the new addition to their family. Giggling and whispering as young girls do, they tiptoed closer to stare at the exotic little girl sleeping soundly. She was tiny but beautiful even as an infant. Her beauty was evident. Her hair was thick, dark as midnight, and curled wildly around her cherubic face. Her skin was darker than their alabaster complexions. She was the color of warm caramel-like her father, the Egyptian, they supposed. She stirred, opening her eyes to stare at the three girls who returned her gaze. Her eyes were stunning, a clear, crystalline turquoise.

"She does not look like the all-powerful." Lachesis thought, her sisters nodded. The Moirai or the Fates did not need to speak to communicate. They read each other's thoughts and often spoke as one. Clotho, the speaker of the past, nodded.

"She is so powerful. She is the daughter of our sister Nemesis, Goddess of Vengeance, granddaughter of our mother, Nyx, Goddess of Night, the oldest of the gods. Only God himself has more power than this child." She reached out and stroked the baby's cheek.

Cooing, she grabbed Clotho's finger and put it into her waiting mouth. Clotho grimaced but didn't pull away. She let the girl gum her finger in the way that babies did.

"Still," Lachesis, the speaker of the present, mumbled aloud. "She just looks like a fat baby to me. She's cute but-"

"She will become the most powerful goddess ever born." The most dower of the girls said. Atropos was the speaker of the future and the most serious of the three. She was the keeper of all things to come and could see the divergent paths that the world could take. She knew the hour of the end of the world, just as Clotho knew the second of the birth of existence. "She crosses pantheons, sister. Not only does she possess the power of her mother and grandmother, but she is also the daughter of the Egyptian God of War. She alone could be the key to our survival."

They turned their eyes to the sweet, innocent babe who gurgled and smiled at her aunties. "Our little Caelestis," Atropos said, stroking the child's soft hair and gave her a rare smile. "Will either be our savior or ... our destruction."

* * *

She stood in her temple, her head throbbing as the baby wailed in her crib. Unable to stand it anymore, Nemesis rose from her bed and went to the squirming bundle, lifting her against her breast and walked toward the small basin her servants had filled with warm water to bathe the child. With her eyes filling with tears, she held the baby down. Water splashed to the pale marble floors as the infant kicked and fought against her. She had not believed that it would cause her pain to do this. She hated this infant, but it was her blood. She had given birth to this creature. Sobbing, she closed her eyes to block out the look of sheer terror in those neon blue eyes as the little girl struggled for her life. She turned her head, wiping the tears away on the shoulder of the pale green silk gown she wore, when she felt the pain rocket through her body, tossing her across the room. The burst of energy exploded inside of her body, cracking bones as she ricocheted against the beamed ceiling and walls. She came to rest on the floor, her body crumbled against a large marble pillar sobbing from the pain of it.

For a second, the child hovered, her dark head dangling in midair, before being pulled into slim arms that emerged from the silver-gray mist.

"How dare you!" The woman who emerged shouted. The mist seemed to draw into her, defining her petite body. Her blue-black hair lifted around her face, and her skin glowed as if she were lit from within. She screamed in anguish as she coaxed the barely breathing infant to live. Finally, the baby choked and spat water before clinging gratefully to the woman who'd saved her life, whimpering in exhaustion. Her entire body vibrated with fury as she stood over the crumpled heap of green silk and auburn curls. "How dare you harm this child? And here on Olympus, to kill a child of the divine, you could be cast out, or even worse, made mortal. How dare you!" She spat, cradling the wet, squalling babe to her chest.

"I curse the day she was born. If you take her, I vow that she will have to feed on the blood of those like her. She will never be truly loved, she will fuel their lust and passion, and that is all. No man, no love ever will save her, no matter what the fates say. She is poison.

"She will find love, despite your vitriol. This child will be loved. She is loved now. I love her. And I believe her father would have loved her if he knew her birth to be true."

"He abandoned us, mother. He tossed us aside for his Nubian, and I will never forgive him for that. I will kill her before I allow him to have her, to love her. I will -" She snarled, rising to her feet. Nyx narrowed her eyes and shook her head. The anger in her eyes faded to something closer to pity, and she sighed, heaving the now quiet child to her shoulder.

"He did not abandon her; he left you. Your vicious nature poisons everything around you. You will not harm this child," Nyx growled.

"I will kill you both-" she spat.

"You have no power over me, Nemesis. You should remember that," Nyx said in a voice that was as cold and hard as stone. "You only see your pain, your jealousy. Your anger has turned you into such a hateful creature, and it hurts me to look upon you. That is why I must do this." Nyx lifted one delicate hand, and Nemesis could feel the power drain from her. Everything that made her the goddess she was slowly faded from her, leaving a useless immortal in the realm of the gods.

"No," she screamed, her eyes wide in horror as the soft

glow left her skin, leaving her ashen and gray. The shine from her thick auburn hair faded to a dull, mousy brown, and the bright blue of her eyes faded to a flat, lifeless gray.

"Mother, what have you done?" Nemesis bellowed, falling to her knees. "What have you done to me?" she sobbed.

"What was gifted to you in birth has been taken away. You still have some, not enough to do any real harm, but enough. I'm afraid I am the reason you are such a hateful and selfish child. I will not burden this child with such a curse."

As she turned to leave, Nemesis rose to her feet, seething with a bitterness that cut Nyx to her soul.

"Wherever she goes, death will follow. Whomever she loves will betray her. She is Kere, death itself. She will destroy us all."

"Enough. You have made your choice, and you have sealed her fate as well as your own. You chose very, very badly, daughter. And for that, you alone will pay." Nyx's voice was no more than a whisper, but it seemed to vibrate, filling the room. "Mark my words, Nemesis, you touch one hair on this child's head, and I will find you, and I will destroy you."

And just as quickly as she'd appeared, she was gone, a trail of silver-gray mist in her wake.

❊ ❊ ❊

CHAPTER ONE

Mandeville, Louisiana
July 2005

She couldn't breathe. Her chest felt tight as if some heavyweight pressed down on her, pushing the air from her lungs. Icy water assaulted her skin, chilling her to her bones and numbing her limbs. The poison in her system weakened her, the boulders tied to her waist dragged her deeper. She opened her mouth and tasted the salty rush of seawater and began choking in earnest. She sat up, trying to open her eyes, but they were caked with salt and sand, sealing them shut. She was floating away, darkness surrounding her as she drifted deeper into oblivion. She thrashed violently, fighting against the weight that was pulling, lugging her further into obscurity, further from land and air and sunshine, her life. She screamed, the sound lost in the vast emptiness that surrounded her, and she was gone. There was no one to help.

"I have you," a deep baritone whispered close to her ear. She stopped moving, feeling rigid arms encircling her waist, holding her body still against a very masculine, very naked body. His hands were large, strong as they moved up her ribs, his lips brushing the tender flesh just beneath her ear.

"I have you, love." He spoke in an extended dead language, so ancient it had no name, yet she understood. It was the primordial language, something that she had known when she was younger—the language of her grandmother.

"Give me your lips," he said, and she felt her body turn into liquid heat, melting against him. She turned her head in the gloom, and his lips captured hers. Soft full lips pressed

against hers, his tongue sweeping past her lips, tasting her. She moaned, leaning back into him, her hand moving up to cup the back of his head, holding him, bringing him closer. His head was smooth and cool beneath her fingertips.

"Open your eyes and breathe," He breathed into her mouth, his fingers tracing the curve of her breasts, his body hot and erect against the small of her back. She did as he said, slowly opening her eyes and gasped in surprise.

His skin was so dark that she could not see any real detail; she could only make out the strong line of his jaw, the full softness of his lips, and his eyes, brilliant glowing neon.

He let his head drop to her neck, sharp fangs brushing the jumping pulse in her throat before sinking in. She groaned, her body slick, every nerve ablaze. She felt herself go liquid all over him and called out into the blackness. Her fangs extended with the need to sink into him, to drink of this delicious man. He held her tighter, those arms of his holding her close, his body rigid, and his hips grinding into her. He stroked her core, and she could no longer control her limbs, her body moving, edging closer and closer to the fringe.

"Come for me," he whispered against her heated skin. *"I'm waiting for you to come for me,"* he said in that lilting language, his mouth searing and sweet with the taste of her blood. She was just about to come apart, her heart racing as the slow burn began.

❈ ❈ ❈

"Hey, Ce." Strong hands were shaking her, her head bouncing on the mattress. She rolled onto her side, away from the bastard who had the nerve to wake her from the most delicious dream. If she were lucky, she would get back and finish the best orgasm she'd ever had. Real or not, she could feel the damp of her panties against her skin, the teeth in the flesh at her neck, and the massive swollen cock filling her.

"Wake up." The shaking became harder, more persistent, and she growled, slapping away the person ruining the best dream she'd had in centuries. Hell, it was the first dream she had, in she couldn't even remember how long, that hadn't devolved into a nightmare. And now she was rudely interrupted by this person who seemed to want to punish her for some reason. He pulled the covers off of her and tossed them in a pile on the floor.

"Out of bed, Princess, " he said, and she groaned, pulling a pillow over her head to shield her eyes from the increasingly bright sunlight being forced upon her. He sighed and pulled the pillow away, tossing it into a chair, before he continued throwing open the heavy burgundy curtains.

Shielding her eyes, she saw the slim but muscular frame of Remy Kent as he moved around the room with a grim determination that she usually adored, but now she wanted to kick him. The sunlight picked up the flecks of gold in the gilded wallpaper casting a cheery summer glow across the much too large bedroom.

When he was done, he turned, his hands-on narrow hips, his hair standing on end in a shock of dark curls that pointed in every direction. Remy, the youngest of her adopted siblings, was at times her best friend and others her worst enemy. Today, it seemed, he had chosen the enemy. She lay flat on the mattress, exhaling as she stared at the ceiling, the reflection from the pool downstairs casting strange shapes that danced like shimmering water above her. She sighed heavily as the last pang of lust seeped out of her, and she lay frustrated and more than a little annoyed. This, she thought, was why she rarely slept at the family home. She preferred the solitude of her penthouse in New Orleans. At least there, she could have a wet dream in peace.

She rolled onto her side before, sliding her legs over the edge of the bed, where her toes dangled mid-air for a moment before they sank into the deep, plush snowy white carpet. She stared at Remy for a second, standing backlit by the early July sun, his arms folded across his chest.

"You had better have a helluva good reason for coming in here like this. I was -"

"Having one monster of a sex dream when I came in. I know. It was pretty sexy to watch. The writhing and moaning got me a little hard. I can still smell it on you," he said, slinking closer to the bed. She noticed it as well, the scent of spice and fresh male mingling with her natural scent of lavender that always floated on her skin. She buried her face in her shirt, inhaling the smell, burning it into her senses. Remy bit his lip and started making soft purring sounds, running his hands along his chest. "So, fucking sexy," he leered.

And now this, she thought. Perfect.

"You are a horrible human being." There were days when he thought of her as a sister, and then there were days like this when Remy was, well, Remy. His older siblings, Gaston and Lisette, saw her as their sister. In every sense of the word, Remy had never been so inclined. They shared no bloodline, and he was well aware of it. He had made it clear that if she ever had an itch, he was more than willing to scratch it enthusiastically. Over the years, he'd been forced to curb his rather inappropriate advances toward a woman the outside world only knew as his little sister. In public, he obliged, but in private, it was no holds barred. In Remy's world, nothing was taboo.

He came to sit next to her on the bed, one strong hand moving up her exposed calf, feeling the smooth skin with practiced ease. Slapping his hand away, and pulled at the hem of the plain white t-shirt and bright green Tulane University gym shorts she had chosen as bedclothes.

"Well, then I guess it's a good thing I'm not human." He leaned back on his elbows and stared at her.

"Not now, Remy," she grumbled, drawing her legs away from him. Her thick dark hair rested over one shoulder in a tangled, matted mess. Her eyes narrowed suspiciously as she inspected her 'brother.'

His skin glowed like burnished bronze, his dark hair was a little too long, curling at the collar of his shirt. She watched as brown eyes shifted to deep green, then amber, his face relaxing. Remy was a pretty man, with soft, almost delicate features. He was sort of androgynous in some ways, with full pouty lips and high cheekbones, a straight Moorish nose, and eyes that were gently slanted upward. He moved with the grace and elegance of an animal. She had known him long enough to know that his effortless grace and sexuality were disarmingly dangerous. It was part of who he was, of what he was, a hybrid. Remy was a shape-shifting Dhampir, giving him more animalistic tendencies. His brother and sister were pure Dhampir, vampire-human hybrids or day-walkers. His mother, Jonas Kent's second wife, was a special breed of a shifter, an element of nature that was so pure that Remy was an even more complex entity.

"Why are you in uniform?" she asked, eying the deep grey button up and darker grey slacks. His shoes were shiny and black, polished until she could see her reflection staring back at her. The uniform of the Grey made him look like a 1950's communist, especially without the jacket. This was not normal. Remy was skinny jeans and t-shift shirt kind of guy.

"That's why I came to get you. The Collective has convened. Your presence is requested, Commander."

* * *

She stood in the shower, letting the heated mist wash over her. She closed her eyes and was immediately bombarded by images of neon blue eyes and soft lips. Her heated skin tingled, and her nipples tightened at the memory of strong hands stroking her in the dark.

"No, you don't." She turned the hot water off and yelped when the spray turned icy. No time for daydreams. She had work to do. She quickly washed and dried herself, stepping into the bathroom's artificial heat to dress in her uniform. As Commander of the Grey, she wore a slightly modified version of Remy's uniform. She slipped on her plain white bra and panties before sliding slate grey leather slacks over her muscular thighs. Remy wandered into the dressing room and slumped against a wall, watching her fasten pants that hugged her ample curves and molding to her long shapely legs. Tucking a fitted camisole into her pants, she searched for her uniform shirt and coat. She spotted the gunmetal silk top hanging on the wall that housed what had to be the entire spring collection of Jimmy Choo shoes.

"What's taking so long?" Remy grumbled, his eyes roaming the room. He was always a bit taken aback by her dressing room size and the sheer volume of clothing it housed.

"I'm hurrying." She mumbled before turning to the mirror to deal with the issue of her hair. She leaned forward, letting the black silk curtain of hair fall forward so that she could comb out the tangles, before securing it in a ponytail, which was neatly plaited and twisted into a bun. Remy's eyes landed on the mark that peeked out at him at the nape of her neck. He moved forward, brushing aside the curls that framed the dark red tattoo at the base of her skull, and stared. It was a delicate and intricate design of a heart encircled by tribal wings sprouted on either side. She had been branded with it years ago but had no idea what it meant, let alone the when, why, or even how she ended up with it.

"What's wrong with your tat?" Remy brushed aside the curls to get a better look at the irritated flesh. "It's all red," Remy said. It wasn't just red; it seemed to pulsate with a dull red glow.

She reached up and touched the slightly raised area wincing, when her nails moved along the mark. It was tender and hot, like she had been burned or, better yet, as if she'd been branded.

"I don't know. I must have scratched it when I was combing my hair. It's fine," she said. Or maybe she was branded by

17

her dream lover. She quickly slipped on the silk shirt, button-ing it with rapid ease that would have been unnerving if Remy hadn't known who she was. She slipped into knee-high leather boots and reached for her gunmetal trench before heading out of the dressing room. She stared at her face in the mirror and smiled a little. Not bad, she thought. Not bad at all for a nearly two-thousand-year-old deity. She turned to face Remy, who smiled at her the way he did so often.

She entranced him. She glowed about her, and with her face scrubbed clean, she didn't look a day over nineteen, maybe twenty. Her eyes were a startling blue, not blue, more turquoise, with thick, long lashes, high cheekbones from her Egyptian father, a straight nose from her Greek mother, and soft full lips that were all her own.

"Come on. Do you know if this is business as usual or something else?" He obediently followed her, slipping on his own heavy woolen pea coat as they moved out of the room and down the long and winding hallway that was her wing of the third floor of the massive fortress their father called home.

"I think they are adding a new contingent to the Collect-ive. By order of the Council, and you have to be there. They won't decide without a full vote," he said, and she rolled her eyes and sighed before rounding a corner and walking down another winding hallway. The soft gold paint of the walls made everything in the house feel warm and inviting. The artwork was all original and expensive, collected over centur-ies by their father, Jonas Kent. She absently touched the tat-too again before her mind wandered to the Collective and her work there.

The house was enormous, decorated in French Baroque style, everything in deep reds and rich golds. The grand stair-case was right out of a palace, complete with hand-carved marble banisters. The house itself had been moved stone by stone to Louisiana when the Kent's had relocated from France what felt like a million years ago.

Remy matched her step for step as they marched across

the marble floors, the click of heavy heeled boots, making a staccato rhythm that echoed through the cavernous hallways. He glanced at her. She was tall, six feet in her stocking feet; the heel on her boots gave her another three inches. But she seemed delicate, with all of that power radiating from her; there was a vulnerability to her, a softness that made him want to protect her. Shaking off the thought, he looked at her uniform then at his own. She made the drab grey look sexy; hell, she looked like a fucking superhero, making him her sidekick.

"Why do you get to be all bad-ass in the leather?" Remy grumbled.

"Because," she said with a smirk, "I am a certified badass."

He smiled. It was true; Celeste was indeed a certified, card-carrying, natural-born badass. One of the most dangerous and sometimes vicious warriors he had ever known, and that was saying a lot. Remy had been a soldier in every war from The Crusades through World War II.

Watching her in battle was a visceral experience; her brutality was legendary. It surprised such brutal force and complete savagery could emerge from such a delicate, beautiful package. She had been the only logical choice to lead the Grey, an army of bloodthirsty preternatural creatures. They had slaughtered hundreds, yet they cowered when she approached.

They moved quickly through the foyer of the mansion towards a small door hidden beneath the stairs. Remy put on his garrison cap and waited until she had slipped leather gloves over her hands and secured her beret before opening the door.

"Are you going to tell me about the dream?" he asked as he waited.

"Nope," she said before stepping across the threshold into the awaiting mist.

He followed closely, pulling the door closed behind them. The mist surrounded them, making them queasy as they moved from one plane to the next, traveling through time and space in a blink. She hated using the portals, but it was the fastest and easiest way to the Collective's compound.

"Was I in it?" He ventured.

"Nope," she said, not looking at him.

"Would you tell me if I were?"

"Nope," she laughed.

* * *

The air became colder, light spreading before them as the mist cleared. Their silent footfalls became audible as they stepped on something slick and hard, stone, she thought. She shivered, her feet crunching on ice, snow blowing across her face. The compound came into view, and she groaned while glancing around. They had moved the entire place again, this time to some tundra.

The Collective, a paranoid bunch of preternatural beings, frequently moved the headquarters, making it nearly impossible to track, therefore rendering any plan of attack a non-issue, for the most part anyway. There had been a few spies from the Dark Fae who'd been able to gain access to the fortress, but none since she had been made commander. But as long as there were Dark Fae and treacherous double-dealings, anything was possible. She had learned that most horrifically.

"Norway? Germany?" she asked, staring at the keep that was half-buried in the side of a snow-covered mountain. The bridge that they walked across emerged from the mist, grey and deteriorating, with cobblestones worn smooth with age.

She looked back to see that everything behind them had fallen off into nothingness. The mountain was dotted with snow and frosted pine trees; the keep surrounded by an ice-covered lake. The wind tore through her trench, and she wished she'd grabbed the heavy fur-lined poncho she had tossed aside. She could see it lying across the chaise in her dressing room, the soft grey mink beckoning her. She exhaled, and the poncho appeared, replacing the trench, and she sighed, snuggling into the warmth of her collar. Remy rolled his eyes, looking around to try and gauge their location.

"How did you do that? I can't transport when I'm in the compound," he mumbled.

"We're not in the compound yet. Besides, I'm a freakin' goddess. Does this look like Greenland? Switzerland?"

"I think we may be in Siberia or on the dark side of the moon," Remy mumbled, quickening his pace to keep up with her. The cold did not affect him as it did others. Being a shifter, his body ran a few degrees hotter than most. Shifters, skinwalkers, and Lycans were easy to spot because of their elevated heat signature, just as vampires and demons leaned on the colder side. All those between, like Celeste, on the surface, passed as human.

"I don't guess it matters. I just wish for once they would pick somewhere warm. What do they have against Bali or Tahiti?" She said. "Let's go before they send someone out here to retrieve us." She looked heavenward, trying to get her bearings, before giving up on the endeavor. They were where they needed to be, and that was that.

"Did I even make a cameo?" Remy asked

"No!" She laughed.

* * *

The Collective compound, to the naked eye, resembled a ruined turret of a castle, falling stone lying scattered in some isolated place in the world, hidden by the mist—an unassuming memory of times long past. In reality, the ruin was only the entrance into the state-of-the-art stronghold; most of the compound ran deep underground.

They crossed the icy slick cobblestone portico, waiting at the massive stone gate. Celeste looked up at the camera she could not see but knew was up above them somewhere. It took a moment, and then the heavy doors parted, slowly opening just enough for them to slip inside. She and Remy stepped into a foyer as the doors swung closed behind them and waited for the steel door opposite them to slide open.

The wall slowly rose, revealing a spiral staircase carved into the wall that led down into the heart of the compound. Celeste stepped down. First, a light illuminating each level, Remy following closely behind. The steel door slid closed, and they were sealed into the base of the turret's cylindrical stone walls.

When they reached the bottom of the staircase, another heavy metal door greeted them, this one with a retina scanner. She leaned forward and let the electronic eye sweep her face.

"Good Morning Caelestis, granddaughter of the primordial Nyx, Daughter of the Goddess of Vengeance Nemesis, Daughter of the God of War Anhur, Goddess of Redemption and Justice, Commander of the Grey," an electronic voice sang before the door slid open. She frowned but made her way into a small alcove, Remy, hot on her heels. She had asked several times to have that changed to Celeste, just Celeste. Or Celeste Keegan Kent, which was the name she went by in the human world. Instead, they had uploaded her entire identity into that stupid machine.

At the next door, Remy pressed his thumb to the fingerprint scanner.

"Good Morning, Remy de Noe Laurent Kent, House of de Noe, Lieutenant Commander of The Grey." He gave Celeste an apologetic shrug.

"You have a longer name than I do, Caelestis," Remy said with a slight degree of amusement. She didn't bother with a response. The second door slid open, revealing a long marble corridor lined with pale marble columns and floor to ceiling windows that opened into a lobby that could be found in any office building anywhere in the world. As they walked towards the guards that manned the entrance, the two men stood quickly, saluting as they passed.

Celeste returned the salute, not looking at the young men but was immediately struck by Lycans' earthy scent. She never really noticed the soldiers, only out of necessity. She didn't want to know the men and women she sent into battle. It was too hard on her when they didn't return.

Remy, on the other hand, paused, staring at one of the young guards. He was huge, with crisp green eyes, bright red hair, and a smattering of freckles across a fresh angelic face. The uniform stretched over muscle, the buttons on his shirt straining against the sheer mass of him. Celeste watched Remy take the young man in, closing his eyes to inhale his scent.

"What is your name, soldier?" he asked, his eyes moving down the immensely muscled body. Even for a Lycan, he was large, but his face was open, innocent. She rolled her eyes and looked away, knowing what was coming next. Remy was going to soil that innocence with his Remy-ness. It was unique to her how quickly Remy could shift gears. Just moments ago, he was watching her ass and flirting with her. Now he was all about this soldier. Lust had no limits, she supposed.

"Briar ó Flannagáin, sir," he spoke with a surprisingly deep Irish brogue, using the Gaelic pronunciation of his name, and Remy's body began to tingle. His fangs extended slightly, and the Lycan's body tensed his breath quickening. She could smell the arousal in the air coming from both of them.

"*Good Lord,*" she thought, rolling her eyes.

"Well, Briar, I think perhaps when the Commander and I have completed our business with the Collective, you and I should talk. I may have a task for you. Meet me in my room in two hours. It's on the fifth level." The giant Briar smiled and blushed beet red, making him look even younger, if that were possible. The elevator pinged, the doors sliding open. Celeste stepped inside and watched Remy, the glint of wanting in his eyes.

"Yes, sir." Briar saluted again, trying to cover the deepening blush.

"Two hours, Briar. Don't keep me waiting." Remy stepped into the elevator beside her, coolly linking his fingers in front of him as the doors slid closed. The soldier watched Remy until the door closed, completely flushed, a smile lighting that faces. She had to admit, Remy had remained calm and nonchalant, even though the lust was radiating from him in overpowering waves. His scent was strong, sugary sweet thick, filling the elevator car.

"You're not fooling anyone, you know," she said, taking her gloves off but avoiding his eyes. Remy managed to look completely innocent.

"I have no idea what you're talking about." He managed to look wholly guileless and somewhat insulted. Celeste turned to face him, her expression blank. "I do love those redheads," he whispered, and Celeste couldn't help but smirk.

Once the elevator began to move, he broke out into a spontaneous dance routine. He started thrusting his hips, his bottom lip between his teeth, his face twisted as if he smelled something terrible. He shimmied up to her, and she placed a hand on his chest, gently pushing him away. He smacked his ass, watching as she stifled a giggle. He turned around, popping his butt against her hip until she'd backed into a corner to get away from him. She finally broke into a fit of giggles when the doors opened, and their father stood staring at them.

He was not amused.

Jonas Kent was a powerful presence, imposing and filling every space he occupied, yet he wasn't a large man. He stood about six feet tall, narrow in the shoulders, his dark wavy hair going grey at the temples. What made him such a force was the laser focus of his gaze and his regal bearing. Nearly seven hundred and fifty years old, Jonas had the bearing of a king, his head held high, with piercing deep brown eyes.

They followed him down the hall toward a small library off the Collective's usual, larger meeting room. Celeste looked at Remy, who shrugged, just as surprised as she was by the change of venue. Jonas held the door open and stepped aside, allowing Celeste entry into the darkened library first. She entered, staring around the room with its dark wood paneling and thick Persian rugs. A fire blazed in the hearth, warming the room and filling it with the smell of expensive cigars, burning wood, and bourbon.

The heavily embroidered Victorian furniture was occupied by members of the Collective and a couple of new people. She stared at the back of two heads, one a vibrant red that hung past milky white shoulders, the other dark and very male. She was staring, straining to hear the conversation across the room, but was only able to make out laughs and the deep voice of Collective member Julian Onder. Julian leveled his gaze at her and smirked, his fangs showing and his yellow eyes giving her an uneasy feeling in the pit of her stomach.

She was so unnerved that she nearly jumped out of her skin when the butler began removing her cape. She let the dwarf take it with a tight smile, handing him her gloves and hat as well. Remy had drawn his coat and began a slow stride towards the group with Jonas. She turned back to Julian, who smiled wider and even managed a wink.

"They have arrived," Jonas said in his heavily accented baritone. Even after three hundred years in the states, he kept the deep French accent. Celeste had the feeling that it was all for show. "I would like to introduce our guests to my youngest children, Remy, and Commander of the Grey, Celeste Kent," Jonas said, and the two with their backs to them rose.

The woman was tiny with skin so pale that it made her hair seem more in-depth and bloodier a red. Her eyes were hard, white irises rimmed with the same deep red, and her face was a cross between a pixie and elf. Yet, Celeste knew from the moment she looked at her. This woman was a pure demon.

"This is Lilith," Jonas said. The woman nodded towards Remy and Celeste, her smile ethereal. Celeste felt Remy stiffen beside her, yet his face remained relaxed and calm. Remy and his redheads, she thought, waiting for him to make a move, say something wholly inappropriate, but he didn't. He simply smiled and nodded in her direction. Celeste nodded to their guest.

"And this is,"

"Karim," she exhaled and stopped short. Her mouth had suddenly gone dry. He was tall, with a slim muscular build, his skin a tawny gold. His dark hair was slicked back tight to his skull, his face slightly angular and one she wouldn't call handsome but striking. His eyes were the thing that captured her attention every time she saw them. They were branded on her memory, so pale they were like looking into sunlit ice. She had seen those eyes in her dreams for centuries. And now, here he was, in the flesh. After all of this time, she was face to face with him again.

The newcomer smiled, and his face became beautiful, his fangs exposed, and that twinkle appeared in his eyes. She knew that twinkle, and she hated it. She hated it, and she hated herself for reacting to it. After all, he had done, he had the balls to show up here.

"Good to see you, Ce-" Before he could complete the sentence, she punched him in the face with a right hook that knocked him flat on his ass.

"Good to see you too," she growled.

* * *

Chaos had ensued the moment Karim hit the plush carpet of the library floor. He crumbled like a ton of bricks, his nose exploding in a bloody mess. Julian burst into surprised laughter, reveling in the violence. Lilith stepped back, avoiding being crushed under the falling weight of the man, her hands going to cover her delicate mouth.

The Collective members sprang to their feet in shock, not knowing how to react to Celeste and the unexpected attack and not wanting to get in between her and her mounting rage. She moved forward, preparing to continue her assault on the fallen man, when Remy wrapped his arms around her, pinning her arms to her sides and backing her away.

"What are you doing?" He asked against her ear. She fought against him, struggling, her legs flailing as she growled in anger.

"I'm going to kick that piece of shit's ass into his fucking neck." She was practically foaming at the mouth, and Remy was struggling to hold her. Karim sat up, those frosty green eyes alight with mild amusement.

"I see you still have a nasty right." His soft Persian accent filled the room, making her knees go weak. His voice was thick and slurred slightly, but it was still the sexy purr that always made her stomach twist into knots. Damn, she wanted to punch him again, knock the sexy right out of him. She surged forward, dragging Remy with her as he dug his heels in to keep her from attacking.

"Little help!" He called to Julian. The other members of the Collective would be of no help holding back a blood-thirsty goddess. They stood in silence as she charged, not daring to get in between Celeste and Karim, who was wiping the blood from his nose and lip. The High Regent moved forward, only to be held back by her ever-present security. Two large men materialized from the shadows and stood in front of her, protectively blocking her from any harm, or a good view, as the melee continued. Jonas was busily assisting their fallen guest, apologizing for his daughter's actions, which meant only the powerful lycan alpha was left to help Remy contain her growing rage.

Julian stepped forward, catching one of Celeste's legs before she connected with his crotch. He shook a finger at her in warning, taking both of her calves in his firm grasp. "Careful Tanrıça, you may have use for that later. I'm excellent at burning off excess aggression,'" he purred, one hand moving seductively up her leather-clad calf.

"Not now, Onder," Remy warned.

"Take her to her suite," the High Regent said, her solemn black dark eyes watching the scene with something close to confused horror. Her perfectly coiffed hair glowed deep chestnut, her skin a soft amber in the firelight. Her long delicate fingers moved up to her throat as she watched the scene in stunned silence.

"Yes, mother," Remy mumbled, gritting his teeth as he and Julian carried the enraged woman out of the library.

* * *

Remy and Julian pushed her into the living room of her fifth-floor suite, slamming the door behind them, both panting heavily after the strain of containing the fury of an angry goddess and getting her safely into her room. Both men sat heavily on the sofa, beads of perspiration dripping from their faces, and panting from the exertion, leaving her to pace the room. Remy looked up at her, watching to make sure she didn't sprint for the door. Her neat bun had fallen free, hanging down her back in heavy, unruly waves, her cheeks were flushed, and her eyes blazed with blue fire. Remy loved her like this, breathing fire, ready to eradicate anyone who crossed her path. She was exquisite.

"Damn, she's even hotter when she's pissed," Julian mumbled.

Remy looked at Julian in disgust, rolling his eyes as the man tugged at his pants, trying to adjust himself. Julian's nostrils flared, and he moved closer to the edge of his seat, those yellow eyes smoldering as he watched her move back and forth across the room. Julian's eyes stayed on the sway of her hips, the way the leather cradled the curve of her ass. He was growling, a low soft hum that vibrated in his chest.

Remy could smell the scent of his arousal, strong and pungent, and it made him angry. This man was not worthy of Celeste, and he had the nerve to lust after her in front of him.

"Not now, Julian. Mind explaining what that was about?" Remy asked, rising and stepping in front of Julian to break his visual contact with her. If he didn't, Julian would pounce on her, and then Remy would have to put him down. He didn't have time for that.

She stopped pacing long enough to look her brother in the eye, her anger evaporating, and her shoulders beginning to shake. She wasn't crying; it was as if a chill had set into her bones and her body trembled. She opened her mouth, snapped it closed, and then opened it again.

"I trusted him, and he ..." she choked on the truth she'd never spoken to Remy. A reality that she had denied to all except one.

"He sold me," she whispered.

CHAPTER TWO

She sat on the starkly decorated room sofa, a glass of scotch in her shaky hands. She was fuming, unable to quell her fury and overcome by profound sadness. It was now Remy's turn to pace. His sinewy frame wound tight. His body made slight popping noises as he tried to keep himself from turning into some ferocious animal. Beside her, Julian sipped a glass of vodka, his amber eyes on Celeste as he inhaled her scent. Lycans were drawn to aggression, and she was throwing it off in waves that had him hard and hurting for her. It also made him angry because there was an underlying feeling of hurt with each wave of anger.

"I'll kill him," Remy grunted over and over, his pupils elongating, giving him a serpentine look as he slunk back and forth across the plush white carpet. "Why didn't you tell me? Why didn't you tell any of us? Celeste- you - you told Nicky, right? Does Nicky know? Of course, he does. You tell him everything," he sighed, jealous of the closeness she shared with her best friend. And not for the first time.

"He sold you?" he repeated, his anger resurfacing with ferocity. His hands became claws with thick dark talons that looked as if they could shred a man to pieces.

"For a fucking camel." She snorted laughter and sighed. "A camel," she whispered.

"I would have been better off if he'd left me to die in the desert. At least then, maybe Anhur could have found me. Or Nyx. Hell, I could have found my way given enough time. But he traded me for a camel instead. Can I pick them, or can I pick' em?" she asked.

The men were silent, and she could feel their pity, and

it angered her even more. She didn't need pity, she had survived, and she would continue to do so. Seeing Karim had only brought all of those memories to the surface in such a primitive way that she hadn't had time to process it. So, she'd attacked.

There was a soft knock on the door, and they all froze.

Remy turned to look at Celeste, who stared into her empty glass, her mind a million miles away. When neither of them moved, Julian grunted and went to answer the door. He wasn't sure whom he was expecting, but it certainly wasn't Karim.

Julian stared at the man, his growl, which moments ago had been sexual, turned to a fierce rumble. He grasped the vamp by the neck and tossed him into the room, his body already beginning to change into the beast he was. Karim landed on the rug with a thud right at Celeste's feet.

Remy turned in an instant, his fingers elongating, the nails shifting into razor-sharp, black talons. His eyes turned deep green and every muscle in him tensed.

Karim rose quickly, his fangs extended, and those intense eyes that sparked with anger narrowed as he prepared for the onslaught that was sure to follow.

"Stop," Celeste said in a low voice. "I'm not in the mood to clean the blood off of my sofa."

Remy stopped growling and stood clenching his fists as he tried to contain his anger. "Please," Celeste whispered, and his shoulder sagged in defeat.

He turned away from Karim, stomping across the room as his human form returned.

"Can I speak to her alone?" Karim finally asked once he realized that there would not be a fight. Not today, anyway.

Remy was about to say something, and she held up a hand.

"You can leave." She met Remy's eyes.

He stared at her for a moment, then seeing something in her that seemed to satisfy him, he turned to Julian, and they headed for the door.

"I'll be right next door if you need us," he said, and then looked at Karim with a smirk of utter disdain. "I hope when she tears your head off, the process is as slow and painful as possible."

* * *

Behind him, the door closed with a gentle snick, and Karim's body relaxed slightly. He could never wholly relax in her presence. She was strong enough to rip him apart, and if he'd truly done something to hurt her, he probably deserved it. Even if he hadn't known the consequences of his actions had been devastating in some way, he had been asked to protect her, to see her out of Persia safely. But his attraction to her had driven him nearly insane, and he had wanted nothing more than to be rid of her before he'd fallen too profoundly. He'd made a promise, bound by a blood oath to Nyx, that he would not seduce her, but he couldn't keep himself away from her.

He hadn't laid eyes on her since he'd entrusted her to the merchant would who promised to take her with his wife into the city of Pelusium. She would meet an envoy there and a ship that would take her to Thebes. The man and his wife had guaranteed her safety on the short journey. Nyx had never told him otherwise, so he had no earthy idea of why she was so angry.

No one would speak of it to him, not even Nyx, who feigned ignorance. When he'd broached the subject with the Collective, they had looked at him with horror in their eyes. Something profound had happened to her, something that had changed the sweet girl he had known into an angry, violent woman before him.

* * *

MARK OF THE FALLEN

Remy sat on his sofa, his eyes closed as he savored his drink, and soft R & B that filled the room when the knock on the door drew his attention. Two hours exactly, he thought as he opened the door to his guest.

Remy closed the door softly when Briar eased past him into the darkly decorated suite. Celeste's rooms were done in stark white with clean lines, Remy's suite was done in all blacks and deep blues; a hint of Turkish tobacco still wafted in the air from the snuffed-out cigarette Julian had left upon his exit.

Briar moved further into the room, his eyes going over the dark leather sofa and a deep pile of the sapphire blue rug before landing on the open door and the big round bed beyond. He could see the heavy black duvet and pillows in the same sapphire as the rug and knew that he would eventually end up there. His eyes moved to Remy standing barefoot, shirtless, that long ragged scar that curved around his left shoulder, smooth and shiny in the dim light. He never really spoke of the scar, which looked as if his arm had been removed and then sewn back on, and Briar knew not to push. His pants looked as if they were clinging to him by sheer will, and Briar couldn't help but think about what lay beneath the soft cotton material.

Remy was slender, but every inch of him toned muscle, smooth save the smattering of fine hair across his chest. He didn't have facial hair, and Briar wondered if he could even grow any. His skin was so soft.

"Drink?" Remy asked, moving past him only to be grasped around the waist and pulled hard against the granite wall that was Briar. Every muscle in Briar's body was rigid, demanding, and tense against him. His mouth was hot and moist against the bare skin of Remy's throat. His big beefy hand slipped low past the waistband of Remy's pants, thick fingers sinking into soft curls before slowly wrapping around his growing erection. He stroked slowly at first, his hand a silken fist playing with him.

"Oh, I have missed you, B." Remy moaned, his arm going up to cup the back of Briar's head while the knot of want low in his stomach burned through his body like a wildfire. Briar pressed his hips into him, his erection just as thick and massive as the rest of him.

"I missed you too, baby." Briar sighed. Remy turned to face him, his eyes on the soft sweetness that was Briar's incredible innocent face. He pulled him closer, their mouths meeting, his tongue slipping past his teeth into the delicious sweetness that was Briar's mouth. His taste always reminded Remy of a fresh orchard, sweet, fresh, he tasted wonderful.

He moved away just long enough to put his glass on the table before he began unbuttoning Briar's shirt, pulling it from the waist of his slacks. Remy put his lips to smooth, hairless skin, watching as the muscles tensed and released, his sex pulsating against his pants, begging for release.

Briar's entire body felt as if it were seared with each kiss. When Remy's lips moved over his nipple, his teeth grazing the skin, he sucked in sharply, his hands slipping into the luxurious curls at Remy's nape, pulling him up so that Briar could capture his mouth.

Remy was vibrating with need, pushing the shirt off Briar's arms and then reaching his belt. His abdomen flexed in anticipation, and it excited Remy to no end. Slowly, he moved down, pushing the pants and underwear down as his mouth left a trail of heat down the center of Briar's chest, his fingers sinking into the soft thatch of moist curls in an even brighter hue of red than on his head. He knelt before him, his hand around the immense thickness that twitched excitedly in his palm. The stroke was slow at first, steady as silken beads of moisture appeared at the tip, coating his hand and making Briar's skin slick and hot.

He moaned a guttural sound that came from somewhere deep inside of him. When Remy took him into his mouth, Briar's knees buckled, but he remained on his feet. The feel of

Remy's tongue, the sleek heat of his mouth as he sucked him, he thrust forward, his body moving in a rhythm to match the pull and retreat of his mouth. Remy reached out, cupping the heavyweight of his balls in his hand, gently squeezing, and his body came apart.

"Oh, fuck me." He groaned, trying to keep himself from falling back. Remy reached around, holding his ass, his fingers digging into the tense muscles as Briar bucked against him. He grabbed a fist full of dark curls, holding Remy's head still as his hips moved faster, pushing into the beautiful pressure of Remy's sweet mouth. He held tight, moving more quickly, pulling harder until Briar exploded into his mouth. He continued to draw, milking the big man who was still, every muscle straining as his organism took him, all six foot three, two hundred and sixty pounds of him, to his knees.

He sank onto the sapphire rug, his chest rising and falling as he tried to catch his breath. Remy sat up, pulling Briar's boots off so that he could undress him completely; he wanted to see him in all his massive, rippling, muscled glory. He wanted to stare at the beauty of Briar's taut, tawny skin against the deep blue of the rug. He was beautiful, so big, and so wonderful. His arms were the size of Remy's thighs, his thighs like tree trunks. Except for the soft, neatly trimmed pelt of hair of this crotch, he was sleek, hairless. Remy watched him, his arm thrown across those emerald dazzlers he called eyes, his mouth open as he sucked in great gulps of air.

"Shit," he whispered, peeping at Remy from beneath his arm. "I was hoping I could last a little longer than that, but you and that fucking mouth ... you do it to me every time," he said in his rolling brogue.

"Oh, you're giving up already?" Remy teased, rising to slip out of his pants. He was hard, his erection pointing straight up, swollen to the point of pain.

Briar lifted himself on his elbows, watching Remy with a focused intensity that would make anyone else nervous.

Remy lifted his hand to his mouth. He licked his palm, his tongue languidly moistening his palm before he began to stroke himself. His hand moved slowly, his eyes on Briar, who watched silently until his own body sparked back to life. He sat up, his back resting on the cool leather of the sofa, his knees drawn up.

"Do you want it?" Remy asked. Briar nodded. He came closer, straddling Briar until his sex bobbing near Briar's face. He continued stroking, looking down at the redhead, his bottom lips caught between his teeth. Instead of reaching for what was so close and aching to be touched, Briar pulled him down so that he was sitting across his chest.

He ran one beefy finger over Remy's kiss swollen lips before slipping into his mouth. Obediently, Remy sucked, pulling in the digit, his tongue looping and dancing against hard calloused skin. The finger was replaced by Briar's tongue, dipping into to tease him.

"Stand up. I want to suck you," he said in a low voice. Remy rose, sliding easily into the sweet mouth, his body shivering. He closed his eyes, thrusting slowly into that sweet mouth that always tasted of strawberries and cherries and such wonderful, beautiful things. He moaned, placing a hand on one beefy shoulder, his hips moving back and forth slowly. Briar's hands cupped his ass, separating toned cheeks, his fingers teasing, slowly moving around him in gentle circles until one finger moved inside of him. Remy leaned forward, his body arching as he pushed back, wanting more. Briar continued to lick, his tongue teasing the head of his cock. Remy pushed forward, straining to keep his body in check as another thick finger entered him. He groaned, every nerve exploding with such pleasure that he could make no sound.

"I want to taste you," Briar said, shifting and Remy found himself on his knees bent over the sofa. He grasped the cushions, his breath coming in harsh bursts when the first stroke of Briar's tongue touched him. He moaned, his face pressed to the cool leather.

Briar ran his tongue from the small of Remy's back, down the crack of his perfect ass, not stopping until his lips closed around the tender weights beneath his sex. He sucked gently, his mouth so hot that Remy felt himself dripping, his sex wet with his moisture, and he had to pull away for a moment to collect himself.

"Stop, you're going to make me come, B," he whispered.

"That's the point, baby," Briar teased, his teeth grazing the flesh at Remy's hip. He chuckled then returned to his delicious torture. His tongue teased, slipping into Remy's tightness, tasting him, his hand stroking his erection until the only sound Remy could make were helpless whimpers. He pulled back, rubbing the tip of his erection against Remy's ass; he rocked, loving the feel of the friction. He held Remy's hips, pulling him against him as he did.

"You want me to fuck you, baby?" He whispered next to Remy's ear.

"Yes," he whispered.

"Say it." He pressed the tip of himself against his hole, and Remy pushed back, rubbing against him.

"I want you to fuck me," Remy said, looking back at him, his arms shaking. Briar held himself still, slowly easing the tip into Remy's tightness, his body drenched with sweat as he kept himself from plunging into him. He paused, and Remy pushed back, loving the feel of Briar's thickness, massive inside of him. Briar closed his eyes, feeling Remy's muscles clenched around him, drawing him in so deep that he felt ready to come.

"Son of a bitch," he cursed, holding Remy's hips still. "You're going to make me come," he breathed.

"That's the point, baby." Remy teased, mocking Briar's heavy accent, and was rewarded for his effort. Briar pulled back until only the very tip of him was inside, then pushed forward, deep and smooth, and Remy groaned his approval. He gripped the sofa again, his nails digging into the leather as Briar's hips moved, pushing in drawing out, the rush of heat and pleasure hitting him in waves. Briar continued, his body rocking against Remy.

"You feel so good, B," Remy coaxed, leaning back to capture Briar's mouth. "I miss you so much, baby. Oh god, oh shit, don't stop. Just like that, just like that." Sweat dripped from Briar's brow as he pumped, his hips undulating like a piston, faster and faster, his breath catching in his chest. He leaned forward, his arms on either side of Remy's face as he drove harder and faster.

"Come for me, Remy," Briar said. "Come for me, oh please, let me hear it." He took Remy's earlobe between his teeth, just applying enough pressure to pinch but not break the skin. Remy groaned, loving the gruffness of Briar's voice, his heavy body pressed, hot and wet to his own. To help him along, Briar reached down and grasped Remy's sex in his hand and began to stroke, the rhythm of his hand matching the rhythm of his thrusts. Then his teeth sank into the tender skin just above Remy's shoulder, and it was all over.

Remy felt himself rolling over the edge, his body on fire, every nerve singing as he came hard in Briar's hand. He vaguely recalled hearing his big man follow, only felt the incredible sensation of every bone in his body melting away to nothing, then slowly coming back together.

Briar collapsed onto him, his breathing labored against Remy's shoulder, his lips brushing Remy's slick skin. Every few seconds, an aftershock rocked his big body, then settled. They stayed that way for a while, still, sweaty, clinging together in the afterglow. Remy smiled, loving the feel of the gentle giant on him, the pressure of his massive body covering him, his arms around Remy's waist. He sighed, his eyes drifting shut. In his way, he loved this big man.

After what felt like hours, Briar rose and stumbled towards the kitchenette, where he downed four bottles of water in quick succession before returning with one for Remy. He took it, sipping slowly, his eyes on Briar's too sweet face.

"I was thinking," he started, not knowing where this was

coming from, but he was going to say it. He was going to suggest that they go public with their relationship. But Briar put up a hand before he could get it out.

"No," he said. "It would be a disaster. I love being with you. You are one of the best people I know. But if this got out, it would be a problem. Not just for you, but me. How would it look a soldier dating the brother of the Commander?" Remy nodded.

It wasn't like people didn't suspect, but to know that he was sleeping with a subordinate could get him court-martialed or worse. It could get Briar kicked out of the Grey; as much as he cared for the kid and wanted to be with him, he was right. It was better to keep what they shared between them, just them.

"Besides," Briar said, nudging Remy's shoulder. "You like the lassies way too much to stick with just me."

"But I like you the best," he said, realizing just how much he meant that. He did like Briar the best. He was such a gentleman, so sweet and good-natured, he made Remy laugh, which was something only a few had been able to do. And most of all, Remy trusted Briar implicitly. Of all of the people he knew, there were only two names on that particular list. Celeste was the other.

"For now. But I saw the wee redhead they brought in. How long before you dip your wick into that fire?" Remy thought about that for a moment. She was cute with flame-red hair and a sweet little face, but he got a distinct impression that she was trouble. It was something about the way she smiled when Celeste had cold-cocked Karim. And she was a demon, after all, a skittish bunch at best. There were only a handful he knew of that were remotely trustworthy. He would not risk it. No matter what people thought, he did not think with his dick. Well, not always.

"It's not all redheads," he said, his eyes roaming over Briar's sweat-slicked body, goose flesh rising on naked skin. He ran a hand over the corded muscle of his thigh, his finger tracing little patterns as it dipped closer to his pelvic bone.

"That's why you liked me," Briar teased, watching Remy's long fingers move with a degree of interest. Remy's hand-dipped, and Briar's skin tightened, everything in him hard and hot and wet. The feel of skin on skin made him shiver, but he liked it. He moved closer, brushing his lips along Remy's collar bone.

"Not just that." Remy looked at him, his warm tobacco brown eyes softened, and he smiled. "You are so much more than that to me." He leaned forward, his lips brushing Briar's in the sweetest kiss. "So much more, love."

❊ ❊ ❊

Celeste poured herself another drink before easing onto the sofa, waving her hand at him to speak. Karim eased onto the sofa beside her, his hand slowly caressing her back through the silk of her shirt.

"I'm so sorry, Calie, for whatever I did. I didn't know," he whispered, resting his chin on her shoulder.

She didn't like him being that close and feeling that familiar after all of this time. He acted as if nothing had happened, as if they had a little spat over some minor issue. Not that he had sold her. He fucking sold her like a rug or a car. She could rip his throat out with her bare hands, but she didn't want to soil her pristine white furniture.

Instead, she stood, putting space between the two of them; the glass clutched so tightly in her hand, her knuckles had turned red. She swallowed the amber liquid, feeling the burn in her chest.

"Tell me what happened," he said, his hand dropping to his lap at her retreat.

"No. not. I will not discuss that with you. And you have no fucking right to ask." She stared at the empty glass in her hand.

"I need another drink." She marched toward the bar on

the far side of the room and poured herself a glass of Evan Williams' 23-year-old collection over ice.

Karim's brows rose at the sight of the expensive bourbon, it cost over three hundred dollars a bottle, and she seemed to be stocked with at least five, Not to mention the bottle of Jack Daniel's Macallan Fine & Rare Collection worth over ten thousand dollars. He took in the expensive decor, the designer rugs, and original artwork, then passed her to the open doors and swallowed hard. The bed was white quilted leather, the fluffy duvet white with gold trim, pillows piled high. It looked as if it filled the room, and all he could picture was her naked caramel skin against the white of the sheets.

After all of these centuries, he wanted her just as much, if not more, than before. The years apart had done nothing to tame his want, and it made his heartache. He reluctantly turned his eyes toward her, and the need tugged at him from somewhere deep inside.

She tugged at the top button of her shirt, freeing it and inhaling while pouring another drink. He turned to look at the bed again, and then his eyes drifted around the room, landing on anything other than her. He couldn't look at her without feeling his need pulling at him. He hadn't come here for that. He'd come to make amends. He hadn't expected the kick to the gut at being so near her. He continued looking around the suite, his face calm as he noted the lack of color here. This was not the Calie he knew; there was no reflection of her fire here. This wasn't her home.

*   *   *

She watched him scan the room and frowned. Draining her glass in one swallow, she poured another and wondered. The vampire clans had always remained neutral, never siding with the Dark Fae or the Collective. Now all of a sudden, they were eager to join one faction. And they had chosen Karim as their representative. Why?

"Why are you here?" She asked, turning to level him with a steady, steely gaze, her tears dry. "Why did you come here, Karim?"

"Because you were so upset..."

"No," she bit, "Why are you here? With the Collective? Why of all of the vampires in the world are you the one being suggested as a new member? It is why you and that demon are here, right? The last I heard, you were allied with no one, yet you show up here, out of the blue. I find it suspect that they sent you and that Lilith, so what is the plan, Karim? I mean, you don't do anything without a solid reason. So, what is it? Do the Vamps know something that we don't?"

He looked at her with those hypnotic eyes that always seem to cut right through her, his face as serene and sincere as she had ever seen it. He wore dark jeans and a white button-up under a battered leather jacket. She stared at the hint of the tattoo peeking from beneath his collar, knowing that he had Persian artwork running from his neck, down his right shoulder and bicep. He'd had the tats since before she'd known him, remembering how she'd been fascinated by the vamp's body art.

"I don't have a plan. I never have a plan when it comes to you. Calie-"

"Don't call me that, don't you dare. Calie died a long time ago."

He was suddenly standing before her, so close that she nearly stumbled backward.

She held her ground, meeting his gaze, her tone as cold as she could make it even as her body became wet and heat rose in her cheeks. She cursed her body for reacting to him, even after all he'd done.

"You will always be my Calie." He brushed a wisp of hair off of her face. "My sweet, sweet Calie." He leaned closer, his lips brushing hers in a whisper of a kiss, and every part of her melted into him. He drew her closer, his arms encircling her waist, his body ready for more. She held her arms out, not letting herself hold him. She may not have control of much when he kissed her, but she refused to embrace him.

His fangs nipped her bottom lip, his tongue slipping into the warm burn of her bourbon-soaked mouth. His hands moved to her lower back, pressing his hardened shaft into her. He ground into her, his hips working as his need grew. He held the back of her head while his tongue dove deeper, a slow moan escaping him as memories of her taste came back to him. She dropped her arms, placing the empty hand on the waist of his jeans, her body relenting to the onslaught pulling him closer.

He took a step, then another, until she was pressed against the wall, his hips pumping as he drove against her, his sex straining against his jeans.

He could feel his moisture against his skin and knew that he would come in his pants if he did not stop this insanity. Yet, he continued, unable to stop, until his body begged for more. His hand cupped her breast through the silk of her top, feeling the lace of her bra beneath. She smelled of lavender and vanilla, tasted of bourbon and her sweetness. He wanted to bite into that tender skin pulsating at her throat, to drink of her and mark her as his own.

Then he was gone, the air in front of her still smelling of him. She opened her eyes and saw him standing across the room, his eyes nearly white as he panted, his face flushed.

"I should go." His voice was rough, and he was avoiding her eyes.

She stared at him, trying to read him, but as with most preternaturals, she couldn't get an exact fix on his thoughts. Not that she was very experienced with reading minds; it was a new gift that she had developed around the time she got the tattoo on her neck. Absently, she reached up to touch it and found it to be hot, searing her fingertips.

"I'm sorry." He stumbled backward, turning, and practically running from the room. She was stunned still, unable to wrap her mind around what had just happened or how quickly it had ended.

She poured another drink with hands that trembled and swallowed it, wanting to burn away his taste. Damn, she hated how she reacted to him, hated the fact that she had succumbed to him, allowing herself to return his kiss. She could still feel him pressing into her, the soft noises she made when he thrust against her. The scent of him, sand and ocean, lingered on her skin. He had been back for less than an hour only to bring back a nightmare that she had just about put to bed, waking feelings that she had all but forgotten. She hated him.

Growling from the torrent of emotion, she stared at the bar, the empty glass and bottle of bourbon waiting for her to make a move. Abandoning the glass, she grabbed the neck of the bottle and put it to her lips, drinking long and hard until it was empty.

* * *

She lay on the sofa, her legs drawn up to her chest, the bottle of bourbon long emptied lay on the floor having slipped from her fingers. She rolled over, her back pressed to the back of the cool leather sofa, her face buried in the crook of her elbow, her dreams plagued by memories that Karim and his damned eyes had brought to the surface, tossing her into a tailspin of depression and anger within seconds. Now he even invaded her dreams with his charm and sexy smile, how she hated him for making her remember. When that hadn't dulled the feel of him pressed against her or the ache in the pit of her chest, she reached for another bottle and slumped onto the sofa, drinking until she fell asleep.

* * *

She had known something was off that morning as they packed up camp and headed towards Egypt. She was to be delivered to her father's temple to live under his protection. Since the ouster of his wife Menhit, he had insisted that she be brought to him. Her cousin, Amazonian Queen Hippolyta, had entrusted three of her most skilled warriors to escort her to the seashore where she would board a waiting ship. They had been protective but distant, not knowing her true identity. It was only within the few days of her journey that she felt something was amiss. It had only taken one to be corrupted before it spread to the others right under her nose. She did not know what had been promised or by whom, but it hadn't mattered in the end.

It had been the wine, she realized, as her eyelids grew heavy. The wine she sipped during her afternoon meal on the Cyndun River's riverbanks, less than a day's ride outside of Tarsus. It was supposed to be poison, but being who she was, it had only weakened her to the point of helplessness. She felt the effects as the sun beat down on her making her light-headed, then a current moved through her, followed by a sudden and debilitating numbness. What did that mean, she wondered before her mind became foggy and she fell. The next thing she knew, she was sinking into the darkness of the Cyndun River and over the falls that led to the vast nothing of the salty Mediterranean. Something heavy had been tethered to her with a thick heavy rope that was knotted around her waist, pulling her down into the murky depths. There was no light, no air, her body paralyzed, but her mind still active. She was helpless.

Yet, she would not die.

She wasn't sure how long she'd drifted when she felt strong hands under her arms, pulling her from her watery slumber. Her eyes opened when she was laid on the sand, and she found herself staring at the stars in the night sky. The air was chilling her skin, but the sand still held some of the heat from the day, warming her back and soothing her. She was on land again, dry unmoving land. She blinked once, twice, then again before trying to use her lungs again. She inhaled, but nothing happened, only the slight sting of *the cooling night air on her salt burned throat. She began to cough before she was rolled onto her side. Everything in her poured from between her lips in a torrent that seemed to shock her rescuer because, from somewhere behind her, she heard a litany of curses followed by hands-on her shoulders.*

It was a man, not a regular man, but a male nonetheless with large hands that patted her back as she heaved. He spoke in a foreign tongue, but it slowly transformed from garbled gibberish to actual words. He was soothing her, his rich tone even and calming, his hand surprisingly warm on her cold skin. He was from the desert. She knew that from the lilting rhythm of his words. Was he a Persian? She wondered why else he would be in the desert.

When she finally was able to inhale the clean, cool night air of the desert, her entire body began to shake from the shock of it all. She tried to focus her thoughts on something, anything other than the sting in her lungs and the burn of her eyes when a shadow crossed her face. Turning to see what fate was to befall her next, she peered into startlingly beautiful pale green eyes. They focused on her with startling intensity, but she could not turn away. Then she saw nothing at all.

When she next awoke, she found herself in the shelter of a tent, lying on satin pillows, dressed in a plain cotton tunic that reached her ankles, with nothing underneath. She sat up, feeling as though she had too much drink, her head foggy and her eyes dry from the salty sea. There was a plate of fruit and cheese on a low table nearby and a pitcher full of cold, freshwater. Lanterns burned, filling the tent with a soft amber glow. The tent itself was made of heavy black linen that shielded her from the sun, but she could see rays creeping between the slit that acted as a door. She rose slowly on unsteady legs and made her way outside.

A black stallion was tied to a post in the tent's shade, a small bowl of freshwater set out for him. There was a small fire pit just beyond the tent's entrance full of ashes, and the faint smell of roasted meat filled the air. She stared into the horizon, the sun burning eyes that had spent so much time in darkness, and saw nothing for miles but smooth, unmarked sand. It was late after-

noon; the sun was just setting behind a high dune, and everything was still. Confused, she spun in a circle looking for signs of life to find nothing, no one. Other than the horse, she was utterly alone.

And she was starving.

The sun had set, and the moon hung large and low in the sky as she lounged on the pillows contemplating her next move. She had spent most of the evening trying to contact Nyx or summon Anhur, her mind reaching out to them until it throbbed from the effort. She wasn't sure if her presence was shielded or if she was just lost to them. Perhaps this was the afterlife, and this was her hell. She reached for a grape, popping it into her mouth, and thought that her hell wasn't that bad when something in the sand to her right stirred. She froze, her heart racing as it moved again, then something large rose from the dirt. Her eyes stretched as he shook the sand from shoulder-length dark hair and then pulled himself out of the ground, as naked as the day he was born. And it was a male; there was no doubt about that.

She nearly screamed, the grape slipping down her throat and choking her. She pounded herself on the chest, assisting the fruit down her throat. She swallowed hard and tried to catch her breath, watching as he coolly moved toward a large vase, pouring water into a basin, and began to wash.

He splashed water on his face before turning his eyes to her, and she gasped. The pale green eyes she had seen before, he had pulled her from the murky depths. She sat slack-jawed, watching him lift his face and pour the basin of water over his head. It ran down his dark hair and the column of his spine, over his firm buttocks and muscled legs. She watched the journey with fascination. He filled the basin again and doused himself once more. This time her eyes landed on his sex, and she could not look away.

She had seen naked men before, but not one of this magnitude and never this close. He was mere feet away, and she could see every detail of him, the ripple of muscle beneath his skin, the wide expanse of his back, and the markings that had been etched into his skin. He was lean, but every inch of him hummed with raw power and sexuality. She swallowed again, her eyes latched onto that part of him that made him male, and it began to grow beneath her gaze. She frowned as it stiffened, jutting up towards his stomach, a fine patch of hair that looked as smooth as a baby's hair. It jumped, getting harder, and she licked her lips, wondering what it would feel like to touch it. Would it be rough or silky smooth? What would it feel like if she allowed him inside of her, surely it would hurt? That was what the others had told her in the camp. They said that it hurt, but only at first and only if the male was unskilled. She did not doubt that this male was very skilled.

A chill went through her as she realized that they were in the middle of nowhere, no other soul for miles, and she had no way out. He could take her right now, and in her weakened state, she wouldn't be much of an opponent. He could force himself on her, and no one could save her. She took a chance and glanced at his sex again, gasping in surprise when it moved.

"Do you see something you like, Caelestis?" At the use of her name, she started, her eyes going to meet his. He was smiling, eyes dancing with delight. When he smiled, she noted his fangs? It was something that should have captured her attention, but she had been so focused on his body that she had not paid much attention to anything else. The fact that he'd buried himself in the sand, shielding him from the damage of the sun's rays, should have tipped her off as well, but spending so much time underwater had clouded her senses.

Vampire.

Sure, she knew they existed, but this was her first encounter with one. He flashed those teeth again, and she wondered if she should be worried about her throat as well as her virginity.

He chuckled.

"'So, you mean to rape me then?" She asked in her matter-of-fact way.

He laughed, a hearty, full-bodied laugh that took her by surprise, but she remained still. He shook his head and turned to look at her.

"No," he said simply. "I do not mean to harm you in any way."

She leaned back against the silken pillows that had been her bed and crossed her arms over her chest.

"How do you know my name? Who are you?" she asked sharply. Her regal bearing returning.

He quickly slipped into a pair of trousers, tying them at the waist with a strip of leather before turning to her. His hair was still wet, leaving trails of water over that tattoo that ran from his right shoulder down his arm to his elbow in beautiful scrawl.

"I am Karim. I was sent to find you, protect you. I am your envoy until Pelusium, by order of your grandmother; I am to keep you unharmed," he said, coming to sit beside her. "I gave Nyx the blood oath that I would see you safely across the desert." He was staring at her, his eyes so intense that she felt herself backing away from him.

"You are a Persian?" she asked, her eyes drifting back to the dark inky pattern on his tawny skin.

"That I am, Caelestis."

She pursed her lips and looked him over for a moment longer. So, this was her first encounter with a Persian and a vampire. And he didn't seem to mind as her eyes roamed over his form. He was virile and made her think things she had thought of in the presence of no other male. She found herself wondering what his skin would feel like if she touched it. Would he be cold like the long-dead or warm like the living, breathing man she saw before her?

"Not what you were expecting?" he asked.

"I expected nothing," she said honestly.

"I hope I do not disappoint." His tone was teasing, and a shiver when through her. It was a shot of electricity that made her heart beat faster and her palms sweat. She felt an exciting stirring and pushed it away. What was happening, she thought.

"Where are we?" she asked, swallowing around the lump that had formed in her throat. She had not been around many males, growing up in the Amazonian village. There were some, during mating times and celebrations, but none like this creature. He was looking at her, watching her eyes move as if he were trying to memorize her features, burning them into his memory.

"We are outside of Hamath."

She gasped, rising suddenly.

"Hamath? But-we were just outside of Tarsus - nearly to the shore. I do not understand." She was hundreds of miles from where she'd begun. Hamath was a port city halfway between Egypt and Tarsus. She had floated nearly across the Mediterranean Sea. She sat still for a moment; her eyes closed as she tried to will herself to Egypt. Nothing happened.

Shrugging, she tried to again, this time willing herself to Nyx's temple. Again, nothing. She looked at Karim, her brow furrowed.

"Why can I not go to Nyx? Why can't I feel her? Why can't I feel any of them?" She could hear the rising panic in her tone and swallowed to keep herself calm. He was before her in a blink, kneeling in front of her.

"Be calm, little one. Whatever was given to you bound your abilities. As soon as we get to Nyx, she will fix that. It is only a temporary issue. That's why I am here." He ran a hand over her hair, intent on calming her. She looked at him with those big bright eyes, and he melted. Damn, she was gorgeous.

"What has happened?" She took a deep breath, trying to reign in the panic that threatened. Why could she not use her teleportation? Why was Nyx unable to find her? What had they done to her?

"Nyx lost contact with you on the day you were to arrive. That was when she sent scouts in search of you. Somehow, your bond was broken. Your escorts, the women you thought of like sisters, had been corrupted. You were poisoned, and your body was tossed into the Cyndun River. You were carried out to sea. Many believed you were dead. Nyx did not believe so." He pulled a tunic over his head and ran a hand through dark hair. She could see more of his face then, a beautifully chiseled face with eyes that made the hairs on her skin rise.

"Why did she not come herself? I have not been away that long, have I?" she asked, sipping from a goblet of wine. It was sweeter than any wine she'd had before and made her feel slightly lightheaded. She supposed it was from her lack of food and so much time in the sea. She'd been in the sea, she marveled. She stared at her hands, her fingertips still pruny from being submerged.

"Caelestis,"

"Calie. If we are to travel together, I prefer Calie," she said absently before meeting his gaze. Again, that soft, sexy smile made an appearance, his fangs illuminated in the candlelight. She ran her tongue over her tiny fangs, feeling her need to feed returning. The sooner she fed, the stronger she would be, but if she drank from him, that meant she would have to return the favor, and she was not sure she wanted the male's mouth anywhere near her tender parts.

"Calie, you have been lost for a long time. Your presence has been hidden from the gods; we believe that whoever poisoned you masked your existence. None of them could find you, and I have a very special talent for tracking. Many who started the journey with me gave up once the Amazon camp was destroyed."

"Destroyed?" she whispered. "What of Hippolyta?"

"She was saved, but she was one of only a few. Nyx released the Kere when she discovered what had been done to you. They are gone. Hippolyta met her glory many years ago now; you have been gone for a very, very long time, Calie." She felt tears bring a fresh sting to her eyes and avoided his gaze. He placed a long, cool finger beneath her chin, forcing her to look at him, her eyes glistening a brilliant sky blue in the dim lighting.

"Do not shed tears for them. They do not deserve your tears, my sweet Calie. I am your protector now. I will make sure you arrive in Pelusium safely. I would give my life for you, Caelus- Calie," he said, his voice a whisper as he gathered her close.

"How long? How long have I been gone? Did they even mourn for me? Did my father mourn for his loss?" she asked softly, her voice catching as she spoke into his bare chest. This close, she could h smelled of sand, water, and desert air. And he felt good.

"He did. He has. They all did, and Nyx still does. But ..."

"How long, Karim?" she pleaded.

"It's been over two hundred years," he said, stunning her speechless.

❈ ❈ ❈

Celeste woke with a start, her heart thrumming in her chest. She looked around the suite and cursed under her breath. She needed to get out of here and go where she felt some semblance of normalcy. She needed to go home.

* * *

CHAPTER THREE

When Lilith had come to this place, she had expected the staid and stately appearance of Jonas and Arbor Kent. She had known that the Collective were a regal and reserved bunch, stodgy and buried in old-world sensibility. What she hadn't expected was the fire that had burned through the room when Celeste and Remy entered the small space.

Of course, Lilith had heard of the Caelestis. Who hadn't?

She was infamous, the goddess who'd defied even death, not once but time and time again. Her brutality in battle was as legendary as her beauty, but to see her in person was not at all what she'd expected of the storied Commander of the Grey. She'd blocked out the inane chatter around her, focusing on the task at hand. She was going to meet Caelestis. It was something she had waited centuries to do.

When she'd entered, Lilith felt a wave of heat rush over her, and her mouth went dry. She, like the others, rose to greet the new arrivals. But unlike the others, she nervously wiped her sweaty palms on her pants and swallowed hard in anticipation of their introduction. She was going to be face to face with her in a matter of seconds.

She had seen Remy first, looking dapper in the grey wool coat and creased uniform. He was what she had known he would be. He was gorgeous in a masculine way, with a swagger that oozed confidence. She had heard rumors about Remy and his proclivities; tales of debauched parties and brawls in dive bars had swirled around the youngest Kent son for as long as she could remember. He had bedded so many that his prowess was somewhat legendary, yet all spoke fondly of the fun-loving shifter.

Just one look in the direction of Arbor Kent, the current High Regent, and anyone could see that her only biological son was adored. He nodded towards his mother but stayed close to Celeste's left side, a smile threatening to make his pretty face beautiful.

Celeste, on the other hand, was not at all what she expected. Sure, she knew that she was beautiful, but to see her in person was something she had only imagined. Celeste was striking in that deep grey uniform, shedding the fur-lined cloak with a natural ease that Lilith had practiced for years to achieve. Lilith was pale, almost sickly looking with her brilliant red hair. Celeste looked as if she lived in the sun. She was taller than Lilith had imagined, with a more curvaceous build, but her face was flawless. Her face was what caught her by surprise. She expected someone with stronger features, a fierce look of a warrior woman, not this pretty girl. That was it. She looked like a girl, not a storied, battle-worn soldier. She looked more Vogue than Soldier of Fortune, with her perfectly coiffed hair and immaculate clothing. Celeste was not at all what she had expected, and the woman immediately enthralled her.

Everything about her read leader, the way she moved through the room like a general, her presence filling the space with the sweet smells of lavender and vanilla. Lilith nodded when Jonas introduced her, unable to form any words as the firelight danced across her soft caramel-colored skin. She had been incomplete and utter amazed at the woman standing before her. Her eyes, her magnificent eyes, shifted from the vibrant turquoise to a color that could only be described as neon cerulean when the vamp turned to face her. Lilith barely had time to comprehend what was happening before the room erupted into noise and movement as Celeste knocked the vamp on his ass.

Of course, Lilith had noticed the Persian when she arrived. She couldn't help but notice him. He sat like a brooding prince in a high-backed chair, his beautiful face tight with apprehension. Not that she blamed him. Vamps were not known for mingling, so sending someone to act as the attaché for the Collective was a significant coup. She was surprised they had even let him in, most vamps being somewhat opposed to the Collective, as a whole. Yet, there he sat, looking oh so sexy. He had been polite enough when they were introduced, but he had been distracted and slightly nervous as well. She wasn't sure if it was in this place or their impending meeting with Celeste.

When he was introduced, everything in the room went still and cold for half a second before Celeste struck him, and hell broke loose.

Lilith had finally taken her seat when she was handed a glass of brandy. She took it with shaky hands, smiling tightly at Arbor, who sat beside her. Lilith remembered looking at the woman, her calm and exterior comforting, and she found herself relaxing in her presence.

"Don't worry, hon," Arbor said in her easy tone. "She's more bark than bite. Remy will calm her down," she assured her, and Lilith thought about that for a while. She watched as everyone else seemed to calm and even chuckle to themselves. They had not intervened, and they hadn't seemed overly worried about the situation because they knew. They knew that Celeste would never hurt someone she truly cared for, no matter how angry.

Now, as she sat alone in this room, Lilith thought about that again and smiled. The goddess who defeated death had given her the key to her weakness without even realizing it.

* * *

Karim wandered through the Collective's compound's winding corridors for what felt like hours before realizing that he was lost. The compound was larger than he'd been aware of when he'd left Celeste's suite on the fifth level. In his wanderings, he'd discovered four additional levels of living quarters that were set aside for the Collective and guests in need of refuge. As a hotel, there were two rooms set aside for balls, parties, and various rituals. The levels closest to the top were for business, places you would find in any office building, board rooms, courtrooms, and the like. More people milled around on these levels, going about their business, socializing, and greeting each other. A few cast sidelong glances at the vampire as he moved through the halls. Not because he was particularly imposing, but because vampires had never been a part of the Collective.

It wasn't until he ventured to the lowest levels, those so deep underground and so well protected, that no sound escaped them, that he realized he was utterly alone in the corridors: the prison and punishment levels, the levels where executions and severe judgments were carried out. The cells on these levels were impenetrable with solid titanium walls and twelve-inch-thick vault doors that would take a year to get through. There were the rooms with silver, iron, and other metals in the bars, and those with double-paned reinforced glass, each designed to keep certain species from escaping. He felt a chill on these levels and went back to the beginning.

If things had been different, he could have ended up in one of these cells. He absently touched his lips, remembering the itch, the spark of electricity that ran through him whenever he kissed her. He had gone centuries fantasizing about her taste, her scent, the way her eyes shifted with her moods. She was sharp and funny, and such a sweet girl, and his actions had somehow changed her.

The elevator doors opened, and he found himself right outside of the room where his night had begun with such promise. He was not at all surprised to see the room empty, the fire dying in the hearth. He moved deeper into the room and took a seat on the sofa, watching the shadows playing across the walls in macabre pantomime.

"There you are. Such a dramatic exit, I thought you might have gone. Or been tossed into a torture cell. I guess you're wilier than I gave you credit for. Impressive." Her voice was deeper than expected, coming from one so slight and fair. Karim rolled his eyes, not at all surprised that she was lurking in the dark.

"I went to speak to Cal ... speak to Cal-Celeste. I wasn't trying to impress you," he said, feeling strange calling her by that name. She would always be Calie to him, Calie with the dancing eyes and a laugh that sounded like the flutter of butterfly wings. He wondered if he would ever hear that laugh again.

"Ah, the beautiful warrior goddess, she is quite fierce in person. And they weren't kidding about the eyes, the way the color shifts. Gorgeous. I have never seen anything quite like them. Or her, for that matter. She pretty much lives up to the legend, wouldn't you say? It was kind of sexy the way she went all Amazonian. Frightening. You must have done something awful." She slid easily into a seat nearby, a drink in her tiny hand, her hair tossed over slim shoulders. Her brilliant red hair, which looked darker in the dim light, was brushed away from a surprisingly cute face; her eyes colorless in the pale firelight. She stared at Karim the way a tiger might eye a weakened gazelle.

"And did the Commander forgive you for your misdeeds?" she asked. "Tell me, what did you do?"

He looked at her for a long moment, his eyes narrowing suspiciously. She was close, her eyes like blood rimmed ice, and her skin was the true definition of porcelain, pale white as if she'd been carved with a delicate hand. Her lips were thin lines stained red. Her hair was such a vivid shade of crimson that it made her skin seem transparent even in the dimness of the room. Something about her filled him with unease. Even her small stature and the slight frame was off-putting to him.

He slid away from her. His hip pressed into the wooden arm of the sofa. He felt that if she touched him, he would somehow be tainted, poisoned by her.

"Why should I tell you anything? Why are *you* here anyway?" he asked, hearing Celeste's voice echoing in his mind. She had asked him the same thing, and just like this creature, he hadn't answered. Yet, he felt that his reasons were more selfish, more personal than this demon's reasons. He had come in part to see Celeste again. When he'd heard that there was a goddess with brilliant blue eyes working as the Commander of the Grey, he needed to find out if it was her. He'd convinced the vampire elders that he would be the perfect candidate for their proposed merger with the Collective.

After all, he'd been a messenger of the primordial, he was one of the oldest and strongest vampires, and he had a pure and regal bloodline. Who better than the fallen prince to redeem the good standing of the vampire clans within the Collective? He had avoided any mention of Calie, her well-being, life now, or even the possibility of seeing her again. Because he knew that his curiosity, all of his want of her had not died in all of these years

And although his motives were less than noble, he got a distinct impression that Lilith's motivations were much more sinister. Something in her smile and the glint in her eyes, or perhaps it was the way the fire cast shadows across her face that made his blood run cold.

"We are alike, you and I, Karim. We have come to this fortress with similar tasks in mind. If we work together, surely it could be beneficial. You already have a relationship with the goddess. She wields such power and respect that they will do anything she asks. These creatures revere her, and even though they won't admit it, she is truly the leader. With your influence over ."

Karim rose to feel sick to his stomach. He did not know if it was her presence or how she spoke, but something was wrong. He could feel a pressure, a building headache, growing behind his eyes as she spoke. The tone of her voice was almost hypnotic, and his natural urge was to fight against it. He stared into her crystal eyes and watched as the red from the rim of her eye bled into her irises, making them as blood-red as her hair. It was a startling effect, and he found himself feeling queasy the longer he stared. She was doing something to him, something that felt nasty and wrong.

"No," he snapped, backing away from her. "You will not bend my will to suit your needs, demon. Stay out of my head because you will not like what you find there." He practically roared. "Don't pursue this, or you will end your days in a torture cell."

He left the room, feeling unclean and ill. It had taken him a moment to figure out that she was trying to influence him to help her. Bending his will to act as her minion, do her bidding. He realized that she managed to attempt in a place that was void of magic. The compound was a bound place. No magic allowed, not by anyone. So how had she managed that?

The demon Lilith didn't know was that you could not bend the will of one of the *Seven*, especially one as old as he.

Karim left and immediately felt the need to warn someone. His only problem was who to go to with this information? He paused at the elevator bank and realized there was only one person he could talk to about this.

✳ ✳ ✳

She ran, the wind blowing in her face as she made her way through traffic to jog past the convention center toward the French Quarter. In skin-tight shorts that showed off long toned legs and a tank that emphasized full breasts, more than a few heads turned as she moved with effortless grace down Decatur towards Jackson Square. She loved the burn in her lungs, sweat dripping down her face and under her breasts while Green Day blasted into her ears from her iPod. Her head was clear, memories of Karim lifting away as she pushed harder, her muscles straining.

She began to slow her pace as she saw the black wrought

iron fence surrounding the square and heard a beautifully melodic male voice. It was a soft tenor, singing something bouncy, and the crowd around him clapped in rhythm to his acoustic guitar. She moved closer and saw his platinum hair and deep tan above the swaying crowd and smiled.

He spotted her too because he began to walk through the crowd, which parted in his wake, clearing a path so that he could make his way to the beauty with the bright blue eyes. Not blue, really, more of a cerulean with bright violet flecks. Her long dark hair was in a ponytail that swayed as she bobbed from one foot to the other.

He moved closer, changing his song from some made-up jaunt to one of her favorites, *Fat Bottomed Girls by Queen*. The crowd seemed a bit taken aback, but she laughed, shaking her head. He wore Hawaiian print board shorts, a faded and rather well-worn t-shirt, and flip flops. He looked more like a surfer dude than a singer. He circled her as he sang, *'Are you going to take me home tonight? Ah, down beside that red firelight. Are you gonna let it all hang out? Fat bottomed girls, you make the rockin' world go round,"*

She turned, a blush creeping into her cheeks as he moved closer. He sang loud and clear and began to follow her as she slowly backed away, waving at the crowd that voiced their disappointment as she left. The performer held out his hands to the public then followed her, singing as he did.

The crowd followed him.

The troupe had grown until they reached Cafe du Monde, and she could no longer stand it. She looked at him over her shoulder, his eyes dancing, and his smile infectious. More people were turning to watch her being serenaded, and she could take no more. She stopped, turning to face him, and the parade halted. The singing didn't.

"Ladies and gentlemen, how about a round of applause for the one and only Nicky Sky." She clapped, and the horde went insane. Without his leather pants and dark eyeliner, without the glitter and glam, they had no idea that the playful street singer they were enjoying was none other than rock god Nicky Sky. Her best friend of six years now.

He narrowed his eyes as the crowd closed in, moving closer for pictures and autographs. He smiled and signed, not wanting to be rude; he was never disrespectful. But he watched Celeste as she moved away from the crowd to continue her jog back to her apartment and a nice hot shower.

"I'll get you for this, CeCe!" he yelled.

She waved her fingers and put her earbuds back in as Billy Joe Armstrong sang *American Idiot.*

* * *

She heard the pluck of guitar strings in her living room when she exited the shower. She paused while she was drying her hair as he picked out a familiar melody. She knew he'd chase her down after what she'd done to him. She was sure he would have gotten to her apartment a little later than he had. She dressed quickly in baggy sweats, fuzzy green socks, her hair hanging in damp waves over her shoulders.

She left her bathroom, a large room in white with a clawfoot tub that was big enough to fit two people and always smelled of lavender. She crossed her bedroom, an elegant affair in soft yellows and lavender, the skylight casting bright rays of summer sunlight across the pillows, giving the entire room a sun-kissed glow. She left the room, taking the stairs two at a time, and spotted the platinum spikes of his hair on her sofa.

"How did you get in here?" she asked when she reached the bottom step. Nicky turned and looked back at her, smiling deviously. He looked like a little kid surrounded by the museum-quality decor. Celeste had so many artifacts and souvenirs from her many years on earth that many didn't even fit into her relatively small apartment. What was here now ranged from Japanese samurai armor in her office nook to medieval tapestries and a nasty bit of modern art that hung on one wall, long metal spikes pointing outward. One had to be careful not to slide into it or risk the possibility of impalement.

Nicky had often joked that the warehouse that stored the remainder of her collection would make any curator, historian, or archaeologist go moist if they ever got a peek at it.

"You know," he rose slowly, still in his t-shirt and board shorts, his feet bare, "that is the advantage of being a rock star. I can get in just about anywhere. Do you have anything to eat in here besides carrot sticks and chocolate chips?"

"I haven't had a chance to get to the store. I was supposed to go this morning, but I got called in. Wanna come with me?" She went through the cabinets making a mental note of everything she needed to stock up on.

"Sure. Is this the Collective?" he asked. Nicky knew of Celeste's true identity. He'd known for years, and she had been grateful for his friendship. He was the one person outside of the preternatural world who knew the truth about her. He was her rock, her saving grace, her connection to the real world where magic and monsters didn't exist. He allowed her to have a real life.

* * *

When she had met him in a small, very elite, very private college six years ago, Nicolai Skylar Novachek was an outcast. A scholarship kid stuck in a dorm surrounded by blue bloods who looked down on him. Everyone except the gorgeous Celeste Keegan Kent. She had appeared, like a fantasy on a chilly fall morning in his junior year. When she moved across the small campus, it was as if the world had stopped. He remembered the way the air smelled, fresh and crisp with the coming winter. Her hair was blowing in the breeze, leaving a trail of black silk behind her as she followed two dark-suited men into the dormitory. She'd glanced his way, only for a second, but when she did, he got the full blast of her beauty. He had was instantly captivated.

The first time he'd made her laugh, he'd fallen in love. It hadn't even mattered what she was by the time he'd accidentally seen her feed from her oldest brother's thick wrist. He had walked into her room, talking while he read a pizza menu, and seen the bulky man sitting calmly as Celeste sank her delicate fangs into his wrist.

He'd dropped the menu and stared until Gaston barked for him to close the door. Terrified, he'd obliged but stood pressed against the closed door, his eyes as wide as saucers, his jaw slack as Celeste continued to feed.

When she was done, she'd looked brighter, healthier, refreshed almost. Gaston shook his head, rising as he looked over Nicky. He was tall, over six-three, a wall of heaving muscle with eyes that were a mossy greenish-brown and sharply focused on Nicky, who cowered too frightened to run. He did note that Gaston, though large and intimidating, did not have a stern face. He had a rather kind yet strong angular face, severe mouth, and skin the color of a perfect cappuccino. But an aura of danger radiated from him. Gaston Kent was raw power and menace in a three-piece suit.

"We should wipe his memories," Gaston said.

He remembered Celeste looking at him, her eyes neon as she inspected him. He met her gaze, feeling calm, and suddenly relaxed. She moved closer at lightning speed. Her fangs bared as if she were going to attack. He was startled, then he started to laugh, a weird high-pitched keening that turning into hysterical giggling. Gaston and Celeste stared at each other.

"This is new," Gaston said with a curiously lifted brow.

Nicky slid down the door, his knees drawn up, hands resting easily on their peaks as he chuckled and snorted, tears streaming down his face.

"Okay," Gaston sighed, kissing her forehead. "I'll be going

now. I believe you can handle - this." He pulled the door, shoving Nicky to the side before he squeezed his massive frame through a crack in the door.

"What are you?" he'd finally calmed enough to ask.

She'd sighed and took his hand in hers and told him everything. It seemed to pour out of her, and he took it in, wanting to hear all she had to say. It started a long conversation that lasted until the early hours of the morning. There had been no secrets between them since. Not even the fact that Nicky was entirely in love with her had been held at bay. Even though he knew that it could never be, he still loved her. And in her way, the only way she knew how she loved him.

* * *

"Collective." He nodded, leaning easily against the kitchen counter.

"That was a cute little stunt you pulled in the Quarter. It took me nearly an hour to get away from those people. It turned into a mob scene. The police had to come. I hope you're happy with yourself." She peered at him from over the open pantry door, her eyes twinkling, and he knew she was smiling even though he couldn't see her mouth.

"Extremely. That's what you get for embarrassing me like that. *Fat Bottomed Girls*? Really?" She closed the cabinet door, a bottle of water in her hand, and went to sit on the sofa. He followed, grunting indignantly, his eyes on her ass.

"You love that song." He laughed. "It was the only song I could think of when you came jogging up looking all hot and tempting. You have a great ass; besides, the only other song that came to mind was *Me So Horny*." She nearly sprayed him with the water that came shooting from her lips in surprise. "I thought you would appreciate *Queen* more. Anyway, let's go on vacation. Ditch your classes and less go to Tahiti. You and me, drinking fruity drinks and getting massages on the beach.

It's summer. You're hot, and I'm young, let's go. Why do you need school anyway?"

"I want to be a doctor. I want to do something meaningful with my life." Celeste was enrolled in Tulane as a third-year medical student with hopes of going into genetic research. Both Nicky and Remy had scolded her about going to school when she could manifest a medical degree. It wasn't like she couldn't obtain the intelligence, but she insisted on being an actual student with her human counterparts. It was what made her unique in her world. She enjoyed her interaction with humans, relished it. She cared for them more than mere playthings or curiosities. She loved the human world. She fit there, much better than she did in her world. It was part of the reason she kept Nicky around. He kept her grounded in reality.

"You being you is meaningful. You're a goddess, for Christ's sake, how much more meaning do you need?"

She rolled her eyes and sighed.

"I want to be more ..." she said, knowing he would understand. Nicky always understood.

"So, what did the almighty Collective want?" To him, the work of the Collective always sounded as if it were some shadowy faction like the CIA or MI5. Everything they did was covert, and Celeste was always being summoned, night and day. She would disappear for an hour of a day, sometimes for hours, sometimes days. When she returned, she was always a little tense; today, she was just about humming with tension. Her run had done nothing to quell her jangled nerves. Something out of the norm had happened.

"They wanted to introduce us to potential new clans joining the Collective. There were two crossovers from the Dark Fae. Well, one was from the Dark side. The other the other, I don't know what he wants." She picked at the label on the water bottle, worrying it with her thumbnail until it came free. She kept her eyes down, watching as the paper fell to the rug in a gentle spiral. Nicky's well pedicured, flip flop adorned feet came into view, and she took a chance, looking up. He'd perched himself on the edge of the coffee table, those sky-blue eyes of his, solemn as he quietly waited for her to speak. She exhaled and debated whether or not she would say anything. Nicky was the one person she had confided in. The one person who knew all of her demons.

He was silent, his face an expressionless stone wall. He didn't move, didn't breathe as he waited. She reached out, taking his hand in hers, and sighed once more, a deep sigh that pushed out all of the bad, stale air that had collected in her lungs.

"It was him, Nicky. Karim. He's here," she said and felt the brief tightening of Nicky's fingers around her own. He was going to speak, and then he didn't. Instead, he gave her a quick tug, and she was pulled into a steady, gentle hug. They stayed that way for a moment, on their knees in the middle of the living room in a strong and silent embrace. As usual, Nicky always knew just what she needed.

"So how badly did you kick his ass?" he asked, and she laughed. He held her at arm's length and smiled.

"Not as badly as I wanted to. Remy and Julian pulled me off of him. But they came to my room afterward. He is there is just something..." She stood up, turning away from him as she prepared to let this next piece of news fly.

"He made a move on you."

She turned to look at him. Nicky had eased onto the sofa and sat with his hands behind his head, staring.

"How...?" She stared, and Nicky snorted.

"Of course, he made a move. He would be insane if he didn't try something." He patted the cushion beside him, and she came to sit with him. He draped an arm around her shoulders and sighed. "He doesn't have a desert or ocean separating him from what he wants. He had to make a move."

"Nicky, he abandoned me in the desert. That is a pretty clear sign that he's just not into me. Not anyway. Whenever he gets close, he pulls back like he's I don't know. Like he's playing with me. I don't like it. I don't like him. I just want to pluck his eyes out, rip off his head, and break him in half."

"But you didn't, and it's not like you didn't have a chance. And believe me, he wants you, Ce." Nicky sighed, kissing the top of her head.

"We all do," he teased, and she managed a rueful chuckle.

❊ ❊ ❊

CHAPTER FOUR

Persia, 466 BC

Karim packed their things, strapping them carefully to his horse, his eyes on Calie as she put out the fire she'd started when the sun had begun to set, and the air turned chilly. Her tunic material was dark but very sheer, allowing her body to be cooled during the day when the sun blazed across the sand. At night, it gave nearly no protection, the wind cutting through the thin cotton gauze, emphasizing the fullness of her breasts and the gentle curve of her hips. She leaned forward, and the neckline pulled away from her body, giving him the full view of bare breasts, her nipples tight from the cold.

For the better part of a week, he had traveled with her across the desert, sleeping during the grueling day and traveling at night. The more time he spent with the goddess, the more enchanted he became by her. She was sweet and honest to a fault. She asked questions that would make any other woman blush, but her innocence, gentle nature, was disarming. He had not expected to find such purity in a warrior goddess.

He had only witnessed her ferocity once. On their second night together, two marauding thieves had invaded their camp. The men had arrived just at dusk, just as he was rising from his slumber. He could hear the voices, men barking orders at a delicate woman alone in the desert. By the time Karim had risen entirely, ready to charge into the night with his sword drawn, Calie had taken one of the men to his knees. He watched as she fought, barehanded against two brutish men. She was magnificent in battle, agile and graceful with a speed and viciousness that would make the strongest Amazon proud.

When it was done, she looked back at him, her eyes a steely grey, her chest rising and falling as she tried to catch her breath. Her long dark hair caught the breeze and flew behind her like a great black cape. She smiled, her delicate fangs dripping with the blood of the fallen men.

"We now have two horses. There was a third, but he ran off. They are still warm if you need to feed," she said with a blood-soaked smile. Karim lost his heart in an instant.

He watched her shift, and his gaze went from the tops of her perfect breasts down the plain of her stomach to the soft hint of curls at her center. Swallowing, he averted his gaze, cursing himself for looking. He cursed the fact that his body responded. She was his charge, and he was to protect her, not lust after her.

"How much longer do you think it will take?" she asked suddenly, and he nearly jumped out of his skin.

"What?" he asked, his tone much harsher than he'd intended. He was staring again. Damn him. He couldn't help himself. He was drawn to her. That sweetness pulled at his heart. He'd stay awake until well after the sun had risen in the shade of the tent, listening to her speak of her home with the Amazons and being one of the primordial. He would tell her of his home in the desert, answering her questions until well into the afternoon. She was so curious and excited by everything in a world she had lived in for centuries but had barely seen. She was smart and funny, a little too honest and completely beguiling. He was done for, and he knew it.

He avoided eye contact, busying himself by packing the tent. She sighed in exasperation, a sound he had grown accustomed to overtime. She did it whenever she felt the slightest bit of frustration.

"Until we get to Pelusium? How long?" she repeated, wrapping her arms around herself. She was freezing, her lips turning slightly blue. He reached for a bedroll shaking it so that the blanket opened with a flourish. They had traveled together for over a week now, and he cared for her more and more with each passing day. He'd seen her strip down to bathe, watching her when he should have been asleep. She was always so warm, and he could not stop think-

ing of her hot, sweaty body writhing beneath him in the sun-warmed sand. Shaking off the image, he took two steps closer.

"Another week or two. It depends on how often I get to feed." He wrapped the blanket around her shoulders, coming close enough that he could smell the vanilla of her hair and the lavender of her skin. She looked up at him with those magnificent blue eyes, and he could no longer breathe.

She hadn't seen him this closely before, but now she openly inspected him, his ice green eyes, long dark hair that fell forward as he wrapped her in the warmth of the blanket. He smelled of sand, and though there was none within miles, the ocean. He had a trace of stubble that gave him a rugged look. His angular face was tense, his jaw clenched and unclenched as he stood looking down at her.

"Do you need to feed now?" she asked, trying to read his expression. "You can take from me if it will help." She brushed her long braid over her shoulder and tilted her head. He stared at the delicate curve of her neck, watching the gentle pulse of her heartbeat in the throbbing vein there. He wanted to taste her, to have her in every possible way.

"No." His voice was low, a strained whisper. He looked down, his hair falling forward, masking his eyes. She reached up, gently brushing his thick tresses off of his forehead so that she could see those fantastic eyes.

"You have the most glorious eyes. They are the most beautiful and kindest eyes I have ever seen. When you pulled me from the sea, they were the first thing I saw, and I knew that you would protect me," she said.

He grasped her wrist, the movement so swift that she was left breathless; she felt her heart hammering in her chest.

"Did I repeat the wrong thing?" she asked.

He met her gaze; his body coiled tighter at the slightest touch of her silken skin. He ran a thumb over the pulse point that matched her erratic heartbeat, his fangs extending. She moistened her lips, her pink tongue darting out to caress her full top lip. He held in a groan as his body went hard and hot. He wanted to kiss her mouth. Everything about her made him want her. The arrogant tilt of her chin, the way she flipped her mane of dark hair over her shoulders. Her constant prattle as she asked question after question and her brutal but completely innocent honesty. Standing so close, her smell was intoxicating, and he could only imagine that she tasted like fresh peaches and berries.

"If you don't need to feed, why are your fangs getting longer?" Her voice was a croak, pushed through the tightness in her throat. He moved closer, his body nearly pressed into her, those eyes lightened, if that were possible, until they were the color of moonlight and her breath caught, "Do you mean to have me now?" she asked on an exhale.

'Do you want me to have you, Calie?" he asked, his lips close to her cheek.

"I see the way you watch me when you think I'm not looking. I see your body react to my gaze. You want to take me, lay with me in the sand, brand me as yours. Yet you do not. Why is that? Do you not find me pleasing?" She asked, her voice a warm whisper against his ear.

"You are very pleasing, Calie." Every hair on his body stood on end, and he could feel his arousal throbbing against his trousers. How had someone so innocent made him so hard without even trying? He closed his eyes and fought the urge to lift her tunic and drive himself into the moist folds of her sex, feel her heat around him, welcoming him.

Against his better judgment, he stroked her cheek; the feel of soft, smooth skin beneath his fingertips was like a shock to his system. His fingers sank into jet colored hair that was softer than silk and darker than moonless midnight.

"Oh, hell." He pulled her close, his lips covering hers, and all of the air left her lungs. Her lips were softer than he imagined. Her mouth tasted of honey and something so sweet he had no name for it. His tongue slipped into that sweet honey, his body pressing into her. He could feel the heat from her core through the thin tunic, the moisture as she went wet and limp against him. She gripped his shoulders, her mouth pliant, and her body willing to accept him.

He pulled away, taking a step back before turning his back on her, his body shaking from the need for more. He could still smell her arousal, strong and delicious. Vanilla and sugar wafted around her like an aphrodisiac. Her body was so soft and willing, and he cursed his weakness.

"Why did you stop? Did I not do it properly?" she asked, confusion in her tone.

Karim could not look at her without his body enacting a revolt. He had promised not to do this, and here he was, ready to have her in the moonlight. He groaned, his body aching for the need of her.

"You did nothing wrong." He moaned.

"Then, why?" She was coming closer. He could feel her, smell her scent getting stronger though her feet made no sound on the sand.

"Because I cannot." He choked, his erection straining, his body aching for the release that would never come.

"I do not understand." She stood before him, those luminous eyes staring up at him, and his erection twitched, pulling, straining against his trousers. His fangs were extended, and his pale eyes cold, hard as he stared at her, his brow furrowed in agony and need.

"If we continue, I will not be able to stop myself from taking you, Calie." She was puzzled by that statement.

She pulled the blanket tighter around her body, a new chill running through her.

"I want you to," she said, and he looked as if he were going to explode. His jaw tightened, and his body just about vibrated at her words.

"I cannot have you," he said through clenched teeth, "Do you not understand? The reason I was sent to find you is that I owe your grandmother a debt. That is the only reason." She looked at him, her face stony.

"You are a task, Calie, a task that I intend to complete. Once I deliver you to Pelusium, you will never see me again. Do you understand? You are a duty to me, nothing more."

"I see." She nodded calmly. "I see that your mouth says one thing, but your body tells a different story." She mounted her horse, *ignoring his hand of assistance. He swung himself onto his stallion, his straining arousal making him uncomfortable. She glanced back, a knowing smile on her kiss swollen lips. Just a duty indeed, he thought again, hating his body for betraying him.*

* * *

He could hear the wind picking up as he climbed the stone staircase out of the compound. His hands were always cold, but his fingers were downright icy with the added chill in the air. He pulled up his collar as he exited, moving slowly across the crumbling remains of the stone bridge. He stood looking over the precipice, his brow furrowed as he contemplated his next move. Below there was nothing but darkness, ahead of a thick fog. He knew what lay ahead if he continued into the thick haze. He would return to his point of entry, an abandoned warehouse in Miami. If he went down, well, he could get to his destination a lot faster. Karim looked back over his shoulder at the remains of what was once the keep of a castle. Now it was a ruin that acted as camouflage.

And she was in there. Or she had been.

Exhaling, he knew that he had no choice. He had to seek help from the only person he could ask. He closed his eyes and silently called out, his mind searching for his target. When he felt the calm roll over him, he said a silent prayer then stepped over the edge, falling silently into the abyss.

* * *

He materialized on the steps of the temple, hidden deeply in the aromatic darkness beyond Olympus. His skin was immediately warmed by the summery air that always surrounded the place. He mounted the steps quickly before he lost his nerve and ran like the coward he was. Before he reached the large marble doors, they swung open, welcoming him inside, with the heavy perfume of the ever-blooming garden within. He stepped inside, and his senses were overloaded by the fragrance of flowers blooming in the sanctuary. The cloying scent of the large white moonflowers that crept up the stone walls and across the ceiling wafted down to him. The honey and almond scent from Night Phlox swept in, reminding him of the taste of Celeste's mouth, and the smell of lavender lingered as it had in her hair and on her skin. There were other things in there as well, creatures that lurked in the night. He could see yellow eyes peering at him from the shadows created by the greenery. The leaves would rustle every once in a while, letting him know that they were in there, watching him, lurking in the shadows. He could see yellow eyes peering at him from the shadows created by the greenery.

The deep green foliage made the hall even darker, blocking out the pale light that managed to creep in, but the colors, the colors of the flowers were unique. It was as if he'd stepped into the Garden of Eden. He walked along the narrow path that led to a room drenched in light, passing a fountain filled with water lilies in every beautiful color of the rainbow. He hadn't seen the need to come here for nearly a millennium, and nothing had truly changed since his last visit.

He made his way into the open, airy room that she occupied, her back to him as she sat on a lounger reading silently. She wore capri pants in a shade of deep green and a white polo shirt. Her thick dark hair was in a ponytail, her feet bare. If he didn't know better, he would think she was nothing more than your average soccer mom. He knew better than that.

"So, what was so damned important that you needed to see me right now? I'm trying to finish my latest Harry Potter." She closed her book with a resounding snap before turning swirling silver eyes on him.

"Dumbledore dies," he said.

She let out an exasperated groan and rolled her eyes before slamming the book shut. Placing the now useless book on a nearby table, she turned her full attention to her guest. Petite and pale, she looked as if she couldn't harm so much as a fly. But Karim had discovered that this little female, yes female because she was beyond a mere woman, this female was by far the most dangerous creature he'd ever encountered. Her presence filled the space even if her body did not. She was powerful and electric and like Celeste in so many ways.

"Fucker," she said without malice. "So, what happened? Tell me everything." She folded her arms across her chest.

He straightened and cleared his throat, not exactly sure where to begin.

She rolled her eyes again, frustrated by his procrastination.

"You were right." He sat, taking the seat opposite her. "The Dark Fae are planning something."

"Of course, I was right. I wouldn't have sent you otherwise," she said matter-of-factly.

"It's a demon. I don't know what kind. She's tiny but powerful. I could feel her pushing into my mind, trying to anyway. She made me queasy. For a moment, I thought that she might succeed. By the way, she spoke, the way she tried to convince me that we should align forces, I think that a plan is already in action. Her name is Lilith."

"Lilith." Nyx whistled. "Of course, they would send her. She's actually the only daughter of Lucifer, or whatever he's calling himself now. And she didn't realize you were one of the *Seven*? Of course not. She wouldn't have tried to influence you if she had."

"So, you do know her?" he asked, a strange itchy feeling began in his neither regions.

"I know of her." The way Nyx looked, the tightness in her posture lead him to believe that this Lilith was one he should worry about. He was also thankful that Nyx seemed to understand his anxiety at the thought of someone like her being in the Collective. Not just that, but she would also be close to Celeste, and that was what worried him more than anything else.

"What are they up to? What's the end game?" Nyx pondered, worrying her thumbnail with her teeth. "I wonder who is calling the shots on this one."

"Didn't your spy tell you? What exactly did he say?"

She looked at Karim and sighed.

"He didn't say much. He didn't have time. All he had time to tell me was to make sure Celeste is protected. I just wonder how they found her. No matter what, she needs to be protected. Now that the Dark Fae know where to find her, they will probably try to get closer," she mumbled, her wheels spinning as she tried to piece together their plan. Her delicate fingers went to her throat. She'd made a point to cloaked Celeste's presence from so many, and they'd found her. Damn it.

"You honestly believe Lilith's going to move on Ca-Celeste?"

He cursed himself for the slip. He had to remember that she was Celeste now, not his sweet Calie. Making her the target of whatever they were planning made him uneasy. Everyone knew of the Fates prophecy regarding the Caelestis, and if they could turn her, they would use her for their own needs. But which would it be destroyer or savior?

"Not if she has any common sense, she won't. But then again, the Dark Fae aren't what I would call sound decision-makers. Keep an eye on Celeste, get close, and for heaven's sake, make sure she stays out of trouble."

Karim snorted and shook his head. Celeste was a homing beacon for trouble. It was ingrained in her DNA to be a shit starter.

"At least until I can get a handle on what those cretins are planning." Nyx continued, ignoring his interruption.

"That's not going to happen. She knocked me on my ass within seconds. There is no way in hell she's going to let me get that close to her. She's already questioned my motives for being there."

"What did you tell her?" Nyx asked. That was the only tricky thing about sending Karim in as a spy. He was one of the originals, a prince of the Seven Houses, vampire royalty. His house, the House of Tyre, was only second in strength and number to the first house, the House of Judea. Like most of the original vampires, he could not willingly lie or be affected by other preternaturals. The Seven were incorruptible.

"I'm telling you she fucking hates me. She'll never trust me. She sure as hell won't let me follow her around. I am not the right person for that job. What happened to her, Nyx? Why is she so pissed?" he said.

"You are the perfect person to do it," Nyx mumbled, leaving the room in a haze of pale grey smoke, her voice floating from another place in the temple. "I would have chosen someone else if I believed otherwise. Lilith- she worries me."

Karim followed the sound of her voice through the corridors until he found himself in a hallway that looked as if it could be in any suburban home anywhere in the world. The walls were painted sunny yellow, and the hardwood floors buffed to a high gloss. He rounded a corner and found a staircase, descending as the sound of her voice trailed away.

He finally found her in a bright, airy living room with floor to ceiling windows that looked out on white sandy beaches. Outside he could see people playing in the surf, children building sandcastles, and sunbathers basking in the heat. He moved closer, staring at the sunlight and wondering why he wasn't burning from the heat. He lifted a hand and let it land in a beam of light that crossed the room; feeling the warmth of the sun on his skin was something he hadn't done in an eon.

"How is this possible?" he asked, his vision blurring from the tears that threatened to spill down his cheeks.

"What?" Nyx looked up at him as she pulled a book from a large bookshelf in the corner of the room, "Oh, the sun? Nothing can harm you here, this place between dominions. Just think of the view as a huge TV." She patted his arm, watching as he basked in the sunlight, something that he would never have the opportunity to do if he weren't in this place, under her protection.

He moved closer to the window, feeling the sun on his skin. He imagined himself out there, letting the sun bake his naked skin. He thought of he and Celeste out playing in the waves, the taste of salty water on her skin, the sunlight in her hair, and other things that he knew would never be. He felt a tightness in his chest as the ache of not having that hit him like a dagger to his gut. He would never have that with her. It was something he could never give her unless they found a place like this, somewhere in between worlds but touching neither.

Finally, when the sky began to change from vibrant blue to dusky orange, he turned to her, his eyes still watery, but a calm settling over him.

"Back to work then?" Nyx asked, sipping a cup of tea while sitting on a large sofa, a weighty leather tome in her lap, waiting for him to get his fill. She'd made him what he was, taken so much from him, the least she could do was give him a few hours of happiness.

"What you need to know about Lilith is in here." She pointed to the book, and it opened, flipping to a page, then stopping. "Apparently, there are all sorts of rumors about her, like she may be a princess of hell or some cursed angel. It's not very clear, but what is clear is that she is a succubus. Well, she holds dominion over all of the succubae and incubi, and her father is Lucifer." She lobbed that little nugget at him as an aside before rushing on. "It's probably how she was strong enough to try to bend your will. I don't like this at all, Karim. From what I know of her, she's very close to the Queen. I need you to watch Celeste. This could be bad."

"I wasn't right the first time, and I sure as hell am not right for it now. Whatever happened before, whatever I did broke something inside of her. I can't take a chance on doing more damage, Nyx. She has brothers and friends around her who would be better--"

"They are also corruptible. You are the only one who can protect Celeste because you are one of the *Seven,* and you're still in love with her. You would die before you let any more harm come to her. She may be angry with you, but she knows you. Sending someone else in will alert the Dark Fae, and we don't want to do that until we know more. Besides, you have to protect the progeny of the primordial. You will do as you're told, Karim, Prince of Tyre."

He stared at Nyx, his face tight, his fists clenched. He couldn't deny Nyx anything. He had pledged his fealty to her long ago, now was not the time for a battle of wills.

"As you wish," he said, knowing that any argument would be fruitless. He stood looking out of the windows at the sky beyond. It had turned dark, and he saw the ever-present moon high in the starry night sky. This was where he belonged, in the darkness with the other slinking and hidden creatures.

"She'll be at her home in New Orleans. You can find her, can't you?" Nyx knew that he could. It was one of the things he was good at. Karim was an excellent tracker, a finder of lost things. That was why she had enlisted him to find Celeste when all others had long given up the search. He was one of the few who could find her, and he had. He nodded and turned to leave when she spoke, halting him in his tracks.

"It wasn't your fault," Nyx said after a long silent moment. Karim's shoulders tightened, and he turned his head to look back at her.

"I don't even know what happened to her. She won't tell me, and I feel horrible. Was it truly as awful as I imagine?"

Nyx placed a gentle hand on his shoulder, her swirling eyes like the clouds before a thunderstorm, her perfect mouth tight. She took a deep breath, but no words would come, and Karim realized that even for her, the wounds were still fresh.

"What happened to her, Nyx? Tell me." He could hear the pleading tone in his voice and felt his heartbeat quicken. "Please, I need to know."

She touched his cheek, her voice as soft as the grey of her eyes. She could feel his hurt, and he could feel hers. Was the truth so devastating that even Nyx wouldn't speak of it? Had his selfish act broken her? What, for god's sake, had happened? His chest hurt, and he felt sick when she began to speak, only to have the wind knocked out of him.

"It is not my truth to tell, agápi," she said solemnly.

* * *

Lilith's head hurt, and her stomach felt queasy ever since the vampire had run out on her. She had never experienced such pain while trying to take control of another. She'd never failed either. She didn't know if it was due to the compound's binding or something unique to Karim. No matter, she had news to report, and she needed to get back home now. There was much to discuss and very little time. The vampire was going to be a problem; she knew from the moment he pushed her out of his head.

She slipped out as quickly and quietly as possible, making her way to the compound's upper level before she was missed. She did have to avoid being spotted by the vampire, but only once. She watched with curiosity as he debated with himself before he stepped off of the edge of the broken stone bridge disappearing into the foggy ether. For a moment, she thought to follow him, to try to figure out how he'd bested her. But decided against it. He could be returning to his clan for all she knew, and the last place she needed to be was in a den of vampires.

The thought alone made her skin crawl. Instead, she decided to go to an equally abhorrent place. She was going to see the Dark Queen. How she dreaded speaking to that female, but as with most things, it was a necessary evil. She tugged the hood of her white fox fur coat over her head before strolling into the wooded countryside in search of the portal that had brought her to the compound several hours ago. *"Here we go, into the woods,"* She sang softly before she disappeared into the atmosphere.

She knew she was close even before the fog cleared. It was the smell, the cloying overpowering scent that always seemed to cling to her clothing and hair. It wasn't an altogether unpleasant smell. It was a more unique and rather pungent aroma, a combination of violet leaf and bergamot, which on their own were quite lovely, but together made her slightly ill. Home, she thought rather ruefully. It had been home for an eon, but now she always felt like an unwelcome guest.

Before she could lift her hand to twist the knob, the door was opened by a rather severe-looking faun, a man with the horns, ears, legs, and hooves of a goat, but then all fauns had the dower face of a sad goat to her. He looked down at her with dark egg-sized, expressionless eyes. He wore a dark suit. His fur brushed away from his long face until it shone his horns shorn to near stumps atop his narrow head. The effect was both terrifying and comical, to say the least.

"She is expecting you," he spoke in a deep monotone that was just a step above a grunt.

"Of course, she is." Lilith sighed, handing him her coat as he allowed her entry into the main foyer. She frowned as she looked around the place, her eyes going up to the new chandelier. Yet another tasteless monstrosity that had been added to the once understated elegance of the home. She sighed and shook her head at the blinding brightness of the crystal-encrusted atrocity. It was like staring into a disco ball. Well, she supposed, the taste wasn't something we were all born with.

"Come with me, madam," the faun grunted, his hooves clattering on the marble floor as he led the way.

She found herself staring as he tried to maintain his footing on the ballroom floors. It was a task that seemed to have his entire body clenched in concentration. For a moment, she felt sorry for the poor guy. This was not a life he was meant for. He belonged outside, frolicking in the woods, not trussed up like a circus chimp trying not to face plant on the hall floor. It was completely unnatural. Then, the Queen was not known for being the most understanding or sympathetic being.

She was led down the hall to a sitting room where she would wait to be seen, her eyes roaming the ever-changing decor. The last time she was here, the theme was an amalgamation of postmodernism, shabby chic, and classic styles that made everything look like a tacky mess. She had never understood how someone with so much personal style had allowed that gauche styling of their home. Today, she thought it was closer to what she'd expected when the Queen had decided that this would be her new residence.

Lilith hadn't cared at the time, having long ago forgone the realm of the Dark Fae for the sultry decadence of New Orleans. What she had taken offense to was the way the Queen had removed the charm of the place with her expensive trash.

The decor reminded her of castoffs from some low budget 80's porn. Shiny and white, with gaudy silver accents, neon throw pillows that held a strange sheen. From the white furniture to the white shag carpet, the whole place proved that money didn't cure awful taste.

"Lilith, I hadn't expected you so soon." The woman breezed into the room, her distinctive hair hanging to her shoulders in loose waves. Her hair was snowy white but slowly faded to an almost black on the ends from the roots. It was even more striking against her usual uniform of all white clothing. It had become her signature. The only color came from her jewel-encrusted Manolos. She looked at Lilith with sharp pale blue eyes while crossing the room with a slow, easy stride. Smart and ruthless, she could also be benevolent and gracious, and in some cases, even seductive when it suited her needs.

Behind her stood a male, quiet and contemplative, but very alert. He did not speak, only stood, waiting, and watching with shrewd intelligence. His skin was a pale blue and reminded her of faded denim, his eyes obsidian, and he was also impeccably dressed. One of her guards, Lilith supposed, or a new bedmate for the Queen. This one was different from the mates she usually chose. He was slight of frame, wearing black slacks and a black shirt opened at the collar. He watched Lilith suspiciously, his face expressionless. He was giving Lilith the creeps.

"I'm honored that you would meet with me, my Queen." She bowed low, her eyes on the intricate Persian rug. The Queen snorted, sitting in a high-backed chair, crossing her legs at the ankle, then snapped her fingers.

The male who'd hung at the entrance moved to a bar at her back and began to pour a drink. He moved with a speed and elegance that was unnerving, his eyes never leaving Lilith as he worked.

"Cut the shit, Lilith. Why did you return so quickly? Did they kick you out?"

Lilith reclaimed her seat, smiling as she did.

The male handed Lilith a drink before turning to the Queen. She took what was offered, her eyes never leaving Lilith as she did. It was as it always was. The male was just another prop, an accessory that made the Queen feel more desirable.

"No, they found me quite charming. I do have charms, you know."

"As limited as they are," she agreed, "So, did the great and powerful Arbor Kent deem you worthy? I guess not. You wouldn't be back so quickly if she had." The Queen's smile was evilly wicked and turned her face into a sinister mask.

"Actually, I never got that far in the process. It seems the Commander of the Grey took offense to the other prospect, knocked him right on his ass."

"The Commander of the Grey?" The Queen lifted one perfectly arched white brow before sipping her drink, trying her best to remain calm.

"It was a vampire of all things. A Persian named Karim." Lilith sipped her drink slowly, deliberately letting her words hang in the air.

"Karim?" The Queen repeated. She was easing forward in her chair, her fingers gripping the glass in her hand until her knuckles turned bright red. Lilith took great pleasure in making the Queen squirm in her seat. The Queen sat back, absently running her finger around the rim of her glass, her white eyes dancing with excitement.

"Did you see her? Was she there?" The Queen's voice was tight, almost a whisper, as she forced the words out. "Did you speak to her?" She asked, her emotions playing across her face as she tried to reign them in.

"I didn't get a chance to speak with her, but I saw her."

"And?" She was practically jumping out of her skin.

Lilith had never seen the Queen like this before, and in all honesty, it was making her a little nervous. She heard the crackle of the glass the woman held as it began to splinter. Tiny droplets of dark ruby blood dripped down her hand, marring the sterile furnishing and puddling on the toe of her immaculate shoes. She paid no notice, her face tightening as she listened.

"She is just as the legend says. She's more. She is fierce and beautiful and ..."

The glass exploded, and blood splattered on the Queen's flawless clothing, shards of glass buried in her palm. The male moved forward, a towel in his hand ready to aide his Queen, only to be waved away.

"The mark? Does she bear the mark of *The Fallen One*?" She barked, and Lilith swallowed.

"I don't know ... I didn't see it. Everything happened so quickly. - I - "

In a blink, the Queen was across the room, grasping Lilith's face with blood-soaked fingers, one knee pressing into the center of her chest. She could feel fingernails and glass cutting into her cheeks, her breath coming in labored gasps. Lilith's glass tumbled to the floor, spilling clear liquid and ice across the thick Persian rug. The male made an audible noise but offered no assistance. He just watched with a sort of morbid curiosity. The Queen's face was so close to Lilith's that their noses touched, her fingers cutting into her.

"You find out! You go back, you get close, and you do whatever you must to find out if she truly has the mark! She is useless to me without it! You do whatever you have to and do not return until you can verify that she has the mark." She growled spittle, sprinkling Lilith's face with each word. The Queen stared into Lilith's pale eyes, and her own eyes narrowed with intensity. She released Lilith, quickly regaining her composure, leaving the demoness shivering in shock.

The Queen straightened her jacket, leaving bloody fingerprints on the already splattered hem. She ran a hand over her hair, leaving an equally macabre streak of garnet, and glanced at Lilith once more, her scarlet speckled face serene and lovely once again.

"You find out, or you don't return," she said as she exited the room, the male hot on her heels.

Lilith didn't dare move or as much as breathe until the sound of the Queen's heels on the marble floors faded into the distance.

CHAPTER FIVE

Celeste sat with her knees drawn up, her chin resting on her fist as Nicky tried to figure out her television remote. The large multi-buttoned device was giving him fits. Since the movie they were watching ended, Nicky had used the remote to turn the lights off and on, open the blinds and turn the stereo on. When he'd finally managed to turn it off, he had pushed the volume on the television to somewhere just above deafening. By the time he pressed the off button, he was completely flustered and agitated. He groaned and tossed it aside, placing his hands-on-hips to stare at her, his brow furrowed.

"Well, now what?" he asked.

She shrugged, then looked up at him, a slow smile spreading across her face, her eyes twinkling. He knew that look all too well, and it usually ended up with them in jail or an emergency room.

"No, Celeste," Nicky groaned, holding his hands up in protest. "If we get in trouble... this face," he pointed to his own somewhat strained expression, and her smile widened, "will be splashed across every tabloid in the world. The paparazzi will have a field day, not to mention my management team."

"You know you want to. It'll be fun," she teased, and he closed his eyes, shaking his head. She stood slowly, her oversized sweats making her seem innocent and almost childlike.

"No. Absolutely not." He shook his head.

"Come on, Nick. Please? Pretty please?" She batted her eyelashes at him and made her bottom lip quiver. He rolled his eyes and continued to shake his head.

"Not gonna work. Nope, nu-uh. No Celeste, no."

* * *

Coming to this place had been a mistake, but he couldn't think of anywhere else to go. Nyx had returned him to his starting point, the edge of the broken bridge, the chill settling into his bones after his glorious reprieve in the sunlight. He'd thought of returning to the compound, of searching for Lilith, but he needed a game plan for that. He needed to think, get away from this place and everything that had happened. He needed a drink, and he needed to feed.

He looked at his watch, the hands spinning wildly. He'd forgotten the effect the compound's cloaking had on electrical devices. There was no time, no night, no day, just endless dusk that settled wherever the Collective was. He looked over his shoulder and thought of going back to Miami, to his high tech, high rise apartment. He could go back to his isolated life there or return to the castle in the highlands with its protective stone walls and family. And the endless line of nameless, faceless women paraded before him as the possible mate for the next Vampire King. But that was precisely the reason he'd left Ireland to begin with. No, he needed something else. And then he smiled and realized he knew exactly where he wanted to be.

Now he stood near the bar, the dance floor packed with bodies moving to the beat of the heavy bass of hip hop and rock blasting from the DJ booth. He'd made a beeline for the bar at the back of the club in the VIP section. Jinxie's was a little piece of their world right in the middle of the human world. The building looked like an abandoned warehouse off of a dirt road out in the middle of nowhere. But inside was a decadent three-story playground for the supernatural and the few humans allowed within the secret haven.

The walls were covered in dark textured wallpaper, the bar an antique from the 1920s, a highly polished art deco deal with gold light around the foot rails. The whole place reminded him of The Great Gatsby but with a hip-hop make-over. The bar's back was a roped-off section of black velvet booths hidden behind heavy dark curtains that allowed its occupants to view the party but kept out the prying eyes. High tables lined the massive dance floor, and a DJ spun from a platform that looked down on the sweaty bodies that populated the dance floor. Jinxie's was the perfect hideaway if you could find it. The location tended to be in motion, the theme in constant flux. One night it could be a space-aged techno bumping rave. The next was a Reggae dance hall. Tonight, it was on the Northshore of Lake Ponchartrain in the middle of nowhere. Next week, it could be in the middle of a subdivision in Metairie or on a French Quarter hotel's rooftop. It all depended on the whims of the proprietress, a devilish little pixie named Jinxie Monroe.

He could watch people entering and exiting the building from the heavily guarded main entrance from his carefully chosen position. He could also see the crowd on the second-floor balcony lounging on plush sofas as brightly colored fairies with iridescent wings moved between them with heavily laden trays of food and beverages.

The bass from the music throbbed, making the floors vibrate as bodies moved to the tribal rhythms, human and preternatural and everything in between, moving as one to the hypnotic beat. He relaxed, all of the stress from the day easing out of him as he bobbed his head to the music. He had no thoughts of the Collective or Nyx or anything other than the music and the Day-Glo orange drink in his hand.

While he watched the crowd move on the dance floor, a towering redhead caught his attention. He lumbered from a back hallway, through the crowd towards the VIP booths. Karim turned and watched him. That red hair was unmistakable. It was the soldier he had seen earlier in the day. When he pulled the curtain out of his way to enter the booth, he saw Remy Kent with his eyes half-closed and a lazy smile on his lips.

'*Shit,*' he thought. He was hoping to avoid all Collective drama tonight. He wanted some time to get Celeste out of his fucking head, and here was a blatant reminder of her seated fifty feet away.

Remy must have been either very high or very drunk because he lifted his glass to Karim and nodded. Karim, a little surprised, returned the gesture. That must have amused Remy because he leaned closer to the redhead and said something. The big man looked his way and began to laugh. Yeah, that was at his expense, all right. Remy was probably regaling him with the tale of Celeste knocking him on his ass earlier. That had probably been quite a sight.

He watched as two Lycans began a violent pushing match on the dance floor. The large males growled at each other, shouting insults, baring claws, and fangs before their packs separated them. He shook his head and sighed. This had definitely been a mistake. The last thing he wanted was to be a vamp caught in a fight between two Alphas and their packs. He'd just paid his tab when a chill ran through him, and the room went still. He turned to face the entrance, and his skin prickled with goose flesh.

She stood on the staircase, her hair hanging in deep, dark waves against caramel skin. Those long muscular legs were covered in what could only be red latex that hung low on her hips and cupped her thighs and ass as if they had been painted onto her, and black stilettos that made her ass defy gravity. Her blouse, which was a generous term, was a piece of dark cloth draped over her breasts. It dipped in the front, and when she turned to the side, he saw that it was only held on by two thin ties, one around her neck and the other across her back. He stared, knowing without a doubt that beneath her barely-there clothing, Celeste was completely bare.

"Don't even think about it." He didn't turn around at the sound of Remy's voice suddenly so close he could smell the whiskey on his breath. He also didn't have to turn to know that the behemoth was right beside him.

"I don't know what you're talking about," Karim said, sipping his vodka, but his eyes stayed on Celeste as she laughed with a platinum blond emo type, complete with guyliner and skinny jeans. The emo god said something into Celeste's ear, his hand on her lower back just above her pants' low-slung waistband. Karim's body tensed in a surprising flair of anger when the blond squeezed Celeste's bottom, and she didn't slap him. She playfully pushed his shoulder, only to move closer into his embrace, her face alight with pure joy. Karim felt his jaw clenching and counted to ten, his eyes on the now empty glass in his hand.

"It would be a shame for me to have to rip out those pretty green eyes of yours or mess up that lovely face," Remy whispered close to his ear with a somewhat seductive chuckle.

Karim didn't move, didn't speak, but his eyes shifted back to the goddess who'd captured his full attention. He hadn't even realized Remy and the giant had gone. He was so entranced.

Damn, she looked good. He had never seen her dressed like that, and fuck, if she wasn't a walking wet dream. He groaned as his erection sprang to life, his chest hurt, and the molten heat in his lower belly moved lower. With every bass beat, his sex throbbed. As casually as he could, he tried to adjust himself, but it only made it worse.

He watched her with the blond, unable to tear his eyes away as they rocked together on the dance floor, the rock star's hands-on red leather hips. Karim found himself becoming angrier as the other man wrapped an arm around Celeste's bare waist and said something close to her ear. She leaned closer and laughed, one hand sinking into his platinum blond hair, before draping her arms around his neck. They were close, intimate, and Karim was feeling an emotion that he'd never experienced before. He was jealous.

Her date danced with Celeste through one more song before saying something to her and walking away, leaving her to sway alone on the dance floor. Karim watched him cut through the crowd, easily making his way to Remy's booth, where a gaggle of women stood near the velvet rope, begging the bouncers for entry. He watched with interest as a cloud of pinkish smoke rose from the table, and the smell of sweet spice floated across to him. It seemed that her fully human guy was familiar with the mist, which meant he knew that Celeste and her family were not human. Interesting, he thought.

He turned his attention back to Celeste as she danced alone in the center of the dance floor. The crowd had given her a respectful breadth, and no one approached her. He scanned the crowd, seeing eyes on her, stalking her every move, but none dared approach. His eyes drifted over her in the flashing multi-colored lights that illuminated the dance floor, zeroing in on a single bead of sweat that rolled slowly down her spinal column before disappearing into the waistband of those pants. She lifted her arms above her head, her hips rocking back and forth, making her ass look like a candied apple, and damn did he want to take a bite. She turned, and he could see the under the curve of her bare breast exposed, her stomach taut and shimmering from sweat.

Unable to hold back any longer, he downed the remnants of his drink before stalking towards the dance floor.

✻ ✻ ✻

The DJ changed the record, and the music began to thump with a heavier bass beat. Celeste rocked her hips, swaying from side to side to the rhythm when strong hands gripped her hips, pulling her back against a very male, very aroused body. The smell of the ocean and sand assaulted her, but she refused to let him ruin her vibe. Instead, she allowed him to rock with her. She could feel his breath sweet and warm against her cheek.

"Why isn't anyone dancing with you?" he asked. "How could they keep away?" His lips touched her hot, sweaty bare skin of her shoulder and her breath caught. Giving in to the feel of him hard and heavy against her, she relaxed into him. His hands moved up her sides, his fingers dancing along the curve just beneath her breast, his breath searing at the nape of her neck as the mark began to throb. She wondered about that, but only for a moment. It felt good to be so close to him and not think. For once, she could just feel and not worry about what it meant or the past. She could just dance.

She turned, her lids low as she locked eyes with him. He thought for a minute that she was going to hit him, but she just continued rocking her body against him, the heat of her seeping through the leather, yes that was leather, pants that were molded to her like a second skin. He ran his hands over the smooth, heated skin of her bareback, his eyes trained on her face as she moved against him. He gently placed a knee between her thighs in an attempt to get closer, pushing against her. His hands splayed against her back, pressing her against him, as they moved as one, slow and hard.

* * *

Nicky sat against the plush black velvet of the VIP booth. His eyes nearly closed as he took a long pull on the blunt between his fingers then passed it to Remy. He remembered the first time he'd ever tried mist. It wasn't long after Celeste had told him about her family. Nicky had come in with blunt between his teeth, the smell of flowers and herbs wafting around him.

"Mist," Celeste had explained. "All natural. Not a narcotic, non-addictive, and it's like six hits of Ecstasy without any weird hallucinations or side effects. Try it. It will mellow you out. Trust me. I would never give you anything dangerous." Mist, he discovered, was a pixie weed that had been soaked in nectar. He didn't partake often, but when the mood struck him, like tonight, he indulged.

He held the smoke in and then slowly exhaled, his eyes finding Celeste in the crowd. She was locked onto someone, a man, with long dark hair and a tattoo creeping up his neck. He had his back to them, but with the position of his body and the way he moved against her, Nicky knew that they weren't just dancing.

"Hey," he coughed, "there's a guy dry humping your *sister* on the dance floor."

Remy stared at him in confusion for a tick, then followed Nicky's finger as he pointed. It took him a minute to realize what he was looking at. Celeste had her head close to Karim's, her heavily lidded eyes glowing, her lips parted as they rocked together.

"Fuck." Remy stubbed out the blunt, the pink mist that had fogged his brain clearing.

"That's Karim. Son of a bitch, I told him-" He rose but didn't have a chance to do much because all hell broke loose in the blink of an eye.

* * *

With his mouth deliciously close to hers, Karim let his hand move up her back to the nape of her neck. He felt something sharp and hot, like an electric shock rocket from his fingertips up his arm. She winced and pushed him as the sting from his touch gave her a sudden sharp pain in her neck.

"What the ... what is that?" he asked. The mark on her neck was burning, and his touch made it ignite in waves of pain that radiated from the base of her skull to the front of her head. It also broke the spell, and she looked at him with renewed hatred. What the hell was she doing? She was practically fucking him on the dance floor. Her legs trembled as she looked at him, her fingers grazing the stinging mark.

"What the hell was that?" He grasped her wrist, and she pulled away, her face twisting into an expression he couldn't place.

"Don't," she growled through clenched teeth. She looked up just as Remy stood, his face contorted with unabashed rage. This was going to be bad, she thought.

"You weren't saying that a second ago, *azizam.* Upset that someone made your cunny wet?" He looked at her with a self-satisfied grin, and she wanted to scratch his eyes out.

"*Motherfucker,*" she whispered before shoving him, her eyes stinging with angry tears. "You keep doing this to me. Why don't you just leave me the fuck alone? I hate you," she said in a low, shaky voice. He grabbed her arms to keep her from pushing him, his mouth covering hers in a hot, bone-melting kiss, which both aroused and infuriated her. She pulled away and punched him, her fist connecting with his cheekbone and sending him reeling.

Karim fell back into a female, his hand reaching out in an attempt to balance himself. He only succeeded in ripping the skirt from the woman behind him. That enraged her boyfriend, who charged him. When Karim dodged the blow, the boyfriend stumbled into a male lycan who spilled his drink on the female he talked to, who immediately slapped him. The melee became a confusing ball of fists and blood as bodies rolled across the dance floor. Karim dodged blows and falling bodies, making his way across the club to Celeste. He managed to get halfway there when Remy took the opportunity to jab him in the gut. He was struck hard enough to make him wheeze and bend at the waist, which Remy relished before dancing off to hit someone else. He was enjoying this way too much.

Karim dodged a wild punch from a Lycan, the one he'd witnessed nearly start a brawl earlier. He was shoving through the crowd, his teeth bared as he searched for someone, his face shifting from man to wolf, and Karim cursed under his breath. Suddenly, he'd found himself in the middle of a pack war, Not a good place for a vamp. He needed to get out of here before sunrise. And according to his watch, sunrise was little more than an hour away. Damn it, he thought and made his way over fallen bodies on his way to a back door when he saw Celeste being grabbed around the waist and headed back. She fought the person holding her, breaking free just as the front door was kicked in by half a dozen trolls in dark suits swinging clubs and tasers at any and everything that moved. Jinxie's muscle was on the scene, and unless he wanted to be stunned, clubbed, or worse, they needed to get out of there now!

Karim grabbed her arm and pulled her with him out the back door.

"Wait, Nicky!" She turned to look for her friend just as he was hauled over Briar's shoulder before he barreled through the crowd, clearing a path for Remy to follow.

"He's fine. Your freak of a brother has him. Let's go." Karim practically lifted her as he dragged her out into an alley. He looked confused for a second until she tugged him to the right, laughing as he stumbled after her.

"Here. My car is over here!!!" she said, and they sprinted around a corner, away from the commotion and a possible night in jail.

She retrieved a key fob from some secret location, and headlights illuminated the darkened corner where the car was hidden. He slowed his pace a little as they approached the headlights, his eyes gleaming at the sleek Aston Martin V8 Vantage in the exact shade of candy apple red as her pants.

"Come on, or do you want to go up like a flair when the sun comes up in like, twenty minutes?" she barked.

He slipped into the passenger seat as she revved the engine. She looked at him for a second before pulling out of the parking space at breakneck speed. The car veered onto the dirt road that ran behind the club and into the night. He watched her handle the vehicle with calm confidence and was amazed. As they left the dirt road, the moonlight played across her face, the car climbing onto the smooth highway that led from the Northshore to New Orleans.

"Celeste, we need to talk-" he began, but she flipped on the stereo, the car filling with the sounds of *Snoop Dogg and Pharrell's Drop it Like it Hot.* She whipped through traffic at top speed with the precision of a trained race car driver, her head bopping to the beat. He knew that if he spoke, she would hear him, but why to bother. She kept her eyes forward, but he could still smell the lavender and vanilla of her skin. He simply stared as she sang along with the music and couldn't help but smile. Hot damn, if she wasn't the sexiest woman ever.

* * *

"Be still," she said, looking at his bruised face. She touched his swollen cheekbone, then his nose, which was bleeding but not broken. She sighed and straightened, placing her hands on her hips.

"You'll live," she said after a while, giving the bruised cheek a nice slap. He winced at the sting but said nothing about it.

"Yeah, thanks," he mumbled, taking the towel she'd given him to clean the blood from his face. "I'm surprised you came up. Hell, I'm surprised you brought me home," he said.

"Well, as much as I can't stand you, I don't want to see you disintegrated in a jail cell. I want to be the one to kill you," she smirked. Turning, she looked around the kitchen, her eyes wandering around the new space, running her hands over the white marble countertop. The apartment wasn't elaborate, but it was comfortable. It smelled clean, like lemon, and freshly scrubbed by a housekeeper, no doubt. The sofa was leather, dark brown, the decor all beige and blue. There was a large armchair beside a bookshelf, television, and knick-knacks. The only thing that made the place look lived in was the artwork.

"I want to show you something," he'd said when she pulled her car to a stop at the curb in front of his building. She stared at him in the darkened interior of the vehicle.

"I know what you want to show me, Karim. I've seen it," she'd mumbled, and he couldn't help the smile that spread across his bruised and bloodied lips.

He flinched when the smile reached his bruised and swollen cheek. Feeling a twinge of guilt, she agreed to come to his apartment, but only for a moment.

These paintings, these beautiful, emotional works of art, were what he'd wanted to show her, and she'd found them scary and heartbreaking. There were canvases on every wall, beautiful spiraling abstracts, in rich tones with the familiar PT signature line. She stared, her eyes moving on the different works, but there seemed to be a theme, deep blues and black with deeply etched features that could be male or female. It was entrancing, like looking into someone's aura. She'd seen similar works in galleries worldwide, and they were worth thousands. The artist had never been revealed but was based somewhere in London, she believed. Works so elaborate were highly sought after, so why did he have so many in this tiny, barely used apartment.

"These are yours?" She asked, pointing to the walls.

He nodded and sighed.

"It's what I do," he murmured, pressing an ice pack to his bruised but rapidly healing lip.

"I would have thought you were a mercenary," she teased. "What does PT stand for?"

"Prince of Tyre," he sighed, a bit sheepishly.

She smirked, her brow lifted in surprise.

"Prince? Claiming your throne, your majesty."

"It is who I am," he assured her, moving closer. "Disappointed?" He returned her teasing tone, and she fought the urge to smile. Instead, she turned and saw one door, which she assumed led to his bedroom. That was not a road she needed to take right now. She looked around the living room, avoiding his gaze and thoughts of his bed. As apartments went, this one was acceptable, she supposed, but she knew this wasn't his home. This was just a place to sleep, eat, bathe, and occasionally work, but it wasn't home.

"Calie, I have to tell you," his tone had become suddenly sincere.

"I didn't know you had a place in New Orleans. I live a couple of blocks from here. Is this what you wanted to show me? Nice," she said, cutting him off. She didn't know why she was telling him where she lived. But she did know she didn't want to hear whatever he wanted to discuss.

"I only use this place when I need to. I live in Miami, mostly. This is what I wanted to show you.'" He pointed to a painting that seemed to hold a place of honor on an easel in a shadowy corner of the room. The canvas was draped with oilcloth, and when he removed it, she stared with her mouth slightly agape. It was a starry desert night, a lone body standing in the moonlight. The face was turned up to the silver moon, the profile of a beautiful woman with caramel-colored skin and dark hair blowing in the night air. Her eyes were soft, her face fresh and innocent and full of promise. Celeste stared at the painting, swallowing hard at her youthful face. That, she noticed, was the face of Calie.

"Do you like it?" he asked, and she nodded, walking around the small living room.

"It's beautiful. But that girl ... that girl died in that desert a long time ago." She looked at him, and for a moment, he saw a shadow cross her face.

She looked away and continued to look around the room at the artwork that filled the space with light and color. Karim sat at the bar, the towel in his hand, watching her. She was startled when his custom window shades began to lower, making the already dim room even darker.

Suddenly, the space felt too intimate, and she needed to go before he decided to reenact their little dance floor escapade. The thought of it sent a rush of warmth between her thighs, and her cheeks flushed.

"The sun is up." He rose quietly, moving to stand closer to her. She turned and nearly bumped into him. She felt entirely off-balance around him. It made her feel weak and awkward. He was staring at her, those cold eyes practically glowing in the darkness of the room. He watched her like a predator, his fangs lengthening, and she could almost see what he was thinking.

"I should go then." She moved to leave, and he blocked her path. Closing her eyes, she sighed. "Karim, just because I can be in a room without snapping your spine doesn't change anything," she said.

He took a step forward, gently brushing her hair off of her forehead. She looked up at him, watching the bruises fade from his lovely face.

"I know," he said. He reached up to touch her cheek, and she ducked away, slipping around him. He grasped her wrist, and she flinched as if he'd burned her.

She pulled away, her eyes wide with an emotion that he had never seen before. Was that fear in her eyes? Or pain?

"Don't," she said, rubbing her wrist and hastily walked to the door.

He beat her there, blocking her exit.

"Tell me what happened," he said, searching her face for a clue, a hint of what it was. But he was slowly getting an idea in his head, one that he immediately pushed away.

"No, I have to go. Karim, get out of the way." She had her hand on the knob.

"Not until you tell me," he said.

He was too close, filling her senses with the smell of sand and ocean and male excitement. She didn't know if it was her proximity or the panic in her that he liked, and she wasn't willing to stay and explore. She pulled on the door, and he slammed it shut, locking it with his mind.

"You can't keep me here." She closed her eyes and tried to transport herself out of place. She concentrated on the hallway outside of the door, willing herself to be there. But something was wrong because she didn't feel the tingle that accompanied transportation. She exhaled, opening her eyes to glare at him. She couldn't leave. He had her right where he wanted her, and he knew it. He watched her with a self-satisfied smirk, and she wanted to smack him right in the face.

"The shades have an extra feature. You can't materialize in or out while they're down. Safety precaution. Don't want angry goddesses sneaking in during the day to murder me in my sleep."

"So, I'm not the only female who wants to kill you?" she muttered, and he laughed.

"You're the only one I wouldn't mind creeping into my bed at night. I'd die a happy man," he assured her, and she snorted, turning to stare at his smug expression.

"You're an asshole," she groaned. "What is your problem? You just pop up here after all this time and act as if you didn't just abandon me in the desert. You show up at my suite, then again tonight, and it's still your usual, draw me in to push me away. Why are you doing this to me? Do you like hurting me? Is this your own little sadistic sexual fetish? Or do you just like the emotional yo-yoing? Is this some vampire bullshit I don't understand? Another notch on what I assume to be a well-worn bedpost? You had your chance, and you left." With each word, she gave him a poke in the shoulder. She couldn't keep doing this to herself; she couldn't maintain her hatred when he looked at her with those damn diamond eyes.

"Damn it," she cursed on an exhale.

He pulled her hard against him, his hand going to the small of her back, his mouth covering hers in a heated kiss that made her toes curl. His hands moved beneath the slinky material of her top, his thumb teasing the delicate bud of her nipple. The touch sent a new wave of heat to the center of her. She whimpered into his mouth then pushed against him, reluctantly breaking the contact.

"Karim," she panted, not knowing what to do or say.

He held her face, his thumb stroking her bottom lip. He closed his eyes and took a deep breath, collecting himself before he was able to speak.

"You have no idea how much I want you. I have always, always wanted you. Whenever I close my eyes, I see your face. I smell your scent. I see you and all I want to do is bury myself inside of you. I wake up, my body on fire, my cock aching to be inside of you. I remember everything about you: your voice, your laugh, your taste stays on my tongue, and the feel of your skin is burned into my memory. There is an ache in my chest whenever I see you, and it kills me, rips my fucking heart apart, knowing that my stupid, selfish, childish actions caused you so much pain. I know that I'll never be good enough for you. But when I'm near you, hell when I smell you, I just - shit, I want you so much I can't fucking breathe. Do you know how much it hurts to be so close to you and not be allowed to fucking have you? It's torture. Being around you its fucking torture."

"Just ... stop talking." She surprised them both by pressing herself against him, her mouth moving over his, her hands holding the back of his head. She tasted of vanilla honey, and he could no longer think beyond the feel of her body against him.

They got as far as the pillar between the kitchen and hallway, her back pressed into it, his hips rocking against her. He trailed kisses over her shoulder, his hands cupping her ass as he began to grind his hips into her. She tugged at his shirt, pulling it over his head before her tongue traced the delicate curve of the tattoo that moved up his shoulder to her neck. He searched for the tie that held the asinine piece of cloth over her breasts and tugged at it. It fell to the floor, and he took a moment to look at her. Her breasts were firm and full, her nipples tight and begging to be kissed. She was breathing heavily, her chest moving up and down in quiet invitation.

"Oh man," he cupped them, feeling the fullness in his hands, his thumbs stroking her taut nipples until she arched into him. He lowered his mouth, his tongue tracing one tight bud before he gently bit and pulled. She made a sound that was not a groan or a sigh but something in between, and it seemed to spurn him on. He sucked harder until her fingers dug into the flesh of his shoulders. While his mouth suckled her deliciously soft skin, his hands worked on the zipper of her pants. When he finally released the zipper, he slipped his hand down to cup her. He expected his finger to sink into soft dark curls. Instead, he found more, bare silken skin. Lifting his head, he brought his mouth back up to hers, his breath coming in hard shutters as he touched the hot moist flesh at her center.

"Oh god, you're so wet," he said against her lips. "You feel like velvet." He gently began to stroke her, his fingers moving into the hot folds at her core before he sank one finger inside of her. She gasped, her body bucking against the feel of his fingers. When he found the hot throbbing center of her, she moaned, her hips rising to meet every stroke. She felt the heat building and the release coming sooner than she expected.

"Oh," she purred, her hand tightening around the wrist of the hand that moved inside of her. She rode the wave, her knees buckling as she came hard and long all over his hand. He smiled, his fangs grazing her sensitive nipples, and she shivered.

He pulled away only long enough to peel the pants from her. He tossed her shoes and pants aside and stared at her. She leaned against the wall, her body perfection, even better than he imagined.

"You are so beautiful," he said, kneeling before her so that his lips could touch the skin just above her navel. She inhaled and cupped the back of his head.

"I want to kiss every inch of you," he said, his mouth moving lower until he was on his knees in front of her.

Her pulse quickened in anticipation, and her body felt too tight and hot, every sense filled with him, his smell, taste, and feel. Gently he parted her thighs, his tongue moving up her inner thigh, and her legs shook. He continued toying with her, his fangs nipping at her tender skin as he gently lifted one thigh, draping her leg over his shoulder. He ran his hands up her hips, cupping her ass, just as his tongue touched the sweet, hot core of her.

"Oh, oh god," she groaned, her body slumping against the wall as he continued his assault on her body. She arched into him, her hips moving of their own will, meeting each delectable stoke of his tongue. Karim licked her, his mouth moving over her clef, his lips closing around the tight bud at her center, and she came again. Her hips undulated against him as she rode the wave of ecstasy, her body slumping forward.

He held her, taking her to the carpet, where he rolled her onto her back. He tugged at his pants while moving up her body, her thigh still held tightly against his shoulder. He slipped inside of her, and they both shuddered. She was soft and so wet, her body tightening around him. He growled, pulling back, then driving into her again.

She arched her back; her mouth opened, but no sound escaped her. He felt so good, his long steady strokes, his mouth on the skin between her breasts. He drove into her again and again, her body rising to meet each thrust.

"You feel so damn good," he whispered. "So good." He moved faster, his hips working like a piston. His body was heated, his eyes glowing white in the darkness. She moaned, her fingers digging into the flesh of his ass, driving him deeper, harder.

"Oh, sweet lord, " he whined and groaned, holding his body still as he felt himself unraveling.

Ignoring him, she bowed her hips back, moving to meet his, she swayed her body against him with a need he hadn't expected, and he lost all control. He drove harder, faster, meeting her thrusts, his body working on its own. She felt so damn good, he had waited so long, and she felt better than he could ever imagine.

The slow roll of pleasure started at her core then radiated outward until her entire body vibrated like a live wire.

Every inch of her pinged with joy as she came once again. Her legs shook from the force of it and her back arched, her head thrown back as a long low moaned escaped her.

Karim was not far behind, his body tense as he finally exploded. She continued to roll her body, drawing every ounce of his seed from him, her body tightening, making his orgasm that much stronger. They clung to each other until their trembles subsided, then just lay, spent and exhausted in the cool darkness of the living room.

She turned to look at him, her fingers moving over the delicate tribal symbols that started just below his right ear and moved down his shoulder and biceps, ending just above his elbow. That tattoo had always fascinated her. She'd wondered about it but hadn't dared to ask him about it. If she knew too much about him, then she'd start to care again, and that would be another massive mistake in a life littered with them. This would end badly. Things like this always ended badly for her.

He leaned closer, his lips finding hers in the dark. He was still trying to gather himself, his heart hammering in his chest. He'd never felt so alive, never felt so wonderfully warm. "That was pretty damn fantastic. You are pretty damn fantastic," he said.

"Yeah, it was amazing," she agreed, her eyes drifting closed, her heart aching. He was amazing and beautiful and perfect. She was glad that it was dark and that her body was drenched in sweat. That way, he wouldn't be able to distinguish the sweat from her tears.

❈ ❈ ❈

Karim couldn't remember having a better night in his long, long life. He stretched and rolled over in bed, hoping to make love to Celeste once more, only to find the bed empty. Opening his eyes, he saw her sitting at the edge of the bed. She wore a pair of his sweat pants and an old t-shirt, her hair damp. She was pulling the thick locks into a sloppy bun.

"Hey," he said, his voice hoarse from sleep. They had made love two more times before finally making their way into the shower, and then too exhausted to move, collapsed into bed. He'd watched her sleep for a while, her body relaxed. He'd brushed the hair from her neck, brushing kisses along her skin, pausing only to look at the raised red mark at her nape. It was something he'd seen before, and as he ran his fingers along the skin around it, he tried to remember where. She shifted then, turning to face him, burrowing closer so that they were pressed together beneath the cool of his sheets. He'd stared at her, unable to believe that she was with him, in his bed. He'd wrapped his arms around her, wanting to feel her close, her breath tickling his neck. He had been afraid to move until the darkness took him, and he fell into a deep and contented slumber.

Even now, he awoke, unable to believe that she was really here. He watched her, quietly amazed that she'd stayed with him. She stood, rolling the pants' waistband so that they wouldn't fall off her. She looked incredible, even in his clothes, which were two sizes too big.

"Morning, beautiful," his voice was still heavy with sleep and satisfaction.

"Hey. I didn't want to wake you. Go back to sleep. I'll be out of your way in a minute."

He sat up and looked at the clock. It was still early, not even ten in the morning. Celeste tucked a lock of hair that had escaped her bun behind her ear, her eyes downcast as she folded her clothing. She laid her pants on the corner of the bed and held up the square of cloth she'd wore as a top. His eyes drifted to the leather pants, the pants that fit her like a glove, making her ass look like a candied apple. He was hard in an instant, his body ready for more of her.

"You don't have to go. It's still early," he said, reaching for her hand. She saw the tented sheet and gently pulled away from him. Her gaze moved away from his face down to his smooth muscled chest, then back to the tent in the sheet. He pulled the covers down, exposing himself, letting her take a nice long look at him.

"Come back to bed, *azizam*."

"I ... have a ... class at ... twelve," she stammered, "I'll call you later."

"Well, that was a lie," he said, smiling. "Does this have something to do with the Blondie from last night? Is he your guy?"

She looked at him in complete surprise. The blondie? She thought and remembered that she had entered Jinxie's with Nicky. Was he jealous, she wondered. The thought has quickly dismissed that thought.

"Nicky? No, Nicky is just a friend, and he's probably worried about me," she said, gathering her clothes. "I'll have this cleaned and returned." She pointed to the sweats.

"Keep them. I like the way you look in my clothes."

She gave him a tight smile before heading for the bedroom door.

"Can I get a goodbye? A 'see you later'?" He leaned forward, reaching for her, but she evaded his touch.

"Later. I really have to go," she mumbled. His stomach knotted, and he crawled out of bed.

"Can you even look at me? Celeste, hey, wait, this wasn't a one-night thing, was it? Because it wasn't for me." He was hot on her heels, following her down the narrow hallway. His tone became harder; his volume increased as they practically raced each other to the living room.

"Let's just chalk it up to a night of drinking..."

"Let's not. You weren't drunk. Don't give me that shit." He was getting angrier by the second. She couldn't do this to him, not now. Not after all this time, when he thought that maybe they had reached some sort of an understanding. She was blowing him off. Well, he was having none of that, not after what they shared. He'd be damned if he let her walk away from him.

"Well, adrenaline. Look, it is what it is. I have to go," she said, quickening her pace. He managed to get in front of her, blocking her passage, a large, nude, curiously semi-aroused roadblock in the middle of the narrow hall. He ran a hand over his head, then down his face as he tried to understand what had happened. Just a few hours ago, she was all over him, purring and moaning, her body hot and wet wrapped around him. What the fuck had happened?

"What the fuck does that mean? Was this like a booty call?" he asked, his voice harsher than he intended. He grasped her shoulder, forcing her to look at him. "Talk to me, *dooset*. Because last night you couldn't get enough of me, now you can't get away fast enough. "

"First, never use the term *"booty call"* again. Strike it from your vocabulary. Second, I don't know what *this* was, but it's not a relationship, Karim. It was sex. I wanted it, you enjoyed it, so it happened, and now I'm leaving." She tried to sidestep him, but he wasn't allowing it. So, they stood, staring at each other in the dimly lit hallway.

"So, it was a pity fuck? A way to keep me from chasing you like a whipped puppy? Get me to heel?"

She tried to step around him again, making it as far as the living room before her path was blocked, yet again.

"It wasn't a pity fuck," she said. "It was a tension reliever. It was either that or pummel you to death. I believe you enjoyed the choice I made. It was a mutually beneficial arrangement."

"You can't just…hate fuck me and walk away."

She stared at him, her eyes a deep steel grey, her mouth a tight line, and if he didn't know better, he would have sworn those were unshed tears glistening in her eyes. His anger dissolved, and he wanted nothing more than to hold her in his arms. When she finally spoke, her tone was low, her voice even as she spoke. It sent a chill through him.

"It's what I was trained to do, Karim. Don't you know?

Haven't you figured it out? That, last night, was something I am very good at. I had excellent training, and I am a very quick study, don't you think? It only took a month before I was the best in the palace. I mean, I had to be, I was the favorite concubine of your Persian King. I was so good, in fact, that I'm the reason he was murdered. I was -I was very, very popular." He stared at her, his brow furrowed.

"What are-" he took a step forward, grasping her wrist. She pulled away that look, returning, and he realized why he couldn't place it before. He'd never seen that look on her face before, not ever, and he never wanted to see it again. It was a look of pure, panicked terror. He released her, not wanting to upset her anymore.

"Don't do that. Don't ever do that," she whispered, easing past him to the door.

"What happened to you?" he whispered, gathering her in his arms and kissing her temple. She pushed away from him, not wanting his pity or to feel his touch. She got to the door, her voice shaking as she spoke.

"I didn't have sex with you out of pity or revenge." She didn't look at him. Instead, she focused on the gold-plated doorknob. "I did it because it's what I do. Once a whore, always a whore. Isn't that the saying?" She made her exit, not wanting to see his face, not wanting to see the pity and shame of having spent the night with used goods. He'd put her on a pedestal, thinking she was too good for him when the truth was, she wasn't worthy of having anyone love her, to be in love with her. She was a broken person, and nothing, not one thing could fix her.

She blinked back tears as she sprinted down the hall to the stairs; she didn't look back just in case he was there, just in case he tried to follow. She wouldn't let him see her cry.

CHAPTER SIX

"**W**here the hell is she?" Remy tossed his cell phone down and continued to pace Celeste's living room. He and Nicky had come to her place after dropping Briar off at the house he shared with two other soldiers in Metairie. They had assumed Celeste had gotten out of Jinxie's okay, that she would have made it safely home by now. Remy had been a little wary when they'd pulled into the garage, and her car was missing.

He became anxious when she didn't answer her cell phone, and she hadn't tried to call either of them. Now it was hours later, and they still hadn't heard from her. Near dawn, Remy's cell had chimed to life. Still, it wasn't her, only their sister Lisette checking in to let him know that Celeste hadn't gone to the family home in Mandeville, nor had she been admitted to any hospitals. However, they both knew that calling them was an exercise in futility.

"She wouldn't go to a hospital, Remy. She's a fucking superhuman. She's fine. She probably found some guy to take out her frustrations on. Now goodnight." She'd managed to make him feel as if she'd slammed the phone down in his ear even though she hadn't. You can't slam a cell phone.

Gaston had called a little later, saying that there were no reports of accidents or arrests. Celeste was simply MIA. He also echoed Lisette's thoughts, which pissed Remy off even more.

"As I told you," Nicky said from his position lying across one of the plush purple couches in Celeste's crowded living room," she probably went home with Karim. They looked pretty heated on the dance floor."

Remy snorted and waved off that notion.

"She would never ..."

Nicky sat up and looked Remy in the eye, his tone even and clear.

"Don't underestimate the power of hate fucking, my friend." Nicky yawned. "And by what I saw last night, she was ready to hate fuck the shit out of that man-"

"Vampire. He's not a man, "Remy grumbled.

"Man, vampire, fucking chipmunk-whatever-it doesn't matter. There was something; some pull that draws them to-gether. There was a mutual attraction, and maybe last night she couldn't fight it anymore. Hell, maybe she didn't want to." He went into the kitchen to start a pot of coffee before re-membering that she hadn't gone to the market. "I'm ordering groceries so that when she does show up, which she will, she'll have actual food in the apartment." Sighing, he grabbed her phone and ordered a grocery delivery from one of the local markets.

"She wouldn't," Remy said, sinking into the deep cush-ions of her sofa. He knew, somewhere deep down, that Celeste probably was with Karim. He'd seen them locked in an em-brace. The way Karim looked at her, his hands cradling her hips as they swayed. There was love there; Karim was in love with Celeste. He ran a hand over his face, scrubbing his stubbly cheek. He remembered what she had been like when they'd found her when they had taken her from the hell she'd been trapped in for so long. She was better now, but behind that bravado and fierce anger, she was fragile. She couldn't possibly believe that Karim was worth her trust, that he wouldn't hurt her again.

"She wouldn't," he repeated. The elevator pinged, and Ce-leste stepped into the living room, her clothes clutched to her chest. She stared at Remy then Nicky before lifting a hand to stop their verbal assault.

"She did." Nicky sighed.

"I don't want to talk. I need a hot bath and a cup of coffee."

"Where were you? We've been looking for you for hours. Celeste, you scared the shit out of me."

She dropped her clothes on the sofa and moved across the room, ignoring Remy's outburst.

"You're out of coffee. You're out of everything. I called for a delivery. You'll be stocked up and a fresh pot brewed by the time you get out of the shower," Nicky said, stroking her cheek. He looked at her and frowned. "Ce, have you been crying?" He asked in a whisper. It was a useless effort because the look on Remy's face told Nicky that he'd heard every word. Damn supernaturals, Nicky thought. Celeste gave him a tight smile and kissed his cheek.

"I'm fine," she said. "I just need a hot shower and a cup of strong black coffee."

"So, you fucked him?" Remy barked, and she visibly flinched.

"Hey, hey!" Nicky yelled at him. "What is wrong with you? It's none of our business."

"You did. That's why you smell like him, you reek of sex, and you're obviously wearing his clothes. Celeste, what's wrong with you? After what he did to you, you fuck him?"

"It's none of our business," Nicky warned, watching Celeste's face. She had her back to Remy so that he couldn't see the fresh tears welling in her eyes. He couldn't see the pained expression or the way her chin trembled. She was in so much turmoil, and Remy was browbeating her. He was also beginning to change, his eyes going bright yellow and his fangs elongating in a face that looked much more feline than it had before.

"The fuck it isn't. He's the reason we had to pull her out of hell, Nicky! You don't know the torture and pain she went through because of him! Every fucking thing that happened to her was because of him. And she goes and spreads her legs for him like a trained whore!" Remy bellowed, and she recoiled. It was as if he'd slapped her in the face. She lowered her head, her shoulders shaking as she began to sob silently. Without looking at either of them, she rushed up the stairs to her bedroom, slamming the door behind her. Nicky, the most even-tempered, laid back, mellow person they had ever known, exploded with rage.

"Are you out of your fucking mind?! What the fuck is wrong with you?! Are you that pissed because she slept with Karim instead of you? You enjoy seeing her cry, or are you just a son of a bitch in general? Why don't you just shut the fuck up and have a fucking seat, stupid, insensitive piece of shit."

"You have no idea," Remy began, and Nicky's entire body tightened, his face a brilliant red. He took a step forward so that he was nearly chest to chest with the rapidly changing Remy. He lowered his voice, and an icy chill ran down Remy's spine when his friend next spoke.

"I know more than you can imagine. I know everything that happened to her. I have been with her when she wakes, screaming in the middle of the night. I've been the one she calls when she's gone too far and hurt some random hook up. I've been the one to talk her down when she's scrubbed herself raw under a boiling shower. Me. Not you, not Gaston, not Arbor- me. So, don't you tell me what I don't know because you have no fucking idea what I've done for her, what I've given up for her. I love her more than anything in this world; I'm eaten alive every time someone else touches her. I know what she's suffered, and I would never speak to her the way you did. I'll die before I let you do it again."

"You of all people should be furious. You've been in love with her since you met her, you've always been there for her, and she gives it up to that piece of shit, *comme une putain commune*," Remy muttered to himself.

"Stop calling her that!" Nicky shoved him, surprising Remy.

"You speak French?" he asked incredulously.

"Among other things, *zlo chlen*," Nicky mumbled, walking away from Remy before he struck him.

"Did you just call me an *'evil dick'* in Russian?" Remy

snorted.

"Yes, I did, you pretentious twat. What gives you the right to talk about her like that? You're her brother. You're supposed to protect her. You're supposed to care about her. You are not supposed to make her feel like shit." Nicky couldn't even look at him anymore. He'd never wanted to choke another person until that very moment.

"Because ...she fucked him. Of all people, it's just wrong," Remy said.

"Goddammit, what the hell is the matter with you? Couldn't you see that she had already beaten herself up over the entire situation? She'd been crying, Remy. Have you ever known her to shed tears over anything? Ever? In like eight hundred years, have you ever? Asshole."

Remy sat down, his jaw slack, his eyes on Nicky's, whose smooth tawny skin was now brilliant red. He had never seen his friend this angry. Hell, he'd never seen him angry at all in all the time he'd known him. Nicky raked his hands through spiky platinum hair and paced back and forth, seething. The intercom buzzed, and Nicky went to answer it. He spoke in low, even tones before turning back to Remy, who sat with his head in his hands.

"I don't like it when you attack her like that. She and Karim have a twisted history, I know. But Remy," He paused and looked at the closed bedroom door then came closer. "Karim was her first love, her first kiss. And even though he did what he did, she still feels something for him. So back the fuck off."

Remy nodded. He hadn't known that, but of course, Nicky would know. Nicky knew everything. She trusted him because, unlike Remy, Nicky accepted everything about her, no questions asked. He loved her unconditionally, and unlike Remy, he would never say the things to her that Remy had. Remy Feeling like even more of a jerk, shoulders slumped, the anger easing from him.

"I am a cunt, aren't I?" Remy mumbled.

"A great big one," Nicky agreed just as the elevator doors pinged open to allow the delivery man into the apartment.

* * *

Lilith sat on the edge of the bed, slipping her feet into a pair of sleek heeled sandals when she felt him watching her from the doorway. She sighed but didn't bother looking at him, knowing that he was here on a fishing trip.

"Good morning, Lovely," he said in his crisp, high-bred English accent. She hated that accent and the fact that he had developed the effect a few years ago. He didn't need it, but he insisted it made him seem friendlier, more open, and relatable. She thought it made him sound like a high-born ass.

"Morning, Daddy," she mumbled. She didn't have to look at him to know that he would have a smile on his handsome face, a face that was made for movies or politics. He'd chosen politics, of course.

His thick dark hair, which wasn't dark enough to be considered black, was brushed away from a perfectly tanned face. The tan was somewhat natural but gave him an outdoorsy feel, as if he spent a lot of time outdoors, which she knew he did not. His eyes were the only thing that took away from his movie idol prettiness and made him seem intense and foreboding; they were dark and gleamed like highly polished coal. When he wasn't smiling, which was rare these days, he could be quite intimidating, almost frightening. Senator Alexander Prince was the poster boy for his party, JFK reborn. He was their Golden God. Little did they know, she thought, they were putting their trust in the Prince of Darkness himself?

"I hear you had a run-in with the Queen," he chuckled. She looked up at him then. He was standing as he always was, just inside the door. His suit was dark and crisp, his shirt was white, and his tie was a vibrant, lively shade of lemon yellow. He said the *queen* as if it were a joke.

"Your wife put her hands on me. She cut up my face, growling and frothing at the mouth like a rabid dog," she said, and his smile faltered, but only for a second. Even with her, he was the perfect spokesman. His smile never wavered as he looked at her, his eyes twinkling brightly. That was why the women in the neighborhood found excuses to come over with casseroles and baked goods. They wanted to get a look at the handsome and seemingly single Senator Prince.

"I told you going into this scheme of hers was not a good idea. You can't trust her, Lil. She will tell you only part of the story, make you do all of the hard work, then step over you to grab the glory." She stood, her head only coming to the center of his chest, and she had to look up to stare into his eyes.

"Why is she so dead set on finding this mark on the Caelestis? What does it mean?"

"It means that she could be the key to ultimate power. If she bears the mark, you won't get close enough to her to find it. She's protected, and she's dangerous, volatile - she could kill you without breaking a sweat." Alexander stared at Lilith as she fussed with her clothing. She looked pretty, even with her bright red hair and pale skin. His smile faded, and the intensity of his glare made her uncomfortable like he was looking through her. She ignored his glare while smearing lip gloss onto her pale pink lips.

"I've seen her in action, and I'll be fine. Don't worry. The queen isn't the only one with plans, father." She reached for her purse, a wicked smile teasing the corners of her mouth as she left the room. "Oh, the plans I have," she chirped happily.

✹ ✹ ✹

He'd woken to find the tent empty, Calie nowhere to be found.

He'd wiped the sand from his body before dressing in dark trousers and going in search of the wayward goddess. They were still a few days outside of Pelusium, but they had managed to stop in several small cities on their way for supplies, sleeping at inns that made it easy for him to keep his distance from her. On this particular night, they were camped at an oasis in the center of miles of a scorching desert.

He moved through the lush greenery, the sound of gentle splashing, drawing him closer to the heated lagoon beneath shady palms. He saw her clothing first; her new tunic and trousers' pale white against deep green grass caught his attention. The smell of water and sand and the unmistakable scent of Calie wafted on the night breeze. He saw her then, her dark hair wet and cascading down her bare back, her caramel shoulders glowing in the moonlight. She kept her back to him, treading water and staring into the starry indigo sky.

"You found me," she said, slowly turn to face him, "it is beautiful out here, Karim. Even in this entire nothing, there is such beauty. Join me. The water is still heated from the sun. You can wash all of the sand from your naughty bits. I got some sapoúni from the last village. It will take the stink off of you," she teased.

"I do not stink."

She lifted a brow and swam around the pool of shimmering water, giving him hints of naked flesh beneath the surface.

He watched her for a moment, his brows raised, then agreed, a bath would be refreshing and was probably sorely needed at this point. "Turn around, dooset. Don't want you ogling my bits," he said with a grin. She tilted her head at the endearment, and he realized he'd called her 'love.' It had been natural and comfortable, and he wondered when he'd started to do that.

"I've seen your bits every night since I met you. Don't get shy on me now, Karim."

"Can I have even the illusion of modesty?" he asked, and she rolled her eyes before turning her back. He stripped his clothes off and eased into the delicious warmth of the fragrant water. She was right. The water felt wonderful on his sandblasted skin. After spending the day baking underground, the warmed water felt refreshing and cleansing. The sand was being washed away from places he could never quite reach, and it felt amazing.

"What is that smell?" he asked after dipping his head into the water to rinse the sand from his hair and face. It was terrific, like flowers and honey but sweeter. He inhaled deeply as she drifted closer and realized it was her. It was the sweet scent of her arousal, and he knew immediately that he was in deep, deep trouble.

"What smell?" she asked, moving much too close. The smell was more pungent now, and she looked so delectable. Her skin was like liquid gold; her hair brushed away from a face that was both angelic and devilish. Full berry-colored lips shimmered, and she was so achingly naked just inches away from him. He was hard and hurting within seconds of her moving towards him with something in her hands.

"Come here," she said, "turn around,"

He turned instinctively, and she began to massage the sweet-smelling soap into his thick hair gently. He closed his eyes and leaned into her touch. Her fingers, gentle and firm, felt wonderful. She came closer, her bare breasts brushing his back. Her hands moved down his neck to his shoulders, lathering his skin with the rich scents of irises and almonds; combined with her natural scent, it relaxed him. Her hands moved down his back beneath the surface, pausing just above the curve of his spine, gently massaging his sore muscles.

"Turn," she said, and he did so without qualms, facing her. She reached for a small clay jar and scooped more of the smooth clay-like soap into her palms until it lathered and began at his throat. Her hands, soft and soapy, moved over his collarbones and down his arms. He stared at her while her hands worked over his chest and the tattoo on his neck and shoulder, then slowly down his sides, pausing at his hips.

He held his breath, waiting for her to do something, the thick, fragrant soap on her hands, making them slick and warm against his heated skin. She looked into his eyes, her hands circling his waist before coming back to run along his lower abdomen. Karim sucked in the air, his heart racing and his body tense. He wanted her to touch him, to stroke him with those delicate soapy hands. He was stiff and achy, his body primed to explode if she would only touch him.

Then she did, her hand slick and smooth, moved over him, and he groaned, his eyes drifting closed. She moved her hand slowly, up and down, from the base to the tip in sweeping strokes that had him weak and shivering.

"Should I stop?" she asked, her voice tight.

He opened his eyes and looked at her; her face was soft, her lips parted, and yet she continued her extraordinary torture.

"No, please don't," he whispered, his mouth coming down on hers. Her hand tightened on him, and he bucked forward, his arms tightening around her, wanting to feel her closer. He trailed kisses across smooth bare shoulders, his hands moving down to cup her firm rounded bottom, then to the mound of wet, silken curls. He stroked her with warm fingers, slowly slipping one into the tight heat at her core, and she swayed against him, her lips touching the top of his tattoo.

He licked the throbbing pulse point on her throat, aching to sink his teeth into her as his body begged to slip into the sweetness at her center. He nipped her with his teeth, not breaking the skin, he couldn't bring himself to do it, and he wouldn't burden her with his mark. Instead, he lowered his mouth to the gentle swell of her breasts, brushing his lips across her skin. He continued to move his body, pushing against her, imagining himself inside of her. His fingers moved into the soft, tight sweetness of her, his body pumping against her hand, and everything in him sang.

*   *   *

She'd gasped in shock when he touched her and clutched his shoulder when he moved deeper, her body sliding against him. She met his stroke as he met hers, their bodies creating wakes and waves in the small lagoon. This was not what she had expected.

This was much better than she had been told. She gasped as a new wave of something unfamiliar rolled through her, a slow burn that started at her core and moved outward in wave upon delicious wave of pleasure. He held her until the mild tremors roiling through her ceased. She'd continued her fervent fondling of him until she felt his release warm on her hand and stomach. He made a noise that was something like a deep growl, and she continued her delicious torture, even though he'd stopped his wondrous exploration of her body. His body was still, every muscle standing out in stark relief; he was beautiful in his release, she thought.

When he was able to, when his breathing had returned to normal, he looked at her. He stared at her, those eyes like sapphires in the moonlight. She looked so sweet and innocent, beautiful and so very, very dangerous. She stared at him with a devilish spark in vibrant blue eyes, her lips curving into a cunning and knowing smile, and he knew he'd been ambushed. She had seduced him, the cheeky little minx; she had set the scene and proven that he wanted her. Of course, he did. He was in love with her.

The realization hit him like a stone wall, and he pulled away, unable to breathe anymore.

"We can never do that again," he whispered, backing away. "You should not have done that."

"But you enjoyed it. I know you did," she said, and he watched as confusion and pain danced across her face. "You liked it, and you know you did. You wanted it, and you want me as much as I want you."

"It was wrong," he bit, and she started from the sharpness of his tone. "It was wrong, and it will never happen again. Never."

She stared at him in disbelief as he hurriedly climbed from the water and covered himself.

"Clean yourself and get dressed. We leave within the hour. The sooner I get you to Pelusium, the better. I need to rid myself of you as soon as possible," he barked and stormed away, leaving her stunned and angry.

He decided then that he could not complete this journey without more happening. He could not risk giving in again. He was too weak when it came to her, too weak and too much in love with her to continue to fight temptation, especially when she was as deter-mined to bed him as he was not to allow it.

"Damn you, Nyx," he'd muttered as he'd marched back to the tent. Why had he made such an impossible promise? Because he told himself, he hadn't expected to fall so deeply so quickly.

* * *

Someone was in his bedroom. He could feel them when they entered the bedroom, but he waited, not sure of what to do. Karim could feel the eyes on him as he slept, his body tensing in preparation for battle. He thought as they moved around him, females. He could smell them, three distinct scents that were very feminine and somewhat familiar. Then he heard the whispered voices arguing above him, speaking to each other with a bizarre cadence that could only mean one thing.

The Moirai had stopped by for a visit.

He rolled onto his back and slowly opened his eyes to stare at the three sisters. Eons old, they still looked like dewy twenty-somethings, with their large creepy eyes on him. Soft, pale Clotho, vibrant Lachesis, and dark Atropos all stared at him expectantly. They were kneeling on the edge of the bed, a trio of very distinct and very pretty women. He'd seen pornos that started like this, he thought. He'd also seen horror movies that ended like this. With this group, it could go either way.

"Afternoon, ladies," he yawned, stretching his sex-ex-hausted body, and they smiled at him. Even with the three in his room and the devastating end to what had been a magnifi-cent night, he could still smell Celeste on his skin. She was on his sheets, his pillows, and he wanted to keep it that way for as long as possible. Now his day had taken a turn to the bizarre.

"How did you get in here?"

"Your little charms are cute, but the magic here doesn't

effect primordials," Lachesis said. He sighed and wondered how Celeste had been unable to phase herself out of his apartment. His heart jumped a little as it struck him that as much as she protested and assured him of her complete disdain for him, she hadn't wanted to leave. She wanted to stay, and she would have felt the magic when she crossed the threshold. She had stayed because she'd wanted to. She'd wanted him.

"To what do I owe this pleasure? Let me guess, big mama Nyx sent you." He sat up, the covers pooling around his hips. They stared, eyes alert, observing him. He didn't know why he bothered asking. He already knew that would be an exercise in futility. Getting a straight answer from the Fates was just something that was never done, especially when they were together. And they were always, always together.

"She is in danger now. You know she is," Lachesis said.

"You've seen with your own eyes, and you know that trouble will come," Clotho sighed.

"It is only the beginning," Lachesis chimed in.

"It will become much worse," Atropos said.

He tried his best to follow their speech pattern, gleaning what he could from their cryptic message. There was always a pattern to them, but it was gone if you lost the thread. He knew that *she* was Celeste, and the trouble he knew had to be Lilith. He nodded and thought, perhaps they could help him.

"The wheels are already in motion. But you must act quickly," Lachesis said.

"Before what happened in the past retakes hold, before the anger consumes and changes her forever."

"Can you tell me what happened to her?" he asked.

They looked at each other, then back at him. Lachesis opened her mouth then snapped it closed. She and Atropos turned to Clotho, who stared at her hands as she debated with herself.

"Please." He could hear the pleading in his voice and rubbed his eyes. "I just need to know."

The three women held onto each other, rocking gently as

Clotho stared at him. They reached for him, taking his hands and sending a current of electricity through him. Clotho's pale blue eyes became beacons of bright light, her voice a hollow ethereal monotone as the sisters began to speak as one, and he was privy to their memories as if watching a movie in his mind. He watched as their lips moved in unison in some strange ventriloquist's act with the three speaking with one voice and became hypnotized at the visions they provided of what once was.

* * *

"Her curse of lust has followed her, her entire life. That is why she was entrusted to the Amazons and then to you. You, Prince Karim of House Tyre, noble and steadfast, Nyx charged you to retrieve her progeny. You, Karim, untouched by magic, were a perfect choice until your heart and your body betrayed your word. You were forced to choose. You chose poorly, and once the covenant was broken, once she was left with the merchant on the outskirts of Pelusium, her fate was set. And so was yours.

The merchant's wife, watching her husband lust for the girl, rid herself of such a rival. The slaver took her and two others to the palace at Persepolis, and she took top price. King Xerxes became immediately enamored with the feisty slave girl. She was not made to live in the harem. She was given her suite and treated as the king's consort. She fought him, but the punishments were so brutal that she found it easier to bear the humiliation over the constant pain. As she was hidden, still affected by the poison that had doomed her, she had no help, no hope of rescue, so this became her life. She had not returned to her protector, and she had not regained her divine gifts; she was unable to defend herself from the horrors at the hands of one who yearned to possess her heart as well as her body. Her visits with the king became nightly as his infatuation grew. He loved her, obsessed over her to the point of neglecting his kingdom. The queen became jealous and tried to have her executed, but her attempts failed as the slave girl was guarded nonstop. Instead, the queen herself was punished for such treachery.

He showered her with gifts and love while keeping her locked away from prying eyes. She was his prized possession, and he watched her, stalked her, and loved her above everything else in his world. As his obsession deepened, he became angered because she did not return his ardor. To punish her for not returning his love, he became depraved in his treatment. He tortured her and degraded her, making her do the most horrific things for his pleasure. No longer satisfied with making her his sexual slave, he began to let others use her as they pleased to punish her for not returning his love.

In the palace, she was shunned and looked upon as lower than trash, an outcast locked in a room for twenty-three hours of the day. Her only friend was the soldier who guarded her door, who made sure she was fed and clothed. The soldier became her confidant and, like all mortal men, fell in love with her. He watched over her and protected her the best he could, but when the whippings and rapes began, he could no longer stand it. He, with the help of an accomplice, assassinated the king as he lay with her. The kingdom was in turmoil as the king's son took reign, yet she remained locked in that place, the new plaything for the soldier who felt that he owned her.

When she would not come to his bed, when she was too beaten and broken down to want another to touch her, he prayed for release from his obsession. That was when the woman appeared, the woman with the eyes of a cat and the skin as deep brown as coffee found him while he was deep in the drink. She, the wife of the father, had been sent by her conspirator, the one who birthed the living reminder of her husband's lost love. She wanted to remove any memory of the love that came before her and eagerly accepted the task. She gave him an elixir to weaken Celeste's resolve, and so would be his. He believed the woman and poured this new elixir into the girl's drink, but it did not work. It only made her weak and sick. He was frustrated and angered by the lie he had been told, and he was determined to have her. When he forced himself on her, she *could not fight, only lay and cry as he used her body over and over, leaving her shattered. He bound her ankles and wrists and used her most brutally, overcome by his own fervent need. The torture lasted for days, days of being tied down and abused with no savior in sight.*

Then when he saw what he had done, saw that now she would never love him, that he had succumbed to his lust like the others, he slit her throat and slashed her delicate and tempting flesh until she lay dead. Then he took what he had longed for. He took her heart. The elixir had not only weakened her; it made her mortal. Her body was cast into a pit where those that wished her dead and celebrated her death found her and desecrated her body so that her soul would be forever cast into hell. She was cast as the villain in the downfall of a once great and powerful kingdom.

She spent many years in hell, so many years trapped and chained in a cell, living her nightmare over and over. She was still lost to those who would protect her, lost in death, in the deepest part of Tartarus for so long that she was all but forgotten. Only one continued the desperate search for her. The only one knew that she was somewhere and would not relent in her pursuit. That was when the deal was made with the Fallen One. The destroyer of gods found her and leading the way. He cleared a path for the family that would be her world. When he saw the broken girl, he was taken by her beauty and her spirit's strength. A new deal was struck, and he marked her for her protection, marked her so that she could be found when the time came. She bears the mark now, and she holds the scars of all that was done to her."

* * *

Karim sat stunned, tears stinging his luminous eyes, his mouth open in abject horror. He jerked his hands from them and pushed himself back on the bed, making sure that his nakedness was covered. His chest burned, his heart aching as tears fell onto the bedsheets. The horror she suffered because of his actions made him wretch, the agony tearing him apart. What had he done? Dear gods in heaven, what had he done?

CHAPTER SEVEN

"**N**yx!!! I know you can fucking hear me. And I know you can get in here if you want to. Your fucking daughters have been here. Nyx!" Karim paced his bedroom, checking the clock every minute, waiting for the sunset. He needed to get to Celeste to tell her - what? He had no idea, but he needed to see her, talk to her. God, how could he have been so stupid? How could he have been so selfish and thoughtless? No wonder she hated him. He hated himself for what she had gone through. Damn it, why hadn't Nyx told him? If he had known, he could have helped her. He could have stopped her from being sold to a slaver. He could have - he could have kept her with him. Would that have been so horrible? Breaking his promise to Nyx would have been the lesser of two evils. Instead, she had been repeatedly abused and finally murdered.

Before they had gone, it was Atropos who'd left the lasting impression, and her eyes narrowed as she studied him while the other two exited the room. She sighed as if she'd decided something significant and touched his stubbly cheek and said, "Fate is flexible. You are not *the* one, but you are *one*. She has a trusted circle, and you will gain entry, perhaps. You and she will be linked for an eternity, not always good, not always bad. But soon, you will find it bearable." She'd given him a somber look before they faded from the room.

"Nyx!!! I swear to Christ if you don't answer me," He didn't know how he was going to finish that statement, but he needn't worry. Nyx appeared in a swirl of blue-grey smoke, her ageless face tense.

"What are you screeching about?" she asked, folding her

arms across her chest. Her annoyance quickly dissolved into curiosity.

Karim stalked toward her, his eyes hard, his face a mask of thinly veiled anger.

"Why didn't you tell me?" he said, and her face fell. She opened her mouth and shook her head. "You knew what happened to her, you knew what had been done to her, and you send me of all people to protect her."

"When she left here this morning, she looked ...if I would have known I wouldn't ... FUUCCCKKK," he screamed, and for a second, Nyx was afraid that he was going to strike her. Instead, he stabbed his fingers through his hair, then settled his hands-on denim-clad hips. For the first time, Nyx paid attention to Karim and his state of undress. He wore old jeans, inside out and undone, no shirt, and his feet were bare. He smelled slightly of the ocean but more like lavender and vanilla.

She stared as he stalked across the living room, pausing at a painting before kicking the easel to the floor. The painting fell face up, and she was struck by the beauty it captured—Celeste in the moonlight.

"You slept with her," she said in a whisper. "Oh, Karim ... that ..."

"Was a mistake? No shit. Do you know how it feels to be hate fucked? Do you have any idea what it's like to have something you've wanted for so long only to be told that it meant nothing? That I meant nothing? I was wracking my brain trying to figure out what I could have done that was so wrong, what made her hate me so much. I mean, as far I knew, she had been returned safely to you. I thought she was pissed that I left her with the merchant and his wife. I had no idea-but, now I know why. I know everything. How did you ever think it would be a good idea to have me protect her now when I did such a bang-up job the first time? You knew her seeing me again would open so many wounds..." He stood still, watching. His glare was unwavering as he stared Nyx down.

She returned his glare, her eyes suddenly cold, her expression giving nothing away but spoke volumes.

"Oh my God, you knew. You knew where she was the entire time. From the moment I left her, you knew. Your daughters, those mind-bending fuck heads, told you exactly what was happening to her. You knew that she was broken. You were counting on it. How could you?" he asked, his stomach churning as if he were going to be sick.

"You don't understand." She said evenly as if speaking to a child.

"You left her in hell!" He growled. The tears that had threatened finally ran down his cheeks as he moved closer to Nyx, who nearly cowered before him. She took a step back and stiffened defiantly.

"And I would do it again in a heartbeat. She has a destiny Karim, that doesn't include you. She will have more than you could ever give her. She will be the most powerful goddess ever born, and I did what I had to do to make that happen," she snarled, her eyes swirled white, her dark hair streaked the purest white, and his blood ran cold. He looked at her in utter disgust, shaking his head in disbelief.

"You're a monster. You pretend to care about her, but you did this. You made sure she was broken before you helped her. You're more evil than Nemesis ever was. At least she didn't pretend to care about her," he said. "If you think I will let you continue to hurt her…"

"You have no choice. You pledged fealty to me, and I will hold you to that. If you so much as breathe a word of this to her, to anyone, I will destroy your entire race, and I will make sure they know that you are the reason why. Then," Her voice was even, smooth and as gentle as a late summer breeze, but her face was a mask of pure hatred. "I will spend an eternity killing you."

He stared at her, his cool green eyes never leaving her face. Slowly, his scowl lightened, and he smiled. The smile gave way to a chuckle and finally rose to a demonic maniacal laugh that made the hairs on the back of her neck rise.

"Do you find me amusing? Do you think my threats are idle?" Her expression softened in her confusion.

"No, I believe that you would kill us all to punish one. I realize that you have a dark, empty hole where your soul should be, you hateful cow. I laugh because when she finds out what you've done, and she will, it will all be for nothing. All of your schemes and plots, your pitiful life won't be worth shit," he chuckled, taking a step closer with each word. "She already mistrusts me, so I will probably get off easier than I deserve, but you ...she'll unleash an unending hell on you, the likes of which you could never imagine. And I will revel in watching you burn." He turned and stormed into his bedroom, slamming the door behind him, leaving Nyx shaken by his quiet fury.

* * *

Lilith was late, but fashionably so, per usual. In the human world, she was the striking daughter of a state senator; her flashy grand entrance always garnered her photos on gossip blogs and in shiny tabloids that lined the checkout aisle of grocery stores. Sighing, she took out a compact, checked her makeup, deemed it acceptable, and waited for the driver to get out of the car to hold her door open for her exit.

Slipping Chanel sunglasses on before easing out of the black town car's back seat fully, she emerged to the pop of flashbulbs. She acted as if she hadn't seen them. She wore a bright teal sundress; a wide-brimmed sun hat covered her crimson hair and shielded her delicate skin from the harsh rays of the July sun. Feigning a sigh of disdain, she walked past them into the posh eatery on St. Charles Avenue. She managed to glance at the paparazzi when someone called her name and was immediately bombarded by camera flashes. She groaned and shook her head, acting as if she were irritated by their presence. In reality, she loved the attention; being a celebutante was almost as much fun as being a movie star. All of the perks, none of the work, just the way she liked it.

Sauntering to the hostess, she looked around the dining room, watching the human faces that turned to see who'd entered the room. She smirked as a group of men nodded to her as she sashayed by, her skirt making a soft swish as she moved. Humans had such an obvious stench when they were attracted to a female. She inhaled sharply; the stench wasn't the correct word, she decided. There was a distinct scent, but it was far from unpleasant on most. It reminded her of freshly baked bread and sugar. If she weren't in such a hurry, she might be inclined to indulge. There was no time for that right now, she thought. And though lust was one of the strongest weapons in her arsenal, it would be useless on her lunch date. For this date, she needed something a little different. She needed charm and grace, a certain vulnerability to make her date think that she needed protecting.

She moved past the linen-covered tables and saw her guest had already arrived and was seated with a glass of water in her hand. Lilith lifted her glasses so she could rub her eyes until they were red and raw. When she felt the sting of irritated eyes, she lowered her shades and mustered up a few tears, just enough to give her eyes a watery look, not enough to spill over. Not just yet.

She took her seat, taking the hand that was extended to her in both of hers.

"I'm so glad you could make it," she said breathlessly. "I'm so sorry, I'm late." She ordered a drink, and purposefully averted her gaze as she removed her glasses. She couldn't help but feel grim satisfaction when a look of concern floated across the ever-serene face of Arbor Kent.

"Not at all. Are you alright?" She placed a comforting hand over Lilith's. Her voice lowered as to dissuade eavesdroppers.

"I don't want to burden you with my problems. This was

supposed to give us a chance to get to know each other, Mrs. Kent." Arbor waved her hand, dismissing the notion.

"Please, you can tell me anything, sweetie. Now tell me, what's wrong?" The waitress returned then with Lilith's drink and their lunch orders. Lilith hid a smile behind her menu as Arbor rattled off her choice. The Queen wasn't the only one who could scheme, she thought. While the Queen dominated the Dark Realm with a velvet fist, Lilith had learned long ago that there was always a better way. Vulnerability was key when trying to garner trust in others. Perceived weakness had a way of opening doors much faster than aggression. More flies with honey, her father had always told her, more flies with honey.

* * *

He didn't know when she'd gone, just that she had, and he was relieved. If she'd stayed, he wasn't sure what he would do or could do to Nyx. She'd known and had been partly responsible for all of the pain Celeste had suffered. And why? Because of some centuries-old prophecy made by a trio of prepubescent whack jobs? No, Karim thought, running a hand over his face. She'd done it because she didn't want to lose control of Celeste. She didn't want to lose the power of having one of the most powerful deities ever born under her thumb. That was all the gods cared about. That was all any of the preternaturals cared about, power and adoration. Many children were afraid that they would be forgotten and discarded by the humans they claimed disdain for. Secretly, they craved adulation and praise. They wanted that attention, needed it. After all, what is a god if no one worships him?

He needed to see Celeste. He needed to -what? Tell her what Nyx had done? That was the one thing he couldn't do. Nyx held power over him. He couldn't break his oath no matter how much he wanted to. Yet, if Celeste asked, he couldn't lie. His stupid honor trapped him. And Nyx knew that. She was using it to keep him from confessing all to Celeste. Damn it, how did Nyx expect him to be around Celeste knowing the truth?

If only he'd bitten her that night in the oasis, if he had taken from her, they would be connected, and he would have felt her pain. If he had taken from her, if he had made love to her that night, she would have been his, and he wouldn't have been able to leave her. Vampires bonded when they fed on their lover, and they remained connected until death. If only he rubbed his eyes and sighed. If.

Sitting on the edge of the bed, he considered his options. He could just manifest in her apartment lobby, but that would cause an uproar. Not to mention that he had no idea what the lobby looked like; it could be floor to ceiling windows for all he knew. And if it wasn't and he managed to get into her apartment, who was to say that she wouldn't kill him as soon as he crossed the threshold. Not that he could blame her.

His best-case scenario would be another session of mind-blowing sex, but you could only get hate fucked for so long before it started to affect your performance. Not that he didn't deserve anything she decided to do to him. He'd do anything to gain her forgiveness, even burn in the afternoon sun. He sat up, letting the thought settle over him, making his decision that much easier.

"Shit," he said and pushed a button on a small remote to lift the shades. He heard the motor begin just as he grabbed the blanket from his bed and made his way into the bathroom. He was willing to risk it, and whatever happened, he damn well deserved it.

* * *

"What the fuck is up with you and this new hip hop obsession, Ce?" Nicky leaned back, taking a deep inhale on the blunt between his fingers, and exhaled the sweet-smelling pink smoke into the air. He took one more hit, then passed it to Celeste, who lay with her head in his lap, her bare feet propped up on the arm of the sofa they shared. Across from them, a shirtless Remy head bobbed to the blaring music that rocked the apartment.

"Aren't you supposed to be rehearsing? I thought you had a tour to prepare for," she said, her eyes drifting closed. Nicky ran his fingers through her hair, watching the strands fall in inky waves.

"You should come with me on tour." Nicky choked. "It's been a while. You could use some mindless fun. And I'm going to South America and Japan. You love Tokyo." He looked down at her. She had her eyes closed as she thought about it.

"What about the Grey?" she asked, but her mind was already on the lights and sounds of downtown Tokyo, the smell of Cherry Blossoms and taste of the world's best unfiltered Saki.

"I can handle that," Remy piped up. "I'm second for a reason, Ce. Go have fun. You're just about done with the semester. I can manage for a couple of weeks. I'll behave and everything." He glanced at his watch and rose slowly. "I have got to get home. I've spent way too much time around you two burnouts, and I need a shower." He pulled a t-shirt over his head, kissed Celeste on the forehead, and fist-bumped Nicky.

"Later," he mumbled, slipping into the elevator.

"You'll be back before the fall semester starts. Come on." Nicky bounced his leg, jostling her head. She looked up at him, slightly annoyed.

"What about the band? Would they be okay with me tagging along?" Nicky hooted as if she'd said the most ridiculous thing he'd ever heard. He had a band of five that traveled with him and had been with him from the beginning.

"They would love it. Hell, if they could, they'd go on tour with you and leave my ass here. Come on. I need my number one fan. "

She thought for a minute, her eyes drifting closed as the Mist took her. She nodded, but Nicky wasn't sure it was to the music or an affirmation. After a second, he realized it was to the music and that she had mellowed out to the point of sleep.

* * *

She was floating somewhere between heaven and earth, her body drifting in the ether. She reached out, in search of something, in hopes of gaining some sort of perspective. What she found was the hard-muscled chest of a male, a large male. He grasped her, crushing her body to his, his pelvis grinding into her. She looked up into impossibly blue eyes, skin so dark and smooth that it reminded her of glass. She could barely make out his features, but she felt safe in the arms of this giant. He smelled of sandalwood and a slight spice that she couldn't place. She ran her fingers over smooth skin and taut muscle, his body hard, making her wet at the slightest touch.

"Kiss me," he whispered in a deep baritone in the old language, and her body grew hot and liquid against him. She lifted her lips to meet his and was stunned by the tenderness of the kiss. He explored her mouth with a skillful tongue, tasting of something so deliciously addicting, she held him tighter. His head was bald. Her fingers moved over the smooth pate to hold him closer. She wrapped her legs around his hips and pushed against the hardened length of him. She wanted him, rigid and thick inside of her.

He broke the kiss, his hands on her face as she breathed against her.

"You are mine. You have always been mine," he whispered, his voice thick and fervent against her skin. She rubbed her core against him, needing to feel him, coaxing him. He held her thighs and slid easily, smoothly inside her, and her bones turned to nothing, her body molded to accommodate him.

She opened her eyes to look into the darkness that hid his face and was stunned. His eyes were no longer brilliant sapphire, and now they were cool, pale green.

"Azizam," he said, and she found that she could no longer breathe.

* * *

woke when her face smacked against the cool wood of the floor, a high-pitched buzzing ringing in her ears. Groggily, she sat up and looked around the dimly lit living room. She was dazed slightly, confused by the drawn curtains, the smell of something burning mingling with the lingering floral and spicy aroma of the Mist. Nicky was no longer in the apartment, but someone else was. She stood slowly, realizing that she'd rolled off of the sofa and onto the floor. She soon discovered the buzzing was the smoke alarm, and someone was sitting on the sofa opposite her, silently smoldering. Smoke rose from a male body which sat completely still, breathing deeply and evenly through clenched teeth. She waved her hands, clearing the air with a great whoosh, and the alarm went blessedly silent.

She rubbed her eyes and turned on a lamp to see the figure sitting on the sofa Remy had occupied before she'd dozed in her Mist haze. His head and face were a mask of burned flesh and muscle that had already begun knitting itself back together. His lips and ears were returning, but his hands were still smoking, as was the skin scorched through the holes in his t-shirt and jeans. He was sitting perfectly still, concentrating on breathing through the pain.

Unlike the mythology, Vampires, truly born vampires, were born human but changed somewhere in their mid-twenties, when they were at their physical peak, and remained that way until death. It was a painful transformation that lasted for four or five days, the agony of which was nearly unbearable.

But once the transformation was complete, they remained in that form until death. It had been that way with the original Seven and was that way for all of their true progeny. They could also bear children and had beating hearts and souls, and they weren't cold to the touch. They looked human to the untrained eye, the only hint being the paleness of their eyes, the sharpness of their canines, and the fact that they burst into flame in sunlight.

He would regenerate, but it was going to be painful. Almost as painful as his transformation.

"Karim?" She turned to look at the clock. It was just after four in the afternoon, hours from sundown. "What are you doing here? Are you insane? Of course, you're insane. Why else would you come here during the day?" Without thinking, she sliced opened her wrist with one sharp fang and thrust it towards his cracked and bleeding lips.

"No," he croaked, "No, I've taken enough from you, Calie. I'll be fine. I deserve this for what I did to you. But I didn't know, she never told me. She never told me that you didn't make it back. I thought you were upset because I left you. If she had told me, I would have gone back. I would have come back no matter what if I had known." He wanted to say more but began cough choking as blood began a slow trickle from his cracked lips.

"Drink." She cringed at the rasp of his voice. It was rough and pained, but he refused her wrist. His wounds would heal.

"I would never have come here. I would never have agreed to be your protector again. I would never have agreed to any of this if I had known what I did, what I caused." He mumbled. Celeste listened, trying to understand he was rambling about, protector? She didn't need a protector in the Collective. She didn't need a protector, period.

"I deserve this and so much more. I deserve this." He looked up at her, deep green eyes in a scarred and smoldering face that were slowly returning to normal. As he spoke, the flesh at the corners of his mouth cracked open, blood oozed onto non-existent lips, and she felt her chest tighten. As often as she'd wished death on him, this was just too heartbreaking to witness. She rolled her eyes in frustration and re-opened the wound.

"Drink," she said. He looked down at the wrist she'd thrust beneath his nose but remained stoic, ignoring the scent of fresh, warm blood. He lowered his eyes, too ashamed to look at her. Instead, he concentrated on breathing and the pain as his body healed.

"You're in pain." She pleaded.

"I deserve it more than you know," he croaked. She sat beside him and gently guided his chin up, forcing him to look into her deep blue eyes. He relaxed a little. It was like looking into an endless ocean, the scent of her wafting around him. Her eyes, her smile, he could get lost just looking into her face. He would die for that smile.

"Karim, sweetie, if you die on my sofa, I will find a way to resurrect you so that I can kick your ass. Now drink," she said in the sweetest tone she could muster.

She gave him a gentle, almost loving smile, and he parted his lips slowly, every muscle movement bringing fresh blood and pain. With nimble fingers, he held her arm, reluctantly bringing her wrist to his mouth. He sucked deeply, his mouth filling with the most exquisite taste he'd ever experienced. She tasted so good, warm, and smooth, like rich red wine. It flowed down his throat, renewing him, healing him.

He held her arm tighter, tugging her forward until she was seated beside him, her body pressed close to him. Her scent invaded his nose as her taste filled his mouth, and he was suddenly consumed with an all-encompassing need for her.

Celeste leaned forward, her lips parting as he continued his slow, steady drink. Reaching up, she brushed the hair from his face so she could see him. The cracks and blackened skin had healed to red, sunburned flesh then settled into his natural tawny tone.

"I've always liked your hair. It is so soft and always smells like the ocean," she said, stroking the back of his head, her voice thicker than she'd intended. Unconsciously, she leaned forward and inhaled deeply, the smell of burning replaced by that beachy smell. He moaned, his tongue moving over the delicate flesh. She ignored her body, knowing that it was only a side effect of the feeding. It was why she didn't allow anyone to feed on her, and she only fed on Remy or Gaston and, in extreme cases, Nicky. There were boundaries that none of them would cross with her. Karim was a different entity.

He sat up and inhaled deeply, the stain of her blood still on his lips, his shimmering eyes pale seafoam. He turned to her, his chest heaving as he tried to collect himself, but she could tell this had gone further than she intended. His movements were so swift that she hadn't even noticed until he covered her mouth with his, pulling her forward until she was nearly straddling his hips. He thrust upward, pushing against her, his body begging for more. She was shocked by the quickness and the ferocity of the action, the basic need. His hands moved beneath her shirt and cupping her breasts, his mouth moved down the column of her throat, pausing at the thrumming pulse in her neck. His teeth grazed her skin in preparation for the bite that was sure to follow. She gasped in surprise and felt herself relenting before she came to her senses.

She pulled free and sprang to her feet so quickly that she bumped into the coffee table and sat down with a thump. Her fingers went to her kiss swollen lips still tingling from the assault, her eyes a shade of blue he had only seen on that last night in the desert. He closed his eyes and inhaled her scent, sweet and bold, filling the room. He reached out, and she scooted back, afraid that if he kissed her again, she would give in. He dropped his head and buried his face in his hands, and let out an anguished groan.

"Karim," she spoke quietly as if she were afraid to spook him.

"I didn't come here to do that. The last thing I wanted to

do was a force - I know everything. I was supposed to protect you, and I failed you. I failed you in the worst possible way. I never knew. I thought- I never knew. If I had known, I would have come back for you. I would have risked the sun for you. But she never told me. She never said a word, that's why I came when she called this time- I didn't know the truth until today."

Her heart stopped beating for a moment, and a chill went through her. She never wanted him to know what had happened to her, never wanted him to look at her with pity and disgust as so many had when they discovered the truth.

"How?" she managed through her suddenly dry lips.

"What?" he asked, a bit confused.

"How do you know? I know Nyx would never tell you." She swallowed hard, trying to keep herself in the room. Everything in her said run, leave this place, leave this conversation. But she couldn't. Looking at the expression on his face, it was still new for him, still raw. She felt tears well in her eyes for him. She'd had centuries to come to terms with what had happened. She understood his pain, and she felt for him.

"How do you know?" she repeated. "Who told you?"

"Your aunts paid me a visit."

She cursed under her breath. The Moirai, those fucking lunatics, of course, they would be the ones to tell. The three of them couldn't help but talk. It was what they did. The original shit-stirrers had been at it again, causing chaos wherever they went. One day very soon, she was going to take great pleasure in slapping all three of them.

"So, now you know all the facts." She ran her hands along her thighs, a nervous habit she'd developed without realizing it. He took her hands, his thumbs caressing her knuckles as he spoke.

"I came here to beg for your forgiveness and to apologize for the hell I put you through because of my stupidity. They were only supposed to take you to the next village. Pelusium was less than a day's ride, and they -she, because it wasn't him, it was the wife, wasn't it? Not that I could blame her for being jealous. Calie, Celeste, I would have burned before I would have let that happen to you. I will burn now if you wish it. I will gladly give my life if that's what it would take for you to forgive me. I would do anything to take that pain for you. I never wanted to hurt you. I just..." He looked at her with those wonderful eyes, his face so tortured it broke her heart.

"I will gladly give up my life if it will take away the pain. Just say the word, and I will walk into the light of day for you."

She knew that he would, but she could never allow that. As much as she threatened to maim or kill him, she knew in her heart, she would never do such a thing. She was justice and redemption. Why condemn a man before allowing him a chance at redemption? She owed him a chance because Karim had made a stupid mistake when he honestly believed that he was doing the honorable thing when it came right down to it.

"I can't let you do that, Karim. I would never allow you to sacrifice yourself for a common whore."

"Don't ever say that!" He was on his feet, looming over her, his face twisted in disgust.

"Don't ever speak of yourself that way again. I won't allow it. You are smart, funny, beautiful, and amazing. You are not a whore, nor can any circumstance ever make me see you as one. Do you understand me?" he yelled, and she nearly jumped out of her skin.

"But I was Karim. I was made to do the most demeaning things; if you only knew what they made me do."

"Then show me," he said, and she stared at him in confusion.

"What?" Was he saying what she thought he was saying?

"Use me the way they used you. I deserve that. I deserve to suffer as you have, and I will do it willingly."

He was, she realized. He was willing to let her take out all of her hatred and pain, and aggression out on his body. She wasn't sure she could do that to him. Not just because of the sexual aspect, because it wasn't just about sex. It was about control and domination over another. She didn't know if she had it in her, nor did she think he understood what she had endured. But he was willing to go to such extremes to earn her forgiveness.

"You have no idea what you are asking for, Karim. It was painful and humiliating. I can't. I would never inflict that kind of pain on anyone," she said, lowering her head. "I could never ..." She didn't want him to see that part of her, that part that made her feel unclean and damaged. "It won't fix anything."

"It could be a start."

She remained silent when he took her hands in his, turning her palms up to expose her delicate wrists. He lifted them to his mouth, kissing one, then the other. She wanted to pull away, but the gentle caress of his lips felt good, warm, and soft against her skin. No one had ever done that before; the sensation sent a shiver through her. The touch was simple, sweet, and she felt her anxiety giving way to need.

"Please, Celeste. Use me." He lowered her hands, resting them on his thighs, careful to hold her fingers because he knew, he knew it all. She stared at him. The intensity and determination in his face told her that he would not give up on this. He was desperate for her forgiveness, bound by some half-cocked sense of duty and repentance to her. This was the plea of a man looking to forgive a grave sin, pain for pain, and flesh for flesh. He cupped her cheek in his palm, his thumb running along her bottom lip.

"Please," it was a whispered appeal. She didn't know if it was the look on his face, her want to forgive him, or the Mist that clouded her mind, but she heard the word slip from her lips before she knew what she was doing.

"Okay."

* * *

CHAPTER EIGHT

Karim sat on the edge of the bed, waiting in nothing but a towel. He'd rested for most of the day before showering in the guest bath. He'd even considered using one of the electric razors in the medicine cabinet to cut his unruly hair. But he'd remembered the feel of her fingers when she played with it, stroking his scalp, and decided against it. There was aftershave, male shower gel, deodorant, and extra toothbrushes stored neatly. He assumed that these things were for her one of her brothers or Blondie; that was what he was hoping, at least. He couldn't imagine these things were purchased for a random hook-up. Celeste wasn't that type of woman.

He found himself wondering about the rock star, thinking that perhaps those two were the couple. They seemed to spend as much time together as possible. Obviously, the human was I love with Celeste. Anyone could see it by the way he watched her. He recognized the expression on Nicky's face that look of longing he was all too familiar. He'd let that train of thought go and simply sat on the edge of the bed waiting, his stomach in knots at what was going to happen.

There was a quiet knock on the door, and his palms began to sweat. He cleared his throat and stood, slowly going to open the door.

Celeste stood waiting, shifting from one barefoot to the other, the heavy bag tossed over her shoulder, her robe cinched tightly at her waist. She was scared and nervous, her stomach doing flips of anticipation when he opened the door.

"Ready?" She asked, and he nodded, allowing her entrance into the room. She'd decided that the guest room would be the best place because, unlike her bed, this one was a four-poster, and she needed that. Also, it was the only room in the house that had no windows. She didn't look at him as she sat the bag on the dresser and began to take out its contents. "Are you sure about this?" she asked.

"Yeah," he said quietly, brushing his hair off of his forehead. She looked at him over her shoulder but said nothing. She didn't have to; he could smell her growing arousal and anxiety, filling the windowless room with the familiar sweetness that was pure Celeste.

"I think I need a drink. Do you have any wine?" Karim asked in a voice that was tight and high pitched.

"Yes, in the kitchen." She didn't look at him. She couldn't. Instead, she continued her preparations leaving him to go in search of something to calm his nerves. Once he was gone, she exhaled, placed her palms on the dresser, and counted to ten. Slowly, she looked at her reflection in the mirror over the dresser and sighed. She could see the bed behind her. The indentation of where he'd been seated was still visible.

"You can do this, Celeste. It's not that big of a deal," she said, looking at herself in the mirror. "It'll be fine. He wants to do this." She reached into the bag and removed four large, hinged golden bangles. Near each hinge was a short length of chain attached with a clasp on the end that she would use to fasten him to the bedpost. She stared at them for a long time, swallowing hard at the memories of these tools. She closed her eyes, took a deep breath, and continued to prepare for what was sure to be an interesting night.

* * *

"This bottle was already open, so …" his voice trailed off at the sight of her. Everything below his waist grew heavy and dense. His skin felt as if it had tightened, and he made a low noise deep in his throat. She turned to look at him, her eyes deep indigo, her face gold in the glow of the dozens of beautiful white candles that had been stacked on every surface of the room, giving the room a soft glow. She had fastened the slave bracelets to the bedposts and laid out things he had never really seen outside of adult movies across the nightstand. She had a small assortment that intrigued him and made his stomach tighten in anticipation. There was a whip, a cat-o nine tails with a heavy braided handle, a large wooden paddle, oils, and something that looked to him like miniature jumper cables. She was just laying the last of her tools, a long thin baton that he soon recognized as a riding crop, on the bed. He swallowed and wondering if perhaps this was the way she preferred sex.

"No," she said, reading his expression. Or maybe she had that mind-reading glitch tweaked, she thought. "I got this while you were resting. I've never used this kind of thing. Well, the bracelets were mine," she touched the gold hoops with trembling fingers. "I removed the bells. I don't think we need them," she said and then smiled, "The riding crop is mine, though." To emphasize her point, she held it up and gave a quick downward swipe, the movement so fast that it made the air crack, and he jumped.

He looked at her, and he found it hard to think because there was no more blood flowing to his brain. He hadn't been sure what he'd been expecting, leather and chains he supposed or something along the lines of what she'd worn that night at the club. This was something softer. She wore a deep green camisole in a shimmery satin that clung to her curves and matching boy shorts that rode up, exposing the soft underside of her ass. Her hair had been allowed to air dry because it hung around her face in loose heavy curls that she raked her fingers through nervously while he stared. Her face free of makeup, making a light spattering of summer freckles visible, she looked delectable.

"I keep forgetting how stunning you truly are," he whispered, his erection moving in agreement. "Close the door," she said, her tone authoritative and just a little shaky. He realized then that he was still holding the bottle of wine and two glasses. He hadn't made it into the room either. Instead, he'd stopped just inside the doorway, staring with his body thrumming and his mouth dry. The towel shifted, and he tried to hide his sudden excitement, but it was useless, and he would be at her mercy in a moment anyway. She crossed the room, taking the bottle and glasses from him, and placed them on the bedside table.

He closed the door behind him, wiped his sweaty palms on his thighs, and crossed the room to join her beside the bed. She let out a shaky breath before turning to him, her eyes on his.

"They would usually give me something I don't know what- to make me more - cooperative," she said, picking up the paddle, testing the weight in her hands. "I would be washed and dressed, painted, and perfumed. Then ..." She slapped the paddle against her thigh hard. The smacking of wood against skin made him cringe.

"Hands and knees." She said. "Or would you prefer over my lap? Or against the bed?" She tapped her lips with her finger, then smiled.

"Come here." He went willingly, his heart racing, a rush of excitement welling inside of him. She motioned for him to join her at the foot of the bed, and he did. She made him turn his back to her and grasp the bedposts before securing the cuffs around his wrists, tethering him to the posts.

"Do we need a safe word?" He asked, meaning to lighten the mood and ease his nerves.

"No safe words. I never had any say, and neither will you. Don't worry. I won't hurt you," she said, her lips close to his ear just as she pulled the towel from his hips. He wasn't sure if it was her attitude or being naked and on display, but he moaned involuntarily, the tip of his penis moistening. When the first blow landed on his backside, his knees buckled as the sensation assaulted him. He stifled a grunt but was soothed by the caress of her hand.

That was unexpected, he thought, closing his eyes. He hadn't expected his body to ignite so completely, either. She repeated the action, a solid thwack of the paddle followed by a smooth stroke of her palm over his stinging flesh. Sweat beaded his forehead, his body aching from the need of her. She struck him again, harder, and his grip tightened on the posts, his knuckles bright white. Each new blow was harder, swifter, and he felt himself weakening, his body going limp. Her final blow was loud and made his entire body rock forward, and he was barely able to remain on his feet or control the force of his impending orgasm.

"Oh god," he moaned. He could hear labored breathing, and for a second, he thought it was his own until she moved closer, touching him with trembling fingers. She ran her hand from the nape of his neck upward, grasping a hand full of hair; she pulled his head back, her mouth at his throat.

"Are you about to come?" She rubbed against him, her own body humming in excitement. She licked his face, and for some unknown reason, he shivered, turning to look at her. She tugged his hair even harder, pulling his head in the opposite direction. "Are you?" She asked, biting his earlobe hard.

"Yes," he whispered, his throat tight.

"Don't. I didn't say you could." She released him and continued her exquisite torture, each strike bringing him closer to the edge, yet he held on, trying to obey. She made it that much more difficult when she reached around him, cupping him with a silken hand while she continued to whack away at his backside. He thrust into her palm with each new strike, biting his lip to keep from exploding, soft groans escaping him until he could no longer hold back. He came against her hand, his knees giving, and he fell forward, his breath coming in hard, heavy gulps.

She released him from the restraints, and he gratefully sat on the edge of the bed, trying to quell the tremble in his thighs.

She moved closer, stepping between his thighs, her body pressed to him, sinking her hands into that thick dark hair. He was breathing heavily, his arms around her waist, as she lowered her mouth. Her breath smelled of wine, and she reeked of vanilla and that unique sweetness that was all Celeste. He opened his mouth, inviting her tongue, but she didn't kiss him. Instead, she grasped his face, her fingers biting into his flesh.

"No. I was never allowed to use my mouth. No one was allowed my mouth, but they could put their mouth all over my body. They could lick, and bite, and taste every inch of me, but my mouth was never to be shared. Understand?" She asked. He nodded. "Say it." She tightened her grip, and he grunted at the sting of her nails.

"I understand," he mumbled. She released him, shoving his face away, turning his head so that she could run her mouth down the column of his throat, her fangs grazing his skin. She moved her hands down his bare chest, raking his nipples with her nails, moving down his ribs to rest at his hips. He wanted her to touch him, to feel her hands on him again, only she didn't. Instead, she reached for the towel and tossed it to him.

"Clean yourself," she said, her throat tight. Her heart was racing, and she was so wet, she hadn't expected to be so excited by this. She had thought it would disgust her, but his reaction, his moans of pleasure, had spurned her on.

"Lay down." She said, keeping her back to him. She gripped the edge of the dresser and tried to collect herself. She could feel his eyes on her, feel him staring as he moved behind her. She swallowed and took a deep breath. You started this, she told herself, and you better damn well finish it.

"I was always tied down," she said, using the second pair of bangles to secure him to the bed. He lay, face-up, and spread eagle on the bed, trying to control his breathing while she secured his ankles with the bangles that had just been at his wrists.

"Always." She tested the restraints, ensuring that they

were tight but not painfully so. "Now the fun part," she whispered with no real humor. She began with the cat-o-nine tails, holding it in her hand, giving it a few test swings before she struck. There was a loud whoosh and then a smack as the soft leather trailed across his chest. She wasted no time building up her strength; the first blow was quick and hard.

He grunted, his sex coming to life again. She continued her delicious torture until his body arched up to meet the leather tongues as they worked down his torso to his abdomen, then across his aching groin. He rolled sideways, struggling against his restraint, his balls tightening when she repeated the action. With each grunt of approval, she struck him harder, her excitement getting the better of her. His skin was red and raw, but he didn't seem to care. As a matter of fact, he seemed to get off on the pain. She dropped the whip, turning away from him so he could not see what she was doing.

When she turned back, she held a thick white candle in her hands, her teeth worrying her lip as she considered what she was about to do. She looked at him, blowing until the flame disappeared, and he gave a short, pained nod of agreement.

The hot wax touched his skin, and he felt every nerve alight with a pain that was sharp and surprisingly wonderful. A long deep hissing escaped him as she lay a trail from his chest down the center of him, stopping just above the soft curls below his waist. He watched with bated breath as she did it again, covering his nipples and collarbone with the last flow of liquid. With her fingers, she traced patterns in the hardening wax, making his skin feel as if it were on fire, each touch making him harder until the pain was a dull constant ache.

She reached back to her table of toys as he now thought of it, coming back to him rubbing her slick, shinning hands together. She placed her palms on his hips, sweet-smelling oil cooling his heated skin. A small smile started at the corners of her mouth, and he found himself smiling as well. The room filled with the scent of was that...? "Is that coconut?" He asked.

"Yes," she said, her hands massaging every inch of exposed skin. He stared at her, caramel golden skin shimmering from the glow of candlelight and oil, the smells of vanilla, lavender, and coconut filling the room. She stroked his thighs, ran her nails over the hypersensitive wax caked nipples, down the contracting muscles of his abdomen, but avoided the place he wanted her hands most. She lubricated her already slippery palms and reached for him. Instinctively, he tilted his hips toward her, silently begging her to soothe his angry erection. She touched him, her slick, vulpine hands moving over the stiffness of his shaft until he practically hummed and vibrated like an engine being revered but given no way to accelerate.

"Look at me," she said, and he turned his eyes to her, licking his lips as each stroke brought him closer to fulfillment. With each caress, he thrust into her hand, his eyes on her face, watching the delicate hitch in her breathing, inhaling the aroma of her arousal; he imagined that he was pushing deep inside of her. He would take the pain; he would take it all over and over if it would make her want him again. She tightened her grasp, tugging at him until his hips lifted, licking her lips, her cheeks flushing at her growing vigor. Harder, faster, the oil on her hand felt like a satin glove on his fiery skin until lids drifted shut from the sheer bliss.

"Look at me. I want to see your eyes when you come." Her voice was tight and strained as she tried to keep her own emotions in check. She wanted to mount him, to straddle him, sink onto him until she could feel the heavy weight inside of her. She wanted to take him into her mouth, taste all of him, warm and sweet on her tongue, but not just yet. He wanted her to use him, and she was going to use every inch of him tonight. Her hand moved faster, her eyes locked on his when his eyes rolled back and his body twisted, hips pistoning faster. He grasped the bedposts and made soft choking noise with each euphoric sweep of her hand.

"Oh- My-fuck," he came again, his body shaking from the sheer pleasure of it all, his eyes closed as waves of ecstasy overtook him. Celeste took great joy in having complete control over him. With each new experience, his body roiled with desire, and she wanted him more.

"Oh god, I need to touch you, azizam," he pleaded. "Please."

"Do you want to taste me, Karim?" She leaned forward, biting his bottom lip, abandoning her rule of him not using his mouth. She wanted his mouth all over her; she wanted him all over her, inside of her. She wanted to taste him, to run her tongue over every delicious inch of Karim's body. Only not now, now he was wound too tightly, his body tense, every muscle standing out in strained relief. He was on fire; she could feel the heat rising from him, smell the pungent aroma of a sea breeze and sand. He mumbled a response, fighting the restraints until the wood creaked under the force.

Celeste climbed on top of him, sleek, damp warmth brushed his lips, and he licked, tasting her through the silk of her panties. She made a soft purring sound, her hips rocking against his mouth, her hands in his hair. He lifted his head, trying to get closer, the bracelets cutting into his wrists as he pulled in an attempt to go deeper, taste more of her. Then she was gone. He followed her with hungry eyes. She stood above him, slipping the silk from her hips, gently placing them on the bed before returning, her hips lusciously close to his mouth.

"Beg," she said. He looked into her eyes neon eyes and licked his lips, savoring her taste.

"Please," he whispered. She went to her knees, and his tongue touched her, a velvet stroke against her feverish skin. She pitched forward, bracing one hand on the wall, the other knotting in his hair as he continued the smooth, irresistible movement of his mouth against her. When he found that tightness at her center, he began a gentle sucking; the feel of his sharp fangs against hypersensitive skin sent her reeling.

His fangs grazed her inner core, and she trembled. He did it again, wanting to sink his teeth into her, to drink from her and mark her in the most intimate of places, but he couldn't. Something was blocking him, deterring him from the thing he wanted most. But he continued, using his tongue and teeth to make her thighs tremble as she rode him hard, her hips rocking against his mouth. When he began the whirling, twisting assault again, she held his head tightly to her, thrusting her hips against him until his tongue slipped into the honey at her core, and she exploded against him. The sweet nectar of her poured into his mouth, filling him in a rush, and he swallowed, reveling in the sweet essence of her. The wood of the bedposts protested as he fought against them, wanting to touch her, to hold her as she came all over him, into him. She was gone, leaving him panting for more, his eyes shining bright white, his fangs bared in a disappointed hiss.

"Come back," he growled. "Please, come back." He hissed through clenched teeth while his sex strained achingly hard against his stomach. He felt like an addict begging for one more hit, just one more to relieve the thundering throbbing at his hips. She trailed kisses down his body, moving lower until she was crouched between his thighs. He looked down at her, her eyes like beacons of light before her lids drifted shut when her tongue traced the tip of his sex before she took him deeper.

"Oh, sweet Jesus." He choked. His body went rigid, and the twin weights heavy and tight beneath his aching shaft. As if she could read his thoughts, she cupped the throbbing spheres in her hands, the pull of her lips stronger. His body arched upward with each pull of her lips, the pressure building in him so quickly that he couldn't hold on. The feel of her soft lips, the gentle scrape of her fangs against his skin, and the steady rhythm had him writhing in divine agony. The creaking of wood and the gentle sounds of her wet, hot mouth were only interrupted by his gasps before his tenuous hold snapped. He exploded, and she continued to suckle, pulling everything from him, milking his seed from him until his body bowed and shook uncontrollably.

She sat back on her haunches, licking her lips, a devious smile on her swollen lips as she struggled to contain himself. She touched him, and he quailed, every nerve in his body on fire with an all-consuming want. She ran her fingertips along the smooth contours of his inner thighs, up to his hips. He cursed as his body grew hard under her gaze, the feel of her fingers on the tender skin tantalizing him. It was like he truly was an addict, and he needed more. He wanted to be inside of her, filling her tightness, making her moan and writhe as he'd done for her.

"What have you done to me? Why can't I get enough of you?" He whimpered, watching her straddle his hips. Convulsively, he thrust upward, easily slipping into the tight heat at her core. He opened his mouth to say something, to have them filled with the moist silk of her discarded panties. He expected her to start slow and easy, giving her body a chance to stretch to accommodate him, but she was already beyond that. Digging her nails into the red tender flesh of his chest, she lifted her hips, then slid back, taking the full length of him into her. Her eyes closed as she began intense, heavy thrusts that left him breathless. She rode him hard; her body slamming against him. He thrust upward, trying to catch her erratic rhythm only to be thrown back against the bed, the taste of her in his mouth, the feel of her around him as she tightened and rocked. She grasped him around the throat with one surprisingly strong hand, stealing the air from his lungs. A new level of unexpected pleasure rocked him when he grew light-headed, and his eyes drifted closed.

She let go just when he thought he'd pass out from a sweet agony he'd never known existed. She continued to move over him, slick and hot; she rolled her hips, the friction of his heavy pelvic thrust touching the tender nub at her core until her body moved on its own. She made a soft whining noise, and he could feel her near the edge.

"Oh yes, yes, oh god, yes." She moaned, her head thrown

back as she moved like a woman possessed. He thrust up hard, wanting more, needing more, and she matched him until her legs tightened at his hips, and a rush of moisture poured from her. She shook; her legs trembled as the force of her organism sent him into overdrive. He continued to buck against her, not wanting the pleasure to end; he closed his eyes and drove up hard and long, each stroke deeper and deeper, until she moaned again, her head falling to his shoulder as she panted against his sweaty chest.

She peppered his chest with tiny bites, her nails digging into him, leaving points of bright red blood on his skin, as she rose and fell against him until the sound of their bodies meeting filled the room. She inhaled sharply, and another uncontrollable wave moved through her, and he was filling her with his heat, a muffled groan escaping him until his body relaxed and he lay still beneath her.

She collapsed onto him, her breathing a pant against his skin, her own body damp with sweat. When she collected herself, she removed her panties from his mouth and released him from the cuffs. She was going to roll off of him and free his ankles, but he held her steady, kissing her neck, cheeks, and finally her lips, his hands moving from her shoulders down to cup her bare backside, holding her still.

"Don't move," he croaked, "I want to stay inside of you as long as possible." She sat up and looked at him. He was a mess covered in his seed and sweat, his hair plastered to his flushed face, red welts and blood rising on his skin. Angry red marks were beginning to rise on his chest and legs, and she could only imagine how his backside looked. She had done so much to him, and he still wanted her. He was insane. Or she was.

"Did I hurt you? I got carried away, and I didn't even use everything..." She sniffed back her tears. Karim brushed her hair from her face and looked into her eyes. "Was I too rough? Was it too much?"

"No, a*zizam*. You didn't hurt me. You could never hurt me. What you did is temporary. What I did ..." She shook her head, kissing him, her mouth sweet and hungry against his. He didn't need to apologize anymore; he'd just let her take out years of aggression on him. All apologies were made; there was nothing left to say.

"I don't want to talk about that." She sniffed and hid her face as the tears continued to flow. She couldn't stop them, it was as if something, some wall inside of her had cracked, and now the emotion flooded out, pouring from her in a wild torrent. She began to silently sob into the pillow, not wanting him to see. All of the hurt and anger poured from her, her body shaking from the release. She didn't want him to say anything, fearing that she would be completely inconsolable if he spoke. Instead, he sat up, holding her close, stroking her hair until she had no more tears.

* * *

Remy crossed the condo's lobby, waving at the concierge who greeted him pleasantly as he made his way to the elevator. As usual, the elegantly decorated white marble foyer was empty, save the evening concierge. He was grinning from ear to ear as Remy approached, standing a little straighter at the approach of one of the building's more gregarious residents. Unlike most of the staid, upstanding individuals who lived here, Remy was by far the most popular with staff. He threw wild parties and gave the biggest tips; he greeted everyone by name and acknowledged them as people, not just fixtures in the exclusive high rise. Two of the condo association past presidents had tried to have him evicted. The first had given up when he discovered that Remy Kent was *that* Remy Kent. The second had not cared about his pedigree, insisting that he was bringing down the property's value. One time he'd nearly been voted out until he'd made his entrance into his first and only association meeting. In true Remy fashion, he stormed into the room wearing a towel around his hips, barefoot and still dripping from his abruptly ended shower.

"Mr. Kent," the pious little woman pulled at the sleeve of her pink Chanel suit as he entered, his face twisted in anger. "We are about to hold a vote," she said.

"You can't vote me out, you prudish old bitch. If you would have taken time to read the charter or dug just a little, you'd know that." he'd bellowed.

"I assure you I can," she retorted with a haughty snort.

"I promise you can't ... but I can have you tossed out of here on your Chanel knockoff wearing ass. I have more rights here than anyone else. I own the fucking building, you pretentious twat," he'd yelled before stomping out. That had nixed any future talk of Remy Kent ever being kicked out of his building.

"Good afternoon Mr. Kent. Good to see you. Your guest has arrived." Remy tilted his sunglasses down to stare at the fresh-faced kid who passed as the concierge today. Danny was his name, and he looked all of nineteen years old. His dark eyes shone with knowledge and a mischievous glint as he watched Remy.

"Thank you, Danny," he said, dipping into the elevator as the doors silently slid open. "Make sure I'm not disturbed for the rest of the night, please." He smiled at his reflection in the polished metal of the elevator door. He'd come to spend the night, Remy breathed. He'd asked Briar to spend the night with him, to share a night away from prying eyes in luxury and comfort of Remy's condo, which overlooked Lake Ponchartrain. They could make love in the moonlight, then go down the street for a nice dinner at a restaurant right on the water or take a ride to a nice place downtown. It didn't matter, as long as he got to spend uninterrupted time with his giant without thoughts of Celeste and her twisted sex life. He had his own sex life to deal with.

He couldn't unlock his door fast enough, his eagerness to see Briar making him a little giddy. Perhaps it was the remains of an afternoon of smoking Mist with Nicky and Celeste, and of course, being up all night. But that didn't matter. He was going to have an entire night alone, uninterrupted with Briar. A rare event indeed.

When he and Briar had begun their relationship, it wasn't a relationship at all. It had been a fling; they would meet in Remy's suite at the compound, spend a few hours together, and part ways. Those hours of sex had led to pillow talk, which lead to talk and friendship. Then eventually Remy realized, he was in a full-blown relationship, something he'd avoided for years. But when he fell for his sweet guy, he fell. He felt light and excited, and for the first time in so long, free. For years he'd been wrapped up in his truly inappropriate feelings for Celeste. Unable to have her, he was determined not to let anyone else get close to her until Nicky.

They'd all loved Nicky from the start. How could they not? Yet, his obsession continued until he had become enamored with the very opposite of Celeste. The large, muscle-bound beauty that was Briar had made him believe that his happiness did not lie with Celeste. Hell, he wasn't positive that it would remain with Briar, but man, was he enjoying it while he could.

"Honey, I'm home." He threw the door open, expecting to see Briar filling the space. Instead, he found her, flipping through a magazine as if she belonged. She didn't even look up, only continued reading as if it were the most interesting thing she'd ever read. She flicked her dark hair over a shoulder, and flipped the page, but ignored him completely. He froze, watching as the other came in from the kitchen eating a Popsicle, her pale eyes bright. He didn't even have to look to know the other was there, somewhere. They always traveled together, like fucking cockroaches; if you saw one, the others were always nearby. They also always meant that trouble was coming. Danny hadn't said a guest. He'd said *guests*.

"Aww fuck." He kicked the door closed with a wall-shaking slam.

* * *

CHAPTER NINE

Karim lay on his side on fresh linen, his hair still damp from his shower. Celeste stood in the bathroom doorway in an old t-shirt of Nicky's, or it could've been Remy's who knew anymore, drying her wet hair and staring at him. He was naked, uncovered, his breathing slow and easy as he slept, his body spent. She had often thought of him like this, imagined what it would have been like in the desert under the canopy of a million stars. If only he'd stayed if he'd made love to her instead of running away, how different their lives could have been. If he had stayed, perhaps she wouldn't live with the hole that had carved its way into her heart, the aching pain and shame of knowing that people knew what she was, what she had been, the favorite courtesan of a once-powerful king.

He shifted, and the bangles that still clung to the bedposts rattled against the wood, and the knot in her chest tightened. She thought the tears would come; they always did when she saw the shackles, but oddly enough, they didn't. Instead, the old memories were dulled by the sound of cracking wood and moans as Karim pulled against them, trying to touch her. He'd begged for release, but not the way she had begged; no, his begging was from sheer need. He needed her to touch him, to prolong the delicious agony, and she had been more than happy to oblige.

Well damn, she thought, he'd been right. The pain was still there. It always would be, only now it was muted. She stared at Karim on the bed and wondered if this had finally begun her healing. Seeing him after all of this time had triggered so many emotions that she could no longer bury. She had to face them, or she would be angry and broken forever.

Now, if only that damn scar would heal or fade—anything to stop the consistent throbbing at the base of her skull. The agony had reached its peak when she was making love to Karim, but she'd blocked it, ignoring the pain for the pleasure of being with him. Now it was more annoying than anything else. She rubbed it and tried to remember something Karim had said when he'd first arrived. She couldn't quite grasp the words, unable to focus on anything at the time but the smell of charred flesh and him nearly dying, too distracted to register what he was rambling about. What had he been saying? Why was she having such a hard time remembering?

Karim rolled onto his back then, giving her the full view of his toned, muscled body. His skin was smooth, tawny, and perfectly made even more beautiful by the intricate tattoo that decorated his right arm and shoulder. She'd tasted that skin, had his scent invade her senses, and felt the power of that body moving with her, inside of her. She swallowed hard and smiled to herself. As if he could read her thoughts, his manhood began to wake under her gaze. Oh yeah, she thought, that's the reason.

She tossed her towel into a hamper; her intention to climb back into bed with Karim quickly died when she heard it. Someone was entering her apartment. She could hear the slow, steady hum of the elevator as it rose to her penthouse apartment. Even after she'd locked the elevator and left instructions at the front desk that she was not to be disturbed, someone was coming up.

"Shit," she grumbled while searching for a pair of shorts or sweats. Someone was going to get fired; she thought as she eased out of the room, carefully closing the guest room door.

* * *

The elevator door slid open quietly, casting a pale-yellow shaft of light across the darkened living room. Nicky stood, waiting for his eyes to adjust to the absolute darkness that shrouded the room. He sighed, realizing that he didn't even have the moonlight to guide his steps.

He toed the table just to the right of the elevator, his fingers moving over the smooth surface before clinging to the wall in search of a light switch. He eased along the wall, taking short close steps, being careful of her artwork, and collected knick-knacks. That was why it was no surprise when he tripped on the three short steps that led down into the living room. He went heels over ass down the stairs, cursing like a sailor, finally landing with a heavy thud on her living room rug.

The room was illuminated in a soft pale glow, and he turned to find Celeste standing over him, her arms folded across her chest, her barefoot tapping the floor. Nicky looked up at her and groaned, rolling onto his hands and knees.

"What are you doing here? I locked the elevator and told the front desk not to let anyone up," she growled through clenched teeth. "Why are you creeping around in the dark?"

"Why do you have the curtains drawn? It's like a fucking cave in here. And I have a key, remember? I came up through the garage, never saw the front desk." He rubbed the back of his head, struggled to his feet, and faced her. "I came to get my phone and my wallet. Did you barbecue?" He began moving across the living room to the guest room. "I have a flight to New York in two hours, and I called you like twenty times. I have a car and the band waiting for me."

"Nicky. Wait," She didn't have a chance to react before he threw the door open and went into the candlelit room.

Nicky finally emerged, and she audibly exhaled. He looked at her, unable to speak. There was a knot in his stomach, a growing black knot that twisted and made him feel as if he were going to be ill. With one hand, he gingerly closed the door, as if he were afraid to wake the man he had discovered there. No, not a man, he thought, an immortal vampire. He felt his eyes sting, and his heart felt as if it were going to shatter if he didn't get out of this place right now.

"Found 'em," he said and headed to the elevator, his eyes never meeting hers. "I have to go." He breezed past her, unable to stomach looking at her.

"Is that it?" She swallowed, her voice tight and higher pitched than normal. He paused his eyes on the leather wallet in his palm. His voice was low and measured as he chose each word carefully, methodically.

"What do you want me to say? Do you want me to ask if he used all of those toys on you or if they were just used on him?" He turned his eyes to her, his expression as closed as his mind was to her at that moment. Her arms were folded across her chest, the t-shirt she wore brushing thick muscled thighs. Her hair was mussed, her cheeks rosy, her lips kiss bruised. She smelled as she always did of vanilla and lavender, and she looked amazing. It struck him that she would never be this way because of him. She would never wear his clothes after hours of lovemaking. He would never hear her call out his name in the throes of an orgasm. He alone had been there through the nightmares and the sobbing fits, the anger and the sleepless nights, yet she had chosen another to bed, and his anger flared.

"Do you want me to ask if you enjoyed whipping and beating him? Did it make you want him more to know that he allowed you to restrain him with the same shackles that kept you a slave? Or did you want me to say that I understand or congratulate you on your conquest? Would you like me to cheer you on and give you a high five for fucking the man, no vamp, must get my terminology correct, that abandoned you in the desert and left you in the hands of not one but two madmen who used you as their fuck doll?" With each word, she moved away from him.

"I never imagined that you would actually ... I never believed... he's wearing my fucking clothes, Celeste. Did it take him this long to realize that he loves you? That he had made the worst mistake ever known to man when he walked away from you? It took this long for the guilt to finally get to him for selling you?"

"He didn't sell me, Nick," She started when he yelled at her, her mouth snapping shut.

"He left you and never thought to ask about you again! He didn't even make sure you made it to wherever the fuck you were going. And now he comes back as nothing happened, and you let him. Why did it take him centuries to even realize that he had to see you? That he needed you? Wanted you? Because it only took me a minute. A fucking minute and I knew that I loved you, and I never wanted to be apart from you. Only a second, and I knew." He raked his hands angrily through blond spikes, his face contorting as he raced through emotions and tried to contain himself. "I can't do this," he finally said, shaking his head. "I can't do this anymore. I have to go."

"Do what?" She clutched her arms, hugging herself, trying to warm her suddenly cold blood.

"This! I can't be your back up guy or your eunuch or human pet, whatever you think I am. I can't do this anymore. I always knew. When I first saw you, I knew that I would never be enough. When I found out what you were, I made myself into something extraordinary for you. I made myself into a superstar in hopes that you would think I was worthy enough. I have turned my life inside out in hopes that one day you would look at me, actually, look at me and know, but you didn't or you won't, and you never will. You will never see me, Ce." He grasped her face in his hands and touched his forehead to hers, closing his eyes as he breathed. "You will never see me, and it kills me every single minute of every fucking day." He kissed her cheek before releasing her and turning to leave.

"Nicky, wait!" He ignored her, not wanting to look at her, allowing her to see the tears that coated his cheeks. Instead, he placed his keys on a table just as the elevator door slid open.

"Good-bye, Celeste." He stepped into the elevator car, keeping his back to her, and spoke no more as the door closed, blocking her plaintive cries.

❋ ❋ ❋

She felt panicked as the doors closed on him. The center of her world, the most stable force in her life for the last six years, just walked out on her, and she crumbled. Nicky didn't understand that he was her everything, he was her base, her humanity, her conscience, and he held a place in her heart that no one else could touch. Nicholas Skylar Novachek was the center of her universe, and he'd just walked away from her. She couldn't breathe, her chest hurt, and she felt as if she would pass out, instead of sliding to the floor, her body shaking. That was where Karim found her when he finally entered the room. He knelt beside her, wrapping his arms around her as she cried. He stroked her hair and rocked her back and forth, whispering sweet things to her in his native tongue until she calmed, her sobs becoming a hiccup, then nothing.

"When I never arrived, why didn't she send you back? Why didn't Nyx send you back for me?" She asked after what felt like forever, and Karim's heart dropped.

"That is a question I cannot answer. That is something only Nyx can explain," he said.

❋ ❋ ❋

She knew exactly when her grandmother arrived in her apartment, even before she smelled the overpowering scent of jasmine that announced Nyx's presence. Because time had stopped, she knew there was no hum from the city's appliances or sounds outside. She lay on the sofa, her face buried beneath a pillow as she waited for Nyx to make an appearance. It had taken longer than she expected; Nyx usually appeared within seconds of Celeste's summons.

"You have a helluva lot of explaining to do, Nyx," Celeste said, without lifting her head.

"Okay," Nyx breathed, sitting on the sofa opposite Celeste, who'd managed to change into jeans and a well-worn t-shirt. "What have I done now?" She sighed, her tone teasing as it always was when she spoke with Celeste.

Celeste turned her head to face her grandmother, her face swollen, eyes rimmed red from her tears. She sat up slowly. Her hair brushed away from her face in a ponytail, her blue eyes a shade of navy that would have been beautiful had it not been so frightening.

"Why didn't you send Karim back to search for me when I didn't arrive? Why did you wait so long before you searched for Tartarus? Why did you leave me to rot in hell when you knew he could find me?"

"I searched. Your father and I," she stammered.

"Try again," Celeste snapped. "And this time, try the truth."

"What did he say to you?" Nyx growled. "I will skin him-"

"Him? Him who? My father, perhaps? Oh, you mean Karim. He hasn't told me anything other than he never knew I hadn't reached my destination. He believed that the merchant and his wife had delivered me safely. He had no idea that I never arrived because you never told him. So, what happened? Let me guess; the Moirai had something to do with it? And my mother? Was there some curse placed upon me? I mean a new one, other than the blood-drinking and touch of lust because those I know. I mean, the lust thing took some getting used to, but it helped out when I was the King's favorite fuck toy." Nyx visibly tensed at her coarse term. Celeste sighed and rubbed her eyes, exhaling as exhaustion crept up on her. "Just tell me," she said.

"Tell her Nyx. After what you've done, you owe her at least that much." Karim's voice came from behind her. Nyx, who started, rose to her feet.

For a while, Celeste had forgotten he was there. But now,

with his thick hair in disarray and his eyes narrowed in what she could only assume was anger, he waited. She'd never seen him angry, not really. She'd seen frustration and sadness, and of course, his ever-cocky grin, but this was a new Karim. His eyes had gone deep hunter green, and he was standing as if he were prepared for battle. This was not her Karim. This was Karim, vampire Prince of Tyre, one of the Seven.

"You have done enough," Nyx spat, lifting her hand as if she were going to do … something. What, Celeste couldn't imagine, but she knew her grandmother wanted him to remain quiet. That piqued her interest even more.

"What I've done? What about what you've done? You let her believe that I sold her. As if I could or would ever tell her why you didn't send me back, Nyx." Celeste watched Nyx and Karim, the way Nyx tensed at his taunting.

"Do you know why, Karim?" Celeste asked, and he nodded, his eyes still on Nyx's pinched angry face. "Then tell me," Celeste said, her eyes on Karim, who lifted a brow in challenge.

"I can't, can I Nyx?" He spoke simply, but Celeste understood immediately. He couldn't because Nyx had ordered him no to, he was one of the Seven, and he had to obey her orders.

"I warned you, vampire," Nyx said, her eyes deep gunmetal, her teeth clenched tight. Celeste watched as Nyx's delicate fangs cut into her lip and a drop of blood formed on her bottom lip. She didn't even seem to notice. Celeste was just that angry. Tiny sparks of energy traveled between her fingers, a dark gray cloud forming in her hands as she prepared to strike him down.

"There is nothing else you can do to hurt me. Besides, no magic can touch me, isn't that right, Nyx? Not even yours." He put an arm around Celeste's waist, holding her close.

"I don't need magic to kill you," she snarled. "I can destroy you with my bare hands."

"Now, I think it's time you tell her the whole truth for once." He snapped his gaze, locking onto Nyx as the two waged a silent battle of wills. "Tell her, Nyx," he said in a lower, more dangerous tone.

* * *

Karim and Celeste sat on the deep purple sofa, Nyx the other across from the two, shifting uncomfortably under Celeste's steady, unblinking gaze. Nyx cleared her throat and exhaled before explaining the much-lauded prophecy of her path to greatness. She'd always know that she was destined to either save the world or destroy them all. She knew of the curse of lust that followed her for her entire life, she knew of her craving for blood to sustain her, but only the blood of the preternatural sustained her life force. She had not known about the curse of never finding love or that these afflictions had been placed on her by her mother.

Celeste grasped Karim's fingers when Nyx told of the first attempt Nemesis made on her infant daughter's life and her flight to safety in Nyx's arms and protection. Protection that was lost when she had been drugged and tossed into the sea. She remembered feeling weak and ill before being tossed into the darkness of the sea. Something heavy tethered to her waist with a thick rope. She'd forgotten about the rope until now.

Nyx spoke of reasons she needed to be protected, to hide her in the human world as she prepared for her rightful place on the throne. She explained that Celeste was important, but not only to her Greek and Egyptian pantheons, and she was also important to the Dark Fae. She was of the primordial, the first of the gods created by the one true *God*, and she had a destiny.

She had been hidden among humans, allowed to hone her skills as a warrior with the Amazons, who Nyx hoped would teach her humility and compassion, qualities the gods had never mastered. Though trained by the Amazons and one of their most skilled warriors, she was never allowed into battle. There was always the fear that her location would be discovered and used to gain power because she could be the savior. She could also be their destruction if given the proper motivation and provocation. The level of power coursing through her had never been fully established, but she was strong and radiating that much energy would surely give her position away. That was why her abilities, her gifts had been muted by Nyx, to hide her for centuries.

When she reached her four hundredth year, the year she reached her physical peak, Celeste was brought to her father's temple in Sestus, where she would take her rightful place at his side. But she had been betrayed by those she trusted, those who'd been corrupted by the promise of wealth and eternal beauty; Celeste had been lost to the sea. Nyx had sent her foot soldiers, trusted guards, out searching for her, but after years with no hint of her, many had given up. Even Anhur himself had mourned the loss of his one precious child. And for her part in the betrayal, Anhur's bride Menhit had been stripped of her power and banished.

Nyx was the only one, the sole believer that Celeste had not died, that she was alive somewhere. That was when she enlisted The Seven, her most trusted warriors. They spanned the known world in search of clues for the goddess, a goddess no one had ever seen or known even existed. One by one, they returned with no news, one by one, they gave up, except Karim.

"And you made him promise not to ... love me? Why would you do that?" Celeste asked, tears stinging her eyes.

"Tell her," Karim said in a tone that sounded to Celeste as if he was barely able to remain calm. She looked at him to see that his fangs had extended, and his soft green eyes were brilliant emerald. He was furious and ready to attack.

"When you never arrived, I knew that something had happened. I sent another party in search of you."

"But not the one person who'd succeed when all others had failed," Celeste prompted, waiting for the rest—needing to hear the rest from her grandmother's mouth.

"I couldn't track you. I could only feel that you were somewhere. I just did not know where," Nyx said. She was moving to the edge of her seat, his eyes wide. "Even with my blood in your veins, I felt your life force, but that was all."

"But you didn't send him back. The one person who'd succeeded when all others had failed, the one who had the best chance of finding me again," Celeste repeated, hating the angry quiver in her voice. Nyx averted her gaze, but Celeste held steady, watching her expression.

"When Karim sent word of you being in the care of the merchants, I sent the Seven in search of them, in search of you. When we found them, his wife told my men that you had been sold to a slaver. She didn't want her husband lusting after you, she thought you were a witch, and she jealously got the better of her," Nyx said in a very quiet voice. "She paid for that dearly, I can assure you of that."

"Except one. You sent back all of the Seven except one. You didn't send him back for me." Her jaw began to throb, and she realized she was clenching her jaw. She was ready to scream, to throttle Nyx.

"Because of the prophecy, Celeste..." Nyx mumbled. *'She will be the greatest love of kings and gods and drive some men to insanity with her guile and beauty. Her true love will find her once he remembers, once she shows him the way. He will be the destroyer of the gods for her.'* Nyx repeated the words that Atropos had spoken. "Your mate, your true mate, is an all-powerful being, a god. Don't you see, only *he* could be your true match? You deserve to be loved by a god. You deserve to rule the heavens and earth and all in between."

"You didn't send him back because you didn't think he was *worthy*?" Celeste stared at her for a moment, then shook her head as tears stung her eyes. "You let me die because of some fucked up prophecy made by a group of tweens a million years ago? What kind of fucked up logic is that?"

"Celeste, my sweet child, Karim, wasn't a proper match

for you. He isn't a god or..." Nyx knelt before her, holding Celeste's hands in her own. Celeste hadn't even noticed her move, hadn't tracked the movement as she let the realization sink in. She stared at Nyx through tears, her face becoming a distorted jumble of colors.

"But for me, he could have been. I am a goddess. I could have made him a god. I could have done that for him. You didn't send him back because he wasn't who you wanted. *You.* Not me. This is about you not having control anymore. I would no longer need your guidance or protection, isn't that it?" she asked, somewhat stunned by the ridiculousness of it all when she realized a greater truth. Her chest burned, and the tears flowed freely.

"You knew." She stared at her grandmother. "Oh my god, you knew!"

Celeste felt her blood pressure skyrocket. The tops of her ears burned, and her chest stung from the pain of realizing that Nyx had left her in that nightmare for years. She had abandoned her when she needed her most, over a prophecy that was just a bunch of random thoughts pieced together by three children, insane and powerful deities but children, nonetheless. She stared without seeing, her stomach twisting into knots. She was trying to keep her last meal down, but it was becoming harder and harder to do.

"You knew what was happening to me even before I died, you knew...You didn't even tell him I was missing? You never said a word to him? The one person in the entire world who could find me, who knew where to begin the search, and you let him leave me. You knew that something was wrong, but you would rather protect your own selfish needs than help me!"

"He was falling in love with you. I couldn't risk it."

"He wasn't falling in love with me, Nyx. He was already in love with me, and you knew it. You knew that if you sent him back, there would be no turning back for either of us. You were supposed to protect me." Celeste could hear the hysteria in her voice, but she couldn't stop, couldn't calm herself. She hummed with anger, her body feverish in her rage.

"You let them rape me, do unthinkable things to me... murder me and send me to ... you knew I was in Tartarus, and you left me there ... you left me ... to do what they did ... the pain." She reached out, grasping Nyx's face in her hands.

Flashes of memory ricocheted through Nyx's head, images of men, and some women, their sinister, smiling faces close as they did what they wanted to hear. They touched her in the most intimate places, using her as they saw fit, marveling at her beauty, all wanting to leave a mark on her, all wanting a piece of her. She could feel the pain and embarrassment. She could feel the metal bangles cut into her wrists and ankles and hear the ting of bells with each thrust. The palace servants, who'd once felt sympathy for the girl, had taken to spitting and putting shards of glass and animal dung in her food and speaking of her in hushed tones as their king fell deeper into his depravity and obsession for her. She felt a brief ray of hope when the king was killed, only to be used and tortured by another before her sweet release into death. A death that was also plagued with more of the eternal nightmare of her existence.

Nyx's own eyes filled with tears, her body ached, and her heartfelt as if someone had it in a vice, tightening it with each beat. She whimpered, her body going limp, and she began to fall, but Celeste held steady, wanting her to see and feel everything she'd endured, not knowing how she was doing it, but she was. She was sharing her burden.

"They broke me, Nyx. They fucking broke me, and *you* let them," she snarled before finally releasing Nyx's face. Celeste moved away from Karim, not wanting anyone to touch or look at her.

She turned her back to them, going to open the curtains to feel the moonlight on her face. She could feel their eyes on her and hear Nyx as she choked on her sobs. Karim remained silent and still, watching her.

She stared into the sky, wondering how different her life could have been if only she sighed.   "Now," Karim said in an even voice, reclaiming his seat. "Tell her about the mark."

* * *

Karim was going to go to Celeste, but she looked as if she would rip off the arm of anyone who came near her at the moment. She was a ball of vibrating energy, her eyes a pale silver, her nails digging into her palms, leaving little crescent-shaped cuts. He knew this because he could smell her blood; the scent of heated sugar and vanilla may have gone unnoticed to Nyx, but he could smell it. In the last few hours, her every scent, every mood, every hair on her body burned into his memory. He knew that tonight had been an emotional tsunami for her, and this little moment was only the eye before the inevitable storm. He would be here to make sure the wreckage was minimal.

"When you ... when you died," Nyx was saying in a hoarse voice, "The Moirai came to me to let me know that your life force had faded and that you were locked in Tartarus. I couldn't go directly, and Uriel summoned *The Fallen One* at God's behest. He was summoned by using his true name, and he came, but at a price. He was taken with you almost immediately. Something about you -it was like electricity filled the room. When he saw you, he breathed life into you, giving you a piece of him, and I suppose that's where this telepathy and some of the other things come from. He shared a part of himself, connected the two of you, and marked you. He said that when you readily accepted your fate, when you called his name and only then, he would come to claim you. He insisted that you were his, that you always had been and always would be. I knew that I had done the right thing."

"What is his name?" Celeste asked.

"That was wiped from my memory. Only you have the

name of *The Fallen One.* It's locked somewhere within you. When the time comes, you will know, and you will take your proper place. You will become the greatest savior the world has known," Nyx said.

Celeste stared at her, her fingers running along the mark on her neck.

"Or the destruction of us all," she whispered, her eyes on Nyx.

* * *

Celeste stared at Nyx, and fat, heavy tears stung her raw, red eyes before slowly rolling down her cheeks. She couldn't remember the last time she'd cried so long and so hard, but her heart was breaking with each new revelation.

"You promised he could...have me? You are no better than the Persian or Nemesis."

"*Agapité kardiá,* I only wanted to protect you," Nyx started.

"I am not your dear heart. I'm not your anything! Your protection has done nothing but ruin me. If you hadn't protected me so much, maybe I would have had a fighting chance. Maybe I wouldn't have been raped and murdered again and again and again. If you hadn't tried so hard to keep me safe, I would have been able to fight back. Instead, you took my power, and you sold me. *You* allowed every nightmare of my life to happen. *You* could have stopped it at any point, but you didn't because you had a plan. You sold me."

"I didn't sell you," Nyx said, rising to her feet.

"You did it! You promised him he could have me! You gave me to someone I can't even fucking remember, but Karim, who you know and trust, had to keep his hands to himself. Someone who I care about, and you ruined that. Because, just like everyone else, you wanted to use me."

"I just wanted-"

"I swear on all that is holy, Nyx, if you say you were just trying to protect me one more fucking time, I'm going to lose my shit. There is no excuse for what you did. He branded me like motherfucking cattle! How many others have this mark? How many others?"

"He could only leave his mark on one, a chosen one. That's you. He gave you part of himself. Do you realize how special you are? I was ri-" Nyx smiled, a tight, strained thing that she was forcing.

"If you say you were right in doing this, I am going to punch you in the fucking throat." Celeste raked her fingers through her hair in frustration. Karim couldn't help the smirk that teased the corners of his mouth, even when Nyx shot him a stare that would turn a weaker man to stone. "You are the worst betrayer of all," Celeste said.

"The prophecy," Nyx began.

"Fuck the prophecy! I never had a fucking chance. At least Nemesis was honest in her hatred of me, but what you did was so much worse. I can tell you for a motherfucking fact that your good intentions and protection are exactly what led me to hell. Centuries, Nyx. I spent fucking centuries in the dark, being raped and gutted until there was nothing left in me to hurt! Nothing left to break because it was already broken! I am broken, and no matter what you say or do, I will always be broken."

Karim rose, slowly moving away as the temperature in the room rose. Celeste's hair lifted as if she were trapped in a field of electricity. Streaks of silver shot through the jet-black waves. Her eyes blazed pure swirling silver. Her fangs elongated, and her body hummed, lifting off of the ground as her anger poured through her.

They stood stunned, unable to speak as the truth of her power made itself evident.

"I relinquish your dominion over me," she said.

Nyx gasped, her fingers going to her throat.

Karim paled at the proclamation. Celeste relinquishing

their dominion was the same as disowning her family. She was removing any influence they had over her, which gave her all of the powers and gifts she was given at birth. A pulse of air moved through the room, the sheer force of it blowing their clothes and hair as if they were the center of a gale. When it settled, the silence in the room grew, making them both uncomfortable. She was fuming, her lips pursed, and her brows furrowed in pure, unabashed fury.

"No, you can't." Nyx sobbed.

Celeste let out a pure anguished shriek. It was like a sonic boom, rattling the windows and shaking the walls. They covered their ears, trying to keep the shrill siren of her yell from splitting their heads open. The floorboards began to lift, clattering in soft applause as they struggled to pull free.

Celeste lifted higher into the air, and everything in the room lifted with her: furniture, dishes, and even a few small appliances rose a foot into the air.

Karim felt his own feet losing contact with the ground, and his heart raced. Nyx looked terrified but impressed by the power that energized the room. Time seemed frozen, but Karim could see that it hadn't stopped by looking at the clock. It had slowed. The sweeping second hand on a clock that managed to stay bolted to the wall moved achingly slow as it ticked the seconds away. They were in a sort of Celeste-induced limbo.

"I have lost everything because of you. You ruined me. Leave. Now!" Her voice was amplified like she was speaking through a megaphone.

"I do love you," Nyx said, her eyes turned to Karim. "And you will pay for what you've done." She bellowed.

"Go before I destroy you," Celeste said in a voice so cold that it set a chill in the room.

Nyx disappeared in a whirl of silver mist, leaving the scent of lavender and jasmine in her wake.

Slowly, the room settled, and Celeste along with it. But not completely. She was still furious, her body still a live wire of energy, the full force of her power coursing through her. For the first time, she felt alive.

* * *

Remy lay across his bed, his bare legs dangling over one side, his head the other. He wasn't asleep though he'd had to listen to Nicky go on and on for the better part of an hour about Celeste screwing Karim. It hadn't bothered Nicky as much as it had devastated him. Remy had to try to let him vent without adding his opinion or throwing an *I told you so* into the mix. Nicky didn't need him being an asshole. He needed him to be a friend, a brother.

"She used her cuffs on him, Remy," Nicky'd said in a rough whisper. "Her slave shackles. He was all cut and bruised; is that healthy, Remy? Is that something she should be doing?"

"I don't know, Nick." Remy had known of her heavy gold bracelets. He'd been the one who'd pried them from her wrists and ankles. She'd worn them so long, and they'd been used so often they'd cut into her skin, caking them with blood and leaving deep wounds that had oozed and refused to heal for weeks. She had given up then, begging them to leave her in her misery. She had been just a whisper of a thing, starved to the point of emaciation, her hair falling out in great brittle clumps. Her skin, now a rich, silken caramel, had been ashen, the color of dried mud, cracked and bleeding. The vibrant blue eyes were pale and watery, her teeth yellowed and rotting from neglect. She'd stank of blood, sex, and sickness, a ghost of what she had been, yet she had stayed, much too strong to die. Or too stubborn, as Remy had deduced when she'd refused to feed once they'd brought her from hell. He remembered those days with vivid clarity. Even all these years later, he could pinpoint the exact moment he'd fallen in love with her.

Of course, he knew that she would never love him the

way he loved her, and over the years, he'd learned to live with that. It had taken time, but he understood that now. Nicky hadn't had the years Remy did to come to terms with that. Everything was new to him; he was emotionally raw, but hopefully, this trip would help him. Nicky just needed a cooling-off period.

He stared at the ceiling, thinking of the fuck-nutty Fates and their confounding prophecies. It was like trying to decode a brainteaser whenever they spoke. He often thought that they did it on purpose, just to fuck with them. They were just that insane and sadistic. He thought of Briar, his beautiful giant, and wondered if perhaps he would be willing to come and spend the night with him. Absently, he ran a hand over his bare chest, the image of Briar's dancing green eyes playing over and over in his mind. For such a big man, he was so gentle, loving, and he did love him. He hadn't thought it possible to love someone so much, but he would give up everything for Briar if he'd let him. His hand moved lower until he touched the hardening shaft between his thighs. Yes, maybe a call to Briar was what he needed.

He had gotten up to get his cell phone from the other room when the intercom on his land-line rang. He picked it up with one hand and grasped his cell in the other, scrolling for Briar's number.

"Hey," Briar's voice crackled in his ear. "The night guy isn't at the door. Let me up." A chill went through him when Briar's rough brogue came through the line.

"Hey, you," Remy said before quickly punching in the code to unlock the lobby door.

"I'll be waiting, hon," Remy just about purred before disconnecting the line. Even if they just hung out and watched television, he couldn't wait to see him. Other than Celeste and Nicky, Briar was the closest person to him. He was more than a lover; he was his best friend. He opened the door; his excitement was rapidly dissolving when he saw who was on the other side. It was definitely not Briar.

"Wait, what are you doi-" That was as far as he got when a fine red mist was blown into his face. It stung his nose and eyes, blinding him. It tasted of bitter almond. He stumbled backward, tripping over a pair of discarded basketball shoes, and dropped onto his butt on the rug. He was cursing and spitting, tears welling in his eyes when he tried to focus on the person who'd been on the other side of the door. He could make out shapes and colors moving into the entryway of his condo, gently closing the door behind them before speaking.

"You'll be fine," she said. "Just give it a minute." Slowly the blob of red and white began to shift and sharpen until he looked into the white eyes that hovered above him. Her pupils had dilated, and the crimson hair floated around an angelic face that he suddenly found completely captivating. She watched him for a while, her head tilted to one side as she removed a pair of dark red leather gloves. He thought that odd, leather gloves in the middle of one of the hottest summers in New Orleans history. She squatted down so that she was looking into his eyes, one perfectly polished fingernail under his chin.

"Lilith? How?" he coughed, the bitter taste still burning his tongue.

"This?" She spoke in Briar's rich vibrato, which was so odd coming from such a delicate mouth. "Old parlor trick, sweetie," she said, *sweetie,* coming out in her sweet lilting tone.

"What did you do?" His voice felt thick, his tongue numb and heavy. He tried to stand, but he could no longer control his limbs.

"That was just a little assistance. Don't worry, it's not poisonous, just something to help loosen your tongue as it were." She stood, straightening her skirt, and looked around the room, nodding approvingly, then turned back to him as he struggled to stand. "Don't struggle. All you're doing is wearing yourself out. Just relax, and in a minute, you'll be fine," she said, and he felt his muscles relax as if she'd commanded them to do so. He was confused and a little scared. He no longer had control of his body, yet his mind was alert.

"What do you want?" he asked, sitting in the center of the room like a discarded rag doll.

She sat carefully in a chair nearby, and he struggled to turn his head to look at her. It took a great deal of effort, but he finally managed. She was watching him, a smug smile on her perfectly glossed lips.

"I want you to tell me everything about dear, sweet sister Celeste. I want every tiny detail from what she eats to what shampoo she uses, all the way down to the color of the polish on her toenails." She sat back, crossing her legs and drumming her nails on the dark arms of the plush leather chair. She looked like an emperor deciding the fate of a lowly gladiator, and a chill went through him.

"I have all night."

✳ ✳ ✳

CHAPTER TEN

She didn't wait for the faun to stumble and slide through the foyer as she had the first time she'd visited this horrible place. Instead, she rang the bell and immediately burst through the front door, tossing a dismissive hand to the poor creature. He slipped on the floor, his hooves never getting purchase on the marble floor, and fell near the winding marble staircase.

Lilith looked at him, confused and angry in a corner, his bow tie askew. It would have been comical if it weren't so goddamned degrading. She would have helped him up if she thought he'd allow it. Sighing, she rounded a corner, throwing the double doors to the sitting room open with a grand flourish. She just about twirled into the room in bright yellow skin-tight pants and a white ruffled shirt, her hair in a loose braid that draped over one shoulder. She crossed the room as if she were on a runway, a brilliant smile on her cherry painted lips.

"I'm baaaack," she sang, dropping onto the sofa. She looked at the upholstery and nodded. On her previous visit, it had been stained with blood, and now it was pristine.

The Queen didn't even look up as she breezed into the room, her eyes on her computer screen and her face as calm and serene as ever. Beside her stood the man who'd been there before, his features relaxed and his demeanor calm. The only indication that Lilith's grand entrance had moved him was the slight lift of a perfect eyebrow.

"Well?" Lilith tapped one yellow pump against the glass coffee table. The Queen looked at her, rising slowly; she took her time crossing the room. As usual, she was in her uniform of white to match her snowy hair. She took her seat, her eyes cool and her face expressionless, tee-peed her fingers and studied Lilith, who looked like summer personified in her cheery outfit.

"So, the last time you were here, I told you to tell me what I wanted to know or not to come back," she reminded Lilith. She held out her hand for the drink, her *"friend"* handed her.

Lilith snapped her fingers at him.

"Hey, can I get one of those? Heavy on the vodka, light on the ice."

He nodded but didn't speak, his eyes on her while he prepared her drink. "Of course, I remember."

"And since you're here, I assume you have what I need?" The Queen sipped her drink, her eyes on Lilith, who smiled and accepted her glass from the silent male.

"One would assume correctly," she agreed, graciously accepting the drink she was handed. "Does my father know about this one? He seems to have lasted longer than the others," she said, noting the slight narrowing of the Queen's eyes, yet her cool detachment remained.

"Your father and I have an understanding One that is none of your business. Now, about the Caelestis,"

"That's the thing, though, my father is my business, which makes your business my business. So, I suggest that the next time you threaten me, touch me, or so much as snarl in my direction, you remember that I, his only daughter, have his heart as well as his ear, while you only have his dick." She sipped her drink, her eyes on the Queen, waiting for a response.

"Well, it's good to see you're just as crass as ever. Now, if you are done,"

"Done, no, I'm not nearly done. You see, I have found a cornucopia of information, a wellspring of all things Celeste Keegan Kent, so much that I believe that we need to renegotiate our little arrangement. The rules of engagement have changed, my dear, and you no longer have the upper hand." She sipped her drink, watching as the Queen's pale face darkened with anger.

She grasped the arms of her chair, her nails scoring the soft white leather. Her eyes flashed, but she held her seat, and as much as she wanted to throttle Lilith, she remained calm.

"You conniving little bitch," she hissed.

"I learned from the best." Lilith tipped her glass to the Queen before smirking and taking another sip of her vodka.

* * *

"So, you're here to protect me from some sort of shadow plot that's being hatched by the Queen of the Dark Fae, who you believe sent Lilith to infiltrate the Collective to get intel, am I right?" Celeste leaned against the kitchen counter, a cup of coffee in her hands, warming her palms while Karim attempted to explain. He nodded. She stared at him for a second, then continued.

"And Nyx sent you because she felt that enough time had passed and that I was so angry with you that there was no chance that we would end up together? And because you have this nobility curse thing, you can't lie, and you can't go against her? Which was overridden by your emotional attachment to me, right?" Another silent nod.

"And no one thought it would be a good idea to let me in on all of this so that maybe, just maybe, I could look out for myself? Or at least be alert to a possible threat?" Another nod, and she shook her head in exasperation.

"So, you're all just a gaggle of idiots?" she asked.

Karim had to agree. Most of their issues could have been avoided if Nyx hadn't tried to "protect" Celeste from the world.

"Pretty much." Karim sipped his coffee, a smile teasing the corner of his mouth.

She lowered her cup, her eyes drifting to her cell phone, which sat motionless on the kitchen counter.

He watched her eyes shift from the phone back to her coffee. She looked like a lost kid in her men's dress shirt, and tights, her hair a tumble of curls, and her face scrubbed clean. She had freckles. He noticed only a few pale freckles on the bridge of her nose. He had never forgotten that face, and he didn't think he ever would.

"Call him," he said. She looked at him through her lashes and smiled.

"So, tell me about Lilith and her dastardly plan to defeat me." She rubbed her hands together like a cartoon villain and waggled her eyebrows. Karim knew that she was changing the subject, and he let her.

"Honestly, I think this is coming from the Dark Queen, not the little princess.8Something tells me that Lilith is all bark and bravado. The Queen, that's the big dog."

Celeste thought about that for a moment, chewing her lip as she contemplated. She frowned as a thought crossed her mind, a thought she'd never had before. She had no idea who the Dark Queen was. She'd never seen her, didn't know many who had, yet she wielded power. She had so much power in the fact that the Dark Prince, Lucifer himself, or Alexander Prince as he was called now, had just about handed over his entire kingdom to her. She ruled hundreds, thousands of the Dark Fae, yet no one knew where she came from or who she was.

"Who is she?" she asked, and Karim shrugged.

"Never met her or anyone who could tell me much about her. I did know of a vamp who said he'd encountered her a few hundred years ago, but he couldn't tell me anything about her. He remembered that she was beautiful and that she was all white." He said.

"Like a ghost?" she asked, and Karim shrugged.

"Not sure. Whenever he spoke of her, he'd get this glassy look in his eyes, like he was trying to remember a dream. The harder he tried, the worse it became until he became physically ill." Karim remembered the male vampire's look, his dark eyes, and his face twisting in concentration. "I think maybe she put some sort of enchantment or binding on him. I mean, he was in her company for hours, yet the only thing he remembered was that she was beautiful and white."

"I take it he isn't one of the seven then," she asked, and Karim shook his head.

"I do think she's behind whatever Lilith is doing. She's who you need to look out for." Celeste laughed and shook her head.

"No, she's who *you* need to look out for. You're my bodyguard, guard my body. Do your job, man," she teased, and he couldn't help but smile. Her eyes darted again to her dormant phone, and Karim sighed.

"Calie, just call him." He'd seen the look of devastation on Nicky's face when he found Karim in the guest bedroom, slipping on a pair of sweats that had been too snug. Nicky had stared at him, his jaw slack and his eyes wide. Silently, he spotted what he'd been searching for, an expensive leather wallet and a more expensive smartphone. He slid them off of the dresser and then turned watery blue eyes to Karim.

"She's fragile," he'd said in a whisper. "Don't you dare hurt her again."

"I won't," Karim said, but it was to Nicky's back as he left the room. The argument had begun then, and he stayed in the bedroom listening, not wanting to intrude on something that seemed so personal, so intimate, and he felt a pang of jealousy. Nicky Sky had known Celeste better than he ever would; she loved him that was evident. She loved him because, unlike anyone else in her life, he would always be there for her. Many of the preternaturals saw humans as weak, Karim included. But Nicky, hurt and broken, never lashed out at her, never said things or did things that would break an already delicate woman. He saw Celeste for who she was, and he loved her despite that. He may have even loved her because of it.

"Call him," he repeated, and she groaned, scrubbing a hand over her forehead.

"I don't know what to say to him." She sighed, putting her

cup on the counter. "How do you apologize for something like this? He is the one person who's never lied to me, never hurt me in any way. He's always there when I need him, and he never even batted an eye when he found out what I am. He just- he's been my rock. He is the only person who knows everything about me, and I mean *everything*, Karim. I have no secrets from him. He is the best person I have ever known, and I love him more than anything." She felt her chest tighten and closed her eyes to keep the tears at bay.

"Call him," Karim repeated as he took her in his arms, kissing the top of her head. "And tell him that." He had to admit that he felt the unexpected sting at her profession of love for her human companion. He wondered if she would ever love him that way, that completely and unconditionally or at all for that matter.

"What if he doesn't want to talk to me? Or tells me he doesn't want to see me anymore? Or worse, tells me to go fuck myself?" She looked up into Karim's face. She'd somehow forget how good looking he was with his smooth tanned skin, dark hair, and eyes that were such a pale, cool green that it could only be classified as glacial.

"He will. He would have to be insane not to want to see you."

"What about you?" she asked, and he frowned at the question.

"What?" Karim half chuckled.

"You managed to stay away for all of this time. Why didn't you ever try to contact me? Or see me? Where were you?" He sighed and released her, moving to the opposite side of the room. She watched him curiously, his body tense and his mind whirling. She could only read his emotions, not his thoughts, as she could with Nyx and most humans. With most preternaturals, she couldn't read their thoughts. She'd realized that she couldn't read any of them when she was with her family, only feel their presence and emotions. Karim, being a vampire, had a different feel to him. He was going through guilt and shame, which she'd often read on him. Then a thought occurred to her, one she hadn't even considered before.

"Karim, do you have a family? A wife?" she asked, her heart in her throat. She placed her hands on the countertop, her head down as she tried to catch her breath. He wasn't saying anything, and she felt her stomach drop to her knees. She cursed under her breath and felt tears sting her eyes.

"Jesus Christ, you do! Goddammit, leave it to me to fall in love with a married man," she exclaimed, then covered her mouth with both hands, her eyes wide with shock. Had she said that out loud? Had he heard it? Of course, he heard it, she thought, vampires had ears better than canines. He could hear her heartbeat from across the room. Shit shit shit, she thought and chanced a look at him.

He was staring at her, his eyes narrowed, his body as still as a statue. He'd heard her; there was no doubt about it. He started walking toward her, his jaw clenched, and his fangs extended. She could feel conflicting emotions from him now, anger, sadness, relief, and the ever-present guilt. With each step he took forward, she would take one back until she found herself pressed against the kitchen counter. He closed the space between them, his eyes igniting, and his body rigid. He pressed into her, one hand sinking into her jet curls.

"Doosat daram. Lotfaen, daer eshghaem beh to shaek naekon," he said, his intensity making her mouth dry. *"I love you. Don't ever doubt my love for you,"* he'd said, but that was not a denial, and her knees buckled. She pushed against him wanting to vomit, needing to get away from him. She could not handle another blow, not now.

"I'm not married, Celeste," he said, and she exhaled but continued to push against his chest. She needed air, and she needed water. She needed Nicky.

"I have no children. I was nearly once married, but she said she could not compete with the ghost of you and that I needed to get over you before I could love anyone else. I didn't come back because I couldn't bear to see you with someone else, and Nyx made sure that I wouldn't come back until she needed me."

She turned her back to him, trying to catch her breath. She felt as if the ceiling had come crashing down on her. He'd been in love with her for all of this time, thinking she was happy with another, not knowing the truth of the torture she'd survived. He kissed her shoulder and held her as she fought through what she could only assume was a panic attack. It had been so long since she'd had a genuine emotion that she'd let someone other than Nicky witness. She was slowly becoming whole again. She leaned into him, grateful for his presence.

"I stayed away because you deserved better. But I've never stopped wanting you," he said when she finally regained her breath. It was an honest declaration, and she couldn't help but smile at the irony. Karim wasn't good enough for the divine bloodline. So instead of letting a good, strong, and honorable man love her, Nyx allowed her to be degraded and damaged for her own selfish needs.

If she had let things happen as they should have, maybe she and Karim would have burned out. Maybe they would have run their course and parted ways as friends without all of the carnage. Maybe they would still be together because, before Nyx's interference, he had become the *one*. The great love of her life.

"You were always more than good enough for me, Karim." She said, *but now, I'm not good enough for you,* she thought.

* * *

Briar had knocked on Remy's door for fifteen minutes before reaching for his phone. As it rang in his ear, he listened for the echo of his personalized ring tone on the other side of the door. He had been with Remy when he'd chosen Destiny's

Child's song "*Soldier*" as his tone. They'd been sitting on the sofa in Remy's apartment, watching a movie when Remy had smiled and played that tone.

"Why on earth did you choose that as my ring tone?" Briar had asked, laughing but a little confused.

"Because," Remy said, standing over Briar in his black boxer briefs and nothing else. *"I need a soldier that ain't scared to stand up for me, known to carry big things if you know what I mean,"* he sang and danced to the beat, and Briar chuckled.

"What if someone hears it? What will they think?" Briar asked, thinking the song was a little too risky for Lt. Commander Remy Kent. Briar hadn't been ashamed of being gay, but he didn't broadcast it either. He was already a big man and ginger to boot, but now he was big, gay ginger who was essentially banging his boss. The ring tone was pretty much on the nose, and they could get into trouble if it were discovered. Remy had suddenly become serious, his deep brown eyes solemn. He sat next to Briar, taking his hand and lacing their fingers, and smiled.

"When have I ever given even one fuck about what people think?" he'd asked before leaning in to kiss him. He and Remy had been brand new, only three weeks into the relationship. A relationship that had started as a one-time thing but ended up being more than either of them had expected.

He smiled to himself when Remy's voicemail came on the line, a deep, sleepy growl that always sent a tingle of excitement through him. Remy had a very nonchalant way of speaking that was somewhere between Southern drawl and French annoyance, but with an emphasis on neither. He'd once told Briar that it had taken him years to develop the non-distinct accent he affected. Unlike Celeste, who could master any accent after hearing it once, he and the rest of his family had spoken French for so long that it had taken nearly one hundred years to adjust the way they spoke.

"This is Remy Kent. Leave a message. I may call you back. I may not. If I don't.-.you know why." The beep followed it.

"Remy, I've been outside of your door for...twenty minutes. I don't know where you are, but I'm going home. I've been awake for over forty-eight hours now, and I'm dead on my feet. Call me later, babe." He pushed the end call button and walked away. He was halfway down in the elevator when the hairs on the back of his neck stood on end. He couldn't put his finger on it, but something was wrong. He yawned and shook his head. He was groggy. Maybe that was why he was so freaked out. It wasn't like he and Remy hadn't gotten their wires crossed before. It happened often. Remy was often being called away at the last minute. He was second in command, after all. And with Briar being a lycan, he was always being sent out to track rouges and lawbreakers, so today was no different.

He rubbed his tired eyes and sighed. He just needed a hot shower and a comfortable bed, and he would be fine. Remy would call when he got the message, or better yet, show up at Briar's apartment. He always did.

* * *

She hadn't expected this. Not from Lilith. The Queen stood, smoothing her skirt before she began to pace the room, her fingers linked behind her back. She circled the sofa, staring at the back of Lilith's head and wishing injury on her as she contemplated the girl. She was feeding her tidbits of information, bite-sized bits that she wanted to savor, but she needed the entire meal. She stood opposite the sofa and looked at Lilith for a second, her pale eyes narrowing as she sized the girl up.

"What do you have?" she finally asked. Lilith uncrossed her legs and deliberately placed her glass on the table before she spoke. She met the Queen's arctic stare, unblinking, unwavering, and smiled a wicked little smile. She had the upper hand, and the little cow knew it. If her husband hadn't warned her off, she would have snapped Lilith's pretty little neck. But she'd promised Alexander not to harm his precious little princess, for now.

"First, we discuss my terms," Lilith sighed.

"Your terms?" The Queen straightened, her arms folded across her chest. "So, you think it's that good?"

"I know it is." Lilith drained her glass, her smirk still in place.

"I'll be the judge of that. What is it you want?"

"When I give you what you want, I want to leave. You give me what's mine, and I will go. I want to be free of this place," Lilith said, suddenly serious.

It took a moment for the Queen to grasp what she was saying, but her perfect face was creased in confusion when she did.

She dropped her arms and looked at Lilith, a bit dumbfounded, before looking at her companion, who looked just as shocked as the Queen. She sat down slowly, gauging Lilith for some sort of tell, some little tick to let her know whether or not this was a trick. Lilith was full of them.

"You want to leave?" she repeated, and Lilith nodded.

"Yes. I want to be free of this place and you. I want to live my life in the sunlight. I want to be loved." That piqued the Queen's interest, her brow shooting skyward.

"Love?" she laughed, "You would give up the throne, the power, the adoration for love? Love is a myth, my dear. The sooner you learn that, the better. There is no such thing as love; there is only lust and degradation. Love, my dear child, is a human fantasy that rarely ends well."

"You see, that's where you're wrong. Love is very real. I've seen it, I've felt it. To see the way those around your precious Caelestis love her, the way they protect her, that's love. I want to feel that. I want to belong to a world where that's a possibility. I want a male to look at me and speak of me how I have seen males speak of Arbor and Celeste Kent. I want to feel those butterflies when my phone rings and I know it's the one

I love. Have you never felt love for anyone?" She was leaning forward, her white eyes scanning the perfect unmarred beauty of the Queen. Surely, someone as beautiful as she must have been in love at least once.

Instead of answering, she sat back in her chair, smoothing her skirt over her legs.

"What did you find?" The Queen's tone was exasperated with this asinine conversation. Lilith was still a child in many ways, and she understood the misguided judgment of her naïveté. She wanted the fairytale she saw when she was with the Collective, not understanding that she was already the princess. She would learn, and she would come back when everything blew up in her face. She would learn that being the heir to the Dark Fae's throne was her birthright, and soon, very soon, she would realize that. At least the Queen hoped she would.

"Agree to my terms," Lilith said. The Queen nodded.

"Of course, child. You can leave to find love or whatever it is you're searching for. Now, does she have the mark?" she asked, becoming impatient with this entire conversation. Lilith had a way of dragging things out for dramatic effect. She was her father's daughter, after all.

"Yes, she does, and there is so much more," Lilith said before telling the Queen of all she'd learned. When she was done, the Queen looked very pleased and somewhat proud. She rose, brushing at her voluminous skirt, a real smile on her perfect lips. She held out her arms, and Lilith, obedient as ever, went to her. She could smell the light scent of roses and lavender that always seemed to surround the Queen. Even though she doused herself in expensive perfumes, that scent always came through.

"Thank you, Lilith. You're free to go," she said, kissing the girl on her cheek. Lilith turned to walk away, but the Queen grabbed her hand, holding it, a look on her face that Lilith had never seen before. Could ut be sadness, she wondered. "But you will be welcome back anytime you wish," she said, and tears illuminated her crystal blue eyes. Lilith nodded, letting her fingers slip from the cool grasp of the other woman.

"Thank you...*mother*," Lilith choked before exiting the room.

* * *

CHAPTER ELEVEN

His mouth was dry and tasted horrible like he'd been sucking on a dirty sweat sock all night. Sunlight was streaming into the room from the open drapes, boring a hole into his already aching head. Nicky squinted and sat up, sending empty beer cans and liquor bottles rolling to the floor in a clatter. The sound sent waves of pain through his throbbing head. He groaned, dragging himself from the bed and shuffled, naked and hungover, into the living room of the suite to find his road manager, David, coming towards him.

"Good, you're awake. You have an interview in two hours, then you have a meet and greet, then soundcheck. We're leaving for the airport right after the show tonight. Move your ass, Sky," he was saying, and Nicky nodded.

"I need a shower. Is Katie awake? I need her help getting packed," he grumbled before staggering back into the room, David on his heels.

He was in the shower, the hot water rinsing away the stench of whatever he did the night before, wishing the water could rinse away the residue of shame and guilt that seemed to hover over him like his own personal dark cloud. But it never did. It hadn't lifted for three weeks, not since he'd kissed Celeste goodbye and boarded a plane for New York. That first night had been epic, even by rock-star standards. So much so, he barely remembered any of it once they landed. He did have a vague memory of checking into his hotel and even performing, but everything after that was a hazy jumble of color and sound. Everything after that was a blur of interviews, shows, women, drinking, and mornings like this.

He was staring out the window of his hotel, looking at yet another city he wouldn't remember, when the petite girl with neon yellow hair entered. Today his assistant was wearing purple sneakers, black and white striped socks, red shorts, and a black and red tour t-shirt. She stared at him for a moment, her hands on her hips, her foot tapping the carpet in irritation.

"You're all packed and ready to go. You have an hour or so to sightsee if you like, but I know you won't. We're in Bangkok, by the way. You're starting your shows in Japan tomorrow. Are you done being a slut for this leg of the tour, or should I make sure the doc has industrial strength penicillin on hand?" she asked.

"Well, good morning to you too, Katie." He smiled. "How was your night?"

"Painful," she sighed before going to check the nightstand to make sure he wasn't leaving anything behind.

"You had phone calls again. Gaston called. He wants to know if you've spoken to Remy. Lisette called. Have you spoken to Remy? Arbor called. Guess what? She wants to know if you've spoken to Remy. And," She paused, sighing heavily before turning to face him. "Celeste called."

"To ask about Remy?" he joked. Katie was not amused. For such a cute little thing, she was the most petulant person he'd ever encountered in his life. Standing just under five feet tall and no more than eighty pounds, Katie Paulsen was the epitome of cute. She had big bright eyes that wavered between green and grey, her face was round, her mouth small, and her nose button-like. Yet, she was a sarcastic girl of twenty-two with the mouth of a sailor and a surly biker's temperament. She was the perfect personal assistant for him.

"I wish you would call her back, Nick. It's been three weeks; what could she have possibly done to make you so angry?" He didn't answer, as usual. Katie had become accustomed to his response regarding Celeste as of late. He didn't take her calls and refused to discuss what had happened between them to make him freeze her out the way he had.

But how could he? How could he say that the reason he was upset was that she had slept with another man, but not just any man. Karim. Seeing that she had opened herself so completely to someone else was unbearable.

In all honesty, he had no right to be upset. Celeste wasn't his wife or even his girlfriend. She was a friend, a good friend, his best friend, But still just a friend. He couldn't forget the image of Karim in the obvious aftermath of lovemaking. Mostly, he thought he was upset because he was with her day in and day out, yet she never saw him as anything more than good old reliable Nicky, her sounding board, and her rock, but he had been there before Karim, and he would be after that.

"At least call your family. They've been calling you non-stop." Katie distractedly took her phone from her pocket and stared at it. "Your car is here. Call your family and call Celeste. Stop being a dick. She's your best friend, so what if she's got a boyfriend now," she mumbled, and he looked at her, his eyes narrowed in suspicion.

"Don't give me that look. She has a boyfriend, and you're jealous because it should have been you," she said.

"I never said ..." he started, and she looked up, her cute face in its perpetual scowl.

"You didn't have to. Men, you're so easy to read. If you wanted it to be you, you should've made a move. Don't get pissy with her because some other guy beat you to it. You drinking yourself blind every night and being the world's biggest man-whore isn't going to solve anything. Call her and stop being such a girl. Besides," she said, leaving the bedroom to answer the knock at the door. "You'll still be around long after this relationship implodes. Boyfriends are temporary. Best friends are eternal." Nicky managed a rueful laugh as he watched the spritely girl open the door to allow the bellman into the room.

"Maybe I should be dating you," he teased, and she shook her head.

"Nah. Even if I were into guys, you're still too big of a

pussy for me. Call your family!" He couldn't help but laugh. Leave it to little Katie to give him a much-needed kick in the ass.

* * *

The phone was ringing, she could hear it, but dear god she wasn't able to answer it. Instead, she reached out blindly and knocked it off of the nightstand, hoping to dull the annoying buzzing. It fell to the carpet, the constant ring muted, and she relented to yet another wave of pure bliss. She sank her fingers into Karim's feather-soft tresses, her thighs tightening around his shoulders as his mouth continued its delicious torture. His fangs brushed against her, sending a tremor through her, and she arched up, her hips rising to meet his ever-tormenting tongue.

He placed a palm on her taut stomach, holding her still so he could continue the assault, making her writhe against him, her breath a startled gasp. A long deep moan escaped her when he grazed the tightened nub at her center with his teeth. When he began to suckle that same nub gently, she went liquid, her body bucking against her orgasm. Her response encouraged him to continue until she was incoherent, her body feeling wonderfully boneless and weak. The phone began its incessant buzzing on the carpet, and he lifted his head, slightly annoyed.

"Are you going to answer that, *azizam*?" he breathed against her thigh. "It's driving me to distraction." He ran the tips of his fingers over her outer thighs, and she moaned. The sensation made her body heat again. He had learned her so well; it was unnerving.

"No, don't stop," she breathed, tugging on his hair in an attempt to steer him back to the throbbing heat at her core. She could feel his smile as he dropped warm kisses just below her belly button.

"As you wish," he said before his lips touched her again. She reached over her head, grasping at the headboard as her hips rose to meet every thrust of his tongue, every brush of those fangs against the tenderest part of her. She could feel him hesitate, and she knew why. It had become routine with him, the need to sink his teeth into her, but never the will; something always stopped him.

"Do it," she said, and he froze completely, his body tense, his breathing harsh. "Bite me, Karim." She pushed her hips upward, inviting him to do as he wished. "Please," she pleaded. He lowered his mouth again when the intercom began to buzz like an alarm. Karim reared back so that he was kneeling between her thighs, his entire body coiled in frustration. He ran his hands through his hair and looked down at Celeste, who punched the mattress and whined.

"I can't," he said in frustration.

"No, no, no," she yelled, and Karim couldn't hide his smile. She sat up, scooting closer so that she was nearly straddling him. "I'll get rid of whoever that is. You don't move." She kissed him, her hands cupping the back of his head. She could taste herself on his lips and delved deeper, her tongue slipping into the warm sweetness there, her hips moving against the erection that pulled at his pajama bottoms. Finally, he grunted and grasped her hips, holding her still when the buzzer began again, this time in earnest, filling the apartment with the shrill ringing. She nipped his bottom lip with her fangs, drawing blood and quickly licking it away. "When I come back, it's your turn."

She sprang from the bed, still wearing the sundress she'd worn to class, letting the skirt fall around her calves.

She and Karim had fallen into a comfortable pattern in the three weeks they'd been together. She would wake every morning, go for a run, go to class, and do her homework until Karim rose. They would go out, see the city as soon as the sunset, then spend the night either in his apartment or hers. Some nights, they would stay in so he could paint, and she would cook, or they would order in. Some days he would wake early and watch a movie with her to spend time together. She was amazed by how normal, how comfortable and easy they had become.

They spent hours watching monster movies, laughing and making jokes and throwing popcorn at the television, like a couple of kids. He knew about her dreams, the sweaty, sex laden dreams that woke her panting and wanting more. He was more than willing to give it, taking advantage whenever the opportunity presented itself. After a night making spaghetti together, she discovered that he loved garlic. So that shattered that myth. As she tried to force them down one night at dinner, he realized that Celeste hated, absolutely hated, raw oysters. And when they made love, it was slow, deliberate, and careful, him usually letting her take the lead, relenting when she needed to be rough. But when he initiated love-making, he took his time, making sure she felt wanted and beautiful and protected.

Tonight, though, when Karim had risen, he had been of a certain mindset, and there had been no straying from his plan.

She was sitting on her sofa reading, dressed in a pale blue sundress, her hair in a ponytail, when the guest room door was thrown open. She'd looked up from her book, her brows raised in question. He was hard, his eyes glowing deep jade, and his lips pulled back in a snarl, exposing those beautiful fangs. He was shirtless and barefoot, wearing dark drawstring pajama bottoms, his chest heaving. He looked downright dangerous.

"Problem?" she asked. He crossed the room, scooping her into his arms before the word had left her lips. She gasped in surprise when she found herself on her back on the bed. Her dress was shoved up around her hips, her panties discarded, Karim's mouth on her, tasting her before she could catch her breath.

"I've been dreaming about this for nine hours," he said, and that was the last thing he said for a long time. Celeste could only grip the mattress and let the pleasure take her away.

* * *

She was going to answer the intercom. Instead, she found Briar standing in her living room, and she stopped short. The mark on her neck, which had been nothing more than a dull ache for the past weeks, was now singing to life. She was so surprised to see the giant filling her living room that she didn't have time to curse the building's security and its abject failure to keep anyone out.

"Briar?" she asked, and he turned bright green eyes on her. He was pale, paler than usual, making his bright red hair seem redder, more orange than deep auburn. He was in his uniform and shifted uncomfortably, looking as if he wasn't sure if he needed to salute or not.

"I am so sorry to bother you, Commander. I just didn't know where else to go. I tried calling, but you didn't answer your phone. It's been three weeks now, and it's never been more than a day. I just- I'm a little worried because he just asked me to make it official, and he said it was love. He even called me that night, but when I got there, he was gone. He always calls me back, sir. Always."

Celeste held up a hand to stop Briar's rambling. She hadn't been able to catch the thread of the conversation, and his thoughts were echoing in her head, mudding everything. She hadn't realized that she could read Briar, but he was so emotional it seemed to amplify his every thought.

"Are you talking about Remy?" she asked, and he nodded. "I wouldn't worry, Briar. He's probably off on some adventure, or he could be with Nicky in Japan." He was shaking his head, his lovely green eyes filling with tears.

"But I can't get him on the phone. He's not answering. He hasn't been to his apartment or his suite at the Collective, and no one has seen him for days. No one. His bike is still in the garage, and so is his car," Briar insisted.

"Try Nicky's number."

"He doesn't answer either. Commander, Remy hasn't even called his mother, and you know how he feels about her." That gave her a moment of pause. Remy never ignored Arbor's calls. No matter where he was or what he was doing, he would always answer her calls. Always.

"Something's wrong. I can feel it. And have you seen the High Regent lately, Commander?" he asked. She thought for a moment and shook her head. She'd spoken to Arbor on the phone, but she hadn't seen her. She was supposed to have brunch with her a few weeks ago, but that had been postponed. Celeste thought for a while, trying to remember the excuse Arbor had used, but she couldn't. She had been so busy with school and Karim, and she constantly ignored calls to Nicky. She hadn't seen much of anyone. And it was odd that she had gone so long without speaking to Remy.

"She's sick with worry. I didn't know where else to turn. Remy always calls me back."

She gave him a sympathetic smile.

"Briar, I know my brother, and he's fickle. Maybe it's just that he..."

Briar shook his head, his face set in a grim frown.

"You don't understand about your brother and me, sir. He loves me, and I love him. I know you think that he's gone off with some new fling, but it isn't like that with us. He offered to give up his position as Lieutenant Commander to be with me, sir. He asked me to move in with him. He wouldn't just walk out on me without explanation." She stared at him, and her jaw went slack.

"Remy Kent has said he you he loves you?" she asked. Remy never spoke of love, only sex, more sex, and weirder sex.

"Every day, sir," Briar said with a shy smile. "Every day."

* * *

Lilith found the room she'd been looking for in this mausoleum of a house. It had taken some time, sneaking up the massive marble staircase then going to the wrong wing on the wrong floor. She'd wandered from one elaborately decorated and expensively appointed room to the next. She'd found a library on the second floor, stocked with mint condition first editions. She ran her fingers over gold lettering on fine leather spines that looked as though they hadn't been broken. The entire room, paneled in a dark wood, smelled of cigars and whiskey. Not an unpleasant smell, but very masculine, she thought.

She's also found Gaston's classically decorated bedroom that smelled of leather and fresh cotton. His room was like the man, solid, staid with a hint of sexy menace. It was dark and sensual and made her wonder about the most reserved of the Kent siblings.

Lisette's room, on the other hand, had been an utter shock. It was the opposite of the leather-clad diva. Lisette's room was soft, decorated in pinks, and reminded Lilith of 1940's romance, right down to the pink satin bedsheets. It was not what she expected at all.

She found Remy's room on the third floor, and it was neater than she'd expected. It was full of things: motorcycle parts, magazines, old vinyl records, and classic rock posters from the '60s, 70s, and '80s and concerts she was sure he'd attended. The thing that surprised her were the photographs everywhere. They lay across the desk, his coffee table, on the sofa and end tables, pile after pile of photographs of wars and architecture, children in impoverished countries, and lavish ceremonies in exotic places. Some in stark, clear black and white, others in vivid color; all were extraordinary. She found herself looking at them, curling up on the floor, leafing through Remy's photo journal. He had talent, his subjects emoting for his camera, comforted by him. They were breathtaking and emotional, and she found tears streaming down her cheeks. She touched her damp face, staring at the tears on her fingertips in awe. This was not something she did, she realized. Demons don't cry, yet there she was.

She felt ill-at-ease and needed to leave as soon as possible; the strange tears wiped away with the back of her hand as she rocketed from the room. She had not come in search of that. What she had come for was right across the hall.

She stood in the middle of Celeste's suite of rooms and smiled. It was just as she'd imagined it- no, it was better. The drapes on the floor to ceiling windows that lined one wall were open, letting the late evening sunlight cast an orange glow over everything. Everything was beautiful, elegant, and understated, from the plush, white carpet to the gold embroidered duvet cover.

The heavy brocade curtains slowly closed, and soft, warm light filled the room from light fixtures camouflaged in the ceiling. She spun around, taking it all in, before running her hands over the back of the soft creamy velvet of a sofa. She looked at the photos that lined her dresser, all of them smiling. Absently, Lilith lifted a picture of Celeste with her brothers and sister at some sort of festival. They were dressed in 1960's hippie wear, Celeste in blue lensed sunglasses and a white crochet dress, her bare feet off the ground. Remy, who held her, wore a fringed leather vest with no shirt and a pair of low-riding hip-hugging jeans. Gaston looked mildly annoyed in a military uniform, but there was a twinkle in his eye.

Stern and business-like, Lisette wore a peasant blouse, her light brown hair in loose waves as she smiled at the camera and flashed a peace sign with her fingers. She returned the photo and looked at other framed glimpses into Celeste's many years with her adopted and, in some cases, biological family.

There were photos with Nyx on some beach, both in bikinis smiling into the sun. Celeste and her father, Anhur, on a fishing trip, Celeste with Arbor and Jonas on a snowy mountain top in ski gear. She had a family who loved her. Lilith moved away from the photos and into the dressing room, her eyes going wide at the sheer volume of things. She moved past the dresses and furs, the jewelry and shoes to the bathroom beyond that looked as if it belonged in a high-priced spa. Everything in Celeste Kent's life was magical. She thought. Lilith ran her fingers over silk and sequined gowns.

She removed a black dress, silky and flowing; she held it up to her chest and looked at her reflection in the mirror. She could never pull off black, not with her white skin and red hair; it would make her look like some Gothic cartoon. No, she couldn't, but she knew that Celeste looked amazing in it, with her long legs and golden-brown skin, the strapless gown would be gorgeous on her. She returned the dress, her fingers lingering on the satin before moving to the vanity in the rear of the room. It was covered in decorative bottles and atomizers of perfumes; she sprayed the scents into the air to smell them. Florals and masks, delicate spices all smelled wonderful, but nothing could mask the scent that permeated the entire suite, the smell of lavender and vanilla with hints of jasmine and sugar, Celeste's natural smell.

She found hidden drawers lined with silk and satin lingerie, most of which looked new and never worn. Another drawer was full of jewelry: diamonds, emeralds, sapphires, and rubies inlaid in gold, platinum, and silver. Strands of black pearls lay in a special black velvet box. She wanted to try it on but avoided the temptation. She did try on a rather large, cushion cut canary yellow diamond ring surrounded by a dozen white diamonds. The band of white gold was loose on her finger, the weight of the diamonds unexpectedly heavy, but it was flawless. She stared at it for a long time, looking at it on her hand before gently slipping it into the pocket of her skirt. She would never miss it. She would never miss anything in this shrine.

She made her way back into the bedroom where she stood, inhaling the essence of the woman who slept here.

She glided towards the windows, opening the curtains so she could look at the moon hanging high and full like a pearl in the inky sky. She could learn to love a place like this, a family like this. They seemed to like each other. She had no loving siblings, and though she was told that she had several brothers, she'd never really lived with any of them. Her father never took her on vacations; her mother wasn't the smiling hugging type. She had lived in an isolated palace of servants and rules. Her mother had spent more time obsessing over the great and powerful Caelestis than she ever had with her. She hadn't been a wanted child. Her birth had been part of the deal, a negotiation. Alexander Prince, the Prince of Darkness himself, had wanted a daughter, a girl he could mold into what he wanted her to be, and her mother had agreed. If and only if, she were allowed to be the one true sovereign of the Dark Fae. The deal had been made, a marriage had been planned, and a baby was born. There had never been love in her life, and now she knew that her mother didn't believe in such a thing.

Lilith had seen love, she had felt it when she spent time with Arbor, and she could see it in the Kents' pictures. She could tell in the way they protected each other, the way they spoke to each other. She folded her arms across her chest and turned to look at the space. This room and those she'd been in on the lower floors had been filled with pictures and mementos of the life of a family, and it made her feel alone. She wanted to have a life like this. She wanted the love and family; she deserved all of it.

She wanted memories of vacations with a loving, doting family who had time for her, other than as a pawn in their constant power struggles. She deserved a room like this with her monogram on bath towels and inlaid in the marble bathroom floor in gold filigree, a wardrobe full of expensive designer clothing. She deserved the protection and adoration, everything that the precious Caelestis had been given since her birth. She had been born into privilege, as the progeny of the primordial and was seen as such. Even after her ordeal in hell, she had been placed on a pedestal, an extraordinary being in a world of the incredible.

"What are you doing in here?" Lilith turned to see who had spoken to her and found Lisette Kent standing in the doorway, her eyes narrowing as she stared at the intruder. Lisette was beautiful. There was no denying that, with honey-blond hair, tawny skin, and eyes as sharp and focused as a jungle cat's, she had an air of superiority about her that was disconcerting. Though she only stood five foot six, she filled the room with her presence, and Lilith found herself taking a step back even though the other woman remained on the other side of the room. Lisette wore a black sheath dress, not leather for once, but cool linen. Her chunky bracelets clinked together as she folded her arms across her chest and tapped the toe of her strappy heeled sandals, and waited for an excuse.

"Well?" She waited, and Lilith managed a smile that she hoped appeared genuine.

"Sorry, I got turned around in this place. I was told there was a powder room up here. I guess I should have known that this wasn't the right place." She giggled. Lisette was not fooled; she stared. Expressionless.

"Explain why you were in my room then?" she asked, and Lilith would have gone pale if she weren't already deathly white. Her smile faltered, but only slightly.

"I... I have no idea what you're talking about. Why would I be in your room?"

"That's exactly what I want to know." She moved so quickly that Lilith was nearly knocked backward by the sudden closeness. Lisette stood just a few inches above her, but she felt as if she were looking up at her as if she'd grown on her swift journey across the room. She was prettier up close in a surprising way. Everything about her seemed to be illuminated. Her eyes were brilliant amber, and her teeth blindingly white as she sneered at the little demon. Her fangs were exposed, and the irises of her eyes darkened to a sparkling bronze.

"You're not as cute or as clever as you think you are. I see you for exactly what you are." She snarled, and Lilith had to steel herself against the urge to run. If she ran, Lisette would tear into her. She knew it. She was a hunter. She could smell it on her, a true alpha female Dhampir if she had ever seen one. Lisette Kent was more frightening than any other member of the overprotective Kent clan, and she would kill her just as soon as look at her.

"The guest powder room is on the first floor. Arbor is waiting for you in the sitting room. I suggest you return that ring in your pocket before you join her." Lisette turned and walked away, not waiting for the denial she knew was coming.

Lilith stared after her for a while, then exhaled the air that had collected in her lungs. She hadn't realized that she was holding her breath or that she'd locked her knees until they buckled. She leaned forward, a hand on the back of the velvet sofa, the other retrieving the ring from her pocket.

She stared at the yellow diamond, watching it catch the moonlight before returning it to its place among Celeste's other forgotten babbles, and sighed. She glanced around the room once more before closing the door on a dream. She wanted this place, these things, and this life. She was going to have everything that Celeste had and more. She deserved this life, earned it, and by the gods, she would have it all.

Even if she had to take it.

CHAPTER TWELVE

"Celeste, please, I didn't live for a thousand years so that you could kill me in a fiery car crash," he said. She looked at Karim, his fingers leaving deep indentations in the leather of her dashboard, his face tight and drawn. His entire body was one tensed muscle, from his jaw down to his toes.

She looked at the speedometer then and realized just how fast she was going. She was pushing the car near one hundred, and he expected to see the flashing lights of a police cruiser behind them at any moment. She eased off the accelerator and felt Karim relax beside her. Silently, he reached for her hand, lacing his fingers with hers, kissing her knuckles. It was her turn to relax when she felt the brush of his warm lips on her skin. She smiled as the shivers began at the base of her spine, but the throbbing in her neck intensified as well. That dull ache she'd been dealing with for weeks now had amped up to a pulsating throb.

"Sorry," she mumbled and took several deep breaths.

He didn't know what else he could say to her to ease her anxiety. He'd tried to calm her when she dialed Arbor and got her voice mail. She'd tried each family member and received the same. Her frustration got the better of her when she'd dialed Nicky and received nothing in response. She'd even contacted his assistant, Katie, who tried to cover for him, barely. Katie had sighed in exasperation before admitting that she had spent less time with Nicky than usual, and she didn't know if he'd seen or even spoken to the erstwhile Kent progeny.

Karim had tried to alleviate her fears, but she wouldn't be

satisfied until she found her brother. Remy never disappeared for this long, and he never ignored Arbor's calls. Nor would he disappear from her life without a call or email, something to let her know what he was doing. Sure, he was known to take off, but he always stayed in contact.

But most importantly, if Remy had professed his love, something he swore he would never do, he wouldn't just leave Briar behind. The thing about Remy is that he was half sylph, a nature element, and half Dhampir, both of whom, once mated, stayed that way. Something was wrong; she could feel it.

She rubbed her neck, the brand on her skin hot and achy. She had been promised to someone she didn't know and didn't love. The man she loved had yet to mark her as his own, to let the world know that she was his and his alone. It was odd; most preternatural males were a misogynistic bunch, possessive to the point of obsession. When they claimed a lover as their mate, it was worn almost like a badge of pride to say this is mine and mine alone.

Why hadn't Karim marked her? When they made love, she could feel his need, but he always stopped as if he weren't sure. Perhaps he didn't feel her worthy enough to bear his mark, she thought. She glanced at Karim, who was looking at her in the darkness of the car. She could see his cool pale green eyes in the dimness, his expression unreadable.

"It will be fine, *azizam*," he said, and she managed a tight smile. She didn't know if he was referring to her missing brother or his failure to claim her.

* * *

Karim looked out the window, watching the trees fly by while Celeste navigated in the darkness. Celeste relaxed more as they cleared the trees and eased onto a blacktopped road that seemed to spring up out of nowhere. Path lights set in the ground on either side of the narrow road illuminated their route, and he could make out a guard shack and a large stone fence fitted with searchlights in the distance.

They rolled past the guard shack. The wrought iron gate opened even before they approached the small hut on the edge of the property. They sailed past a helicopter pad and what felt like three miles of immaculate lawns before reaching the circular driveway at the front of the house. House was an understatement; it was a neo-gothic chateau that looked as if it belonged in a fairy tale. There were balconies on the second and third floors wrapped around the building's perimeter and at least six chimneys that he could see. All it needed was a princess locked in one of those turret towers, gazing longingly at the horizon.

He caught Celeste's hand and looked at her for a moment. She was wearing a threadbare t-shirt and dark denim jeans that had seen better days and a pair of beat-up old Chuck Taylor Converse sneakers. He supposed she was the princess, even though she looked more tomboy than a damsel in distress. She ran a nervous hand over her ponytail and chewed her bottom lip, a nervous habit he'd noticed.

"Understated," he said, and she smiled.

"It's Castle *De Noe*, built in the 17th century in Perche. Arbor loved it so much when we lived in France that Jonas had it moved here, brick by brick. I know it's a monster, but it's been home for four hundred years." He nodded and followed her up the stone steps to the ornately carved double wooden doors.

"Are you sure they didn't just lose Remy in the house somewhere?" he asked, and she laughed. It was the first chuckle he'd gotten out of her in a few hours. The sound lifted his mood a little, making it easier to face her family and whatever was happening now.

Before she could touch the handle to let herself in, the heavy wooden door was opened by a man who looked as if he could have been anywhere between sixty and ninety years old. He was tall, standing with a straight back, his white hair neat and brushed away from a slightly wrinkled face that could only be described as aristocratic. He wore a black morning suit, complete with a gold double-breasted vest and black and gold polka-dotted necktie. When he saw Celeste, his colorless eyes lit up, and he looked younger.

"Madam, you're here. Thank the gods," he said, and she smiled, releasing Karim's hand long enough to embrace the older man. Karim stared at him and realized that he wasn't a man. He was fae. He looked human, except for the slightly pointed ears and fangs, which weren't demonic, vampiric, or even divine like Celeste's. Yet, he was fae, which kind Karim had no idea, some sort of faery he assumed, but fae, nonetheless. And very devoted to Celeste.

"Good to see you too, Frederick," she said. "This is Karim, Karim -Frederick. Frederick is a Hugtandalf. He takes care of us all."

Karim's brow rose. A Hugtandalf was a Danish elf, they didn't age, and they held a great deal of magic, but no one had ever known how they harnessed or manifested that power. They were a secretive bunch and rarely moved beyond their small villages in the countryside of Denmark.

"Where is everyone?" Celeste crossed the threshold into the two-story foyer, Karim on her heels.

"They are in the sitting room, madam. And they have that creature with them." He made a face, his eyes darting left and right as if he were afraid someone might sneak up behind him. "That demoness," he whispered, and she nodded.

Karim followed her, his fingers linked with hers through the foyer. He stared up at the massive chandelier that glittered against the gold-leaf ceiling, complete with sculpted cherubs in the molding. The floors were imported marble; the staircase had beautifully handcrafted ivory banisters, which matched the steps' cream-colored marble. The walls were painted in warm hues of gold, cream, and brown. He could smell the magic in this place. It reeked of it. No wonder Celeste had been trusted with the Kents. This place was like a strong military hold. She had spent her last few years in a virtual fortress.

Frederick led them into the sitting room, bowing as he left as quickly and as quietly as he'd come. The golden room was cool, lit by soft amber light. There were soft beige rugs on the marble floors and a bright red chenille sofa and love seat. Red Queen Anne chairs were facing the dormant fireplace and an antique chess set that was rarely used anymore. Photos and artwork filled the room, along with the scent of fresh summer flowers that had been brought in from the garden. Celeste gave Karim a gentle tug forward, and he followed her, his eyes scanning the faces in the room.

When she entered, each of her family members was in quiet conversation and paid no attention to the new arrivals. Jonas sat with his arm around Arbor, who looked tired and worried but no worse for wear. She was Arbor Kent, after all. Other than tired eyes, she was just as radiant as ever. Jonas looked haggard; the grey at his temples had spread, peppering his dark hair with strands of silver. Lisette and Gaston sat opposite their parents in matching armchairs. Gaston had a cool, detached look about him, but then he always looked that way. The only thing to hint at his worry was the fact that, for once, he wasn't in a suit. Instead, Gaston wore blue jeans and a polo shirt. She hadn't even known her older brother owned a pair of jeans. And sneakers, he was wearing a pair of Air Jordan sneakers. Did he even know who Michael Jordan was? Hell, did he even watch basketball, she wondered.

Lisette was sitting with a glass of red wine in her hand, her eyes on the person sitting in the shadows of the room away from the rest of the family. Celeste followed her line of vision and saw her then, Lilith. She was dressed in a full white skirt and bright green halter, her hair brushed away from her pale face in sweeping waves, and Celeste thought something about her appearance was off. She wasn't sure what it was, but there was a definite oddity to her already bizarre appearance. Karim's fingers tightened on her hand, and without looking at him, she knew he'd spotted her as well. She had her eyes down, as if she were afraid to meet Lisette's eyes, not that she could blame her. Lisette had a withering stare that made the blood run cold.

"Oh, thank the gods, Celeste." Arbor was on her feet and coming towards them, her face spreading into a radiant smile. She looked better already, Celeste thought, releasing Karim's hand so she could embrace her mother. Jonas stood and ran a hand over his hair, his smile tight and tired. They each hugged her, Gaston lifting her off her feet in a bear hug before greeting Karim. Lisette stood back, staring at them, her eyes narrowing before a sly smirk tilted the corners of full pink lips. Karim recaptured her hand, his eyes on Celeste, who let the remaining tension in her body drift away. It was as if his touch had soothed her. Lisette noticed. Lisette noticed everything.

She gave Celeste a nearly imperceptible nod of approval. Before tilting her head toward the demon. She was standing now, just behind the sofa, her white eyes boring into Celeste as if she were trying to memorize her face.

"You've met Lilith. I take it? She's become Arbor's shadow over the past couple of weeks." Lisette reclaimed her seat, watching Lilith come forward, her tiny white hand outstretched in greeting and her lips parted in a predatory smile.

"It's a pleasure to meet you, Caelestis finally. We didn't get a chance at the Collective. I've heard so much about you. Arbor speaks of you so often I feel as if I know you already," she spoke in a husky, rushed voice. It wasn't what Celeste expected from her. She expected something light, flirty, and if she were honest, a little ditzy, not so deep and sultry. Celeste didn't take her hand; instead, she just stared at her, her face blank. Lilith lowered her hand, her smile faltering a little.

"Karim." She nodded toward him, and he returned the gesture, his face a stony mask of indifference.

"Tea, madam." Frederick was at Celeste's side, holding a tray laden with Arbor's silver tea service. Lilith and Karim jumped, but no one else seemed to notice that the butler had appeared out of thin air. He gave Celeste a wink before placing the tray on the coffee table. Looking for something to do, Lilith moved with him, pouring tea for Arbor and Jonas.

"So," Celeste and Karim claimed the leather love seat opposite the fireplace as their own. "What is happening with Remy?" She refused the cup of tea Lilith held out for her, her eyes on Arbor, who sipped from her cup and made a face.

"Sorry, I forgot the honey," Lilith said meekly, holding a small bowl and a honey dipper over Arbor's cup. She finished and gathered her cup of tea before perching on the arm of the sofa. She reminded Celeste of a parrot resting on Arbor's shoulder, ready to swoop down and serve whatever need Arbor might have.

"We can't find him," Gaston sighed. "No one has seen or heard from him for weeks now."

"Did you check his apartment?" Celeste asked.

"Of course, we did. I even asked the concierge to call me if he made an appearance, but nothing. And, of course, we can't get Nicky on the phone. So, he's missing too." Arbor held her tea-cup up to her lips, then brought it back to her lap. Celeste watched Lilith's eyes follow the delicate china cup with interest, and she found it unsettling.

"Nicky isn't missing," Celeste said distractedly. "He's on tour. Remember I told you he would be in Japan for a few weeks."

"You were also supposed to go with him. Why didn't you?" Arbor asked, her eyes moving from Celeste to Karim then back again. She knew the answer to that question. Celeste could just about make out her murky thoughts. Arbor's mind was not as closed as everyone else's.

"We disagreed. And now Nicky won't return my calls," Celeste mumbled.

"About him." Arbor nodded towards Karim.

They both nodded.

Arbor thought about that, her mind running through several scenarios that Celeste had a hard time tracking. Arbor had an erratic way of thinking; her train of thought seemed to run through six or seven things, none of which connected to the other. Celeste thought listening to her thoughts was like trying to capture chunks of air with a butterfly net. She stared at Karim and sighed, her mind seeming to wind down to focus on the most prominent thoughts. Remy was missing and needed to be found, and Nicky was family. And Celeste was the key to them all.

"Can you still track him? Nicky, I mean? Since you've fed from him?" Jonas was saying, but another voice had invaded Celeste's mind. It was clear, strong, and focused, so loud it was almost as if she'd thought it herself. It was repeating over and over, a relentless mantra of one sentence, the noise slicing through her brain, making her eyes blur. The sudden invasion ignited the pain in her neck, sending waves of shooting pain from the back of her head to her brow.

Drink the tea, and it'll be fine. Drink the tea, and it will all be fine. Drink the tea, drink the tea, drink the tea. She could hear the words and wasn't sure if they were being said out loud or just echoing in her head. Suddenly, there were more voices, more thoughts. Some of them were clear as if several conversations were going on right in this room; others were as if they were speaking underwater, but they were all ear-piercing. Someone was touching her. She was aware of that, but not who the hand belonged to. She could see someone coming close, and then she was looking up at them. Had she fallen on the floor? She wondered as the world axis was tilted. She could taste blood, thickly sweet and somewhat metallic, filling her mouth.

There was a movement in the room, faces blurring until they were nothing more than faded images of her family. She turned, not hearing but feeling that Karim was stirring beside her. She turned to face him and was blinded by pain. She couldn't hear anything other than the voice, worried and strained ringing in her head, the pain in her neck burning, twisting into the base of her spine. She blinked, trying to reclaim her vision, but everything was coated in a haze of red.

Karim was standing over her, his eyes wide and his mouth moving, but there was no sound, only that voice that was so loud, so close that it could have been her own but wasn't.

The tea, the tea, drink the tea, it'll all be fine drink the tea, the tea the tea. Then everything was dark.

* * *

Celeste had tensed next to him, her eyes glassy, and she was mumbling. He looked at Arbor, who had just placed her empty teacup on the tray when Celeste's nose began to bleed, and her body convulsed.

"CeCe?" Lisette was on her feet, the closet to her sister; she closed the space between them in one step. Karim grasped Celeste's head, trying to get her to focus, but she stared blankly at him, her brow furrowed.

"What's happening?" Arbor was nearly hysterical, and Jonas was moving across the room. Karim couldn't answer; all he could do was look at her, his heart hammering in his chest. He thought he'd been scared with Celeste driving like a maniac, but that paled in comparison to the white-hot terror that gripped him now.

"Celeste, *azizam,* look at me. Calie, focus. Calie." She didn't respond, her body going limp in his arms. He was trying to hold her, but she wilted off of the love seat and onto the rug, her eyes darting rapidly from side to side though she wasn't seeing anything.

"What's happening?" Arbor was asking. "What's wrong with her?" Karim shrugged, his eyes never straying from Celeste, whose eyes had taken on a washed-out watery look. She groaned as if she were in pain, clutching his arms as she tried to say something. He was speaking, but he didn't think she could hear him. He stroked her hair and tried to calm her as much as he was trying to calm himself. His body had broken out in a cold sweat, and his breathing was labored as he tried to tamper down his rising panic.

"Love, look at me. You're going to be okay," he was saying when the second series of convulsions began. This time her body thrashed violently, her legs kicking the coffee table over and sending the tea service scattering across the room. Karim vaguely remembered someone yelling, and he could feel Arbor drop to her knees beside him, her hands-on Celeste's chest. There was a flurry of movement and sound, but all he could focus on was Celeste, who lay helplessly on the floor.

"The tea! The Tea! The Tea! The Tea!!!Tea tea tea teateateateatea!!!" Celeste screamed in a voice that wasn't hers. It was hoarse, guttural, almost demonic, sending a chill through the room and pausing Lisette and Arbor in their advance. Tears slid from her eyes, and she reached out, blindly searching. Karim grasped her fingers, bringing them to his lips. She arched her back, her body bowing as she struggled to breathe.

"Celeste." She was making choking noises as if she couldn't get air into her lungs. Karim's eyes filled with tears, his heart racing as he realized that she wasn't moving, and there was no rise and fall of her chest. He leaned closer, listening for breath, but there was nothing.

"Celeste?" He gave her a gentle shake, but she remained still, limp, her heartbeat slowing.

"She's not breathing," he said, pressing on her chest. "She's not breathing!" More movement, more people in the room suddenly crowding the space, and she was being taken from him and lifted into thin arms clad in a dark morning suit. He watched in stunned silence as Frederick held Celeste against his chest with one arm, her limbs dangling limply. She looked like a full-sized rag doll, swaying in his thin arms. Frederick held her face, opening her mouth with slim, elegant fingers, his mouth hovering above hers. It looked as if he were going to kiss her, and Karim felt irrational rage burn through him. Arbor placed a hand on his arm, and he settled.

Frederick didn't kiss her. Instead, he exhaled, breathing a mist, pale and glowing, into Celeste's waiting mouth. Everyone in the room stilled, waiting for something, anything, to happen. She suddenly inhaled a great gulping gasp, followed by a series of coughs. Frederick whispered something in a language Karim did not understand, and her breathing leveled, her body still. He looked at Arbor, who still held his biceps in a death grip, and she relaxed, breathing a sigh of relief, easing the tension in the room. Frederick lifted Celeste's taxed and wearied body into his arms, cradling her like a child against his chest.

"She will be fine. She must rest. She will also need to feed quite a bit. I will take her up to her bedroom, madam," Frederick spoke to Arbor, who'd gone pale. She nodded, and he left the room, Celeste's lethargic but breathing body in his arms. They remained still for a while, just collecting themselves after the chaos

"What was that?" Lisette breathed, clutching her throat.

"Has she ever done that before?" Arbor asked Karim, and he shook his head numbly.

"No, she has the occasional nightmare and a few dreams, but nothing like that. Never that," he said. Lilith moved, slowly righting the overturned coffee table. Her movements were tentative as if she were trying not to be seen, her blood-red eyes matching the vivid color of her hair. Karim turned to look at her, his fangs extended and his eyes glowing a deep hunter green.

"You!" he bit, trying to contain his growing fury. "What did you do?" Arbor tried in vain to hold him back, but his rage had taken control. Gaston and Jonas blocked his path, their hands held up to slow his charge, but Karim was much stronger than even the two. He easily pushed them aside, aware enough not to harm them, knowing he could cut through them if he wanted. He was one of the *Seven*, an original vampire prince. There were very few creatures alive or dead that could tamp his anger.

Lilith stumbled backward, her irises bleeding from red to white, her lips trembling from sheer terror. She sidestepped a chair, her hands searching blindly for some sort of protection. She had learned from their last meeting that her magic did not affect Karim; without someone intervening, there was no stopping him.

He grasped her upper arms, lifting her into the air, turning over tables and chairs, making her lose a shoe before slamming her body against the wall hard enough to dislodge art and photographs. Several crashed to the ground, glass shattering and spreading across the marble floor like chunks of ice. He was cursing her in his native tongue, the words foreign to her, but she knew a curse when she heard one, no matter the language.

"You evil little twit, tell me what you did, or I will rip your throat out." He growled, his mouth dangerously close to her face. He shook her, her feet dangling, her remaining shoe falling to the floor. She fought, her nails clawing at his face, but he easily avoided her, his teeth lengthening even more.

"I didn't do anything!" She screamed, trying to kick him away from her, his fingers digging into her arm, cracking the delicate bones beneath.

"You did something. That was why you were sent to get close to her. Why?" He pressed harder, his hands like steel bands around her biceps, enjoying the sound of her bones splintering.

"I don't know what you're talking about! I didn't do anything!" she screamed, and tears rolled down her cheeks. He stared into her bulging eyes and repeated his question, this time through clenched teeth. He banged her head against the wall again, sending more expensive, pretty things crashing to the floor and cracking the wall in the process. The lights shook, and there was a rumble behind him, people coming into the room, he assumed, but Lilith had his full attention.

"What did you do? Why are you here? You can answer, or you can die. Either outcome is fine by me. Why did they send you?" He growled.

"I never did anything to her! I didn't do anything! I don't

know what you're talking about!" She stared at him, her lips trembling, her breathing harsh gasps, pain running through her broken shoulders. When she didn't answer, he lowered his mouth, his teeth sinking into the delicate white flesh of her throat. It hurt, stinging like hot blades being sunken into tender flesh. He twisted, making sure she felt every ounce of pain. He widened his mouth until his bottom teeth pushed on the gentle bones of her larynx.

She could feel the pressure of his jaws closing in on her, and breathing became harder, her mouth filling with the taste of her blood. He was crushing her, pushing his body into hers until she could feel her ribs cracking one by one, her thin frame nearly hidden by him. She couldn't move, she couldn't breathe, and the terror left her whimpering helplessly, unable to fight against him. There was a startled gasp from someone at his back, but Karim was not going to stop until she either confessed or died. Blood, thick, dark cloying and smelling of sulfur rolled down her skin, staining her top and dripping onto the floor; the pain was unbearable, and he could feel her heart rate triple.

"The mark!" She screeched. "She wanted to know if she had the mark! That's all! I wasn't to touch her, I wasn't to hurt her, and I didn't. All she wanted to know was whether or not she had the mark!"

CHAPTER THIRTEEN

When Karim released her, Lilith had fallen to the floor in a bloody and broken heap like a marionette whose strings had been cut. Cowering in the corner, she watched the vampire with wide, terrified eyes. He looked truly horrifying, his thick dark hair hanging in his face, shielding his malevolent glowing eyes, his blood-stained fangs still exposed as if he were ready to attack her again. He wiped the blood from his lips with the back of his hand and stalked away from her as if he were unable to look at her without attacking.

Arbor placed a calming hand on his chest, her eyes meeting his in silent understanding, and then she stepped aside so that he could follow Lisette to Celeste's room. There was not much discussion while Jonas and Gaston silently righted the room, and Arbor spoke to house staff in hushed tones. They practically ignored the crushed girl in the corner until Gaston gingerly gathered her in his arms and followed his mother and father to a second-floor guest room.

* * *

"I didn't do anything to her." Lilith croaked, then flinched. "I didn't do anything that would hurt her." Arbor glanced back at her, giving her a tight smile but said nothing. Gaston placed her on the bed, carefully arranging her so that she sat with her back against the white headboard, her feet, one still missing a shoe, on top of the navy and white striped comforter. He looked at her, his face completely void of any emotion, his deep brown eyes on her bloodied neck. He met her eyes, staring long enough to make her uncomfortable before smirking and leaving the room. Jonas was speaking to Arbor in a corner, quiet and serious. She kissed his cheek, nodding her agreement to something Lilith had not heard, and then he too left the room.

Lilith hurt all over. Her arms, back, and neck were bruised a deep purple, blood had caked on her healing neck wound, and her head throbbed from being slammed into the wall. She swallowed, feeling the burn in her raw throat, still tasting blood and smelling of sulfur.

"You were sent here to spy on Celeste." Arbor said matter-of-factly, "I knew you were here for something. I just wasn't sure what, but it makes sense now. The Queen wants to know if the prophecy is true, correct?"

Lilith would have shrugged if her bones had mended, but they had not, not yet anyway. She tried to shift her body but flinched when she awoke the pain that had settled over her like a warm ache.

"Okay, so why did you stay? You know she has the mark, you could have taken that information and gone on, yet you continued to come around. Why did you come back, Lilith? Why would you continue to stay around my family once your task was complete?" Arbor asked, standing at the foot of the bed, her eyes doing a mental inventory of Lilith's wounds.

"Because ... you made me feel like I belonged. Like you liked me. I never had that; I wanted to stay around a family that likes one another. She said no harm would come to Celeste. She just wanted to know. She wanted to know if she was as beautiful as rumored if she was as fierce a fighter. That's all." Tears began streaming down her cheeks, and Arbor softened. She came to sit at Lilith's bedside, gently easing onto the mattress in an effort not to jostle her. She took one pale, limp hand in her warm tawny one, her brown eyes meeting white, and smiled.

"I understand, dear," she said, her voice hypnotic and melodic. Lilith saw something then; a pallor fell over Arbor's sun-kissed skin, washing her out. She looked sick, then it passed, and she was smiling again, her smile as warm and welcoming as always, and Lilith relaxed, her pain ebbing.

"You are welcome here, sweetheart, just like the rest of my children. I will look after you. I will send someone up to help you get cleaned up and to make sure you are comfortable. Don't fret. You will be fine." She stroked Lilith's cheek before rising and slowly crossing the room, her steps forced, stilted like she was unsure. She stopped at the door, turning to give Lilith a curious look before closing the door behind her.

Once the click of Arbor's heels faded down the hall, Lilith waited for a tick more until she was sure no one else was coming to this seascape explosion of a room. When she was satisfied, she rose and stretched, rolling her shoulders with ease. Her bones made soft clicking noises as they snapped painlessly back into place. She kicked off her remaining shoe and went to inspect her reflection in the mirror.

Karim had done a job on her alright. She was black and blue, her neck a raw red mess where he'd chewed on her, but the punctures were healing nicely. She sighed, her hair, her poor beautiful hair was a mess, and her top was ruined. Demon blood not only stained, it burned, and she could see the scorched path of her blood on the Kelly-green cotton.

She hadn't known how Celeste had read her mind or what the hell had happened to her. The seizures were terrifying, and she had been scared that maybe their precious goddess was dead. She had been for a little while- if only she'd stayed that way. But then Celeste never made anything easy. She ran a hand over her rat's nest of a hairdo before turning away to look at the small room she'd been sequestered in; it wasn't bad. It wasn't like the other Kent siblings' suites, but it was pretty enough, and she could deal with the nautical theme. For now.

She touched her bruised arms and shoulder and thought of the vampire. He had been in a full-on animal rage, his restraint barely holding as he throttled her. She had known he cared for Celeste, but to see him so viciously protective of her, his muscled body tense with fury, was very telling. She wondered if he were that passionate about his lovemaking. No matter, Celeste's time was ending as the lady of the manor; it would soon be Lilith's turn to pick up the mantel. Celeste had survived whatever had happened to her, but that was fine.

It didn't matter anyway; her plan had worked, after all. Arbor drank the tea, and soon Lilith would be established as the center of the Kent family. She would be a better daughter to Arbor than Celeste ever was, and Arbor would adore her. The potion she'd slipped into her tea when she'd added the honey had already taken effect. She could see the subtle changes in Arbor when she looked at her. It wouldn't be long now.

She heard footsteps getting louder on the hallway's marble floor outside of her room and returned to her position on the bed. She had managed to look acceptably pitiful by the time two youngish women in white entered, looking at her with large pitying eyes. They silently moved about the room, preparing a bath, and inspecting her wounds. She managed to produce the winces and flinches needed as they undressed her, tears rolling from dry eyes. They would share looks of pity over her head with the discovery of each new bruise. Sympathy had always been one of her weapons; *appearing* tiny and frail always helped with the impression of helplessness.

Lilith Prince Kent. No, *Lilith Kent,* she thought as the women moved her from the bed, careful of her broken arms and bruised body, slowly walking her to the small bathroom within the suite. Why give her father any claim to her? She was leaving that behind her, just as he'd left her. She could go the Celeste route and use Arbor's Americanized human name, *Lilith Keegan Kent, heir to the High Regent of the Collective.* Yes, she decided, that had a very nice ring to it indeed.

* * *

Celeste moaned and rolled onto her side, feeling as if she were going to be sick. Her stomach rumbled, and her head felt ready to explode. She could hear voices, hushed and anxious, from somewhere nearby and tried to force her eyes open. The lights, though low, made her eyes burn, and she groaned, rolling onto her stomach so that she could cover her head with a pillow.

"It lives," Lisette teased. She sat on the bed, her hand on Celeste's back.

"Turn off the lights," she mumbled through her pillow. There were some movement and a tap on her back, letting her know that the lights had been dimmed. She rolled onto her side and felt her stomach protest and her head pound. Lisette held out a juice glass filled with something dark. Celeste frowned, not wanting to drink anything; her stomach was bound to revolt.

"Take it," her sister insisted. She struggled to sit up and took the glass reluctantly; her expression would have mirrored her annoyance if her head didn't feel like a parade had just high stepped across her brain. The glass, she realized at once, was full of fresh, warm blood. Her stomach may have been enacting a revolt, but her mouth watered at the smell. She closed her eyes and inhaled the scent, then brought it to her lips and drank. Suddenly, she had a monstrous thirst, draining the glass in one gulp.

"More," she breathed, wiping her mouth with the back of her hand.

"More? Okay." Lisette silently took the empty glass, her perfectly arched brows lifting in amusement, and went to ring the kitchen for more. When she rose from the bed, Celeste looked at the others in the room. Gaston and Arbor were in her sitting area, and their heads close together as they talked. The curtains were drawn so that she couldn't tell the time of day, but by the heat that radiated from the windows on one side of the room, she figured it was late afternoon. Her bedroom faced the east, and the sun was always on this side of the house at that time of day. She looked around the room; nothing was out of place, everything was clean and neat, but something was wrong. She looked to her left and noted the clear outline of a body, and caught the faint hints of the ocean.

"Where's Karim?" she asked, clearing her throat. Her voice sounded rusty to her ears. Arbor looked at her, a smile on her face as usual. She moved across the room, but even in her groggy state, Celeste could tell that something was wrong. Arbor was a glider. She moved with an effortless grace that made it seem like she floated on air. Today, she was struggling. She looked thinner, her normal perfection off. Celeste supposed it was the strain of Remy being missing and, of course, her little incident, which she could only partially recall.

"He's in a safe room, down the hall. We had to make him sleep and feed. He's been beside himself with worry. He's resting now," Arbor assured. "You've been asleep for four days."

Celeste was astonished. Four days?

"I don't know what you did to him, but that boy has it bad. He stayed at your bedside like a whipped puppy and refused even to shower until you woke up," Gaston teased, tossing a robe to her. She snatched it out of the air, sighing and shaking her head.

"I know exactly what she did to him," Lisette said with a wink. "And I approve." Celeste slipped the silky robe on and prepared to stand when Arbor placed a hand on her shoulder. She would find Karim and lay with him in the safe room to make sure he knew that she was okay. Even in his death-like sleep, he would know she was there.

"No, you don't. You need to rest. You nearly died, Celeste." Arbor's perfect face, for the first time, was showing lines of age. Her hair, normally thick chestnut, seemed thinner, her eyes had faded to the color of whiskey instead of the rich chocolate they had been before. Celeste reached up and stroked a cheek that was surprisingly cold and dry.

"Are you feeling okay?" she asked. From the corner of her

eye, she saw Lisette stiffen. Gaston also managed to look relaxed and tense at once, his eyes hooded. Of course, Celeste thought, she was worried. Her little stunt had only added to Arbor's anxiety.

"Have you heard from Remy? What about Nicky? What happened to me? Lilith." She snarled the demon's name, her headache singing to life as the memories of Lilith came back to her. She remembered watching her while they discussed Remy being AWOL; she remembered the tea brought in, and someone invading her mind. Not just invading, taking over completely, screaming into her until she thought her head would split open from the volume and intensity.

"We haven't heard from Nicky or Remy. Nicky still isn't returning calls, being a diva, I guess. Jonas is commanding the Grey in your absence; he has that Briar tracking Remy. He's very dedicated." Celeste nodded and smiled. She had no idea just how dedicated Briar was, but Celeste had the feeling Jonas did.

"We have people looking, but..." Arbor shrugged, her eyes filling with tears. She inhaled and tried to smile. It was strained and tight and made her look even older and somehow, frail. The worry over her children was taking its toll, the errant Remy and the psychotic Celeste, what a pair they made, she thought.

"What happened?" she asked when no one said anything. Lisette sighed and looked at the other two before she spoke. She replayed the night's events to her, ignoring Celeste's horrified gasps at the knowledge that she had nearly died. Her body had lain lifeless on the floor until Frederick saved the day.

"I always knew Frederick was a freakin' superhero," she sighed.

"Then, once he carried you away, your male went absolutely ape-shit on Lilith. I thought he was going to shove her through the wall and rip her throat out if she didn't talk." Gaston said, rather admiringly. Karim had managed to impress two stone-faced critics in Lisette and Gaston.

"Did she?" She hadn't realized that she was clutching her robe in a knot at her chest.

"She did," Arbor nodded. "She was sent by the Dark Queen to report about your mark." Celeste absently touched her neck, feeling the raised flesh there. It was sore, but not pained, not really, not anymore.

"And?" Celeste asked

"And nothing. That was all she did," Arbor said, brushing a stray curl off of Celeste's face.

"But the bigger question is," Lisette sat next to Arbor on the bed, "what happened to you?" That was the question, indeed. Celeste rubbed her forehead and tried to recall what had triggered the voices.

"It was a voice," she said. "In my head, like a siren. It got louder and louder, splitting my skull in half. Then it was everyone, all of this noise, hundreds of voices all at once, these thoughts echoing in my brain until - I don't know what happened." She rubbed her eyes. "I couldn't see or hear anything other than these hundreds of voices, but that one...the one that was so loud it blocked out everything else." She held her head, remembering the fear, the cold terror that washed over her.

"You kept yelling about tea, do you remember that?" Gaston had drifted closer. She shook her head and immediately wished that she hadn't. She groaned and lay back on her pillow, her arm across her eyes.

"Tea? Weren't we drinking tea?" She asked, trying to force a memory, any memory after the voices began. She could only remember the voices, and then something odd popped into her head. She moved her arm and stared at the family members' faces in the room, and Lilith was watching Arbor with an intensity that bordered on obsessive.

"I think Lilith did something to the tea," she said, "Did you drink it? Did any of you drink the tea?" She sat up, ignoring her headache and new nausea that rolled through her. She knew that Gaston and Lisette had not. She wasn't concerned with them. She stared at Arbor, waiting for a response. There was a moment when Celeste received a clear picture of Arbor's thought patterns and found it to be gone. It was as if someone had drawn a shade, and there was a void. It wasn't like Lisette, who telegraphed broken thoughts, bits that crept through, or Gaston who's thinking was completely linear. It wasn't even emotion-based like Karim. It was just a void. Even when she didn't get clear thoughts from those around her, she always had some sort of empathic connection. She rubbed the mark on her neck, hoping to generate some sort of motor in her head like she had the other night when everyone's thoughts bled together in a cacophony of sounds and images. But there was nothing, just a blank, emotionless emptiness that she would have never associated with the warm, gentle heart of the woman who had been her mother for nearly a millennium.

Arbor smiled; it was bright and beautiful, lighting her face, and for a moment, she was herself again. She tucked strands of hair behind Celeste's ear.

"No, dear. You kicked the table over," she said, rising and running a hand over her skirt. "I will go and see what is taking the kitchen so long with that refill." She laughed. "And you need food, maybe soup? Don't want to force anything too heavy." She looked at Gaston and Lisette, motioning for them to follow her. "Come on, let's allow Celeste to get some rest." She leaned over, kissing her on the forehead, and then followed the others out. When she closed the door, Celeste let out the air that had collected in her lungs. If she hadn't heard it, seen it with her own eyes, she wouldn't have believed it. There had been a shadow, slight and rapid, that crossed Arbor's face. If she had not known Arbor, had not been around her for the better part of eight hundred years, she would have never believed it even possible.

She'd asked the question because she'd remembered seeing her sip from that delicate white china cup with pink roses. She'd made a face like she'd tasted something strange in her honey-sweetened tea. Whether she'd known it or not, Arbor had done something she hadn't done in the eight hundred plus years Celeste had known her, something she didn't think Arbor *could* or *would* ever do.

Arbor had lied.

* * *

After eating two bowls of chicken noodle soup and drinking another glass of fresh blood, she had dozed off again. She wondered who was donating, but it was bringing her back to herself quickly. When she rolled over this time, she felt a body next to her. She felt the caress of gentle fingers on her cheek and the smell of the ocean. She opened her eyes to find Karim staring back at her.

"Good night, sunshine," she said, leaning over to kiss him. He held her closer, kissing the top of her head. "Don't ever scare me like that again. What was that?" He asked, feeling her shrug in his embrace.

"I have this thing I can do," she said vaguely. He looked down at her, his brow raised in question.

"Do go on," he said, and she tried to explain her ability to read thoughts. "So, you can read my mind?" he asked when she was done explaining that night. She shook her head.

"No. With preternaturals, it's different. Humans, I can block. I only hear what I want, when I want from humans- preternaturals, not so much. I can feel emotions, bits of images get through, and sometimes a thought or two, but that night I could hear everything crystal clear. It was like someone turned on fifteen hundred radios, each broadcasting a different wavelength at once. It was overwhelming, and one was like a bull horn in my head."

"Is that why you started yelling about tea?" he asked.

"Something was in Arbor's tea. She said she didn't drink it when I asked, but she lied, Karim. I may not remember much about that night, but I remember her drinking that tea. When

I tried to get something from her, there was nothing there. Her mind was blank, empty. Lilith did something to her."

"I think she did something to you, too." He kissed the top of her head, his hands stroking her bare back beneath the covers. "Are you just in your underwear?" He pulled the covers away and looked down.

"Yes. Why don't you join me?" she teased, kissing his neck. "I understand you did something to Lilith."

"I almost killed her," he said. "I have never wanted to kill anyone more in my life. She did something, and she likes to play innocent. I believe she did more than just tell the Dark Queen about your Mark. She's up to something." She nodded against his chest, getting another whiff of the stench that surrounded him like a cloud of funk.

"You smell awful. What is that? Rotten eggs?" She asked, moving away from him.

"I bit Lilith. I was going to rip out her throat, her blood tastes like sulfur, but ..." He stood and stripped out of his shirt, kicked his sneakers and socks off, intent on joining her under the covers. When his hands moved to the fly of his jeans, her eyes drifted down, watching as he released the first two buttons. She licked her lips, her headache suddenly not that big of a deal. She was suddenly in need of something other than food or even blood. Karim cleared his throat and snapped his fingers, making her meet his gaze.

"My eyes are up here, young lady. After what you've been through, you need to feed and rest. Sex should be the last thing on your mind," he said. She got to her knees in the bed, her head still throbbing and her stomach growling from hunger, but she also wanted to hold him, to feel his skin against hers. She kept her eyes on his as she unfastened her bra and let the straps slide down her arms before she tossed it to the floor. She moved her hands down her hips to the lacy elastic of her panties and watched his Adam's apple bob when he swallowed. She slipped out of them and watched his eyes darken, and his fangs extend.

"Should be, but it's not. Right now, you are on the top of my list." She eased off the bed and came closer to him, her blue eyes gleaming in the darkness.

"I don't think we should, *azizam*. You're still weak," he said, without much conviction. She was so close and smelled of vanilla and lavender, that devious smile on her lips. That smile always did it for him.

"I'm sure we can figure out something that wouldn't be too ... strenuous." She ran her fingers across his bare abdomen, caressing the tense muscles, and continued walking past him into the bathroom. He stood for a moment in the dim light cast by the single lamp in the massive room and counted to ten. When he heard the shower start, he abandoned the countdown and his jeans.

* * *

They lay side by side in her bed, the curtains drawn against the late morning sunlight. When they got out of the shower, smelling like flowers and sex, they slipped into bathrobes that had been laid out on the chaise in her dressing room. A late breakfast had awaited them in her sitting area with fresh flowers from Arbor's garden.

"Frederick," Celeste said with a fond smile. Karim had looked at the gourmet breakfast and purple hyacinths, her favorite flower of course, and shook his head. He knew that it was ridiculous, but he still felt a tinge of jealousy whenever he thought of how Frederick had saved her life. He hadn't hesitated when he'd swooped in like a superhero and breathed life into Celeste. Then he'd calmly carried her up to her bedroom, mounting the grand staircase like Rhett fucking Butler.

"Yeah, Frederick," he sniffed. Celeste caught the sarcasm in his voice but said nothing. It didn't matter now, she thought, moving closer to him in the bed.

"But that isn't what I need. I need you," she said, her fangs extending, and he smiled, holding his wrist out to her. She had his wrist to her lips, her teeth buried in clean flesh as she drank, her eyes glowing vivid cerulean. With each pull on his vein, a small involuntary moan escaped him. Celeste reached out, her hand slipping into the folds of his robe, gently stroking him as she fed. He closed his eyes, his fangs extended, and he ached to sink them into her, to taste her, claim her. Yet, he knew that he couldn't, not now.

When she released him, she rolled onto her side, her eyes like beams of light, and her damp hair in dark ringlets around her face. She looked healthier already, her skin smooth and luminous. She was breathing hard, her hand still moving beneath the folds of his robe. She lowered her mouth to his, filling her senses with him. She intensified the velvety petting, and he moaned into her mouth, his arms encircling her and dragging her body closer. She did him one better, straddling him, easing him inside of her. He made a noise, a deep rumble in his chest, his hands buried in her hair, pulling her mouth back to his.

"Do it," she whispered against his lips, then turned her head, exposing her neck. He watched the pulse point jump against tender skin, and he could feel her heart beating, smelled her blood and arousal, and he wanted nothing more. He opened his mouth, grazing her skin with his teeth, but couldn't break the skin. Something was blocking him - stopping him some magic that he had never known. He kissed the skin there, just below her ear, and tried again, and again he was repulsed.

He rolled her onto her back, and her robe opened, exposing naked flesh that smelled of wanting. She lifted her hips, greeting his body as it moved into her, her eyes and hands on his face. He wanted her so much, needed her. He drove harder, trying to lose himself in her. She moaned, encouraging him as he tried again, this time managing to knick her. It was only a knick, a bloodless scrape, and seared him, burning his mouth and throat. It felt as if someone had stabbed the roof of his mouth with a red-hot poker. He growled in frustration and sprinted from the bed.

"Fuuuccckkk," he bellowed and kicked the bedside table over. Celeste sat up, closing her robe, the hurt evident on her face. Karim turned and looked at her, and his heart hurt even more.

"If you don't want to mark me, it's okay." He was back at her side, on his knees, his face buried in her lap.

"I can't." It was a low, hoarse whisper, and she thought, for a second, that he was crying. "I want to make you mine more than anything in this world or the next, Calie. I have always wanted to make you mine, to claim you as my mate. I should have done it all those years ago when I had the chance, but now it's too late."

With a shaky hand, she tilted his head up so she could look into his eyes. She had never seen him cry, not that she could remember. She'd seen him angry, and she'd seen him upset, but this was something new. She slipped off of the bed, kneeling next to him on the floor, her thumb wiping his tears away.

"It's not too late. I love you, Karim, Prince of House of Tyre. I have loved you since you dragged me out of the sea. I loved you when you left me in the desert and when I punched you in the face. I want you to be yours and only yours," she said, her fat tears rolling down her cheeks. She didn't know if it were a culmination of all of the things that had happened over the last two months, her near-death experience, or the fact that the man she loved was inconsolable.

"Mark me, take me as your mate. Please." The last word was barely a whisper, and he crumbled, dragging her into his lap he cradled her, burying his face into her hair.

"I can't mark you. That's why I've never fed from you without you breaking your flesh. I have tried so many times, but I can't," he whispered into her hair. "You have already been claimed."

"He's dead." She said, shaking her head in protest.

"He's not dead, Calie," he said.

"But we don't..." She stopped when she realized what he was saying. She rubbed the mark on her neck, and cold dread washed over her. Once marked, there were only two ways to remove it, one by mutual release, like a human divorce where both parties agreed to part. The other was if the one who made a claim were dead. That would void the claim, releasing her, but she hadn't been released, not in all this time. Even though she had never seen him and could not remember him, the bond remained.

"You are mine," he'd said in her dreams, *"you will always be mine."*

"No," she whispered. Karim couldn't mark her because *The Fallen One* was still alive, and when the time came, he would come and claim her. She held his head, forcing him to meet her eyes, and brushed the hair off his forehead.

"I love you, and I will be yours for as long as we have, marked or mated or not. I am yours, Karim Tyre. For as long as I can be." She lifted her wrist and, with one fang, sliced the flesh and held it to his mouth. "Take from me, as I have taken from you, and we will be as one." She whispered the vow that would bond them as mates.

He drank, deep and long, filling his senses with her as his tears continued. She ran her fingers through his hair, her body reacting to not only the pull of him drinking but the feel of his mouth, hot and hungry, on her wrist. When he finished, he held her face, kissing her with a longing that she had never felt in him before. He held her tight, his arm around her waist as he looked into her eyes.

"I take from you as you have taken from me, and we will be as one," he said, holding her close. *For as long as I can bear it,* he thought.

* * *

"Sweetie, I'm home." Lilith breezed into the apartment that had been Celeste's at the Collective compound. Acquiring the room had been easier than she thought. All she had to do was waltz in with the only son of the High Regent, and just like that, she was on the authorized list to come and go as she pleased. It didn't hurt that she had become Arbor's constant companion, making her transition here much easier than she would have ever believed. All of the Kents were so willing to trust anything Arbor said, blindly following her lead. And she had Arbor Kent wrapped around her petite little finger.

Sighing in satisfaction, she inhaled the sweet scent of lavender that always lingered in this place. Putting her shopping bags on the floor, she kicked the door closed behind her. She loved this place, the clean lines, lack of clutter, sheer beauty, and elegance.

"Wow, it was so hot out there. It must be at least one hundred degrees in the city," she said, making her way across the living room to make herself a drink.

"Hon?" She called but received no response. She looked into the bedroom, half expecting to see him still in bed where she'd left him, but he wasn't. She placed her hands on her hips and began tapping her foot, wondering if he was in one of his foul moods again. He was always in a foul mood.

"Come!" She barked, and he moved across the apartment quickly and silently, his face twisting in anger. He always had an angry scowl lately, she thought. He was dressed in black flannel pajama bottoms and nothing else. He looked tired and in need of a haircut and shave, but she had taken away the razors a few days ago when he'd tried to cut his own throat. That had been a harrowing experience, she'd fallen asleep, and he had managed to get a straight razor. Unable to harm her, he harmed himself. When she found him, he lay on the bathroom floor, a wound at his neck, and poured blood. She'd managed to heal him, but now he was not allowed anything that could be used as a weapon, not for her safety, but his. He stared at her, his eyes shifting from brown to serpentine green to shark-like black.

"Are we pouting today?" she mocked him, tugging at his scraggly beard.

"Get away from me," he mumbled through clenched teeth. She gave his cheek a gentle pat and shook her head.

"If you're nice to me, I will be nice to you," she said. He sat on the sofa, looking her over and smirking.

She wore dark jeans on her slim frame, converse sneakers, and a t-shirt from Nicky Sky's first world tour. Her hair had been straightened and worn in a high ponytail, and her eyes, normally white, were neon blue.

"You can dress like her, live in her room, wear her perfume, but you will never be her. You are a very poor imitation," he snarled, amusement in his voice. "You're pathetic."

"Be nice, Remy. I have great news. Don't ruin my mood. I have just been made heir to the High Regent. Arbor is so sweet. Did you know that she could add a codicil to her will naming her successor? It's iron-clad, completely unimpeachable. She is amazing, almost like a mother..." she said, twirling around the room. Remy snorted.

"You know, it amazes me how you think that what you're doing is acceptable. I guess it shouldn't, though, because it's the only way you could get anyone to spend more than five minutes in your company. You vapid twat."

"Don't make me take your voice away again." She folded her arms across her chest and regarded the way one would a petulant child. He returned her gaze, his eyes shifting to amber, then back to brown. She wasn't going to let him shift until she wanted him to. He glowered at her, his eyes narrowing as he fought against the magic she used to hold him.

"Fuck you," he yelled. She leaned over him, her face close to his, a wicked smile on her face.

"Be nice, love." She kissed him, forcing a response out of him. He hated it, hated the fact that she could manipulate his body, make him yield to her whims. She had made sure she could control every physical aspect of him, but she couldn't touch his mind, and it drove her mad. If he were human, he supposed, she could control his emotions as well, but he was too strong for that. She had managed to get every ounce of information she could about Celeste. She tortured him by making his heart stop, breaking bones, and forcing rapid shifts between human and animal forms that were both painful and draining.

"You know that the moment you release me, I will tear your motherfucking face off and use it to wipe my ass, you psychotic cunt," he said with a sweet smile. Her smile faded, replaced by the ever-present anger that resided just beneath the surface. She grabbed his face, her nails digging into flesh that already sported healing cuts and bruises.

"I warn you, Remy, don't make me do unpleasant things to you," she said.

"Maybe I'll let Karim finish what he started. Maybe this time, he'll crack your fucking head open." He laughed.

"And maybe this time, I'll slice the skin from your thighs. Or better yet, Briar's thighs. Maybe his back, or his face, he has such soft, tender skin, doesn't he? And those eyes, they would look so good in a little glass jar. Or maybe, I'll just cut off his balls and feed them to you. I can get him for you, maybe give you one last night with him before I put his pretty head on a spike. Or maybe, I will take him for a test ride of my own before I slit his throat." She licked her lips and smiled that evil, wicked grin of hers and laughed maniacally. She truly was a psychopath, he thought.

Remy could feel his rage bubbling to the surface, his eyes blackened, and his teeth sharpened to points.

"Oh, are we angry? Well," she motioned with one finger, and he was on his feet. "Let's use that to my advantage." She pointed to the bed, and because he couldn't stop himself, he turned and went to bed. He stripped down to nothing and lay on his back, waiting.

"You're lucky you're such a beautiful boy." She crawled

across the bed, whispering the words she'd whispered so many times before until his body was hard and aching. She straddled him then, forcing him to caress her milky white flesh.

"If not," she sighed, moving her hips over him. "I would have killed you a long time ago." She leaned forward, capturing his mouth, and he closed his eyes, his mind going to the place it always went as she rode him. Tears streamed from the corners of his eyes as he thought of Briar's beautiful emerald eyes, his soft lips, and surprisingly gentle touch.

She bit his chest, grunting and moaning as she rocked against him, forcing him to look at her. He did, but he didn't see her. He saw nothing through the blur of tears and the agony of knowing that he had betrayed everyone: Celeste, Arbor, and most of all, Briar. How would he be able to look him in the face again, to tell him what was done, how she forced him, and how sometimes, not often, but sometimes, it felt good.

CHAPTER FOURTEEN

"I'm going, and that's that," Celeste said, tossing a pair of jeans she hoped were clean into a duffel bag. Lisette stood with her arms folded, watching her, her face a mask of grim determination. Gaston and Karim sat watching the two with detached interest. This argument had been going on for a day and a half now, and Celeste was not to be deterred.

She and Karim had returned to her apartment the night before because Celeste was determined to find her brother. The last contact anyone had with Remy was when he'd called Briar, and since he was AWOL too, Nicky was the only one who might know something. It was only logical that Celeste go to see him since he was a child and ignoring phone calls from the family, the only family he'd ever known.

Lisette, the rational Kent daughter, thought that perhaps she or Gaston should fly to Japan to talk to Nicky. Gaston had agreed that Celeste had just had a near-death experience, and she needed rest.

"I've died before," Celeste reminded him, "that didn't stop me. What makes you think you can?" She stood looking him in the eye. Gaston turned to look at Karim, who held his hands up in surrender. He was sitting on the sofa, the curtains keeping out the afternoon sun. He wore a pair of paint-stained jeans, v neck t-shirt, his feet bare, and in the brilliant color of Celeste's living room, he looked as if he belonged. He also, Gaston noted, looked extremely happy. He'd never seen a happy vampire in his life.

"I gave up this argument hours ago," he said with a smile and winked at Celeste. Gaston looked at her, shrugged, and joined Karim on the sofa. Lisette would not be so easily swayed.

She stood in a sheer flowy floral top and shorts, a very un-Lisette-like fashion choice. But they were in the middle of one of the hottest August's in Louisiana history. Even in the air-conditioned penthouse, the heat was unrelenting. The thermostat struggled to keep the temperature at a comfortable seventy-two degrees.

"If you won't listen to reason, then at least let me come with you. I will have Frederick pack a bag and meet me at the airport. Shit, I have a charity event I'm speaking at tomorrow. I can cancel it." Celeste held up a hand.

"Lisette, I will be fine. I don't need a baby sitter. Besides, you need to look after Arbor with the wicked witch lurking around. She's done enough damage already, and you're the only person she's actually afraid of. Besides, Jonas has been working with the Council to get her out, and Gaston is taking over command of the Grey until I come back. I will go, talk to Nicky, and fly right back. I promise. Two days, 32 hours, and I will be back," she said and hoped that would be enough time to help. Since she'd seen Arbor the afternoon before, she had gotten worse. Her illness overtook her in a matter of hours.

Celeste ran a hand over her tired eyes and tried to remove the image of a disheveled and dazed Arbor passing out in the dining room the night before. She'd risen from her seat at the head of the table to say goodbye to Celeste and Karim as they headed for New Orleans, just after sunset. Arbor looked drawn, her face gaunt and her eyes a sallow hue.

She stumbled, her hand going to the table to regain her balance, and she had gone down, pulling the lace table cloth and all of the dishes, silverware, and that night's dinner onto the floor with her. They had all moved quickly, Jonas gathering her into his arms before she hit the floor, his face that of a helpless man. In all of their years together, he had never seen Arbor ill, not so much as a sniffle, and now she was bedridden. And she had insisted that Lilith not be blamed. She had even gone so far as to allow the manipulative little rat to move into the room across the hall. They'd known, after Celeste's near-death experience, that the tea had been laced. With what, they had no idea, and Lilith wasn't going to implicate herself; even if they knew she was guilty, she wasn't stupid enough to admit it.

"I can keep an eye on her," Lilith had just about purred as Frederick carried her bags into the room. Celeste wanted to punch her in her smug little face, but she hadn't. She had noticed something different about Lilith Prince, a change that she couldn't quite put her finger on. But she didn't have time for that right now. She needed to find her ass of a brother and bring him home, and when she found Remy, she would wring his neck.

"Look, I can't just sit here and wait while you try to figure out what's wrong. Maybe if I can get Remy to bring his skinny ass back here..." She shrugged, not knowing how to finish that sentence. "I know you don't understand, but this is something I have to do," she said, tossing a pair of sneakers and a clean t-shirt into her bag. She stopped and looked down at the pile of clothing, staring back at her.

What she wouldn't tell them, couldn't bear to tell them, was what she knew to be true.

❊ ❊ ❊

Celeste had stormed into the master suite after her encounter with Lilith, her rage bubbling over at not only Arbor, who was in some sort of haze, but at Jonas for allowing such idiocy. She slammed the door closed behind her, knowing Lilith had been hot on her heels and was pleased by the sound of the door crashing into her smug face.

"What the fuck is wrong with you?" She yelled at Jonas, who was sitting on the bed beside Arbor. The light outside was a rainbow of purples and oranges as the sunset, and the room smelled of roses and whiskey. They both turned to look at her, but it was Jonas who spoke first.

"Celeste now is not the time. Lower your voice." He crossed the room, placing his hands on her shoulders. She saw the worry and anger rising in his serene features, and she tried her best to keep her tone low.

"Now is exactly the time. Why would you think it was a good idea to move that demonic Chihuahua into the room directly across the hall from yours? What kind of fucked up logic are you using, Jonas, when it's obvious that she poisoned Arbor? Are you that dense, or am I losing my fucking mind here? Is that it? Have I lost my motherfucking mind, Jonas, or have you?"

Jonas pursed his lips, his face tight with anger at her blatant disrespect. "Watch your language with me, young lady." She narrowed her eyes.

"Now is not the time for daddy dearest, Jonas. Stop acting like a squirrelly twat and tell me what the hell you think you're doing?" He looked back at Arbor, who'd rolled onto her side, her back to them, then pushed Celeste further away until they were standing near the door. She held up a finger to halt his speech before pressing her ear to the wood of the door.

She could hear breathing, slow and steady, just below her shoulder and smiled before jabbing the wood with a closed fist. The door splintered, and there was a yelp from the hallway followed by curses and the slam of the door across the hall. Feeling satisfied, Celeste turned her attention back to Jonas.

"I know you think I'm sitting by while that psychotic troll does whatever it is she's doing, but I assure you I don't trust her. Every eye in this house is on her at all times because I need to know what she did. I need to fix it before it's too late."

She stared at Jonas, watching as his eyes filled with tears and her heart stopped.

"Haven't you felt the change? The weather? The heat? Celeste, Arbor is dying, and we need to stop it. The Council and I have been working non-stop to find something to help, but it only worsens. So, if that means I have to be nice to that scheming *putain* to find out what she gave her, I will. I will be her best fucking friend if she will tell me what she did to my wife. Right now, we need her, but as soon as I can, I will tear her apart." Jonas's calm demeanor had changed, his eyes darkened, and his fangs extended, but he refused to shed a tear.

"We may not find an antidote in time. That's why I need you to help me. Maybe seeing Remy will help her fight until we can find a cure. He will help her fight. He will make her; he's just - if she dies before he sees her -" Celeste held her father, holding back her tears, as she stared at Arbor's back. It was then when she saw it, the skeletal frame silhouetted by the dying light, the frizzy, damaged hair that had patches of shiny scalp showing through, the way her breathing was harsh and strained.

"No, we can't let that happen," she said, kissing Jonas' cheek. She wiped the tears from her cheek. "I'll get Remy back, I promise. He will help her beat this, right?" She didn't believe her own words, but she hoped they at least sounded true to Jonas.

"Right." He sniffed and managed to smile at her. "We will beat this. Now wipe away those tears and come say good night to your mother." He put an arm around her shoulders and walked her back to Arbor, who opened her eyes and managed a smile when they approached.

✳ ✳ ✳

She had to find Remy if only to say goodbye; she'd made a promise, and she intended to keep it. Then she would deal with Lilith, that little demon had no idea what it was like to be on the bad side of the daughter of war and vengeance, but she was going to find out very soon.

"Are you listening to me at all?" Lisette snapped her fin-

242

gers in front of Celeste's face. Celeste grasped her wrist with reflexes so swift that no one saw her move. She looked at a startled Lisette, her expression stony.

"No," she said. "So, stop talking." The tone of her voice made everyone take notice. Karim leaned forward, his lips parting to speak, when Gaston placed a staying hand on his chest and shook his head. Lisette nodded, and her wrist was released. She backed away, swallowing hard and visibly shaken by what she'd read in Celeste's face.

"We'll be waiting in the car," she said, backing away, rubbing her wrist, which had already begun to bruise. Gaston nodded to Karim before following Lisette to the elevator. Celeste never turned to look at them. She continued staring into her bag, her mind a million miles away.

"Are you okay?" he asked, and she managed a nod. "Are you sure? You seemed kind of rough on Lisette."

"I made a promise to Jonas to find Remy. If I can do that, I won't feel so freakin helpless. I'm in medical school, for Christ's sake, and I can't do anything to help," she said.

"Because Arbor is dying." He finished her thought, and she nodded.

"How did you know that?" She asked, leaning back against him. He sniffed her hair, kissing the top of her head, wrapping her in his arms.

"Because I was there when she collapsed, azizam. I saw her, and I could smell death coming for her." She didn't say anything, only held onto his arms around her.

"Can you smell an antidote?" She was half-joking but wished for a magic cure.

"Whatever Lilith gave her is strong, but I can't tell what it is. The problem is, Arbor is a nature elemental, and what she gave her may not even be poison to us. It's so easy to tamper with their delicate systems."

She knew he was right. Nature elementals were pure entities, never polluting themselves with anything that could throw their delicate systems off balance. Once, Arbor had gotten a contact high from Remy's Mist smoke, which made her ill. They'd suffered three days of torrential rain after that. No, they had no idea what they were looking for, and Lilith wasn't going to tell. Sighing, Celeste patted his arm.

"I have to go. They're waiting for me." She sighed.

"You know, if you just popped in instead of flying, we could send them away and use that time for something else." He teased, cupping her breasts through the threadbare t-shirt she wore, his mouth on her neck. She cupped the back of his head, loving the feel of his touch, her man, her mate.

"You are a bad influence." She turned to face him, wrapping her arms around his neck. His hair had grown since they'd been together, and even though she knew he shaved every night, he seemed to live with a perpetual case of five o'clock shadow. She raked her finger through his hair, smiling at the joy she saw on his face. She'd never seen him so happy and relaxed.

"I would pop in, but then I would sleep for two days after. That's a long trip, Karim," she said, knowing that she would not only need rest, but she would need to feed on an immortal to regain her strength, meaning she would have to call on Nyx or Anhur, and even though she wasn't angry any longer, she was still a long way from forgiveness.

"Anyway, it won't take that long. I'll fly to Japan, fly back, and then you'll have me forever."

He tensed then relaxed, forcing himself to smile even though he knew his time was limited with her. He didn't know when it would end, but it would. He assumed this was how humans felt, knowing that they didn't have forever but lived within the moment. It made their time together that much more special. He kissed her, cupping her denim-clad ass. She kissed him, her tongue slipping into his mouth, her teeth nipping his lip and drawing blood.

"Okay," he said, catching his breath. "You need to go before I'm unable to let you leave." He carried her to the elevator, trying to catch his breath between blistering kisses, her hands in his hair, her mouth on his.

"I'm going to miss you, azizam." He settled her in the waiting elevator car.

"Thirty-two hours," she said, giving him one last kiss. "I love you," she said as the door began to slide closed. He patted his chest, his palm over his heart, and said goodbye.

Thirty-two hours, he told himself, and she would be back in his arms.

※ ※ ※

Something was wrong, Lilith thought as she rushed down the grand staircase, a tray of half-eaten soup and tea in her hands. This was not supposed to happen. Arbor was not supposed to get sick. Her heart was hammering in her chest by the time she made her way to the kitchen to drop off the tray and bring up a bottle of water and something to help her sleep.

Jonas had been called away on a business matter, leaving Frederick to care for his ailing wife. Lilith, insisting on helping, had, in essence, become Frederick's handmaid, running up and down the stairs, changing bed linens, and seeing to anything Arbor might need. Now she was going down to the kitchen for the eighth time in less than two hours with more food Arbor had been unable to eat.

When she entered the restaurant-grade kitchen, Frederick, the cook, and the housekeeper all looked at her. She expected them to ignore her as they always did, but Frederick came to take the tray from her without a word or nasty look. The cook shook his head and mumbled something about Arbor, not eating, worry on his face. He made no effort to hide his disgust, nor did the housekeeper who mumbled under her breath as she left the room.

"She needs water and something to help her sleep." Lilith ran the back of her hand across her sweat-drench brow. The heat outside had crept into the house, making it feel like a sauna. Her t-shirt stuck to her sweat-soaked back, and her shorts were sticking to her thighs. She'd pulled her hair up into a bun to avoid the frizz that accompanied this type of heat, but she still had sweat dripping down her back.

"Here." Frederick handed her an ice-cold bottle of water and a glass full of a cloudy yellow liquid.

"This will help," he said, indicating the yellow liquid. "I hope you're proud of yourself. I hope when this is over, you get exactly what you deserve."

Lilith felt as if he'd kicked her in the gut. She lowered her gaze, unable to look at the people who watched her for news of their beloved madam.

"I'll get this up to her." She was unable to meet his gaze. She rushed back upstairs to Arbor's bedroom. Lilith hurried into the cool dark room where Arbor rested uneasily. She quietly pushed the door open with her elbow.

Arbor sat in a chair near a window that faced her garden. The sun was high and cast a golden glow across the room, which had been decorated in black and white, more to accommodate Jonas than anything, Lilith had assumed. She would have guessed Arbor would have preferred something with a floral motif or at least more greenery. Arbor turned when she entered, a tired smile on her gaunt face.

She wore a Kelly-green robe, her thinning hair covered with an elegant turban that matched her robe. Even in her declining state, her beauty was still evident. Lilith felt her stomach turn at the welcoming smile that greeted her approach.

"Frederick said that this would help you sleep." She handed the glass to Arbor, who reached for it with a shaky hand. Fearing she would drop it, Lilith assisted, holding the glass's weight in her hand and bringing it to Arbor's lips. She watched Arbor struggle to drink, forcing herself to finish every drop, then sat back with a heavy sigh.

Arbor turned her attention back to the garden, and Lilith busied herself with turning down the bed. She stared at a picture of Arbor and Jonas from a wedding ceremony sometime in the 1940s. Arbor looked radiant in a white satin gown, her smile bright, and her eyes on her husband. Jonas smiled brightly, looking down at her with pure adoration. They looked blissful, and even though they had been married for centuries, the picture looked as if they were getting married for the first time.

"That was our fifteenth wedding. Every few decades, we renew our vows. Jonas claims he hates it, but I know he loves it. Just look at that smile," Arbor said when she spotted Lilith looking at the photo.

"You two look so young and happy." Lilith ran her fingers along with the polished silver frame. "So much in love."

"I have loved Jonas Kent from the first time I laid eyes upon that man," she said wistfully. "He was just a boy when I met him, his first wife buried two years, and he was trying to care for two little ones alone. I came to his home to be a nurse for Gaston and Lisette. They were such sweet children. I fell in love with them instantly, such as warm hearts. But when I looked at Jonas," she sighed, closing her eyes in memory of that first meeting, "he took my breath away. I have never wanted another man before or since, and I never will."

Lilith watched Arbor's eyes get heavy and went to help her to bed. She lifted her out of the chair, and Arbor felt she weighed no more than a small child and got to her feet. They moved slowly, painfully across the room until she settled in bed, her lids drifting closed.

"I wish I could find a love like that," Lilith said as they moved. "Not many find a love like that."

"You will," Arbor assured her. "I believe we all have great loves, sometimes more than one. When we find them, we should hold on to that for as long as we can. I just happened to find the right one my first time out. I believe Celeste has reclaimed hers. Karim loves her like no other, and I believe he always will. After all, they went through, they ended up together, so there is always hope," she said, closing her eyes. Lilith felt another pang of both guilt and jealousy, guilt for what she'd done to Arbor and jealous because she'd mentioned Celeste.

"Have we heard from Remy yet?" Arbor yawned. Lilith managed a strained smile and patted her hand, pulling the covers over Arbor's shivering body.

"Not yet," she said, but it didn't matter. Arbor was already asleep. She stepped back and looked at what she had done, the damage she had wrought on a woman she admired and, in her way, loved. It was a simple adoration potion, meant to make Arbor love her as one of her own, to look at her and accept her the way she had Celeste. It had worked to some degree. She had been welcomed into her bedroom suite directly across from this room, but Arbor was dying, and she had no way of stopping it. She wanted to tell Arbor, to explain that this was not what she wanted; this was not supposed to happen.

She wanted to bring Remy here to see his mother and offer her comfort, but that would not happen. They would know what she had done, know that she was the reason Remy stayed away. They would know that she, acting as High Regent, had the royal guard take Briar to the cells in the collective basement where he was tortured out of spite. She'd made Remy watch as his lover had the skin on his back peeled away as he screamed in agony, his eyes on a teary Remy the entire time. She needed help. She needed to prove that she wasn't a monster, like her mother and father before her. She could be a bitch, but she wasn't completely heartless, not really. And when they found out, and they would, there was no way around that, she would have to pay dearly. If she were lucky, she would make it out of this with her life.

"Dear lord," Lilith thought, lifting Arbor's brittle hand in hers. *"What have I done?"*

❊ ❊ ❊

Nicky stumbled drunkenly into his hotel suite with two

women draped on him. He was sweaty, shirtless, and sporting a days' worth of beard stubble. Celeste had showered and changed into fresh jeans and a tank top and ordered room service by the time he crashed in. She stood with her arms folded across her chest, her face grim. The women saw her first, pausing at the sight of the six-foot-tall blue-eyed beauty watching them.

"You have company, dear," one of the women said. She had long dark hair and slightly Asian features, and a British accent. The other, a rather manly looking young woman with close-cropped hair and eyes that reminded her of steel ball bearings, wore a skirt that was barely there and a crop top that struggled to contain her ample bosom.

"Who's the slag?" crop top asked, giving Celeste an accusatory look. It was as if she thought Celeste was intruding. Celeste stared at her, her cold blue eyes sharp and penetrating.

"Nice mouth on this one, Nicky. I'm his sister." She folded her arms across her chest and leveled him with her withering stare. Nicky swallowed and disengaged himself from the women, sobering as he crossed the room.

"Ce, hey-" His face fell. She wondered how he managed to look like such a drunken slob and hurt little boy at the same time.

"I am so pissed off. I have been calling you for weeks. Everybody has been calling you for weeks. Remy is missing, Briar is missing, Arbor is sick, and you're fucking everything in Asia because I have a boyfriend. Well, boo fucking hoo, Nicholas," she'd slipped into Russian without realizing just how angry she was. "You have ignored the only family you have ever known. Grow up, Nicky."

"You knew I was in love with you," he began in Russian before slipping back into English. "You knew that I wasn't seeing anyone because -"

"I never told you not to date, Nicky. I never told you to pine after me like some love-sick puppy. I asked you to be my best friend. I asked you to be there when I needed someone because I trust you above all others, and you run away because of Karim?"

"He can give you what I can't!" he yelled.

"And you give me what he can't! You are my best friend, my brothers aren't as close to me, and you run off like a little bitch because your feelings got hurt? Suck it up, man, get some balls!" she yelled back in English, getting into his face. They stood staring at each other, the heat rising between them as the tension in the room rose.

"Are you going to hit me, CeCe?" he asked.

"Depends. Are you done being a drama queen?" she shot back. He narrowed his eyes and sized her up, then the smile crept in, and he embraced her. She relaxed and hugged him back, still chastising him as they rocked back and forth in the living room of his hotel suite.

"I have missed you so much," he said, taking a step back so he could look at her. "I hate to admit it, but you look good."

"And you look like you dressed in clothes you got at a Billy Idol garage sale. What is this?" She pointed to his outfit of black leather and chains. "You look ridiculous." He laughed and hugged her again.

"Seriously though, Nicky, please tell me you've heard from Remy?" He looked at her face, the worry in her eyes. "Arbor is dying," she said, and he sobered immediately.

"Come on, I'll grab a shower, and you can tell me what's going on." He grabbed her hand and headed to the bedroom, the two women throwing their hands up in frustration.

"What about us?" the Brit asked. "What are we supposed to do?"

"Leave," Katie said from the door. She gave Celeste a wink and ushered the women out. "Come with me, ladies, and I will make sure you get some nice parting gifts." Celeste couldn't help smiling. Hiring Katie was the best decision Nicky had ever made.

* * *

She felt completely defeated on the ride back to the airport, her head pounding and her eyes burning.

"I spoke to Remy the night I left for New York, Ce. I haven't heard from him since. I thought maybe he was pulling a Remy," he muttered while towel drying his hair. Remy was known for taking off for days with only his cell phone and a camera. It was how he relaxed and decompressed when the regimented life of being a soldier got to be too much for him.

"So, you ignoring everyone was just you being an asshole?" She rubbed her eyes and yawned. Nick sat next to her on the bed and patted her leg.

"Yes, and I apologize. I should never have gotten so emotional that I would cut you guys out of my life. You are my family. The only family I know, and I'm so sorry. Tell you what, I'll fly back with you tomorrow."

"I'm leaving tonight. In about an hour, actually. I only came because you weren't talking, and I need to find Remy ASAP. I'm just waiting for the new flight crew and the plane to be checked and refueled. Besides, don't you have like two more shows? You'll be home in a few days anyway. Finish up here first." She kissed his cheek and gave him another hug.

"I know that there are so many reasons you and I are better as friends. I understand. It just hurts to see you moving on." She touched his cheek and kissed him gently on the lips.

"You, Nicholas Skylar Novachek, are the one true, pure unconditional love of my life. No one will ever replace you in my heart," she said. He held her hand to his cheek and smiled.

"Get out of here. I have to talk to Katie and get some things taken care of, and then I'm coming home. Tomorrow. No arguments. My family needs me," he said, giving her a bear hug before he let her go to her waiting town car.

✽ ✽ ✽

Now alone in the backseat, she felt worse than before. Sure, she and Nicky were back on track, but she had no idea where to start in their search for Remy. She looked at her watch, it was a little after three a.m., and Downtown Tokyo still glittered with billboards and neon signs. She stared out of the window as a group of bikers roared by, turning her thoughts to Remy and his bike. He'd had several over the years, but he always had them custom painted to mimic a green tree python's colors.

"It makes me stealthy," he said. "Besides, it's my go-to shift when I'm pissed. Kind of like my spirit animal." She missed him so much, and she was terrified that something had happened to him, something horrible. She closed her eyes and tried not to think about that. She wouldn't think the worst when the worst was already happening to Arbor. She needed to get home and try to help find a cure for whatever was affecting her mother.

Her cell phone rang in her pocket just as the car pulled into the tiny airport.

"I'll just be a second." She motioned to the driver as he helped her out of the car. She handed him her overnight bag and stepped to the side, watching Lisette's face light up her screen.

"Hey Lisey," she yawned into the phone. "Hey, I can barely hear you. Are you on the plane already?" There was a clatter in the terminal. She turned and saw one of the maintenance crew picking up an overturned toolbox while another yelled at him in Japanese. Frowning, Celeste walked outside, running a hand through her hair.

"Sorry about that. I'm not on the plane just yet. I'm about to board in a minute. I saw Nicky, and he hasn't seen or heard from Remy in weeks. Lisey, I'm scared. It's not like him to disappear like this. And Briar..."

"About that, we've found Briar," she said, then in a whisper. "Some of the soldiers said that Lilith had him tortured for some reason. No one knows why, but she brought in some of the Dark Fae to do it, Ce. And Arbor is getting worse. This is getting bad. Hurry home, sweetie. We need you."

"I will. I am," she said, hanging up. She stood looking at the night sky, trying to stop the tears that threatened. Her family was falling apart, and there was nothing she could do. She sniffed and looked down at her phone again. She could call Nyx and ask for help; she should call her. She looked over her shoulder and saw the driver and pilot looking at her, their faces concerned. She couldn't summon Nyx with the two of them staring a hole in her back.

She wiped her eyes and turned her phone on, and began searching for Nyx's rarely used cell phone number. She walked further away from the terminal entrance, her head pounding as she dreaded this call. Stepping further into the shadows, she felt something moving above her. She looked up into the pitch of the starry night sky and saw something moving.

From a distance, it looked like a flock of birds to her. But it was moving stealthily, and they were too large to be birds. As they came closer, she could see their large dark wings moving as one, dozens of pairs of red eyes glowing in the darkness, and she froze. They were coming faster now, swooping down towards her like guided missiles.

"Oh shit," Celeste mumbled and turned to run, her goal to reach the front of the terminal where there would be light and people. They couldn't take her in the light. She felt relief when she saw the plane, the pilot standing on the tarmac just inside the hanger door. If only she could move a little faster, but the gravely ground was wet and slick beneath her feet. Her sneakers, though stylish, offered no assistance in her escape on the shifting pebbles. She slid, tried to right herself as the light from the hanger grew brighter, closer, she was almost there, almost safe.

Almost.

She was yanked backward, her feet leaving the ground as talons dug into her shoulder and lifted her into the air, soaring into the dark abyss. She dropped her phone, watching as it crashed to the ground and skittered across the tarmac, broken. She fought, only to have the razor-sharp claws dig deeper into her flesh. She stilled, closed her eyes, and tried to breathe through the pain as her captors whisked her into oblivion.

When the pilot, ready for take-off, went in search of his passenger a few moments later, all he found was her shattered cell phone a few feet from where she was last seen and nothing else.

* * *

CHAPTER FIFTEEN

Nyx didn't know what to expect when Karim had urgently summoned her. She had no idea what she was going to find when she manifested in Celeste's living room.

What she found was a rampaging vampire, his bare chest smoldering from the sunlight that streamed into the uncovered windows. Nyx snapped her fingers, and the heavy drapes snapped closed, but that seemed not to affect him. He was practically snarling, pacing back and forth like a caged animal.

"She's gone," he said. His body seemed to vibrate, his eyes shimmering emerald when they turned to her. "I can't feel her anymore, Nyx. She just popped out of existence. I should have gone with her. I should have insisted that I went to hell with the sun." Nyx stared at him, holding her hands up to still his pacing as she tried to understand what he was rambling about.

"What do you mean? What are you talking about?" she asked, and he stared at her as if he were just now noticing that she was in the room. He blinked and stared, then swallowed.

"She went to Japan to ask Nicky if he'd heard from Remy. People are missing, Nyx. Remy, his lover Briar, now Celeste and Arbor -" he frowned and shook his head. "She was trying to find Remy before Arbor dies."

Nyx sat down heavily, her eyes wide, her mouth dry. "And she went alone?"

"It was supposed to be a quick trip. Fly there and back. She was getting back on the plane, Lisette spoke to her, and she was already at the airport. Then nothing. They only found her phone. Is she still alive? I can't feel her, Nyx. I can't feel her anywhere." He grasped Nyx's trembling shoulders and gave her a shake, making her meet his gaze. She stared, and when it finally sunk in what he was saying.

"You are blood bound?" she asked. "But you can't- not with the mark- not with her-"

"We found a way. It's not as strong as it would be if she hadn't been claimed, but I could feel her. I felt her. She was tired and a little worried but safe. Then she was gone," he said, sitting heavily on the coffee table. "She was just gone."

They sat in silence, gripping each other's hands as they tried to calm themselves. Nyx looked at Karim, the right side of his bare chest scorched but healing. He hadn't even flinched, hadn't even calmed himself enough to block out the sun that was slowly killing him. His only concern then and now was Celeste. It had always been Celeste.

She looked at his face, the face of a man who had been devastated and was hurt and terrified into a blind rage. Karim loved Celeste, not just loved her. She was his entire reason for being. She was the *one* for him.

"We will find her," she said, patting his hand. "We will find her, and we will destroy anyone who gets in our way," she said.

"And I know where to start," Karim said.

* * *

Lilith paced the living room of her father's Lakeview home, her clothes sticking to her in the sweltering heat. Even here, a few hundred feet from Lake Ponchartrain, there was no cool breeze drifting in from the water. She hated this room more than she hated her mother's entire house. Alexander had decorated the living room in red, white, and blue; it looked like a fourth of July float had exploded. She sat on the bright blue sofa and shook her head at the flags and historical décor; it was strictly pandering, she knew it, and he knew it.

He was on the telephone, that perfect twinkling smile

still in place even though the person he was speaking to couldn't see just how handsome and charming he truly was. He laughed at something, a laugh that she knew to be fake, and she rolled her eyes. He looked at her, and she stared back impatiently, tapping her sneaker foot.

"Skip, I'll call you back. My daughter came in, and she looks like she needs to speak with me," he said. "Yes, daughters, probably some boy trouble." He laughed again, and she groaned.

He hung up and looked at her, his handsome face set in stony emotionless silence.

"What is it now?" he asked, clearly uninterested in whatever had Lilith on edge.

"Arbor Kent is dying, and I think it's my fault," she blurted, and he reacted by lifting his brow. "I gave her an adoration elixir, and she got sick, really sick. I can't fix it; how do I fix it?"

He placed his palms on his desk and rose slowly. His blue eyes darkened, and his tanned skin reddened. She took a step back when thick dark horns uncurled from beneath his perfectly coiffed dark hair.

"You," he said through clenched teeth, "have damned us, you stupid, selfish, insignificant little child." He moved toward her, and she continued stumbling back until she fell onto the sofa. She swallowed and stared up at her father, who had grown in stature and girth. The seams of his dress shirt strained and ripped, sinewy muscles poking through the thin cotton, heat radiating from him bring the temperature in the house to a scorching one hundred and ten degrees.

"Arbor Kent is a sylph, a nature element. She is of the earth, and you have poisoned an aspect of the earth, upset the balance of nature. She must remain pure, or it can be catastrophic. Why do you think she is untouchable? No harm is to ever come to any elemental. "He inhaled.

"I'm sorry. I just wanted - I just -how do I fix it?" she asked, tears burning her eyes.

"You can't. She will die, and you had better pray to whoever it is you pray to that this place, these people, this part of the world, doesn't get blown away with her. What you have done could cause a war. What you have done can cause the Collective and the Council of the Gods to destroy us, to wipe the Dark Fae out of existence. Do you understand? Do you see what you've done with your jealousy? You have brought **WAR** to my door." He grabbed her upper arms, his dark talon-like nails digging into her flesh, his skin burning her, and she cried out. He snarled, exposing a row of sharpened yellow teeth, a forked tongue slithering out and touching her cheek, leaving a thick trail of saliva. He held her closer, his mouth close to her ear, and she closed her eyes, anticipating the next strike. She was sobbing, her chest heaving and her body shaking.

"I would kill you right now if I did not love you. And if you weren't my one true heir. You leave this place right now, or I will end you, Lilith." He released her, and she fell to the floor in a heap. She shook, unable to make her legs work, unable to do anything but truly cower in his presence. He stomped out of the room, dark cloven hooves ripping the fine Italian leather of his loafers and leaving scorch marks on the bright red carpet. She laid there, her tears and her pain all too real. When she could, she struggled to her feet and ran out of the house, never looking back and never planning to return.

❋ ❋ ❋

"Ready?" Katie leaned against the door frame of Nicky's hotel bedroom, her eyes on the useless itinerary in her hands. When Nicky had risen that morning, when the call had come that Celeste was missing, he'd canceled all of his plans, much to the chagrin of the band and his manager. They had been only a little more understanding when he said he'd send the private jet back for them. Only Katie seemed undisturbed by the news. In fact, she seemed to expect it, and she was surprisingly quiet about the entire thing.

He tossed one more shirt into his already overstuffed messenger bag before tossing the strap over his shoulder. The rest of his things would be flown out with the band. He looked around the room, making sure he hadn't forgotten anything, and nodded, his mind on everything going wrong at home.

"Come on then," Katie said, shaking her body the way a wet dog might, shedding what looked to Nicky to be a layer of gold glitter.

"What the fuck, Katie?!" Nicky yelped.

"No, not Katie." She shook again, and a layer of pale blue leaves peeled away to reveal her face, and he gasped. He was staring into a pretty yet dower face with eyes that were much too large and bright. Her skin was pale, her hair midnight dark, and made the hair on his neck stand up. He stared at her, his mouth agape. She smiled; well, he assumed it was a smile, either that or a muscle twitch that imitated a smirk.

"What the absolute fuck?!" Nicky said when he was finally able to speak.

"We don't have time for this. We have to go. I was sent to bring you to the Collective. You'll be safe there," she said, and he stared at her.

"Wait. What? Who are you?" he asked.

"I'm taking you to safety. People are missing, and you, being close to the Caelestis and her family, could be a target. I was tasked with keeping you safe, just until we find the Caelestis and the shifter. Come now, Nicholas." She crooked a finger and claimed his arm.

"Hold the fuck up!" he yelled, pulling away again and moving across the room, the strap to his messenger bag knotted around his fist until his knuckles had turned white. "Just wait a fucking minute. Who the fuck are you? Where's Katie? I can't go to the Collective. I'm human."

"I," she said with a sigh, "am Atropos, the progeny of Nyx, Moirai, and seer of what is yet to come. Katie is fine. She is on another level of consciousness and will think you've already left when she wakes. You are allowed entry into the Collective because of special circumstances. We must go."

He looked at her, then narrowed his eyes and tilted his head.

"You're one of the fates?" he asked, and she nodded in exasperation. "CeCe said you were all fucking nuts. Where are the other two? And why are you speaking clearly? I thought you spoke in ridiculous riddles."

She shrugged.

"Nuts? Maybe a little. We don't always travel as one. And the riddle thing, I just do that to fuck with people. Makes my life a little more interesting. Hold your breath." She wiggled her brow, a truly mischievous smile on her face, making the dower girl look pretty. He stared at her and frowned, ready to ask another question when he was surrounded by swirling mist. He closed his eyes and held his breath, praying that they would get to their final destination in one piece.

* * *

Lilith paced her bedroom, avoiding the flow of traffic in and out of Arbor's bedroom that clogged the hallway outside of her door. The heat outside was stifling, the wind still, quiet. She'd turned off the television long ago as human news only reported on the impending storm heading into the Gulf. She had seen the news feeds, watched people speak of leaving the area while others declared their intent to stay. She closed her eyes and tried to think of something else, something pleasant like Remy and the touch of his skin. Or the fact that she had nearly gotten everything she'd wanted.

She poured herself vodka on the rocks at the mini bar in her sitting area, pacing the room, trying to think. It was so hot, the ice melted in the cup before she'd finished it. What had she done?

She knew that the end was near for Arbor. There was no coming back from this. She should, she knew, let Remy say good-bye to his mother. But with his strong will, he would blurt out everything as soon as he could; he was a risk. She poured another drink, nixing the ice and downing the vodka in one swallow.

She had straightened her hair and wore it in a high pony-tail, a style she had never worn because it seemed too common, too ordinary. Instead of her normal designer clothing, she wore cargo shorts and a plain white tank top she found at Old Navy and plain white low top Converse. She'd done everything she could to make herself more like Celeste. She'd even begun wearing the same shade of lipstick and changed her eye color. She looked at herself long and hard, slowly stripping off the clothes and wiping the lipstick off with the back of her hand. Remy had been correct. She looked ridiculous—a poor, pathetic imitation of the original.

She jumped into the shower, washing her hair and cleaning the sweat and smell of desperation from her body. When she'd finished, she wrapped her alabaster skin in a thick white bathrobe and combed the snarls from her hair, and let the blue bleed from her eyes, running her fingers through her hair until thick silky waves rested on her shoulders. Why try to be Celeste when she could be who she truly was?

There was a banging on her door right before it blew open and slammed shut again. She hadn't seen anyone until Karim had his hand on her throat, pushing her across the carpet, her feet skipping across the floor as she tried to get her balance.

He tossed her down onto the bed, his skin smoking from the late afternoon sunshine that streamed in through the partially covered windows, but he seemed beyond feeling it.

"Where is she?!" he barked, and she flinched, propping herself up on her elbows.

"Where is who?" she asked, crab walking back across the bed.

"Don't test me, Lilith. Where is Celeste?" She sat up looking at Karim in his paint-stained jeans and a dark t-shirt. He was fuming like he had the night he'd attacked her, but he wouldn't kill her. Easing off the bed and staying as far away from him as possible, she went to the bar for another drink.

"I don't know where Celeste is. I haven't seen her since the two of you rode off into the moonlight. Besides, I've been busy with her mother on her deathbed and all," she said.

"A deathbed you are responsible for putting her in," he snarled.

She looked at him over the rim of her glass, pausing for a moment before gently, deliberately placing the glass on the bar.

"I love Arbor. I would never do anything to hurt her. She is family now."

"And we know how loving your family is," he snapped. "Don't play games with me."

"I thought you liked games, Karim." She came from around the bar, a smirk on her lips. "But you're right; I am tired of pretending to be the poor broken princess, especially since we already have one of those. She is good at being the strong, moral, but damaged damsel. But would you consider her a damsel? I don't think so. She's too much of a badass for that. Is that why you love her? Because she's so tough and still so very, very weak?"

"She's far from weak," he said, his anger giving way to frustrated confusion.

"Let's say I tell you what you want to know. What do I get out of it?" She moved closer, filling the space between them with the strong feral scent of her arousal.

"How about I let you live?" He chuckled. "You may not be as pretty, but you will survive." He looked pleased with the obvious fear he saw in her eyes. He wanted to kill her, she knew that, but he wouldn't. He couldn't. No blood could be shed in the house of the High Regent, she thought. He seethed, every instinct telling him to kill her, cut her throat, and let her bleed out on the carpet like the worthless animal she was.

She straightened and stared at him, her mind reaching out to him. He cringed, pushing the feeling of spiders running across his brain out, and she physically recoiled. Like Remy, he was strong, too strong to let her manipulate his mind. Unlike Remy, though, she couldn't manipulate his body. There was more to this vamp than she realized, more power. She moved closer, trying again to push the mental wall out of her way, to drill through the block. But he batted her away like nothing more than an annoyance. How hadn't she seen it before? Because she had never met one of the *Seven* before. She had heard of the seven original vampires, the ones who had special powers, abilities that superseded even those of the gods.

How had she not seen it before? Karim, Vampire Prince of House Tyre, the incorruptible. He grasped her, lifting her into the air, and for a moment, she thought he was going to throw her across the room. He didn't; he only tightened his grip, his mouth near her neck, while crushing the air from her lungs. She could feel her bones, already mending from her father's assault, cracking, her healing wounds re-opening.

"I'll give you what you want if you give me something I want," she teased. He tossed her to the floor, her robe falling open slightly. She looked in his eyes and undid her belt, letting him look at her bare body. She ran a hand across her breasts, watching his jaw tighten and his eyes narrow as she licked her lips and stood.

"You play nice," she let her finger moved down the deep v of his t-shirt, ripping it down the middle. "And I will tell you what I know," she said. He grasped her wrists, twisting, but she made no whimpers of pain. "I know you like it rough. We can get as rough as you like, Karim. All I want is an hour, and I will tell you what I know about your precious, Celeste." She pressed her lips to his chest, and his stomach churned with sickness.

"Get away." He shoved her and turned to walk away. He'd reached the door, his hand on the knob, his anger rolling off of him, adding heat to the already stifling room. The smell of her mingled with the scent of his singed flesh gave the entire room a suffocating feel. He felt ill, his chest burning as he opened the door to leave.

"The great incorruptible Prince of Tyre, you leave now, and you'll never find out what I know. Your pride is more important than saving her, is it? Are you just going to *abandon* her again? Your one true love?" she said, and he paused, looking back at her. "I promise it'll be worth it. It won't even hurt. Unless you want it to," she said, smiling at the defeat she saw in his eyes.

He thought of the night Celeste had said the vow to bind them, the night when he had been hurting and had been willing to do whatever she needed to make sure they would be together, to make herself his and his alone. Angry tears burned his eyes as he thought of her out there somewhere, hurt, alone, wanting to come back, waiting for him as she had so many centuries ago. She had waited for him, and he'd walked away then, leaving her scarred and broken. He couldn't walk away again, no matter what the cost; he had to find her. What else he could do, he wondered. What were his other options?

❄ ❄ ❄

She landed on her knees with a thud on slick cobblestones of a patio in some realm she had never seen before. The sky was white, stark with yellow birds moving across the horizon. She stared at the house just a few feet away; the looming grey stone building looked like something out of an old horror movie.

Celeste began getting to her feet when one of Harpy's taloned feet pushed her back down. Now that she was on the ground, safe from being dropped into the nothingness between realms, she reached back, grasping the ankle of the creature that touched her and flipped it over her head. It landed on its back, its face stunned by the strength and swiftness of her capture. The other Harpies at Celeste's back began to advance, but she was not in the mood.

Celeste stood, looking at the dark-winged creatures. There were five in all. With dark plumage that covered human breasts, torso, and legs, small women's size and shape transitioned to the bird's legs just below the knee. Three-toed feet sported thick black talons and made clicking noises on the cobblestone as they shifted in preparation for an attack. Their arms were adorned with beautiful wings, their heads capped with soft feathers, framing rather pretty female faces. Faces that were bird-like, but lovely, nonetheless. They ranged in colors from deep purple to ebony and stared at her with wide eyes.

She moved forward, and they stepped back, making soft chirping sounds that reminded her of blue jays, but no human sound came from them.

The one on the ground was struggling to her feet and made a low hissing noise at Celeste's back, revealing her razor-sharp teeth. It made a noise at the others, and they took off, flying straight up into the colorless sky.

Celeste caught her breath, rubbing her bruised and bleeding shoulders. She was numb and light-headed, her chest scalding from the movement between realms. She turned to look at the French doors that led into the gloomy-looking house when a movement to her right caught her attention. She turned to see a guard moving toward her. He was tall, dressed in black slacks and a plain black long sleeve shirt. His face was on the stony side and a pale blue. Someone was approaching from the rear, she could hear him moving closer, but she did not turn her head to look at him. Her eyes did dart right to the goblin moving closer, then to her left as another demon, this one a deep purple, came toward her. She noted that they were all in black, all in soft-soled shoes, and all moved with practiced stealth.

"You need to come with us, Caelestis," the blue man said, and Celeste smirked.

"So, it takes four-five now," she pointed over her shoulder to the newcomer, "to escort wittle ol' me into the house that looks like it belongs to the Addams Family? I'm not going any-where until you tell me where the fuck I am and who the fuck brought me here." She sighed and placed her hands on her hips.

"Just come with us," Blueman said, holding out a hand. She didn't move, only stared at him. A hand clamped down on her still-healing shoulder, and she winced and then kicked back. The heel of her foot caught her assailant in the knee; there was a loud pop when the bone broke and a pained grunt when he fell sideways onto the cobblestones. She glanced at him writhing on the ground, holding his shattered knee, but she did not move.

"Well?" she asked, planting her feet.

"Please, don't make this difficult, Caelestis." Blueman moved closer, a retractable baton in his hand. He flicked his wrist, and it extended, his red eyes on Celeste, who smiled widely. Behind her, someone unsheathed a sword. She could hear the metal sliding against metal even with the ogre lying on the ground moaning behind her. She spared him a look, saw that his damaged knee was pointing in the wrong direction, the thick white bone poking through his slacks. She watched him writhe, then kicked him in the side of the head. He fell silent, and she exhaled, her eyes back on the blue man who looked as if he were approaching a feral dog.

"Oh, I'm going to make this extremely difficult." She smiled. Blueman charged, swinging the baton at her, and she stepped to the right, sticking her foot out to trip him and let-ting his momentum carry him. He tumbled over the downed ogre and landed with a thud. While Blueman was falling, the demon at her back lunged forward. She shifted, the blade of his broadsword moving past her shoulder, slicing through several strands of hair and knicking the top of her ear. She grasped the hilt of the sword between her flattened palms and pulled. The demon bumped her back, and she elbowed him in the stom-ach, knocking the wind from him. He loosened his grip on the sword, and she pulled it free, tilting the handle up, hitting him in the chin. His eyes rolled back in his head, and he fell onto his butt, his mouth bloody. She spun, kicking him in the face, and he was out for the count, sprawled on his back on the cobblestones.

The purple demon on her left and the goblin on her right ran at her, both like charging rhinos thundering on the stone patio. She stepped back and let them crash into each other, rolling her eyes at their incompetence. Blueman was back on his feet, the baton ready for action. He swung at her knees, striking her shin with the first strike. She cursed and stared at him, her blue eyes fading to silver. He smirked and swung again, this time aiming for her head and damaged shoulders, but she blocked each blow with the sword, taking a step back with each advance.

The goblin got to his knees and grasped her around the hips. She leaned back, using him as an anchor so that she could kick the advancing Blueman in the chest. He fell backward, his eyes wide from the power of her strike, and landed hard on his back. She turned the sword in her hands, grasped the handle with both hands, and plunged it into something soft and yielding until her hands were slick with thick green, black blood. The arms around her hips went slack, and the goblin fell to his side, the sword buried in his chest.

She tugged at it, but it wouldn't budge. Behind her, she heard the shrill cry of the Blueman who charged, swinging the baton. He caught her in the face, slashing across her cheek. She grunted and fell to the ground, her mouth bleeding. He loomed over her, the baton over his head. She rolled away, springing to her feet. There were only two demons on their feet, Blueman and the strangely pretty purple demon. They charged at once - she leaped into the air, kicking purple in the face and slapping Blueman in the nose with the heel of her palm. Purple fell, dazed, while bloody Blueman continued the onslaught of blows. She smiled while easily dodging his increasingly wild swipes, infuriating him even more.

The purple demon got to his feet at her back, his arms encircling her waist, pinning her arms to her sides. She struggled against his grasp, watching Blueman smirk, his teeth startlingly white against deep blue skin and dripping dark red blood pouring from his nose.

Celeste returned his smirk and kicked him, the toe of her sneaker catching him under the chin. He made no noise as he hit the ground, only a muted thunk, and the baton sailed across the patio and into the bushes. Before Purple could fully grasp what had just happened, she reached down to grab what she hoped were testicles and tugged. He screamed, and she knew she'd hit her mark; even if they weren't testicles, she'd hurt him a helluva lot. He let her go, and she swung a hard-right roundhouse, striking him in the jaw, and he too, went down, his head bouncing on the cobblestones.

"You should have just answered my question," she said to Blueman, who looked up at her with glazed eyes. She wiped the blood from her mouth and touched the bruise on her cheekbone, wincing. The mark on her neck singing to life as someone approached from the darkness of the house's interior.

"I must say, that was quite impressive. Those are some of my best men," a woman said behind her.

"Then you are in a world of trouble," Celeste snarled before turning to see who had brought her to the colorless, airless, soulless place.

She wore all white, today a white cotton bustier and crisp white shorts that reach her mid-thigh. Her shoes were plain white pumps, her snowy hair in a neat bun at her nape. Celeste stared at her, her mouth open, but no words would form.

The infamous Queen of the Dark Fae came toward her; arms open wide in greeting. "You're here. You're finally here." The Queen embraced her, and Celeste stiffened, not sure what to do or feel. Her arms hung limp at her sides, her body tense from the contact. Behind them, she could hear the guards gathering themselves, trying to regain their composure.

"You're dismissed. Go get patched up," the Queen said

without looking at them. She was too busy, staring at Celeste. She gingerly held Celeste's sore shoulders and took a good long look at her.

"Let me look at you," she said, touching the silky dark hair and smooth caramel-colored skin. She ran her hands down Celeste's arms. "Wow, you are absolutely gorgeous," she gushed. "But then I knew you would be. How could you not be? Lilith said you were stunning, but my gosh, you look so much like your father." She tucked a strand of hair behind Celeste's ear before tucking Celeste's arm in hers and walking her towards the house. Celeste went with her, too numb to object, too stunned to speak. She stared dazedly at the Queen.

"I can't stop looking at you. You are really here. Finally, after all this time, you are really here."

Celeste finally gathered herself and stepped back, moving from the Queen's embrace, not wanting the woman to touch her. Finally, she was able to speak through a throat that had closed the moment she'd seen the Queen's face. The words came out hard and clipped through tightly clenched teeth and a bit of a snarl.

"Hello .... *mother.*"

* * *

CHAPTER SIXTEEN

Nicky sputtered and choked, his chest stinging and his eyes burning. He felt as if he were going to throw up or pass out, so he leaned against the wall to support himself. When he finally regained his composure, he looked back at Atropos, who seemed no worse for wear. He looked around and saw that they were in the hallway of what he assumed to be a rather expensive hotel.

"So, this is the Collective?" he gasped, putting his hands on his hips while trying to catch his breath and shrugged. "I thought it would be more...magic-y." He waggled his fingers in the air. Atropos just gave him that twitchy smile and pointed to the door behind them.

"This is Celeste's suite; you can stay here until everything is okay. You can ride out the storm here as well. You will be safe, "Atropos said, opening the door, and Nicky peered inside, smiling at the apartment beyond.

"Storm?" he said.

"Arbor is dying, Nicholas. The storm is going to be massive, dangerous, and many will die. You cannot release an elemental, especially one as old and powerful as our Arbor, to nature without some major damage. Here, you will be safe, protected. Now go, rest well," she said. Nicky stared at her, confused, and a little jet-lagged from the trip. She touched his cheek and smiled serenely. He could see the divinity in her then, that ethereal quality that always surrounded Celeste.

"You are very special, Nicholas. You burn so brightly, and it's blinding. You are so much more than you realize. You are destined for more than this world," she said. He was lost in the swirling color of her eyes, then snorted and shook his head.

"You're just messing with me, right?" he asked and saw the twinkle in her eye.

"Perhaps." Then just as quickly as she had come, she was gone. Shrugging this off as yet another oddity of being "adopted" by a family of mythological creatures, Nicky made his way into the apartment, kicking the door closed behind him.

He dropped his bags at the door and looked around the living room with interest. It was a bright, airy room, even with no windows. He strolled across the living room, running a finger over the hardwood top of the bar. Though lacking in color was obviously expensive, the decor, from the metal artwork on the walls to the rugs on the floor and television, everything was state of the art, top of the line. He stared at a hole in a bare wall behind the bar and noticed a painting on the floor. He stared at the painting and wondered if it had fallen or if it hadn't yet been hung. The hole would suggest the former; either way; he found it odd. He looked at it for a minute, then turned his attention to the bar and found it odd that the liquor had been secured behind a locked door. Odder still, he thought, but then what did he know. He marveled at how neat everything was, especially since Celeste was known to leave things around her apartment. There were books and papers everywhere in that place, but here everything was orderly, not one thing out of place. Whoever cleaned this place did a great job, better than many of the five-star hotels he'd stayed in, and this one even had a kitchen.

He went to look in the fridge to see if there was anything exotic and otherworldly in there. What he found was a well-stocked fridge of fresh, everyday mundane foods. It was better stocked than Celeste ever kept the pantries of her apartment. He found it odd that there were no glasses or silverware; all of the dishes were plastic. Weird, he thought, with all of this luxury that they would skimp on the dinnerware. Strange, but then again, he'd been surrounded by the strange for the last six years.

He looked down at his cell phone, the clock flashing different times as if he were crossing time zones even though he hadn't moved. He dialed the number of members of his band, and the line immediately connected, so at least that worked. What was he supposed to do in this place? And how long would he have to stay? He wanted to get out of here, but he wasn't even sure where here was. Was he even on Earth, or were they on another plane? He needed to feel useful, not like a damsel locked in a tower. If he couldn't help find Celeste, maybe he could track down Remy. He just needed to find a place to start. From a conversation with Celeste about this mysterious floating fortress, he'd known that Remy's apartment was across the hall from hers. He would start the search there right after he had a shower.

* * *

Remy could tell that someone had entered the suite and, for a moment, believed it wasn't Lilith. He thought it was Nicky, but that just couldn't be. He'd had that dream before where Nicky would find him, or Celeste or Gaston and even Briar, but they had always just been dreams, prayers that his nightmare would end. He no longer prayed for rescue, and now, as he lay on the bathroom floor, tears stinging his eyes, he prayed for death. He was naked, his body bruised, broken, and bloody, and he wanted to stay that way. He wanted to die.

And his mother was dying. She was dying, and he was trapped in this hell by that spiteful troll. He heard the door slam closed, and his body tensed in anticipation of her beckoning. He held his breath, praying that the gods would take his life before she reached him, then he would be there to greet Arbor in the heavens.

Lilith had taken everything from him, including his ability to shift, but she had never been able to tap into that place to control his mind. She had his body and sometimes could control his voice, but never his thoughts. She'd become furious when he'd laughed at her when she could no longer force his exhausted body to perform for her. He had taunted her, calling her weak and lacking because even with all the power she possessed, she couldn't get him to do as she pleased.

"With all your magic, you can't even force me to want you anymore. You evil used slag. You've tried so hard to be Celeste, dressing like her, living in her suite, but it didn't work. No one fell at your feet as the second coming because you are a sad, pathetic imitation of her." He laughed. "You are disgusting, and no man worth anything will want you. You are so wretched that you had to poison my mother because even your own parents don't want you." He laughed, and he could see the fury in her eyes.

"I'm warning you, Remy –" She growled, and he laughed harder.

"You can't be her. Even at her worst, Celeste has never had to force a man to be with her. She never had to manipulate or trick someone into loving her. Even your parents are obsessed with her. That's why they sent you here, isn't it? You can find out every detail of her life, report everything about her, what she eats, who she loves because she is the ideal. She is what you have always wanted to be, and you can't. You will always live in the shadow of her perfection. I mean, I didn't even want you, and I've fucked everyone!" He sneered, and it had been too much.

She had taken his voice, and even when she began to hurt him, he silently laughed through the pain, knowing that she was losing control. Her anger had pushed her to the verge of insanity, and she had sent for Briar.

Briar. The thought of him made him hurt even more. What she'd done to him, the way she'd forced him to watch as she had the skin sliced from his broad muscled back and thighs, had broken him. He could only stare, forced to watch as Briar howled in agony. He'd begged her to stop, pleading for Briar to forgive him with each slice into his smooth tawny skin.

"There is nothing to forgive," Briar had croaked, his lips dry and cracked, his eyes filled with tears. She had allowed Remy to kneel beside Briar, to speak to him, but he could not touch him. "This," Briar had said in his beautiful, floral Gaelic, "is not your doing, *álainn*. This is not your fault."

When he thought of all of the pain, he'd caused with his weakness, his betrayal, the people he loved most were being hurt and dying. He had found a way out, a way that she hadn't seen in her obsession to become something and someone she would never be.

He lay completely still, squeezing his eyes closed, when he heard someone approaching the bedroom. He exhaled and turned his head when he heard singing, low and off-key, coming toward him. He knew that voice instantly and turned his head just as Nicky froze in the doorway.

"Holy fuck," Nicky screeched, sliding across the floor to cradle Remy's head in his lap. Tears streamed down his cheeks, blinding him as Nicky searched for a towel to staunch the blood that poured from Remy's wrists and throat.

"Remy, sweet Jesus, what did you do?" Nicky screamed, tying towels around Remy's wounds to staunch the bleeding. "Why aren't you healing? What did you do?" He looked around the room, trying to find whatever had been used to work so much damage. Remy weakly lifted his hand to show Nicky a long, thick, blood slicked nail, the one, Nicky guessed, had been holding up the painting he'd seen on the floor.

"Dumb slag forgot about that." He choked, smiling up at Nicky with blood-covered teeth.

Nicky couldn't figure out what to do other than reach for the cell that was still in his back pocket. He flipped the phone open with one hand and stared at the screen. He couldn't call 911. It's not like he could call an ambulance to this place. He didn't even know where this place was, let alone how to get inside. He scrolled through the address book and stopped at the first name that made any sense to him.

He pushed to talk, holding the phone to his ear as he continued to apply pressure to the cut at Remy's throat. He coughed, blood splattering across his face and Nicky's bare chest.

"Nicky," Gaston began but was immediately interrupted by Nicky, who was near hysterics.

"I have Remy. He's bleeding to death. Come to Celeste's suite in the Collective. Something is wrong. I don't know how to stop the blood. He's not healing. What do I do? Shit. What do I do? He's all bruised, and I don't know what to do. There's blood everywhere." He hadn't even taken a breath when he heard the clatter as the door burst open and voices calling to them. It sounded as if an army had entered all speaking at once; languages he didn't understand came from voices he didn't recognize.

"Here! We're here!" Nicky called as several faces appeared at the bathroom door. Gaston still had the phone in his hand, and Nicky could hear his voice echoing from the receiver. Gaston went pale beneath his tan skin; his eyes were wide and red-rimmed.

"*Chers dieux dans le ciel, Remy qu'avez-vous fait?*" Gaston cried and fell to his knees beside his brother. Remy smiled and touched Gaston's shirt with a blood-drenched hand. Nicky wasn't fluid in French, but that he understood because he had asked the same thing.

"*Dear gods in heaven, Remy, what did you do?*" Gaston repeated over and over, kissing his little brother's forehead, tears streaming down his cheeks.

"She can't use me anymore. That fucking mongrel bitch can't use me to hurt anyone ever again. I win." He began to cough and choke. Nicky and Gaston shared a look before Gaston asked the question.

"Who, Remy? Who can't use you anymore?" he asked in a low even voice, even though he knew the answer. He tried his best to tamp his fury because he could feel Lisette just about vibrating with rage behind him.

"Lilith. I beat that bitch," he said and closed his eyes, waiting for the sweet embrace of death.

* * *

Karim closed the door and turned to face her, his expression stony. She smiled, letting her robe drop from her shoulders exposing silky white skin. Karim blinked and walked toward her with a sexy hip swinging swagger. She smiled and dropped the robe a little more, showing just a hint of cleavage. With large, surprisingly warm hands, he cupped her cheek and looked at her with those pale green eyes and smiled, showing just a hint of fang.

"Stop fucking around and tell me where she is." He moved closer, his breath tickling her lips.

"Fucking around is exactly what I want. I'll tell you what," she licked her lips in anticipation of a kiss and smiled. "If you're a good boy, I'll tell you anything," She ran her hands up his chest, and he caught her wrists, pushing her away.

"I would rather have my manhood removed with rusty pruning shears than to have sex with you. It would be much more enjoyable than being battered by you, you tired, worn-out piece of overused demon ass." He slammed her body against the window, the glass cracking and his arm beginning to smolder as the late afternoon sunlight seared his skin. He didn't feel the pain or even care that his skin was smoking.

"Tell me where she is, or by the gods, I will reach down your throat and rip that stone you call a heart from your chest. I know that cretin is your mother. Nyx told me everything. So now you'll tell me everything, and I may not throw you out the fucking window." He pressed harder, and she could feel the heat from the still air against her skin. Glass pierced her skin like tiny needles, smearing her blood on the glass, the smell of burning flesh choking her.

"Speak," he growled, and she heard a piece of glass fall to

the ground. When she didn't say anything, he pulled back and slammed her harder against the glass, and she cursed that she had one of the only rooms in this mausoleum without a patio. There was a straight drop of at least 50 feet to the stone patio below. It wouldn't kill her, she didn't think, but it would definitely hurt like a son of a bitch. He slammed her body again, and more chunks of glass fell and shattered, some cutting deeper into her back, and panic filled her. One more shove and the entire window would give; she couldn't breathe, and he was staring at her with an intensity that made her heart beat faster.

"I don't know!" she screamed, tears spilling down her cheeks. "I don't know! I never knew! I don't know where she is!!! She howled, and there was a sudden quiet stillness in the room. The pressure at her neck relented, but he didn't release her. She could hear him breathing, the hand at her throat a raw red mess of exposed muscle and bone, but Karim felt none of it.

"I have never enjoyed killing anyone more than this; I think I'll savor it a little longer," he whispered against her ear before biting a chunk of flesh from her neck. She tried to scream but only managed a strangled gurgle. Karim chuckled, a deep rumbling sound that made her chest vibrant, and her body twitched from utter terror.

"You have nothing to say, Lilith? No witty comebacks?" He pressed harder, and she raked at his hands, trying to loosen his grip on her throat and push away the hand on her chest.

The bedroom door blew opened, and the room was filled with soldiers, Lisette leading the way.

"Karim, by order of The Grey, I demand that you release her. We have what we need." He looked over his shoulder at Lisette. She met his gaze, her tone even and stern.

"Let her go. We have what we need," she repeated, and something in her expression made him comply. He stepped back, the smoking flesh of his arm beginning to heal when he stepped out of the sunlight, taking a position behind Lisette in the safety of the shadows.

"Thank the gods you're here. He was going to kill me. He was going to rape me!" Lisette's brow shot up, and then she turned to look at Karim. His sardonic expression was more than Lisette needed to assure her that Lilith had just lied.

"Is that the story you're going with?" Lisette laughed. "Gentlemen, take Ms. Prince into custody." Lilith sputtered, unable to speak as two rather large guards in complete battle armor grasped her arms. "We found Remy, you dumb fuck. You are being charged with kidnapping, false imprisonment, torture, coercion, treason, sexual assault, rape, and if Arbor dies -" She moved closer, her deep brown eyes flashing with barely restrained fury, her jaw clenched, "murder."

The guards half-dragged Lilith from the room as she uselessly fought against them. They didn't even struggle with her, easily lifting her off of her feet to half carry, half drag her along like a petulant child.

"We will find her," Lisette said, taking Karim's hand in hers. He nodded, squeezing her fingers. "Just between us, you should have ripped her heart out." She winked and left the room, her voice carrying over Lilith's shrieks of protest.

"Also, you're being charged with being an unbearable canker on my ass, an annoying twat, and a god-awful lay.

* * *

Celeste stood at the opposite end of the room from her mother, her eyes scanning her surroundings with slight interest. Everything was either black or white and gave Celeste a sick feeling in the pit of her stomach. Like her beaming mother, this was all a facade, masking the sinister truth. Nemesis had taken extra care in making everything around her look perfect, but beneath the pretty decor was the smell of sulfur and evil. Celeste felt ill at ease, but she remained stoic.

She noted Blueman standing silently in the corner, looking at her with unadulterated hatred. His face was battered, and his shirt torn, his eyes narrowed to the point of non-existence. She smiled at him and gave him the finger before returning her gaze to her mother.

"Lilith did not do you justice. Just look at you. Come, sit." She patted the sofa cushion beside her, but Celeste remained rooted in place, her arms folded across her chest. She had no intention of sitting beside this woman, nor would she drink the tea or coffee that were continually being offered. Pursing her lips in frustration, Nemesis pressed on.

"I invited you here so that we could get to know each other better. Try to be civil," she said, and Celeste's brow shot north.

"Sending Harpies to kidnap me in the middle of the night is your idea of an invitation?" She laughed, shaking her head. "Lady, I knew you were crazy; I didn't think you were stupid as well."

"As I was saying, I think we need to reconnect. Don't you see Celeste, with our combined power, we can rule not only the Dark Fae but the Collective. You have the mark, and soon, he will come and claim you as his own. The Daughter of War and Vengeance and the Destroyer of Gods, you will be infinite. We could be infinite.; we could have absolute power. And what a tableau, me with my white hair and skin, you with all your dark exotic beauty and your sister with her bright red-" Celeste frowned, staring at her with a slack jaw.

"Sister? Are you trying to tell me that Lilith-" Celeste felt queasy.

"Yes. The three of us could rule so well together. Just think of it, Celeste, the power, the adoration, and no one or nothing would be able to stand in our way. We could take back the human realm; we could be incredible. All you have to do is remember his name." As she spoke, Nemesis crossed the room, pausing mere inches from Celeste, her white eyes shining with excitement.

"Is this some kind of joke? Are you really trying to Darth

Vader me?" she asked, too stunned to even laugh. Nemesis stared at her, confused by the reference. "Are you honestly trying to bring me over to the dark side? Nyx would never allow -" She clarified, only pausing when Nemesis smiled brightly at her, her eye dancing.

"Nyx?" Nemesis chuckled, "Sweetie, Nyx isn't going to stop this. She's the one who planned it." Celeste stared at her, trying to push her way into Nemesis's mind, but all she could come up with were emotions. Her mother was so joyous that it made Celeste feel sick and dizzy.

"You're lying," Celeste choked, swallowing hard to keep the bile from rising. She closed her eyes when tears clouded her vision and shook her head. When she opened them again, Nemesis was standing in front of her, her fingers toying with a lock of Celeste's hair.

"You know I'm not Celeste. Everything she has ever done has led to this. She knew that she needed to do something to bring all of that anger back but under control. Once you had the anger, once you could manage without exploding into violence, she knew that you were ready. Honey, why do you think she sent Karim and Lilith to the Collective in the first place?" Nemesis rested her hands on her shoulder, and Celeste took a step back, breaking their contact.

She needed to sit now, her knees buckling at the thought of Karim being in on this entire scheme.

"Karim was not a part of this. He would never -"

"Of course, he wouldn't. Not intentionally, but he would reawaken those memories, those feelings- it was why he was sent back to you. Because he could break down that wall that you've built around yourself." She sighed. "Nyx figured if anyone could do that, to awaken those memories, it would be your precious Persian. I see that for once, my mother was correct."

"You twisted maniac," she whispered. Everything made sense now, Karim's reappearance and Lilith's sudden defection to the Collective at the same time. It was because she was using them all. Another one of Nyx's power plays had just taken Celeste down. Of course, Nyx had known who the Dark Queen was. Of course, she knew Lilith's identity. She closed her eyes and mentally counted to ten to keep from exploding.

"We can be what we were meant to be, Celeste. We can rule every realm between heaven and hell if you would just accept your fate and remember." Nemesis reached out to stroke Celeste's cheek, only to have her hand savagely batted away.

"You are fucking batshit crazy." She tried to hold on to her temper, but it was becoming harder and harder to maintain. "You drag me away from my family, my dying mother, to try to get me."

"She is not your mother." Nemesis struggled to remain calm, but Celeste could see the rage rising in her. Beneath her cool demeanor, she was fuming.

"She is the only mother I have ever known. I will not be your puppet in whatever scheme you have conjured up. Now, how the fuck do I get out of this nuthouse?" she yelled, trying her best to teleport the fuck out of this hell. It didn't work. Of course, it wouldn't.

Nemesis snarled, her teeth sharpening, her pale skin darkening, and horns extended from her silvery mane as she showed Celeste her new true face, the face of the Dark Queen. It was a move meant to intimidate, a trick she'd utilize often enough to gain a reputation. It received no reaction from Celeste, though.

"You will not speak to your mother –"

Celeste leveled her with a searing gaze, her body vibrating with anger. She rose, her feet lifting off of the ground as a brilliant white light surrounded her. Electricity danced and crackled around her, her blue eyes a stark unblemished white as she spoke in a tone that was beyond anything either of them had ever heard.

"Do not test me, or I will burn this place, this realm to cinders," she spat, angry tears flowing freely now. To prove her point, the walls began to smolder, smoke filling the room.

Nemesis's eyes went wide, her mouth open, and she clapped her hands with glee.

"Beautiful," Nemesis whispered, indicating the silver that streaked Celeste's hair. "She is absolutely beautiful," she said in a low whisper. Before she could respond, Celeste felt a sharp prick in her arm. She turned to see Blueman with a syringe in his hand. He'd injected her with something, and she felt her head get cloudy. Her feet settled on the carpet, and she stared at them incredulously. She had done this on purpose, instigating a reaction to seeing just how strong Celeste had become over the years. She had felt this before, right before her body had been shoved into the Cyndun River centuries ago.

"What did you do? What did you do to me?" she asked, her speech slurring and her knees go weak. "You better hope I die because if I don't, I'm going to fuck up your entire world." She slurred before slumping into the waiting arms of the man who'd injected her.

* * *

Remy was wheeled into the dim, quiet of Arbor's bedroom. His wounds bandaged, his body still bruised and broken, but he needed to see her. He needed to tell her how truly sorry he was. There were people silently moving around the room, checking her, and making sure she was comfortable. Some were familiar to him; most were not. This wasn't good. He knew that from the silence in the room, the whispers and intense conversations that were happening in clusters around him. Frederick rushed past him, pausing only to give him a tight sympathy smile. Arbor was dying, and there was nothing they could do to stop it.

Nicky sat on the edge of the bed, kissing the back of a skeletal hand, tears in his eyes as he spoke in hushed tones to the woman who had taken him in as one of her own. She had nurtured him, encouraged him, and loved him. She had given him a family. Arbor was their anchor; without her, they would have floated away long ago. Nicky turned to see Gaston pushing Remy's wheelchair into the room and stood. He kissed Arbor's forehead and said something before rushing out of the room, tears streaming down his face. Remy looked up at his brother's tightly pinched expression and nodded.

As they'd made their way to the master suite, Gaston had told him that there was nothing left to do, that she was only hanging on to say goodbye to him, to make sure her baby boy was found safe and returned to his family. She understood what was happening, she was told that Lilith was, and she didn't seem to be upset or even surprised. It was as if she'd known it was going to happen.

She had waited for her baby boy, the last of her children, to say goodbye. Gaston moved Nicky's chair as close to the bed as possible, then cleared the room to give them privacy.

She turned to look at him, and Remy felt the tears immediately. She didn't look like his mother. She was shrunken, shriveled, her skin ashen, and her eyes like saucers in a skeletal face. She gave him a small smile and reached for his hand. He grasped her fingers gently, feeling the bones beneath her thin skin, and more tears came; he couldn't stop his sobs of anguish and held her hand to his lips.

"Shhh," she sighed, releasing his hand so that she could stroke the soft curls that she'd always loved. "It's okay," she said, her voice weak and tiny.

"This is my fault. This is all my fault," he repeated, and she cupped his cheek with a withered hand, shaking her bald head. She inhaled, trying to gather enough breath to speak to him.

"No, Remy, this is not your fault. None of this," she assured him.

"I betrayed you all- I-"

"You did no such thing," she said. "Do you think that I would ever believe that you would ever do anything to hurt this family? To hurt me? This was not your doing. This was what needed to happen. It's just the beginning, my sweet boy."

"I don't want you to go," he said. She smiled, a single tear sliding from the corner of her eye. She was hurting, but her sorrow wasn't for herself. It was for him, her baby boy.

"It's time. You have become such a smart, strong male, and I am honored to have had you as my son. I will never leave you, Remy. I will not be on this plane, but I will always be a part of you. My blood flows through you. My essence is in your eye. You are truly the best thing that I have ever done in a long, long life. Do not ever forget that we share a heart, and as long as your heart beats, so will mine." She closed her eyes and took a deep breath.

"Mother," his voice was slightly panicked, and she smiled, opening those soft brown eyes.

"Don't let what has happened ruin the love that you've found," she breathed.

"You know about Briar?" he asked, sniffing away tears.

She managed a small chuckle.

"You're my son, Remy. I know everything about you. He is good for you, and he loves you like no one else can. Don't let anything ruin that. And remember, there will be bigger battles than this, my son. Protect those close to you as I always have and will always protect you. Remember *Ragnarök*." She whispered the last words as her eyes drifted closed.

Remy struggled to his feet and climbed into the bed; wrapping his arms around her, he kissed the top of her head. He was going to ask her what she meant, but her labored breathing stayed the question.

"This bald thing, it's a good look for you," he teased, and she laughed.

"Je t'aime, mère," he whispered. She patted his arm and closed her eyes, her head cradled against his shoulder. She felt so tiny, so thin next to him, but as always, she smelled of flowers, gardenias today.

"Je t'aime trop, Rémy," she whispered.

Those were the last words Arbor Kent would ever speak.

* * *

The storm came in the early hours of the morning, tearing through the city and bursting the levees with a force none had ever seen before. The damage was devastating and swift, wiping out the city, taking many lives, and destroying families in one fatal swoop. The world watched the destruction with sadness and awe, some not understanding how truly horrendous it would become in the days that followed.

While the global news documented the human loss, the world weeping and praying for those left behind, starving and dying in the unrelenting heat that followed, no one knew of the private pain of a world just beyond that of human existence.

The death of Arbor Kent not only rippled through the human world, but it also shattered the Collective and Dark Fae alike. Remy had been holding Arbor in his arms when she'd taken her final breath, surrounded by family and those who loved her most. There was only one face missing in the sea of red eyes and dower expressions. One face that had been lost to them into the abyss, and they wondered if she would ever be seen again.

* * *

In the darkness of a room that had become like a tomb to her, Celeste lay on the cold cement floor, her wrist and ankles shackled to a heavy chain that was bolted to the floor. She hadn't heard the news, but she'd known. She'd felt a great loss, an emptiness, when Arbor had left the world. She rolled onto her side in the darkness, wrapping her arms around a naked and broken body, and sobbed. Not from the pain of being beaten and tortured, she would survive these wounds and many more. She wept for the loss of her mother, a person who very much made the world a better place just by her being in it. She wept because she didn't get to say goodbye. She knew that once she got over the hurt, the pain of such a devastating loss, she was going to make good on her promise.

She was going to burn this realm and everything in it to ashes.

* * *

CHAPTER SEVENTEEN

I cy water assaulted Celeste, startling her awake. She coughed, opening her eyes, silently lifting her head to look at her tormentor with her one good eye. The other had swollen some time ago, yet the beatings continued. She was chained to a chair that had been bolted to the floor in a room with dark walls and a concrete floor. She had been staring at the drain in the center of the floor, watching blood and water swirl before disappearing. She must have passed out because the next thing she remembered was the water, stinging and icy cold, waking her.

She wore a thin white t-shirt and panties, the metal chair cold against her battered skin. Her hair hung in her face in wet bloody clumps, her mouth bled from a split lip. Several of her fingers had been broken and were now swollen, black sausages at the end of swollen red hands.

"Are you ready to give in?" She looked up into the face of Blueman, whose name she had learned, ironically was Azul. He sported an eye patch now after getting too close on one of these little *"training"* sessions, and Celeste had gouged his eye out. That was before when she had been chained to the wall with some metal alloy that she'd easily broken. Those chains had been replaced by wrist and ankle shackles made titanium with a little dark magic added for good measure and secured to her chair.

This chair had also been a recent addition. When they had foolishly used a wooden chair, she'd simply broken the chair by throwing her body back with enough force to splinter the wood on the cement floor. That time, she'd speared her tormentor, a yellow-eyed demon, through the throat with a piece of wood. As he lay choking on his own blood, she had stood, looking at the door, waiting for her mother to enter.

She never did. But she watched. Celeste knew that she could feel her eyes on her from some hidden location where she monitored these sessions. Occasionally, she would hear her chastise the torturer of the hour outside of the door, but Nemesis had never set foot into this room. Not yet, anyway.

She knew better.

"I'm speaking to you, Caelestis," he said her name as if it were a curse, and she smiled.

"Fuck you," she said and was struck in the face before the words were out of her mouth. She spit blood and started to laugh. "You hit like a pussy," she spat, and he struck her again and again only stopping when she spit teeth onto the ground.

"When I get out of this, you are going to be one of the first people I kill," she said. He shook his head before hitting her across the chest with his baton. She coughed, the wind knocked out of her. She was sure that she was going to leave a bruise. Well, another bruise, but that would heal. They all would heal, she thought. Azul leaned close, his face inches from hers as he spoke.

"We will continue this until you relent, Caelestis. Why not make this easy on yourself and relent?"

She looked at him, one brilliant blue eye to a deep red one, and smiled a bloody smile.

"Why don't you suck my big, hairy dick?" she asked and began to chuckle. He turned his attention to something in the corner of the room, and she followed his gaze to a tiny camera there. She hadn't noticed before, but now, she saw the thin black cord that disappeared into the ceiling, a tiny light shining in her direction.

Nemesis was somewhere nearby. She knew that. Nyx was with her. She could feel the two of them watching, waiting for her to give in, give up. She smirked and turned her attention back to Azul, who eyed her warily. He wasn't succeeding and knowing the power-hungry heifers that were her mother and grandmother, and there would be hell to pay. Good, she thought.

He seemed to be listening to something. Something only he could hear. Celeste was too far gone to try and listen into his mind. Besides, demons' minds were like giant puzzle pieces that didn't seem to connect in any real way.

"The Queen said relent, or she will have to call in reinforcements. She has been in contact with an old friend of yours, and he is desperate to see you after all of these years. Your former King or should I say, master- has missed you very, very much."

She pursed her lips, biting back a comment as cold fear went through her. She shot a glance towards the camera, her fury growing along with her fear and hatred. She needed to stay calm. Showing any emotion other than flippant defiance would give Nemesis an edge. She would continue to dig, to poke at a wound if she thought it would get Celeste to react. She wanted to see how far she could push her, how long she would resist because breaking her was her goal. Breaking her would make it so much easier to control her.

"If she wants to bring that fucker here, she better do it soon. Because before I kill you, and after I kill him in the nastiest way I can come up with- I'm going to slit that bitch's throat and shit in the hole," she said, laughing maniacally. Azul looked at her, then at the camera. He straightened and leveled another blow to her already bruised and broken face, and the world went dark again.

* * *

Remy hobbled down the hall, his wrists and throat still bandaged, his leg healing from a break that he hadn't known he'd had until his rescue. He hadn't been to his bedroom since they'd held Arbor's memorial the day before. It had been an eerie experience. The world outside was silent, with no birds or crickets chirping in the late summer afternoon, no color, as everything had taken on a gray tinge. There wasn't even a body because, as an elemental, she reverted to her true state, a floral scented breeze that tore through the south in the form of a hurricane.

He spent several nights sleeping in her bed, smelling her scent on the pillow and feeling her around him. Jonas had allowed it, lying beside his wounded son as he mourned his mother, and in some ways, his missing sister. Now he made his way up the stairs to the third floor to his room that had been cleaned and freshened for their newest guest.

He pushed the door open and heard the gentle beep of medical equipment that monitored Briar's vital signs. The big man lay on his stomach, his back covered in thick white bandages, the sheets draped over his bare backside. A nurse checked his IV, and Nicky slept on a chaise in the corner. He stirred when Remy entered, springing to his feet at once.

"Hey," he said in low tones, rushing over to assist Remy, who waved him off.

"How long have you been here?" Remy asked his eyes in Briar's still body. He was breathing, he could see that, but he was so still, so quiet that it was scary to him.

"Since they brought him in. His wounds had gotten infected. He's on IV antibiotics and medication for the pain, but he's doing okay. He has been asleep for a while. How are you?" He searched Remy's face, his eyes red-rimmed and bloodshot.

"I am fine. You look like shit. Why don't you go over to Celeste's room and get some sleep?" He touched Nicky's cheek, cupping it in his hand. "You need rest just like the rest of us," he said.

"Have you heard anything?" Nicky pressed. Remy shook his head. They had no idea where Celeste had gone. Lilith was no help, refusing to speak to anyone until she was before the Council. Karim, who'd moved into an apartment in the Collective, worked with the other members and Nyx to locate Celeste. He wasn't doing well either. As far as Remy knew, his guilt was eating away at him. Remy understood that better than the others, which was why Karim had confided in him.

Briar stirred, and Remy's eyes moved back to his prone form on his bed. Nicky squeezed his shoulder on his way out, signaling the nurse to follow him.

Remy eased closer, so he could get a better look at his lover. Briar's face was still battered, the bruises fading from deep purple to a sickly green and yellow. He had his hand under one bruised cheek, his lips slightly parted, a gentle snore escaping with each exhale. Remy couldn't help but smile before easing next to him in bed. He lay on his side, looking at him when one bright emerald green eye drifted open. He smiled, his hand stroking the ratty beard Remy sported.

"There's my beautiful boy," Briar said in a whisper, his voice hoarse and slurred from lack of use and the high doses of pain medication needed for a Lycan. Especially a Lycan of Briar's size.

"Hey, baby. I didn't mean to wake you." Remy moved closer but careful not to disturb him too much.

"I'm glad you did. I'm so happy to see you, baby." He ran his fingers through Remy's thick dark curls and smiled sleepily. "If your hair were longer, you'd look just like you did the first time I ever laid eyes on you. I fell in love with you that day, I think," Briar said, and tears filled Remy's eyes. He leaned closer, capturing Briar's lips with his own. Savoring the feel of his mouth, the taste of him, and he reveled in it. He had missed him. He pulled away and rested his forehead against Briar's, sniffing back tears.

"I missed you so much. I thought about you every single day," Remy said.

Briar cupped his cheek in his hand, his thumb wiping away Remy's tears. He kissed his cheek and winced as pain moved through him.

"Are you okay? Do you need anything? "Remy sat up, ready to spring into action. Briar smiled, shaking his head and placing a hand on Remy's thigh, stopping him. He shook his head, coaxing Remy back into bed, pulling him closer so he could kiss him again, his hand resting on Remy's t-shirt clad chest.

"All I need is you, baby," he said. Remy moved closer, sharing his pillow, breathing his air.

"I'm sorry," Remy started, and Briar closed his eyes, shaking his head.

"No, I already told you, *álainn,* this was not your fault. This was all Lilith. I would never blame you for what happened."

Remy closed his eyes and smiled, the sting of his words cutting through him. Of course, it was his fault because if he hadn't gotten involved with Remy, Lilith would have had no reason to torture him. She would have never noticed Briar, and he would have been safe, his body still intact. Instead, Remy had pushed her over the edge, and she had taken it out on Briar. His beautiful, gentle Briar.

"You deserve so much better than me," Remy whispered.

Briar laughed softly and kissed Remy's nose. "There is no one better than you, Remy. Not for me, you're it. All I ever wanted." He yawned, his eyes drifting shut. Remy began to ease off of the bed, but Briar caught his arm, his eyes opened.

"Where are you going?" he asked.

"I'm going to let you get your rest."

Briar shook his head, linking his fingers with Remy's. "No, stay." Briar yawned again.

"Okay. Whatever you want," Remy sighed, smiling and snuggling close to the immobile giant.

"I want ..." Briar let his hand drift down to the drawstring of Remy's pajama bottoms, waggling his eyebrows. "What I want I can't have right now, so just stay. I want to keep you close, feel you beside me. I miss this." He draped an arm around Remy's waist, pulling him as close as possible without injuring either of them. Briar smiled, drifting back into a drug-induced sleep, gently snoring against Remy's hair. Remy watched him, staring into Briar's face, running his hand over his bare, muscled arms, and sighed. He didn't know what he'd done to deserve such unconditional, unwavering love from this man, but he knew that he wasn't worthy of it. Not just yet, maybe not ever.

"You do deserve better," he whispered before his own eyes drifted shut.

* * *

Nicky couldn't sleep, not in this room that smelled so much like lavender and vanilla, so much like Celeste. He hadn't even taken off his jeans and t-shirt and lay atop the covers. Even though industrial-sized generators purred somewhere beneath the house, pushing cool air and light throughout the house, he couldn't get comfortable. He rolled onto his back and stared at the ceiling and prayed that she was okay, that she was safe. Whenever he closed his eyes, he saw her sprawled on a bathroom floor somewhere, bleeding out and welcoming death the same way he'd found Remy. The thought of that made his stomach hurt. Remy was the strongest person he'd ever known and for him to break like that was frightening. What chance did someone as fragile as Celeste stand? She was physically strong but so vulnerable and sensitive, so human. And maybe that was his fault because he kept her tethered to the human world much more than her world, a place where she was spoken of with reverence and awe.

He hadn't noticed the door open until Karim was standing over him, his intense green eyes staring down at him. Nicky started and clutched his chest, cursing under his breath before bursting into laughter. He sat up, throwing his legs over the edge of the bed and stretching.

"You scared the shit out of me." Nicky groaned. Karim smiled, but it didn't reach his eyes.

"Sorry about that," he muttered, going to sit on the sofa.

"For a second, I thought ..." He pointed to Nicky, who nodded his understanding.

"That she was back." He completed Karim's thought. "I know. It's like being here. It just reeks of her. Not just the smell of lavender, but the pictures and the clothes. I walked into her closet and saw all the things she won't wear. I couldn't tell you how many times Jonas had some big to-do for his business associates, and Celeste would want to wear sneakers and jeans. She would give Arbor fits." He closed his eyes and bit back tears. "She didn't even get to say goodbye. It's going to tear her up."

"She is a fighter. She's strong." Karim was saying, but Nicky shook his head.

"She's breakable. Karim, I know you love her, but you haven't seen her when she's hurting. I've seen glimpses, little peeks of it, and that is so hard to deal with. You want to help her, but Remy has seen her at her lowest, when she was nearly feral, not speaking or eating when she wouldn't let anyone touch her. She's come back from so much, but there is still that softness, that delicate part of her that remains cracked. She has a real hard time believing that she's worthy of love, real love. She has all of that power, but she's so fragile."

Karim nodded, listening to Nicky talk about a side of Celeste that he had never seen. He'd seen the anger and frustration, he'd seen sadness, but he'd never seen the devastation, the depression, the part that made those around her move in closer to protect her.

"That's why you love her?" Karim asked. Nicky shrugged, dropping into a chair. His exhaustion was getting the better of him, but he felt better talking to Karim. At least he had someone to commiserate with over it. Another outsider was brought into the fold simply because they had fallen in love with the same woman.

"I love Celeste for lots of reasons. She's beautiful and smart, strong and sexy. She's also stubborn and argumentative, absent-minded, and dresses like a twelve-year-old boy.

But when she looks at you, really looks at you, it's like she can see your soul. She accepted me, this orphaned foster kid who followed her around like a puppy, made me a part of this family. She gave me roots and hope, and unconditional love. She protects me even when I don't need it and forces me to do better. She says I'm her humanity. She's my compassion."

Karim smiled at that, liking Nicky more for his honesty. Even though he knew Celeste in a way he never would, he understood and appreciated the other man's feelings. Celeste was unique in her ability to make those around her feel both protective and protected.

"When did you know you loved her?" he asked, and Nicky smiled.

"The first time I made her laugh. That laugh." Nicky covered his heart with his hands and fell back into the chair.

"That laugh," Karim agreed, shaking his head. "Is like music, isn't it? It kind of takes you by surprise at first."

"Because it's so freakin loud," Nicky said, and Karim laughed.

"Like a bullhorn. But it's so light and contagious. When she really gets going, it is the best sound in the world," Karim said, looking down at his hands, the smile still in place.

"When did you know?" Nicky asked. "When did you know you'd fallen in love with her?"

Karim thought about that for a moment, scrubbing a hand over three days of stubble.

"It was long, long ago, before ...everything. It was a night in the desert, we were packing our horses, and she was rambling on about something. She was always asking questions and telling stories. She asked me a question, and I turned to look at her, and it hit me. The moon was full, huge, hanging low in the sky; she was facing the horse, her hair catching the breeze, blowing behind her like a silken sail. She turned to look at me with those eyes, and I couldn't breathe. She looked like an angel. That caramel skin was glowing, she was smiling, and that was it. I knew I was gone."

Nicky nodded, watching Karim with interest. When he didn't speak, Karim looked at him and found him staring with interest.

"I can't even sleep without her now. I've gotten use to her stealing the covers and throwing her legs across me in her sleep that I feel naked without her." he sighed, "I'm starved. I think I'll call down to the kitchen for something to eat. You want anything?" This seemed to pique Nicky's interest. He sat up, new questions popping into his ever-churning mind.

"You're a vampire," he said. Karim had the phone to his ear, asking for club sandwiches, chips, and sodas. He nodded at Nicky, his brows raised. When he hung up the phone and reclaimed his seat, Nicky leaned forward in his seat. "You ordered two club sandwiches and soda?"

"That I did," Karim agreed.

"But you're a vampire," Nicky repeated.

"A fact that has been well established," Karim chuckled.

"But you eat food." It was a question, but Nicky had said it as a statement.

"And drink beer and breathe," Karim nodded.

"But you're a vampire. Aren't you like dead?"

Karim laughed and shook his head. "I'm not that type of vampire."

There was a soft knock on the door before Frederick entered with a tray laden with food. He looked at the two men seated in Celeste's room and silently placed the tray on a low table between them. When he turned to leave, Karim stopped him, grasping his wrist.

"Thank you, Fredrick," he said pointedly. Frederick gave him a small, sad smile and nodded. Once he was gone, Karim turned to find Nicky staring at him, his brow furrowed in utter confusion. Karim reached for a sandwich and took a bite while Nicky worked out whatever was clicking in his brain. He didn't have to wait long.

"What type of vampire are you? I didn't know there were types?" Nicky reached for a sandwich and waited.

"I am one of the *seven* original vampire princes created by Nyx. We are the head of the Vampiric Royal Court. I am Prince of House Tyre, second created, second oldest. I was born human but changed by Nyx when I pledged fealty to her a long, long time ago. I eat regular food and drink, but I need blood to survive. I can go days without feeding, but the longer I wait, the worse my hunger becomes. If I wait too long, I become almost feral, dangerous. I can eat garlic, crosses do nothing to me, and I have no problem procreating. The vampires you're familiar with do exist, but I don't have those weaknesses as one of the Seven. Those vamps are created by the descendants of the Seven, sort of like being infected. They must die and be reborn. They must drink of the blood of their creator; therefore, they are tied to that vampire forever." He took a bite of his sandwich and waited.

"You can have kids?" Nicky asked, and Karim nodded. "And you can change people to vampires? Have you ever done it?"

"No," Karim said. "I've never wanted to change anyone. You either have to be power-hungry or have a great love for someone you change. And there is always the risk that they don't make it through. I wouldn't want to risk it."

"And you can't go out in sunlight?" He took a bite of his sandwich, intrigued by this information.

"No, I don't burst into flames immediately, but the exposure will kill me within a few minutes."

"Silver bullet?" Nicky smiled.

"They sting like a mother, but those kill Lycans - werewolves." Karim chuckled.

"Stake to the heart?" Nicky laughed.

"Will kill anything with a heart. Are you planning on killing me?" he asked. "I mean, I know I snaked your girl and all -" Nicky threw a handful of chips at Karim and laughed.

"I just want to make sure I have all of the facts. Just in case I have to shank your ass," Nicky said with a cheeky wink.

Karim nodded and became suddenly serious, his smile

becoming a grimace.

"I'm glad she has you. You're a good guy, Nicky," Karim said. "She's going to need you. She's going to leave me, you know. I know it. I've known for a while, and when she finds out what I did -"

"She already knows, and she understands." Karim was shaking his head, a sad smile on his lips. He stared at the sandwich in his hand and lost his appetite. He tossed it back on the tray and picked up a can of soda.

"It's not just that. I'm just a place holder. I can never truly make her mine. I've tried. That's why I can't feel her anymore. If our blood bond had been a true binding, I would feel her no matter where she was as long as she's alive. But I can't. It's like she just popped out of existence, and I don't even know what to do to find her. I feel useless, unworthy." He shook his head and took a drink.

"If it helps, I know she loves you," Nicky offered.

"I know she does, and I love her to my marrow. But sometimes love just isn't enough. The longer I'm with her, the harder it will be in the end. It should end sooner rather than later because if I wait too long if we have a child, I would never be able to walk away. I would never get over her when he - I just want to enjoy every second I have with her. When it ends, and it has to, and it's going to fucking kill me." He finished his drink and lay across the sofa, his arm thrown across his eyes. Nicky watched the vamp, slowly eating his sandwich and empathizing with him. Yet another soldier in the legion of men who, by no fault of her own, had lost his heart to Celeste.

* * *

She wasn't floating this time, not in the dark abyss or the cloudless sky. Instead, she was still in this room, this torture chamber, and her body ached. She felt gentle fingers moving along her bruised cheek and opened her one good eye, but only a little, only slightly. Hands, warm, strong, and comforting, rested on her shoulders, making her relax for a moment. She looked up and saw the deep blue eyes glowing in the darkness and sighed, resting her cheek on the back of one of his smooth obsidian hands.

"You are injured," he said in that deep vibrato that shook her to her core. *"I can help. All you must do is call for me."* He came around the chair, kneeling between her thighs. He ran a hand along her bruised legs, up her arms, his eyes resting on her broken and swollen fingers.

"He is a good man, and he will love you for as long as he can, but you are mine, and only I have the power to protect you, love. You must allow me to do so." She was looking into his beautiful face, smooth onyx skin and cerulean eyes glowing in the gloom of her cell. Tears came to her eyes, and she sobbed, releasing the hurt and pain, the constant ache in her that had burrowed so deep that she'd forgotten it was even there. It lived in her, like the mark on her neck, reminding her of things that she'd tried to forget.

"Speak my name, and my power will live in you. My legion will be your protection, your shield from those that would harm you and those you love. Speak my name, and I will take the pain away. Trust in me, you are mine and mine alone, and I will watch over you, from this day forward."

"But Karim ... " he laughed, a sound she hadn't heard before, but it calmed her. It was a rumble, deep and throaty, and settled over her. She smiled, feeling safe and loved, oh so loved.

"Karim is your consort ...for now. You are mine for eternity." He kissed her hands, one then the other. *"He has taken the sting out of things you hadn't even realized were hurting you."* He ran a finger across her wrist, and she nodded. She no longer had an aversion to people touching her wrists. She no longer felt sick to her stomach when a kiss was placed on her neck or when she was grasped in a bear hug by surprise. Karim had allowed her to trust again. She hadn't even realized it.

"He is who you need now. I am who you will need forever. Speak my name, and I will protect you." She heard movement in the room, nothing sinister, but a warmth that surrounded her. From the shadows, a grey figure standing at least nine feet tall stepped forward. His face was still, his eyes colorless and serene watched with curiosity.

"Speak my name," he repeated, and she looked down and was immediately lost in the depths of his blue eyes. She spoke a word, a name she hadn't even realized she'd known, but his smile let her know it was the right one. He slipped a long silver chain around her neck - a pendant dangled from the end in the shape of the mark they shared, his on his chest above his heart, hers on her neck.

"Feed and grow strong for the battle to come." The grey male came forward and knelt beside her, lifting his wrist to her lips. *"Drink as much as you need, love. As much as you want."* She closed her eyes, sinking her teeth into hard flesh that tasted of ash and fire, but his blood was sweet, honeyed nectar, rich and delicious. She drank deeply, filling herself and feeling her body grow stronger. This was not the blood of an ordinary preternatural. This was beyond the divine. This was a powerful, healing elixir of those that came before the gods, but after Him, this was the blood of the oldest and strongest, the blood of the Grigori. And she could call upon it whenever she was in need, because she was the *Keeper of the Nephilim*, now and forever. She pulled away, gasping for air. It was so good, like a drug that fueled her, her heart racing in her chest. She was reborn.

"You are mine, forevermore," he whispered, brushing his lips across hers, and she felt a new heat begin in the pit of her stomach. It was as if he'd ignited a fire in her, the electricity that pulsated in her every nerve. She felt stronger and, with her army, unstoppable. He ran a hand over her face, and she felt her lids grow heavy again.

"Now rest, my sweet," he said softly, and she drifted back into the darkness.

* * *

"She won't break, majesty." Azul was saying to Nemesis, whose eyes were trained on the monitor. She was watching Celeste, who was either in a trance or hallucinating, lift her head and say something,

"She will break," she snapped. She needed her to break. She couldn't gain control until Celeste was completely broken, weak, and at her mercy. It would take longer than she thought because even with all of her scars, Celeste was tough. She'd hardened. But only on the outside. Once they cracked that tough exterior, she would have her. She squinted, leaning forward when Celeste leaned to the side and opened her mouth as if she were feeding.

"What is she doing?" Nemesis swore because she hadn't added sound to the room. She tapped a button on the console and zoomed in, but there was nothing there, the room empty except for Celeste shackled to a chair and a single light bulb high in the ceiling. After a while, Celeste's body was limp, her head lolling from side to side, but her lips were moving as if in conversation.

"She's waking, Majesty," Azul reminded her. "And she wants to see you." They both turned to the monitor, watching as Celeste shook herself awake, forcing the one undamaged eye to open. After a moment, she turned and looked directly at the camera, her smile frightening. She mouthed a vulgar term directed at her mother and laughed, before turning away from the camera, her eyes on the drain in the middle of the floor.

She was too still, too quiet, and had been alone far too long. Celeste was too clever, resourceful, and cunning; giving her time to think was never a good idea.

"I'm going in. She will break. I'll make sure of that." Nemesis swallowed hard as she thought of facing Celeste; over the past few days, she'd seen her capabilities. It was terrifyingly beautiful how ruthless her daughter had become, yet she needed her. She pushed her chair away from the monitor and rose slowly.

She stood, tugging at the hem of her white button-down top, and ran a hand over her white jeans before exiting the room. The short walk down the hall to the cell where Celeste was held was nerve-wracking, and she found herself counting to ten before allowing the guards to open the door.

Celeste looked up when she saw the shadow cast by her mother on the floor before her. Nemesis took a deep breath and stepped inside, physically jumping when the heavy door was slammed shut and locked behind her. Celeste smirked and watched her mother come further into the room.

"You came alone? No mommy or guards to protect you from the big, bad goddess?" Celeste asked, not waiting for Nemesis to begin her banal niceties.

"You don't understand the raw power that you hold. I see the potential in you. Nyx was always frightened of you, but I knew from the start that you are destined for greatness."

"Was that before or after you tried to kill me the first time? Because I believe I was an infant at that time."

"I was distraught, devastated - " Nemesis sputtered.

"Or what about the next time, when you had me drugged and tossed into the sea? Did you recognize the power then? Or what about when your mother allowed me to be drugged, raped, and murdered? Did you see it then? Or do you just enjoy trying to kill your children? Wait, wait, that can't be right because you never, as far as I know, tried to kill Lilith. Was that because you didn't recognize any power in her? Or was she just not worth the time to murder?"

"You and she are not the same. You are - you are so special, Celeste. Do you understand what it means now that you have the mark? Do you know how long I have waited to find you to get close to you? When he comes to you, you will hold immeasurable power. Are you ready to accept your fate?"

Celeste nodded slowly, her eye brightening if that were possible.

"But that's not the real reason I wanted to talk to you." Celeste sighed, her tone even, almost relaxed. "I didn't know that you dream when you're blacked out? It's not always just darkness because your brain isn't completely shut down. It's still working. Did you know that? I say that because *the Fallen One*, I suppose that's who he is, comes to me in these dreams. Mind you, most of the time he comes, it's - well - it's quite exhilarating." She gauged Nemesis for a reaction, but as usual, her mother's face was expressionless. "But sometimes, he tells me things, reminds me of things that I have forgotten or locked away in a part of my mind for safekeeping."

Nemesis rolled her eyes and tapped her ballet flat covered foot on the floor, impatiently waiting.

"Are you getting to the point of this story, Celeste?" she asked. Celeste's smile widened, her nose wrinkling as she nodded.

"Oh yes, I'm getting to that part. You see, I must thank you for all of this," she made a stilted hand gesture to indicate the room, her wrists still bound to the arms of the metal chair. "Because of your...care? Treatment? Training? However, you envision these little sessions that you put me through. I remembered something that I never even realized I knew. You know what it is?" Nemesis threw her hands up in exasperation.

"I have no earthly idea, Celeste," she growled.

"I realized that for me to gain this magnanimous power that you crave so much, I would have to remember his name. Do you know that no one has spoken his name in centuries? Eons? A millennium- but it was trapped up here." She lifted her arm easily to tap the side of her head, the heavy metal shackle dropping away like wet tissue. It took a tick for Nemesis to realize what she was seeing, but she took a step backward when she did and called for the guards.

"So, guess what, the blue boy knocked loose when he hit

me in the head?" She crossed her legs and folded her arms over her chest, her shackles clattering to the floor. "A name. One name came to me in bright neon on a hundred-foot-tall billboard. I said the name, I did what you wanted, and I claimed my rightful place. I am the Caelestis, the one claimed by the *Fallen One*. " She stood, her bruises fading, the swollen eye shrinking, returning to normal as she rolled her shoulders and broken bones snapped back into place, much to Nemesis's astonishment. Celeste cracked her neck and stretched her back, smiling more to show that her perfect smile was once again intact. Celeste looked at the camera, made a gun with her thumb and forefinger, and pretended to shoot it. Sparks flew from the tiny device, killing the feed to the monitors. There was noise from the hallway as guards tried and failed to unlock the door, a door that locked from the outside.

Nemesis could feel the cold sweat begin on her brow, her breathing becoming a panicked pant when several sets of brilliant white eyes appeared in the darkness, filling the room. Nemesis stumbled back, expecting to reach the door, only to find her back pressed against a heavily armored chest. She turned to look up to stare into white eyes shining down at her. The face was stony, a dark charcoal grey that reminded her of lava rock. It was chiseled and strong and expressionless. She gasped and moved back, her jaw slack as she realized what these giant stone men were. These were the descendants of the *Fallen One*, the stone army that was the Nephilim. Slowly, one by one, she could hear metal against stone as they unsheathed their swords, ready for battle at Celeste's command. She laced her fingers together and took a step towards her mother; her voice lowered as she moved in to speak.

"Remember when I told you I would burn this place to cinders?" Nemesis' eyes widened when Celeste stepped closer still, her eyes sparkling with unbridled hostility.

"Well, mother dear, I'm starting with you."

* * *

CHAPTER EIGHTEEN

The guards struggled to open the cell door, hearing the panicked cries and unable to assist. Azul pushed through the crowd of armored creatures, a weapon in hand. He intended to blow the lock off of the door, but he needn't bother. As soon as he got into position, the small gun-like electro-taser pointed at the lock. The entire wall exploded in a shower of rock and fire.

Azul was thrown back, a boulder size chunk of cement snapping his leg just below the knee. He wailed in pain, dropping the taser as he pushed at the heavy chunk of wall that pinned him in place. Around him, he could hear the moans and wails of fallen guards hidden in the dust and smoke.

He stared as something moved in the gray mist that settled around them, and his eyes widened in fear. The Nephilim stepped forward, standing ten feet tall, shoulder to shoulder in dark metal breastplates with the crest of *the Fallen* across the chest, and dark leather Praetorian skirts. They wore metal guards on their skins and heavy swords on their hips. If that was what it was, their skin was dark, the color of burned charcoal, cracked and illuminated with deep reds and oranges, like lava flowing beneath the stone. Their massive stone-colored wings tucked against their backs looked like shields protecting them from rear attacks. They looked down, colorless eyes falling on the Queen who lay in the rubble like a discarded, dirty toy.

Somewhere an alarm began to sound, shrill and squealing, alerting the guards that there had been an escape attempt. Azul finally managed to push the stone from his broken leg and drag himself to the Queen, who lay coughing, the right side of her face charred and bleeding

* * *

Her chest hurt, and she couldn't see out of her right eye, which she realized had been damaged in the blast. Nemesis coughed, trying to gather herself when he grasped her arms and half dragged her out of the way of the advancing army that moved through the hole in the wall. She stumbled along, letting the demon pull her past the newly assembled guard as they prepared for battle. Azul managed to get her safely behind her soldiers, dragging his leg bleeding and broken behind him, his lungs coated with grit and dust from the wall, and collapsed. He turned just in time to see the Nephilim advance. Their swords drawn, they moved as one unstoppable machine cutting the Queen's guard as if they were nothing more than paper dolls. They had made it out of the narrow corridor to the loggia at the rear of the house, but the unmovable stone men were still cutting down the soldiers. Swords did minor damage as they slashed through some, burning others to cinders with the mere touch of their skin. Those not in the throes of cutting down the Queen's guard were setting the house ablaze.

Azul wasn't paying attention to Celeste as the goddess sliced through demon after demon, getting closer and closer to her mother. He sat with his back against the wall, a trail of thick dark blood left in his wake, trying to find a way out as the world burned and bled around him. He ripped his sleeve and wrapped it around his leg to staunch the bleeding.

He hadn't noticed her until she was upon him, her sword drawn, a look of violent glee in her shimmering silver-blue eyes. She pressed the tip of her blade into his already throbbing leg, smiling when he yelled in pain. She leaned closer, her face close to his, and he began to sweat.

"Remember when I said you would be one of the first I

kill?" He was anticipating the sword, a swift blow to the heart or his head, the bloodier, the better. Instead, she plunged the sword through his leg and into the ground below, pinning him in a place like a bug. She grasped his face in her hands, her face close enough to kiss him, and licked her lips.

"I always keep my word." She tugged his head swiftly to the right until the bones of his neck snapped. He slumped, his head hanging at an unnatural angle. She pulled her sword from his leg, spinning as her mother charged toward her, skillfully wielding a double-bladed spear. Celeste turned her body to the side, giving her mother a smaller target, spread her legs, and crouched down, her sword raised for battle. She lifted one hand and beckoned her mother forward, her eyes narrow in a warning.

"Come get some," Celeste growled, igniting Nemesis' ire.

She charged forward, her blades slicing the air, her face set in a mask of anger. She swung at Celeste's throat, which Celeste easily dodged, turning on her heel so that she could thrust her sword forward. Nemesis took a step back and twisted the spear, both ends swinging towards Celeste's face like the blades of a fan. She blocked each blow, but they were coming too fast, one blade slicing through the silk of Celeste's shirt, blood pouring from the wound. She stumbled back, looking at her arm. She glanced at it, then sidestepped Nemesis' forward thrust, and Celeste spun away, swinging her blade down and connecting with the center of the spear. The heavy metal snapped, leaving Nemesis with two short knives. She recovered quickly, swinging behind her in an attempt to cut Celeste, before turning to keep her eye on her daughter.

Celeste didn't turn to face her mother as she thrust the sword back, feeling it sink into flesh. She pulled the blade and turned as a blossom of red spread along Nemesis's side, and one of the knives clattered to the floor. She looked at Celeste in shock; she'd never been wounded in battle. Never.

She looked at her daughter, the child she'd tried to kill over and over, and was stunned by her. She stood with her sword in hand and touched the bloodstain spreading across the soot caked front of her shirt. Celeste returned her gaze, set her jaw, and pure energy danced around her, sparking and reaching out like fingers into the airlessness of the hall.

"This is what you wanted, isn't it, mother? To have me reach my full potential? \" Celeste yelled over the cries of the dying and the raging fire at her back.

"I will grind you into the dirt!" Nemesis snarled and charged, her blade high over her head, preparing to strike. Celeste dropped her sword and waited, grasping Nemesis's wrist and punching her in the face.

She stumbled back, blinking as she saw stars. Celeste advanced, another blow connecting with Nemesis' sternum, and she retreated, taking a moment to collect the air that had been knocked from her lungs and left her gasping.

Nemesis swung back, the knife cutting through the air, her fist connecting with Celeste's mouth. Blood flew from her lips, and she managed to look excited and pleased at once. Nemesis charged again, using her momentum to carry her forward, her strength and stamina waning.

"You really need to work on your cardio," Celeste taunted and sliced Nemesis across the throat with the side of her hand, followed by a blow to the back of her neck when she stumbled forward. She landed on her knees, the clattering of the metal on cobblestone reminding her that she still had a weapon, even if she were out skilled by Celeste. She rolled onto her back, just as Celeste's boot heel came toward her face, instinctively grabbed her foot and pulled. Celeste crashed to the ground with a thud, a little surprised by the move. She took no notice if she was hurt because she was back on her feet in a blink. Nemesis rolled to her knees and stood, trying to catch her breath. She was becoming winded and tired, her wound bleeding more than it should, not healing as it normally would.

Celeste took two steps forward, her body low in a practiced fighting stance, and Nemesis noted the glee in her, and she thought she might be enjoying this fight, getting some sort of strange satisfaction from it. When Celeste once again gestured for her mother to come at her, she knew that this was a side of the goddess she hadn't realized existed. Celeste truly was a skilled warrior, and she intended to kill her.

She gathered herself and charged, blade swinging, but Celeste turned, grabbing her mother's wrist and tossing her over her shoulder. She landed on her back and felt the pop as several ribs broke on impact. Her head hit the cobblestones, and everything went out of focus. Celeste sat on her chest, forcing the blade in Nemesis's hand to the woman's throat. The tip pierced delicate white skin, and blood pooled around the wound, dripping down the polished silver blade.

"I told you I would slit your fucking throat," Celeste growled. She pushed harder, but Nemesis fought back, struggling to pull the weapon from her neck. Her strength was waning, her vision blurring. Celeste's face loomed over hers, a mask of horrific happiness as the blade sank deeper.

"We could have ruled the world together," Nemesis grunted, the taste of her blood filling her mouth. "We could have been unstoppable."

Her voice was no more than a gurgle, blood filling her throat as she tried to halt the progress of the blade as it sank deeper and deeper into her neck. Sweat dripped from the tip of Celeste's nose, the heat from the growing fire sweltering, smoke burning their lungs. She reached for the wound in the woman's side, gouging it with her thumb until Nemesis groaned in agony.

"You should have thought about that before you tried to kill me," Celeste growled as Nemesis struggled to breathe. Her hold on the blade wavered, slipping as blood coated the handle

"Take my advice," she said, watching the life fade from her mother's eyes. "Stay dead."

* * *

It had taken a while, but Nicky had finally managed to fall into an exhausted fitful, sleep in the wee hours of the morning when the lights came on. He covered his face with a pillow and chuckled when he heard Karim, who'd fallen asleep on the sofa, began cursing the parents of the person who'd dare to wake him.

"Quiet," Remy growled and pulled the pillow from Nicky's face letting the light shine directly into his eyes.

"What the hell, Remy?" He groaned and sat up. He watched as Karim rose like a corpse in an old vampire movie, his eyes still closed as he called Remy something in his native tongue. Nicky knew it was something off-color because Remy laughed.

"You wish," he said, pulling the covers back and tossing clean clothes at Nicky. "Both of you, up now. We've been called to bear witness before the Council." Karim rolled his eyes and lay back on the sofa.

"Fuck the Council," Karim grumbled as a pair of clean jeans flew toward him. Without sitting up or even opening his eyes, his hand shot up and snatched them out of the air.

"I feel the same way, but you, my friend, are part of the Collective now. You have to." Karim looked at Remy with one pale green eye and sat up, grumbling as he made his way into the bathroom. Nicky watched Remy, now nearly completely healed, wore his uniform, hair trimmed, and the beard gone. He looked almost like himself again, yet there was sadness, a rawness, and anger that hadn't been there before.

"Okay, then I can go back to sleep," Nicky said and pulled the covers over his head. They have ripped away, leaving him exposed in nothing but a pair of boxers. "If you wanted to see me naked, Remy, there are easier ways," Nicky teased.

"Get up. They want you too." Remy chuckled and slapped his foot. Confused, Nicky sat up on his elbows, his brow raised.

"Why? I thought only preternaturals were called to see the Council. Wait, am I dead, and no one told me? Did I die when I was teleported?" He touched his chest, testing to see if his hands went through. "Did it give me some sort of superhuman abilities? Am I like Spiderman?"

Remy sighed and shook his head.

"You're family." He wandered over to a desk, rifling through a drawer as he spoke.

"All members of the Royal Family of the Collective, the family of the High Regent, have been asked to bear witness." He found what he was looking for, a letter opener that looked more like a knife than an office tool, and tested the weight in his hand. "That includes all who share blood with a member of that family. Celeste had shared blood from Arbor and Jonas when she was brought into the family centuries ago. And I assume she's shared blood with Karim."

"You assume correctly!" Karim called from the bathroom. Nicky had fixed his mouth to ask a question when Remy grabbed his hand and slashed the palm.

"Shit, Remy! Goddamn it- " he yelped as blood pooled in his hand. Remy did the same to his palm and grasped Nicky's hand, pulling him to his feet.

"My blood for your blood, we are bound by family. You are my brother, brother to my brother and sisters, son to my father, and have all the privileges to the House of *de Noé* and the Kent Family legacy." He kissed Nicky on each cheek before releasing his hand. Nicky knew that before the Kents became the Kents, they were the de Noé family originally from Roque-brune-Cap-Martin, a small Providence near Monaco in France. That was centuries before they relocated to Perche, then the Americas. He didn't have time to truly react because Remy licked his palm, then his own, to begin the healing process.

"Get dressed, petit frère," Remy said.

Nicky stared at him; his expression was disgusted by what had just happened. He wasn't sure if he was in shock or honored because he could only focus on his wet palm.

"You licked me."

* * *

Lilith felt tiny and conspicuous, surrounded by what had to be four of the largest soldiers enlisted in the Grey. Their armor, she had learned from Remy, was a state of the art Kevlar tactical body armor. The suits had been reinforced with some sort of material that protected them from human-made and magical weaponry. Their faces were hidden beneath dark grey helmets that made them seem alien. She stared at the two's profiles in the lead, trying to make eye contact through their dark visors. They didn't even acknowledge her presence as they moved silently from the darkest recesses of the Collective to the second-level mezzanine.

From here, she could see the lobby above them and out of the windows that made up the lobby roof to see the midnight sky lit with millions of shining stars. It was beautiful. She couldn't remember the last time she'd seen that many stars in the sky. She slowed, and one of the soldiers behind her gave her a nudge forward. She continued, turning to look at Gaston and Lisette, who walked behind her, sneering. Lisette was always sneering at her.

Her sneer spread into a smile that wasn't for Lilith but the three striking men descending the wide staircase from the lobby. Remy, Karim, and a blond she recognized from his countless magazine covers and music videos approached.

He looked at Lilith, staring at her with something that bordered on revulsion. He didn't sneer the way Lisette had, nor did he ignore her like Remy and Karim. Instead, Nicky Sky stared at her with a frosty glare that made her feel ashamed of herself for the first time. He shook his head dismissively before turning back to Lisette, who held his palm in her hand, inspecting it.

"Welcome, *petit frère*," she said and kissed him on both cheeks when the entire building began to quake. It was gentle at first, a slight tremor that rattled fixtures and jostled the small group.

"What the - " Remy started, and the place shook again, this time more violently, mortar and stone falling from the ceiling. The shaking continued, tossing things to the floor. The colonnade ceiling glass began to crack and rain down on them, and people screamed, running for cover.

"Is this an earthquake?" Nicky asked, another bone-rattling quake rumbling the place.

* * *

The windows above them gave way, raining chunks of thick tempered glass down on them. Lisette pulled Nicky with her as the others ran for cover. Remy pulled a radio from some unknown pocket and began rattling off orders in rapid military-speak that sounded like a foreign language to Nicky's civilian ears. Grey body armored soldiers poured into the lobby from elevators and stairwells, some brandishing large black weapons that looked like laser cannons, others with swords. Nicky had never in his life been so terrified and exhilarated.

A sea of red armored soldiers descended from the sky, filling the lobby and the mezzanine with what had to be an army of hundreds. A man stepped forward, his smile jovial, but his eyes darkened with unbridled fury. It was a startling contrast that made Nicky step further into the shadows, his heart thumping against his ribs.

"Lucifer, you're not supposed to be here. You've broken the peace accord; the Council will crucify you for this," Lisette said. Nicky's head snapped around at the mention of the name he'd heard about in bible study from the time he could walk. He stared at the handsome, almost angelic features and remembered words he'd heard in Sunday school that Lucifer had once been an angel and was beautiful to behold. He swallowed hard and crossed himself. Never had he believed that he would come face to face with the devil.

"That psychopath crossed the line first. Now, where is she, Lisette? Give her to me now, or I will tear this place apart brick by brick until I find her." He was practically frothing at the mouth, his skin a ruddy red, his fingers turning into claws as he clutched the hilt of his broadsword.

"Lilith? She's right here," Lisette said, a bit surprised he would demonstrate such a show of force and on a neutral plane, no less. This was tantamount to treason, breaking the tenuous treaty established between the Dark Fae and the Collective.

"Not her, you can have her. I'm looking for the rabid lunatic that murdered my wife. I want her here now, or I will tear this place apart until she is brought to me!" he bellowed.

"You should have let me sleep," Nicky whispered, tapping Remy on the shoulder.

✳ ✳ ✳

She stood on the roof, looking down at the scene unfold beneath her. She'd manifested here when the Nephilim had taken her from Nemesis' realm. From her vantage point, she had a clear view of the red army and wished she were in more than a damp, dirty t-shirt and panties. She paused for a second, but only a second, before she was in her dark grey Kevlar armor, her sword in hand. If he wanted war, he'd get war.

"Where is she? She killed my wife!" Alexander howled. Celeste shook her head and sighed. Lilith, who was hidden in the shadows, made a noise, a low howl that sounded like a wounded animal.

"Mother's dead?" she wailed. "No, no - " she choked before the sobs began in earnest. Alexander continued his tirade, ignoring the heart-wrenching moans.

Celeste stepped through the broken window, landing on

one knee, one hand down to brace herself, her sword drawn and at her side. Slowly, she stood, a smirk on her lips, her brow raised in surprise.

"All you had to do was ask nicely," Celeste said. He growled, reaching for her, but she easily dodged him, slapping at his hands with the flat side of her sword while wagging a finger in his face. "Be nice, Alex," she said.

"I will rip you apart for what you did!" he snarled, looming over her. She looked up at him and sighed heavily as if she were bored with the entire situation.

"For killing my poor excuse of a mother, slaughtering the guards, or burning your house down?" she asked.

"Did she just say, mother?" Remy asked Lisette, who stood with her jaw clenched. "I could have sworn she just said that the Dark Queen is...was her mother."

"It's the least I could do for the woman who did so much for me. You know, in her last moments before I sank my blade into her throat, she didn't speak of you. She didn't declare her love for you or that red-headed abomination you call a daughter. Not once. And here you are - knocking down my front door offering a war. If you would have pulled out, or if mommy had been a good girl and just swallowed-. you could have saved yourself a world of trouble. Instead, your albino weasel wolverine of a daughter murdered the only mother I have ever known. I will enjoy sinking my sword into you, just like I did your psychotic cunt of a wife." She lifted the sword to her mouth, seductively licking the cool metal. "Mmmmm, I can't wait."

With lightning-quick speed, she drew her sword across his face, spraying blood and nearly blinding him. He howled, stumbled back, grabbing his eye, then charged her, but she was ready, fighting back with swiftness and fury that was unexpected and a little frightening.

* * *

Nicky sank deeper into the shadows, Lilith uncomfortably shoved into his personal space. He shoved her aside so he could watch the battle unfold as if he were watching a movie. The red army surged forward, weapons firing pulses of energy, while swordsman moved across the marble lobby.

Lisette roared and charged forward, blaster in hand, The Grey moving with her in waves. From the shadows, what looked like hundreds of giant stone men with bright white eyes emerged. Standing at least ten feet tall, they began cutting through the red army with swords that seared flesh and left the wounded decimated.

Karim and Gaston fought side by side, carving the red army with zeal and vigor that only matched Remy, who fought with his hands and teeth as his only weapons. The half-man -half tiger moved with ease and agility from years of moving between animal and the human form. In battle, he was glorious, enjoying the fight with joyous zeal. He was at his brother's back, his fangs and claws ripping through demon after demon with the excitement of a child, an unstoppable machine smiling with devilish glee.

But it was Celeste that captured Nicky's attention. She moved with a lethal grace that was almost balletic. There was calm in her fighting, a beauty in the way she moved around the large clumsy demons. She silently led the stone giants that cut down more than half of Alexander's army in a matter of seconds, leaving it depleted with many abandoning him.

Alexander let out a guttural roar at the height of the battle and charged forward, his sword swinging in a wild arch as he raced across the floor like a freight train. He stood at least three feet taller than the six-foot Celeste, his speed unnerving for such a lumbering beast. Celeste had her back to him, engaged in battle with three of the demon army when Karim stepped in to take the blow that was coming at her back. The blade sliced across his chest and blood poured dripping onto the cracked marble floor. He fell to his knees, clutching his chest in agony, his sword clattering to the ground.

Celeste turned in time to see him fall, and rage consumed her. She howled and charged forward, burying her sword into Alexander's side, where it burned like heated coal. He screeched and tried to dislodge it, clawing at the handle, which had become blazing hot. She stared for a moment, watching his skin sizzle, smelling the pungent stench of cooked flesh before she removed the blade, letting it clatter to the floor.

"This is far from over, Caelestis," he snarled, clutching at the nasty open gash, his acidic blood burning the marble floor. His army fell back; two of his less damaged soldiers assisting him to his feet as they retreated. "I will have your head before this is done."

"I look forward to it." She sheathed her sword and wiped the blood from her cheek with the back of her hand. She wasn't entirely sure if it was splatter from someone else or if it were her own, but it didn't matter. If it were her blood, she would have healed already anyway, another newly developed power, she healed instantly.

Nicky watched as Celeste turned her attention to the statuesque men, who all turned to face her in unison. As if listening to some silent orders, they all took positions around the lobby and mezzanine. Nicky watched the stone sentinels as their eyes slowly closed, and they remained still, effigies until their mistress summoned them again.

He watched Celeste move to Karim, checking his wound, and exhaled. She then spotted Lilith crouched in a corner. Celeste marched across the room to her sister with a determined stride and punched her in the face. The movement was swift and done with such force that Lilith crumbled immediately, blood sprouting from her mouth and nose as her head bounced on the cracked marble floor.

He'd known that she was a certified badass but seeing her and her entire family in action had given him a new level of respect for her. Celeste was truly a warrior; he'd known that, of course, but seeing it made it real. Celeste was an immortal goddess. Violence and death were her life.

He never stood a chance.

CHAPTER NINETEEN

The Council chamber was still and silent as they waited for the gods to return from the small soundproof room they had sequestered themselves. They had been in the small room for what felt like hours, a god from each pantheon sharing in the decision of how to handle Lilith after her father intruded on the Collective.

Celeste and her family had taken up residence in the gallery of chairs that faced the Council podium as they waited. Only Lilith sat apart from them in a heavy metal chair in the center of the room. Though she wasn't bound the way Celeste had been, she was held in place by several levels of magic. Celeste stared at her and smirked before turning to look at the people sitting with her.

They were a filthy, blood-covered, exhausted mess. Remy sat plucking chunks of flesh from beneath his claws and flinging them at Nicky, who punched him in his arm. Lisette stared at the toe of her boots and fretted over the singed leather, mumbling about demon blood under her breath. Gaston and Karim sat in companionable silence, the latter holding a piece of his torn t-shirt to the rapidly healing wound across his chest. Jonas had joined them shortly after they'd entered this stark white room, embracing Celeste as if he hadn't seen her in years.

"Jonas, father - I am so sorry - Arbor." She couldn't stop the tears that flowed freely, leaving clean streaks on dirty cheeks. Jonas shushed her, held her face in his hands, and shook his head.

"She knew. She knew." He kissed her forehead before pulling her back into his arms. Now he sat silently, his arm around Lisette's shoulders as they waited for Lilith's punishment to be handed down.

Celeste stiffened beside Karim, feeling a strange prickling heat on her neck, her mark searing.

From the corner of her eyes, she saw the tell-tale signs that her grandmother was manifesting beside her. Celeste stood, moving closer to the swirling cloud of silver mist, waiting as Nyx materialized.

Karim rose with her, tossing the bloodied rag to the side, and he tapped Gaston's shoulder drawing everyone else's attention in the process. They all turned just as Nyx fully materialized, her grey eyes large with surprise.

Nyx took a step back, surprised to discover Celeste so close. She stumbled, clutched at her heart, and laughed nervously before opening her arms to embrace her granddaughter. Celeste allowed the embrace but remained still, her arms at her sides. Undaunted, she held Celeste at arm's length to look her over.

"I knew we would find you. Karim, didn't I tell you she would be fine."

Celeste shook her head, tears stinging her already raw red eyes. Gently, much too gentle for the anger she felt, she took Nyx's hand in hers, holding them so tightly that the bones began to crack. Everyone, except Lilith, sprang to their feet, intent on stopping Celeste until they heard her speak.

"Except I'm not fine, Nyx," Celeste was saying. Nyx yelped, dropping to her knees as Celeste increased the pressure on her crushed hands. "But that's what you wanted, right? You wanted me to be damaged. She told me, my twisted fuck of a mother, the mysterious Dark Queen she told me. She told me everything you did. I thought of you just before I shoved my dagger into her throat."

Nyx wept, trying in vain to free herself from Celeste's superhuman grip. The more she struggled, the tighter Celeste held on, crushing the bones in her delicate fingers to dust.

"What I did was for -" Nyx was sobbing.

"The greater good, I know." Celeste laughed. "You did it so that I could reach my full potential. I know. That little fact was beaten into my head. It's tattooed on my brain. Just like this brand is burned into my neck." She released Nyx, shoving her so hard that the smaller woman fell to the floor, holding her gnarled hands to her chest as she wailed in agony. She flinched as Celeste squatted beside her, her tone even as she spoke, sending a chill through the room.

"You'll be happy to know, dear sweet grandmother, that I did what you wanted. I remembered his name. That's why I can do this-" Celeste placed a hand on Nyx's forehead, and the color began to drain from Nyx's dark hair.

"No," Nyx screamed, seeming to forget the pain in her hands. "No! You can't!"

"But I can," Celeste assured her as she drained Nyx's powers. "I will take your power, as you took my mother's. If it didn't throw the entire planet into chaos, I would take your life. But unlike you, I'm not a heartless, selfish waste of flesh. At least, not yet anyway. We'll just see how this goes."

"I will take him from you," Nyx said, her eyes darting towards Karim, who stood by looking nervous. "I still hold dominion over him, and even you can't take my dominion from me."

Celeste looked back at Karim, her expression filled with sudden sadness, her heart aching.

"You did that centuries ago. And he is no longer yours to rule. He and all of the *Seven* no longer answer to you. They answer only to themselves. I can do that too." Celeste winked before rising, leaving Nyx, a crumpled heap on the floor. She stood looking at her, her once-powerful grandmother, the one person who she believed, would protect her above all others who had betrayed her over and over again. The anger and pain dissolved as she noticed for the first time the tiny lines around her swirling grey eyes, the small, frail frame, and hair that rapidly faded to a deep grey.

"I banish you to the realm of darkness. If you ever set foot into another realm, I will end you. Go." Celeste waved her hand as if dismissing Nyx, only to have her slide across the room through the heavy steel doors which slammed behind her.

Slowly, Celeste turned to Karim. He held his arms out, and she went into the warmth of his embrace, silent tears damping his t-shirt.

"Thank you," he kissed the top of her head and held her.

* * *

With his short white blond hair and perpetual surfer vibe, Zeus rubbed his eyes and sighed heavily, his shoulder slumped. He leaned against the desk; his legs crossed at the ankles, his hands shoved deep into the pockets of his shorts. As usual, he wore a vibrant Hawaiian shirt and flip-flops, his skin deeply tanned from hours in the sun. His features remained youthful, but his eyes, those vibrant and twinkling eyes, were ancient. He looked at the family and shook his head before he began to speak.

"A decision has been made, and I must admit, it is not one I agree with, not by a long shot. The Council was deadlocked. Eight voted for death; eight did not. Since we could not agree, it was taken higher, and the decision has been made and is out of my control. It has been decreed that to avoid a war between the Collective and the Dark Fae that would more than likely devastate the human world, Lilith will have her powers stripped, she will be flogged, ten lashes for each charge by someone you deem appropriate, and she will be imprisoned in the Faery realm. With the way their time works, her sentence of three years will be more like seventy, after which she will be allowed to act as High Regent of the Collective as decreed in Arbor's hand in her will. We can't prove whether it was forged, magically or otherwise. We cannot dispute it.

These conditions must be met as restitution. I'm sorry guys, I tried, but some of my brethren -"

"Are fucking idiots!' Remy exploded. "Are you kidding me? That's it? That's all she gets for the damage she's done? She has destroyed my family! She killed Arbor. She should be skinned alive - " Zeus lifted his hands in surrender.

"I agree. But what can I do?" he asked. "She has a very powerful mouthpiece, someone speaking for her who has more pull than I do. Than any of us, apparently. I fought for her to be executed immediately. She deserves to have her head removed from her body. I can promise you this, if she steps out of line, so much as a harsh word, a finger, an eyelash in the wrong direction, I will personally strike her down where she stands. I will leave nothing but a scorch mark, but as of now, my hands are tied."

"I bet I know who," Celeste said. "This is fucking ridiculous. Know what - " Celeste stood, silently removing the bars from her uniform and tossing them to the floor. She removed the holster from her thigh and dropped her sheathed sword with a clatter. "Fuck the Council and the Collective. I have done everything that has been asked of me for the better part of two centuries. I have been poisoned, drowned, raped, tortured, murdered, kidnapped, and beaten. I have seen my brother kidnapped and raped, his lover tortured, my mother killed, and that evil little munchkin twat of an ass hat gets a spanking and sent to her fucking room? Are you all high?" she yelled towards the hidden door through which they'd all retreated.

"I know you can hear me, you weak-willed cowards! This is why I spend so much time with humans because they understand the consequences of their actions. You immortal cockstains treat life like a fucking game. She killed Arbor, Arbor, who was beloved and didn't have an enemy in any known world. It was like murdering a fucking baby bunny. That alone should be worth her head. I don't need this shit. I am the motherfucking Caelestis, the Progeny of the primordial,

Daughter of War God Anhur and Goddess Nemesis, Former Queen of the Dark Fae. I'm an Amazon Warrior, and I could end all of you with a snap of my fingers. That makes me the biggest, baddest motherfucker in this bitch, and I don't need this shit. All of you listening back there can kiss my perfect ass as I walk out the door." She yelled as she walked out, giving everyone the finger.

"Well, with that said, fuck you guys, I'm going home," Remy said, tossing his holster and sword to the ground, limping after her, Nicky at his side.

Lisette eased over to Zeus, a smirk teasing the corners of her mouth. "I guess she told you."

"And she did it spectacularly," Zeus agreed, trying to stifle his smirk.

* * *

Remy stood on his balcony, the cold December air chilling his face as he stared out into the darkness. He could hear the waves from the lake lapping at the shore and see the twinkling Christmas lights decorated the occupied homes and businesses around his building. He inhaled the air's fresh cold scent and sighed, turning to look back at the darkened bedroom.

Briar lay sprawled across the bed, his back to him, his head buried beneath a pillow. Remy couldn't understand how he could sleep that way, but on Briar, it was adorable. His back had healed, leaving thick scars that wrenched Remy's heart every time he saw them. Briar had told him time and time again that he didn't blame him, but it still hurt to know that he'd been the cause of them. It was his fault Briar had been released from service with the Grey as well.

After Celeste's major meltdown, Remy had quit, and they had subsequently decided to release Briar as well, citing his injury as the cause, but he knew the truth. Julian Onder had taken Briar into his pack as a tracker and enforcer, a right hand to the Alpha. It had been done as a favor to Remy, but Julian had praised Briar for his ability. He didn't even mind that the big man was gay, which would have made him an outcast in most packs.

"Do I look like a Neanderthal, *kardeş*?" Julian had clapped Remy on the back, "Briar is a one-man war machine. I would be stupid not to have him to my right. And he's fast, for such a big wolf, he is agile and quiet. It's freaky."

Remy walked back into the room, closing the sliding glass door behind him. He went to bed and pulled the pillow from Briar's head so he could see his angelic face. He slept peacefully, his naked body partially covered by a sheet, the fresh tattoo marking him as Julian's second on his massive bicep.

He leaned over and brushed his lips against Briar's, taking care not to wake him. "I will never love anyone as I love you, *álainn,*" *he* whispered before slipping an envelope on the pillow beside him. He picked up his duffel bag, giving the sleeping giant one last look before leaving the apartment.

On his way down in the elevator, he reached into his pocket for his phone and dialed the one person he always would.

"Hey, Ce, I'm taking off for a while. I didn't want you to worry. I'll call you in a few days. Love you, *mi cœurtendre.*"

❋ ❋ ❋

She came downstairs, pulling her damp hair into a ponytail, only to pause halfway down when she saw him. Karim stood in the living room, a heavy duffel bag over his shoulder as he waited for her to make her way across the room.

"Where are you going?" she asked, wrapping her arms around his neck.

"I have to go to meet with the Seven. We have a lot to

discuss. I'll be back in a few days," he whispered, running the pad of his thumb over her bottom lip before giving her a searing kiss. She held onto him, deepening the kiss, wanting to remember his taste, his scent, the feel of his body against hers.

"But I just got you back," she whined.

"I will be back in a few days. It takes more than a looming boogeyman to get rid of me," he whispered. He reluctantly backed away, reaching for the elevator call button. The doors slid open, and he stepped in for the last time, his eyes shimmering with tears.

"I love you," she said.

"I love you, Calie. I will always, always love you," he said as the doors closed.

Celeste waited until she could no longer hear the hum of the elevator before she sat heavily on the sofa, her head in her hands.

Slowly, the guest room door opened, and Nicky stepped out. He gathered her close to him and kissed the top of her head as he reached for the television remote. She cuddled closer, resting her head on his chest as she let her sadness pour out of her in wailing sobs.

"He'll be back, Ce," he assured her. She looked up at him and shook her head.

"No, he won't," she sniffed. Instead of trying to convince her otherwise, Nicky turned on the television and settled in for a cheesy 80's movie marathon. He would be content to hold her and let her wallow, that was what she needed, and Nicky always gave her what she needed.

"Thank you," she said after a long while.

"Anytime," Nicky said, kissing her forehead. Katie had been right. Boyfriends would come and go, but best friends were eternal.

EPILOGUE

She sat with her back to the wall, her knees drawn up to her chest in the cold, damp cell. The gown she wore barely covered her legs, and she was freezing. Her hair, her crowning glory, had been shaved off when a case of lice had infected the cells in the lower recesses of the Collective, leaving her with a shiny, white pate that made her look sickly. The overhead lights made her look paler than she already was and gave her white eyes a jaundiced glow. She hated this place, hated that they had put her here without her magic, without so much as a book to keep her mind occupied during the unending hours of isolation. She had thought the lashing would have been the worse, but that had only been the start. Those wounds, though deep and stinging, had kept her in the infirmary for a month, but they had healed, and now she was relegated to this fresh hell. She buried her face in her hands and sobbed, as she did every night when the only sound in this hell the wind was whipping through the halls.

"Hey," she nearly jumped out of her skin when she heard a voice, low but very clear, whispering in her ear. She was on her feet looking for that voice source but saw that she was still alone. She ran a hand across her eyes and sighed.

"Lilith."

She nearly screamed, backing up until her back was pressed to the cold metal of the heavy cell door. She covered her mouth with her hands; her eyes were darting around in fear. Did she hear things, or had it happened? Had she gone insane?

"Sweetheart, it's me. You haven't gone insane." She recognized the voice then, the soft charming lilt of her father. She spun around looking for him when she saw him shimmer in the corner of the room. Looking over her shoulder carefully, she noted the red light on the camera monitoring her every move. She went back to her cot, sitting as she had before, her eyes on that shimmer in the corner of the room, her mouth hidden by her folded arms.

"How did you get in here?" she asked and heard his familiar chuckle. She rolled her eyes and regretted that question. Duh, she thought, of course, he could do what he wanted. He was the prince of darkness, after all.

"What are you doing here?" she asked.

"I came to let you know that you are protected, *puellam*. You will survive this, and you will be better for it. This little exercise will teach you patience, and you will need that for what's to come." She sighed.

"So, you're not getting me out of this cesspool?" she mumbled, dumbfounded.

"Of course not. You make it through this, and you will be the High Regent of the Collective," he said.

"A lot of good that will do. They took away my magic. I have no power, and they have made sure I can't have any real power over the Collective."

He tsked, and she could just picture him wagging a finger at her.

"What they took was only the tip of the iceberg, my sweet naïve child. They also took your mother's power, and we both know that she is more powerful than ever." She sat up, her ear pricked by what he'd just said. She looked at the camera and settled back into her slumped position before she spoke again.

"You said *is*, not was," she said, watching the shimmer as it floated across the cell. She could picture him tapping his bottom lip with his index finger. He chuckled and sighed.

"Did I? Must have been a slip of the tongue." He assured her. "You just hold steady, sweets. You are destined for greatness. And if you have faith in me, trust me, I can assure you that you will have all of the power you desire. More than you ever even imagined."

"And what will you gain from this?"

He moved to a blind spot right beneath the camera and materialized. She gasped but kept her head down, trying to mask her surprise with a cough. He had a scar, one she hadn't seen before, running from his hairline across his right eye down to the corner of his mouth. That scar had ruined any chance of Alexander ever being elected to political office. She had ruined him with one slash of her blade, a blade made from the same stone and fire as the Nephilim themselves.

"I get to pay that little *k'ats* back for what she did to me, for what she did to us," he said. "I get to kill the Caelestis."

ABOUT THE AUTHOR

Tanisha Jones grew up in the greater New Orleans area, where she still lives with her daughter. She received a BA from Southern University, New Orleans in Literature.

She still lives in the New Orleans area with her daughter, the Mississippi River on one side, the bayou on the other. When not reading or writing about gods, goddesses, and all things magical, she's cooking, baking, or spending time with her rather large loving family. She is also a proud Breast Cancer survivor.

Follow her here:
Website: www.tanishadjones.com
Twitter: @tanishadelill
Instag

OTHER BOOKS IN   THE FALLEN SERIES

The First to Fall

The body of a Rock star is missing. He is the homicide detective assigned to the case. She is an enigmatic beauty who knows more than she is willing to reveal. Will the chase for the truth lead them on a collision course with destiny?

Elijah Cain has always lived his life according to the rules. But when he is called in on a missing body's bizarre case, it leads him to a woman who attracts him like no one ever has before. As much as he wants, he knows that she knows more about his case than she will tell.

Dr. C. Keegan Kent doesn't trust anyone outside of her world. When Elijah Cain walks into her world, she is terrified by her attraction to him. She also knows that there is more to this tall, dark, handsome detective than meets the eye.

As they grow closer, she introduces him to a world he never knew existed and a destiny long forgot. His connection to the tantalizingly exotic Doc runs deeper than Eli realizes and leads him on a path to the truth. The chase for the truth puts them on a collision course with their destiny or their destruction

The First to Fall is book one in the sexy and exciting Fallen Series. It's an erotic, action-packed story of a goddess finding her humanity and a human finding his divinity during their ascent to love.

Unbound

Someone's trying to kill her. He wants to protect her, but her secrets won't let him.

They must work through their past or lose everything.

Elijah Cain

Eli is still trying to come to grips with who he is. He's overwhelmed about coming into his powers and trying to figure out if what he has with Celeste is real. Everything is in question. If he doesn't make the right choice, he could be the catalyst to ending humanity.

Celeste Kent

Celeste and Eli are finally in a good place. She's ready to reveal her past when her ex-boyfriend pops-up on her patio. He claims he's there to help but only causes strife between her and Eli.

As two worlds prepare for war, can Eli and Celeste forgive old betrayals to save humanity?

Unbound is book three of the Fallen series set in a world of gods and angels. It's an erotic, action-packed story of a goddess finding her humanity and a human finding his divinity during their ascent to love.